Ripples of Infinity

The Dimensional Alliance 2nd edition, Volume 4

Bonnie K.T. Dillabough

Published by The Infinite Publishing Alliance, 2021.

Dedicated to:

First: George C. Dillabough, without whom I would never
been able to complete these books in such a timely manner.
Second: To the fans of my books who encourage me to write.
Their delight is my fuel.

Acknowledgements:

All of my beta readers: Carolyn Hardy Greiner, James Zukowski, George C. Dillabough and Melanie Runyon Nielson.

Also, I would like to acknowledge my copy-editor, Lynette M. Smith. My journey with her has been both pleasant and instructive. Between her ongoing encouragement and her professionalism, I feel confident that the quality of my books and my craft continue to improve, as every author hopes. Highly recommended. You can find her at AllMyBest.com.

Table of Contents

Prologue:

Jenny entered her bright living room with a sandwich on a plate and a glass of cold lemonade. She set her food down on the little table next to her cozy reading chair and greeted the big black cat that was curled up lazily on the window seat, basking in the California sun and watching the birds in the bougainvillea that twined up the wrought iron arch of the gateway in her front yard.

"Comfy, Tidbit?" she asked aloud.

Tidbit replied in mindspeech, *"It's been a long week. The sun feels good."*

Jenny knew what he meant. They had spent the past week at Dimensional Alliance headquarters, working with beings from many different dimensions preparing for the ongoing battles to free the multiverse from the restrictive influence of the Insenium. Although the Alliance had been able to create havoc and chaos on the main Inseni planets, which disrupted the political structure of their enemies in an effort to stop their incursions, there were yet hundreds of planets and dimensions throughout the multiverse that still lived in slavery from the Inseni's previous conquests.

After her wedding to Burt, she and Tarafau, Tidbit's alter ego, had returned to Alliance headquarters to discuss tactics and a reasonable solution to the suffering caused by the Insenium. Then she and Burt and Tarafau, now in his persona of the black cat Tidbit, had returned home. Burt had been able to spend only one night at home and then headed off to Sanglarka to bring the other Earth guardians up to speed. *So much for a honeymoon*, she mused.

Lova, the guardian of the Sanglarka gate in Sweden and the trainer and support for new guardians, had her hands full. She had been assigned to find replacement guardians for both the India gate and the Australia gate, as the Alliance needed Brendan in the space fleet. Brendan had temporarily returned to his gate until such a time as they could locate and vet a suitable replacement. He wouldn't be able to stay long, as there were some major offensives in the planning stages and he needed to be there. Once Lova had located some suitable candidates, she would be coordinating with Jenny before offering them the posts.

The India gate had been without a guardian for nearly a year now and had been temporarily sealed. Although there were troopers stationed within the gate, they were authorized to report back to the Alliance only if there were issues; none of them had the gate key that would allow them to do more than just watch the gate for potential intrusions. The gate-guardian system was strict about that. Therefore, getting a guardian for that gate was a high priority.

Then there was the resettling of Miriha's people to their home world after their having been abducted and relocated by the Insenium. That gate also needed a new guardian.

As the Gatekeeper, it was Jenny's responsibility to oversee not only the Earth gates but also the gates in other dimensions. This included the finding and vetting of guardians, as well as being involved in the finding of new gates, analyzing different cultures that might be added into the Dimensional Alliance as participating members, and generally being the face of the Alliance.

Of course, she didn't have to do this alone. She worked closely with the Dimensional Alliance Council, and she had agents available to be her eyes and ears. All of this could have been overwhelming even under "normal" circumstances, but nothing about Jenny's journey to this post had been remotely normal.

However, while she had been at Alliance headquarters, the chief physician at Dimensional Alliance headquarters had ordered a three-week rest at home before continuing her extensive duties. For the first time since she first moved into the little house on Infinity Loop with all its secrets, she actually would get to spend some quiet time here.

Bob, her neighbor across the street and a newly vetted Dimensional Alliance agent, was also taking some much-needed time at his house, reorganizing his lab, checking in with the various neighbors, and preparing for a project with Mervin, also known as Merlin of King Arthur fame. They were making extensive plans to research and explore the gate system from a scientific and historic point of view, with the goal of potentially finding additional security risks and determining how to prevent them.

Bob was fitting in agent training (something, as had been true for Jenny, that had been skipped by necessity). Jenny had worried about that due to Bob's age, but so far he seemed to be excited about it. And he was admittedly a lot more fit than most people his age, especially because he had spent most of his time since his retirement puttering in his workshop with his bots and other experiments.

He and Merv thought that finding the origins of the gate system might aid them in continuing to liberate those who had been enslaved by the Insenium in other dimensions, as well as in locating potential natural portals that had been missed.

Bob was going to rent his house out to his son in his absence, but he wanted to secure his lab and be sure there were no telltale signs of his recent activity for his son to discover. All of the private projects he had been pursuing for various Earth tech companies had been turned over to those companies' own research labs, as Bob would have no further time for it. He told them all he was taking a research sabbatical. Over the years he had worked for a number of large companies and had put a tidy sum away for just such an eventuality.

His son Chris would be housesitting while he was off on his adventures, but Bob would be taking Ignatius, his hyacinth macaw with him on his journeys. Chris had been told that his dad was going on "walkabout," to coin a phrase from Brendan, the Australia gate guardian. Bob's son, Chris, was a nice young man, a bit older than Jenny and very much like his dad. Jenny knew that Bob had given Chris her cover story about working for an international firm as a ghostwriter and she wouldn't be home much.

Now, before she sat in her cushy reading chair, she wandered over to the dining room table. Sitting down, she invoked a box out of her MDP. The first week she had moved into her aunt Lizzie's home, Bob had brought over three boxes. One of them had contained many volumes of journals and photo albums. At the time, events had moved so quickly that she had never gotten the opportunity to even open the journals. She had idly flipped through a couple of the photo albums, but the journals would have required time and attention that she didn't have available at the time.

She pulled the first volume out of the box. The year on the spine said 1952. Finally, she would learn the full story of her Aunt Lizzie, the former Los Angeles gate guardian who had left her everything, including the key to adventures beyond anything Jenny could have imagined.

She turned to Lizziebot, standing near Jenny's reading chair. "Please take messages for any incoming calls or reports unless there is a true emergency. I will check in this evening with headquarters, per my doctor's instructions," she told the bot before settling into the armchair with a sigh.

"Not a problem, Jenny. Do you wish me to set a reminder? I know it is easy to get absorbed in your reading."

"Yes, please, Lizziebot. Around suppertime would be good."

"Got it," the bot replied and settled herself at the opposite end of the fireplace.

Jenny opened the journal carefully. The pages were yellowing and somewhat fragile. She made a mental note to have Lizziebot scan the journal when she was done with it, so they could keep a digital record of the original, including her aunt's handwriting. She wasn't sure if it would ever be of any interest to anyone else, unless she eventually had children, but it seemed a shame to lose this artifact if it could possibly be preserved.

Of course, she imagined much of it would be somewhat classified, due to the nature of her aunt's adventures, but still, she wanted to be sure it would not be lost to time. Jenny had hopes that the time would come when Earthlings would be ready to know about the gateways. But until then, one of the issues Jenny constantly had to deal with was the necessity to constantly keep her secret. Of Jenny and Lizzie's family, only Jenny's father had any hint of what was really going on in Jenny's life.

Chidwi crooned from the back of the chair, where she had taken to perching whenever Jenny was moving about the house. She had been a delightful addition to her household and liked to help with meals as well as cleaning and straightening. Jenny had made sure she had a comfortable bed in the room they had labeled "the office," which was not the same as the "gate office." Chidwi also had a nest she had created for herself in the little yew tree that hung over the koi pond. Both Chidwi and Tidbit were fascinated by the calming undulations of the koi, sparkling in the light that filtered in through the branches of the little tree.

Chidwi was an unusual creature, reminding Jenny very much of an emperor tamarin monkey with the exception of her coloring which was in various shades of green. A light, almost chartreuse green fur covered most of her body, and she had a long dark green moustache and eyebrows. She had a prehensile tail and tiny gentle hands, as well as feet that she often also used like hands. Her huge intensely periwinkle blue eyes were surrounded by bright white circles of fur under her dark green brows, giving her the appearance of always being somewhat surprised at the world around her.

Chidwi was known as a linkling. She had linked to Jenny permanently during a visit to Tarafau's home dimension and was now Jenny's constant companion. Like Tidbit, she used mindspeech to communicate, but she also had a lovely soft voice and crooned when she was content or when she was trying to soothe someone. Her kind could, however, also create a high-pitched, extremely loud call of alarm when danger happened, something Jenny hoped never to hear again.

Chidwi was careful to "turn her reflection off " whenever she sensed anyone besides Jenny, Burt, Bob, or Tidbit anywhere nearby. This made her invisible, for all intents and purposes. For now, however, she draped herself across the back of the armchair like a large green doily, peering over Jenny's shoulder. Jenny was pretty sure Chidwi couldn't read, but you never knew, as she was constantly discovering new and interesting things about her little companion. Of course, one of the linklings' abilities was the gift of being able to actually read the minds of the beings around them, so whatever Jenny read, Chidwi would also be able to experience.

With a satisfied sigh, Jenny settled in for a nice read. Her aunt's now familiar hand was clean and neat. The cover of the journal was dated 1952. On the very first page it said: "I've been in college for two years already, and it occurred to me that perhaps someday someone might want to know how things were in my time. My study of history tells me that a lot has been lost because ordinary people didn't keep and preserve a record of everyday events "

As she began to read, Jenny nibbled on her sandwich and sipped lemonade without even noticing she was doing it. Her aunt wrote so clearly and with such vivid description that she could picture what was happening in her mind, especially since she and Lizzie had grown up in the same area. Many of the landmarks were familiar to her, and her parents, who were very engaged in family history and genealogy, often told her stories about that time so long ago.

In her mind's eye she saw....

Chapter 1: Lizzie

Lizzie stalked down the long corridor. There were no other students in the hallways this time of day, as classes were in session, but this was her advisory period, set aside for library work and consulting from time to time (as little as possible, in Lizzie's mind) with her advisor or professors for the beginning-of-term planning sessions.

Lizzie thought she knew what she wanted out of college life and didn't relish these sessions with her advisor. She really liked this professor and looked forward to his classes, but these sessions on career advice and evaluations of her performance felt like a complete waste of time to her. She had no desire to fit into some predetermined mold of "success."

So, when she got to his office door, she rapped smartly, waited for his, "Come," and vowed to herself that she would control her eye-rolling in his presence.

Professor Cormier was probably in his late fifties, balding and graying. He was shorter than Lizzie by about an inch, but she never felt she was looking down on him. He was energetic and seemed to look at the world as if it were somehow humorous, a joke that only he understood.

he cocked his head to one side inquisitively. He often reminded her of a bird. His eyes were dark, small, and bright, and his black brows were expressive. When lecturing, he often bounced on the balls of his feet when excited about his topic, which was often.

"Ah Lizzie," he said, shaking his head with a sad smile. "I wish I could say this meeting was to congratulate you on a rise in your grades, but alas. Why do you think you're here?"

"That's a deep and age-old question, professor. Is this a test?"

He shook his head. "Lizzie, Lizzie, Lizzie... what are we to do with you? You have a brilliant and curious mind. You ace every exam put before you, but you seem to do the homework only if it interests you, and you don't seem to be all that intent on even turning it in after you have completed it. You should be the valedictorian of your class at graduation, but your grades are mediocre at best. I don't understand why you are attending this university."

He didn't sound scolding, but rather sad and more than a bit curious.

"I am sorry to be such a disappointment," she replied tersely, looking at the hands in her lap.

"It isn't my business to be disappointed in you, Lizzie. It isn't my business to have an opinion one way or the other. When it all comes down to it, you get to choose. You're an adult. What concerns me more than anything is the potential consequences of the choices you are making now. You could easily have the kind of grades that would get you any position you decided to shoot for after college or to pursue a doctorate in the discipline of your choice. But for now, you would be fortunate to get a clerical job somewhere.

"You're intelligent enough to see this, so I ask you again: why are you here, if not to show your full potential to future employers?"

Lizzie looked up from her hands straight into the bright dark eyes of Professor Cormier and sighed. She felt he really was trying to help her, but how could she communicate clearly and without potential censure?

"Ah, professor, there's the rub, actually. I'm not interested in impressing an employer. I'm willing to pay for my tuition and books for the simple purpose of learning. Between the money I saved up and my scholarships, I have enough to accomplish my true goals.

"I haven't completely decided the specific path I need to take once I leave the university, but frankly I'm not sure I even care if I get a diploma. Learning is the entire point of my time here. Grades are significant only if I care what others think of what I've accomplished so far. I'm still deciding on where I go from here. I'm shooting for a path that involves traveling, studying, and exploring, but that's as far as I've gotten."

"Hmm, interesting. But I notice that your schedule is heavy with sciences and math. Why is that, do you think?"

"Curiosity, professor... sheer curiosity. I am ever curious to know how things work. Science and math are the study of how things work. I think there is so much more out there, so much we don't yet understand. I spend a lot of time puzzling things out, and I find myself feeling like, if I just walked through the right door, the answers would be there. For now, the mysteries seem like they are calling me from a room in my head I have yet to discover. Okay, I know that makes very little sense, but it's how I feel."

Lizzie realized she was blushing. She was unused to being this open about her feelings and somehow felt she wasn't adequately expressing how she felt.

Professor Cormier sat behind his desk his fingers steepled next to his chin in thought. "Lizzie, I have been watching you for the last two years. You have a lively mind, and your papers and comments are insightful, when you actually turn them in, but I suspect there is much more going on in that big brain of yours than you let on. I've been considering how I can help you rise to your potential "

Oh boy, Lizzie thought with a mental sigh. *Here it comes   another lecture about work ethic and seeking security in the world   "*

But the professor met her large brown eyes solemnly with his bright birdlike ones and said, "Are you tired of the classroom environment? Perhaps somewhat bored with the snail's pace of your instruction?"

Lizzie nodded and then realized this honest response might offend her advisor. But it was true. He had hit the proverbial nail on its proverbial head.

"Professor, no offense. I know it doesn't seem like it, but I do put in the work, and I also get impatient with my fellow students who seem to be plodding along. I shouldn't judge, I know, but I really would like to get down to the real stuff. But they won't let me take any of the truly advanced courses until I finish my bachelor's, and it is taking too long to get there. So, I guess the answer is yes. I am impatient with the pace of the courses available to me."

Professor Cormier didn't reply immediately, and for a moment Lizzie wasn't quite sure if he had even heard what she was saying.

"So, what if we cancel your classes for now and get into the real thing?"

"Professor?"

"I have developed a special, somewhat unusual course of study that would eliminate the fluff and get you into the level of science you seem to be so eager to explore. It isn't a certified university course, and you would get no college credit, but you would achieve your goal of learning for learning's sake. It would be self-funding, so no tuition, and room and board would be provided.

"You will recall from your history studies the ancient practice of apprenticeship? This would be like that. You would do the work I set out for you, and you would receive instruction in the sciences beyond what is available at any level in the university.

"Give it some consideration. It would be a major commitment, and I would require you to sign a nondisclosure agreement, as you will be working on projects that require absolute discretion. No textbooks and no lectures. A hundred percent hands-on science on top secret work. If you consider it and wish to pursue it, I will meet with you in a week to get your agreement and allow you to sign the paperwork."

Lizzie realized she must look a bit dazed, her mouth slightly open and eyebrows raised.

"May I ask what prompted you to make this offer?" she finally asked into the silence.

"Among other things, there was a paper you actually did turn in to me in my Physics class. Do you remember? I have it right here."

He reached into a desk drawer and slid the paper across the desk to her. She did remember. She hadn't been sure at the time if she might not get a reprimand for the content. It was entitled, "The Role of Imagination in Science."

"Yes, professor. I do remember. I would have written more, but your instructions were to make it brief. I didn't feel I adequately addressed the topic, and I know that a lot of what I said contradicts some of the philosophies of many scientists... facts versus imagination instead of acknowledging that both are necessary. So, I admit to being a bit confused about why you thought this was a reason to invite me into your special project."

"As I said, I've been following your university career and observing you in my classes. Other professors I have spoken to agree with me that you have great potential that may be wasted on formal classes. You appear to do the best in a lab environment, and your curiosity and outspoken nature mean that they often feel they would prefer to have you in a class of one," he said with a raised eyebrow. And Lizzie found herself blushing once again.

He continued, "The university environment is stifling for someone like you. Ordinarily you would be stuck with just 'doing your time' as if the university were some kind of prison. For you, it probably seems that way, despite the opportunity to spend your time learning. But the timing of this particular opportunity is fortuitous and may not be available in the future.

"I won't lie to you. It will mean a lot of hard work, and where it is taking you may not be clear to you in the beginning. The tasks I set you may not seem to be connected, but I promise you I will never set you a task that doesn't have a distinct and important purpose toward your goals of discovery. Once you begin, you will be committed to continue. The contract you sign will obligate you for a minimum of one year. To keep your options open, I will set you up with a sabbatical status, so you could come back to the university with no penalties or gaps in your student record, should you choose not to continue when your contract is complete.

"As I said, I will let you consider this and come back in a week at this same time."

Looking back, Lizzie would never be sure what prompted her action, but she leaned forward in her chair, looked the professor directly in the eye, and said, "I don't need to consider. I'll do it. You've covered all the bases, and an opportunity like this may not come again. Where do I sign?"

Chapter 2: Apprentice

(Jenny took another bite of her sandwich. She had an idea where this might lead, but it was fascinating to her that she hadn't been the only person somewhat blindsided by an unexpected opportunity.

She realized already that she and her aunt had a number of personality differences. She would have never spoken up to a professor or someone in authority in that way during her college years, and she had been very wrapped up in getting good grades.

She flipped a page.)

Lizzie spent the next couple of weeks moving out of her dorm room into the studio apartment above Professor Cormier's workshop. The space was in a large, two-story, industrial-style metal building in a warehouse district. The parking lot was huge, meant to handle employee's vehicles and delivery trucks, but the only car in the parking lot belonged to Professor Cormier. It was a two-toned Chevy Bel Aire with a black top and white body.

Lizzie had expressed surprise at such a nice car for a man on a professor's salary, and she said so.

The professor's eyebrows had shot up in surprise, and then he grinned. "You don't think this property is cost free? No, Lizzie, this is all mine. Science, done right, can pay very well. Teaching is more a very entertaining and satisfying hobby for me."

He began by showing her where she would live during the apprenticeship. The small apartment had its own entrance on the outside of the building, stairs leading up from the side of the building, just off of the parking lot.

At the front of the main building, she noticed two large metal garage-type doors that would allow pretty much anything smaller than a dump truck to enter the space. Lizzie wondered if the building just came like that or whether the professor ever actually had projects that were large enough to require the use of the big doors. To the right of the large doors on the loading dock, there was also a regular glass door with a deadbolt lock that led into the office area of the space. You could use that door to go through to the workshop/lab.

Lizzie didn't own a car, so she was glad she would have a short commute from the little apartment down the flight of stairs and through the office door. She owned a bicycle, and that would do for her. Any trip that she couldn't handle on her bike meant she would use the "yellow cars" as the electric trolleys in the Los Angeles area were called, or the bus lines. All in all, however, other than trips to a local grocery store, Lizzie had neither the time nor the inclination to go "gallivanting," as her father was fond of saying.

The little apartment was small but didn't feel cramped. The small living area included a couch, a desk, a little kitchenette, and a furnished bedroom that led into a simple bathroom, with a shower stall instead of a bathtub. Since she had been living in the dorm up until now, she didn't have much in the way of possessions to arrange in the space.

When she had finally moved all of her things into her place, she went to the downstairs office to report to the professor, who had returned from the university. "I'm in, professor." she said to him briskly. "When do we start?"

"First, you need to know the rules. Have a seat."

Obediently Lizzie sat, eager to begin, but unwilling to get off on the wrong foot with this man she would be working with for at least a year.

"You have signed the nondisclosure agreement and the contract as an apprentice. This means you follow instructions immediately and with exactness. Often times, for safety's sake, there will be no time for lengthy explanations. At the completion of each project, we will review the process and discuss what you have learned.

"You will keep a study journal and always have it easily to hand. This is a separate document from any personal journal you may already be writing. This journal will be made available to me at my request, so I can correct any misunderstandings or incorrect conclusions you may have drawn, as well as discuss your thought processes as you go along. This will be absolutely required as part of your training.

"Secondly, you will be working much of the time on your own when I am away at the university. This means you will need to be very aware of the safety protocols I have put into place within these walls. We will be building discipline and training your body to quickly respond to your mind. Within a month or two, these protocols should come naturally without thinking. This is vital for your safety and mine, as well as the successful completion of the projects we will be pursuing.

"Finally, everything you see here—*everything*—is confidential. You are not to speak of it to anyone, ever. Even something that may seem insignificant to you may be more than it appears to be. Am I clear?"

Lizzie nodded. "Yes, sir. Clear as glass."

Professor Cormier handed her an essay notebook and a pen. "Come with me."

He led her through the door that led into the workshop. Just outside the door, he reached for a lab coat hanging on a wooden coat rack. "Put this on. There is a pocket protector in the breast pocket for your pens, and the large front pockets below will accommodate your notebook."

Lizzie did as she was told as the professor donned his own lab coat. As she turned away from the little nook just outside the office door, she gasped. She had expected a real laboratory atmosphere, white, sterile, and organized. This was not at all like that. This was more like a haphazardly curated museum with no apparent theme.

From the metal beams of the two-story ceiling hung a disparate collection of things, from a small aircraft to the assembled skeleton of some huge flying creature she didn't recognize. The main room was divided into various sections with different tool sets and assembly areas. Some of the areas had the traditional beakers and Bunsen burners, but most of them looked a lot more like a crafting area with contraptions of many kinds in various stages of construction, most of which were puzzling to her.

He led her over to an area in a far corner, which held what appeared to be woodworking tools. "Over time, you will be introduced to the various ongoing projects in the lab, but for now we will start with the necessary disciplines to graduate you to more intricate projects. In this process, you will learn a great deal about physics and will be able to employ your prodigious math skills. I imagine this all looks like an eclectic jumble, but I assure you that every space of the lab has a specific purpose related to the sciences and invention."

At this point, Lizzie was beginning to wonder if signing that contract was a big mistake. But she decided to withhold judgment for the moment. She had made the commitment, and she wasn't one to go back on her word.

"Do you know how to use basic carpentry tools? Saws, hammers, sanders, and the like?"

"I've worked with my dad on some projects around our home, professor, but I wouldn't consider myself a craftsman, if that is what you mean."

"No, no, that will be more than adequate. For your first project, you will build a simple frame loom. I have typed out instructions for you." And he handed her a one-page document.

"All the materials you will need are in the cabinet behind you. Safety goggles in the drawer of your workbench and tools hanging on the pegboard above the workbench. Assembly table is next to the workbench. Please take notes of your thoughts as you work. Be honest in your notes. Also note any thoughts that come to you about how to improve the process. Once this part of the project is complete, you will be using the loom to create a number of weavings.

"I want you to speculate as you go and to journal about your conclusions and the overall experience. Some of the questions you may want to consider are: Why is he having me do this? What am I learning about physical mechanics? How would I have done this without the instructions? How is weaving relevant to the sciences?

"I will be in and out of the lab, as my schedule permits, and you can ask any questions you might have. At the end of this part of your project, when you are satisfied with the quality of your work, leave me a note in the office on my desk. I'll arrange for us to sit down and discuss it and get you started on the next step in your process. After that, you will begin the actual weaving process. Any questions?"

Lizzie shook her head numbly. At this point she didn't have a clue why this was relevant or what this had to do with science, but Professor Cormier's classes had always been insightful and interesting, and she had never known him to be prone to any eccentricities that would make her doubt his sanity, nor did he seem to be a prankster. Undoubtedly this was a test, and she wouldn't make a snap judgment, as she might normally have done.

"I'll leave you to get on with it, then," he said, suiting action to words and turning towards the office, but then he turned again. He tossed her a key-ring with several jingling keys on it.

"You'll need to be able to get into the lab when I am not here, which is most of the time. The small key is the key to the cabinet. Each cabinet in the lab has its own lock. Oh, and please tidy your area when you are finished each day. I know this place looks like a jumble, but I know where everything is, and would like to keep it that way."

Once again Lizzie nodded and watched as he turned back and went out through the office door. She could hear him walk out the warehouse entrance and then heard the hum of his Bel Aire as he left, probably to that day's classes. She wondered how much he was ever in the lab, considering his class schedule and just taking care of his own basic needs. She knew almost nothing about him—no more than any of her other college professors—but she had a feeling that would probably change.

She sat on the tall stool next to the workbench and began to read. There were lights hanging from the ceiling over each work area, but for now the light was supplied by the intermittent skylights arrayed along the length of the building on either side of the peaked roof. The instructions were fairly simple, so she went to the supply cupboard and began to assemble her supplies. One-by-two-inch wooden strips which appeared to be made of oak, finishing nails, corrugated frame fasteners, carpenter's glue, and sandpaper were all there, as called for in her instructions. She then assembled her tools, a ball-peen hammer and a tack hammer, a hacksaw, a miter box, and some small wood clamps.

She started by measuring the wood and marking it to the desired length. This would be similar to making an overlarge picture frame, and the corners of the wood would have to be mitered for the best fit. The miter box had angles measured out, so it was a matter of positioning the wood on the box and making the cut using the guides.

Cutting the oak with a hacksaw was hard work but she did it carefully, not rushing the process despite her impatience with the time it would take. She knew this was inevitably some kind of a test, and she wouldn't fail it by a lack of attention to detail. Once she had the four mitered sides completed, she put the remaining pieces of wood into the used wood bin at one side of the workbench and decided to take some time out and have a bite of lunch before proceeding.

She made sure her supplies and equipment were carefully put in order and the sawdust swept up and left the building to head up the stairs to her apartment, after being sure to lock the outside door to the lab.

So far, her little place was very plain, simple furnishings and no pictures on the walls. She didn't imagine she would be spending much time there, mostly just to eat and sleep, as she intended to spend most of her waking moments in the lab. The one major benefit of this opportunity was the option to work at her own pace. She suspected that this too was a kind of test. However, one way or another, the opportunity to learn without the restrictions of the pacing of public instruction was something she had yearned for. It would be silly of her to waste it. The more focused she remained and the more hours she put into this first basic project, the sooner she would get to the "good stuff."

Professor Cormier had stocked her cupboards and small refrigerator with all the basics, and she had also brought with her some of her favorite foods, unsure of what he might choose for her. He had a grocery delivery service on contract, and he told her that she could just leave him a list once a week of whatever she needed.

Today it would be one of her favorite lunches, a habit she had acquired early in her student days at the university, a peanut butter and jelly sandwich with a glass of pink lemonade and an apple for dessert.

As she sat at her kitchenette table, she placed her notebook at her side, another habit picked up early in her student days. She almost never ate a meal without either a book or a notebook in hand. She hardly noticed what she ate most of the time. She had a habit of eating alone except when she was home with her family, usually at Thanksgiving and Christmas. She told a friend, "I like to ruminate while I masticate," which brought a puzzled look but no comment. She hadn't made many friends while in school, simply because she spent most of her time reading or studying. And admittedly, most of her fellow students found her a bit odd, something she had become used to, growing up.

It wasn't as though she was antisocial—well, maybe she was, a little—but she was totally absorbed with finding answers that didn't really seem to be out there, or at least not in the detail she would have wished.

This is why she had accepted Professor Cormier's offer. The chance to finally "get her hands dirty," as her father would have said, was worth going through some hoops for.

She considered what to say about her experience so far. Mostly she had questions: What does learning to weave on a rudimentary loom have to do with science? Why build the loom with her own hands, instead of just buying a loom to weave on? How did the process help her move forward with her studies? And, lastly, was this the professor's idea of a great practical joke? She half expected him to jump out at her when she finally completed this first task and cry, "Surprise! The joke's on you!"

As she finished her meal and cleaned up, she went back down the stairs into the warehouse lab, redonned her lab coat, and headed for her work area.

She placed some newsprint on the worktable and laid the sticks in the rectangle shape face down. Using the carpenter's glue, she glued each of the corners to one another and clamped them down to dry. Later she would use the corrugated joint fasteners, pounding one into each corner with the little ball-peen hammer.

While that was setting, she cut another of the sticks four inches wider than the finished frame and sanded the ends to prevent it from snagging on the threads or yarn of the loom. This would be what was called a "shed stick."

She then collected a half-inch dowel stick and cut it the same length as the shed stick for the "string heddle." Between the shed stick and the heddle, she would be able to do the weaving much quicker than simply weaving in and out over the warp. She also sanded the ends of the heddle and placed it aside.

She patiently checked off each of these steps in her notebook. Next on her list were the shuttles that would carry the yarn or thread back and forth through the warp that was opened up by the shed stick or heddle. She would need more than one of these to carry different colors of thread, as she doubted she would be satisfied with weaving with a single color. Already she was forming an idea in her mind as to what she might decide to weave as her first project.

She took a piece of oak tagboard out of the wood supply cupboard and cut out four rectangles about ten inches long and three inches wide. At either end she cut a "V" shaped notch about two inches deep. Once again, she sanded all of the edges and put them aside. This would hold a good deal of fiber, whether yarn or thread, and make the weaving much more efficient.

Once she had this completed, the glue had set sufficiently to allow her to pound in the corrugated joint fasteners. Now she had a sturdy frame. The last step was to measure out the pattern for pounding in the nails at either end that would hold the warp threads for the loom. This meant drawing a line down the exact center of the top and bottom end boards and measuring out and marking quarter-inch increments along the line.

By the time she had completed this much, it was time for supper. To her surprise, once she had once again organized her materials and cleaned up sawdust and put the wood scraps into the scrap bucket and was ready to head back upstairs, the professor showed up, a basket in his hands.

"I brought us some supper. I figured by now the idea of having to prepare a meal would be tiring. We can eat in the office and talk about your first day."

Lizzie could smell the aromas of chicken and potatoes wafting up from the basket and grinned.

"Sounds good to me."

He cleared off an area on both sides of the desk and set out some plates and flatware, a roast chicken that had been cut up for ease in serving, and a bowl of mashed potatoes. He then pulled out a covered gravy boat, napkins, and some cups, which he filled from the water cooler.

"So how did it go?" he asked after they had filled their plates.

"None of it was difficult, just a trifle time consuming. I just have to drive the nails in. I figured I could do that tonight and then go to the next step tomorrow."

"You got that done very quickly and efficiently. However, you don't sound very enthusiastic about it."

"I guess I'm just puzzled as to what this has to do with science."

"Ah, well that's part of the test, isn't it? As you are pounding the nails, I want you to consider that, not just the step-by-step activity of producing the loom or even weaving on it. I want you to find the meaning of it. I know it sounds somewhat mysterious or even a bit eccentric, but I promise you this is not just busywork. I challenge you to set yourself the question just before sleep tonight. Before you sleep you will have created all of the components for a simple and efficient loom out of basic materials much sooner than I had expected.

"Tomorrow you will begin to learn the weaving process. I have a short film on the basics you will be able to view before you begin. Feel free to rewind the film and replay it as many times as necessary. When we finish our meal today, before you begin the last part of today's project, I will show you how to use the projector in the screening room."

"Thank you, professor," Lizzie said, perhaps not as sincerely as she should have. "Thank you for the meal, it is very tasty." This last was more sincere. She seldom ate anything this balanced. She wondered if he had prepared it himself but decided not to ask, as he might be offended.

"You're welcome, Lizzie. In time you will learn there is always method to my madness. In the meantime, you will have to suspend disbelief for a little while longer. I promise you that you not only will understand in time but will eventually appreciate why I did not take you faster. This is vital to the process. There are a lot of ways I could have taught you the vital work habits and mindset that are necessary to what comes next, but I have observed you learn best by working through things on your own."

Lizzie nodded and blinked in surprise when she realized she was scraping the last of the mashed potatoes from the plate and that the chicken she had taken was bare bones.

The professor took her plate and the leftovers and arranged them back carefully in his basket, gesturing to her to enter the lab.

Once again, she donned her white lab coat with Professor Cormier right behind her. "Let's see your progress so far."

She led the way to her work area and was pleased when he remarked at how neat her workspace was. He examined the various parts of the loom carefully.

"Well done," he said with a smile. "I would have expected nothing less from you. This is quality workmanship, and you have followed the directions I gave you admirably. Tomorrow you will be ready to begin learning the weaving process. Come with me."

He led her to the opposite corner of the lab to a door that led into a room that included a low ceiling and no windows. He switched on the lights to reveal racks and racks of reels of film with labels below each reel showing the title of the film. At one end of the room was a large screen, and behind a row of chairs with desks attached to them was a projector on a cart with an organizer tray under it that served to organize film reels if you were going to run more than one in sequence.

He showed her where to find the reel for the weaving tutorial and then showed her how to set it up on the projector and how to thread the film through the little rubber wheels and in between the light and the lens. Then he attached it to a take-up reel below the loaded film reel.

"That's about all there is to it. When you are finished, simply rewind the film from reel to reel by toggling the switch to rewind. Be careful to always turn the projector lamp off whenever you need to pause the film. The heat from the lamp can easily melt the film. As I said, you can watch it as often as you need to or stop the film at various places, do that step, and then return and start wherever you left off. I can wish the process weren't so clunky, but it is what we have to work with at this time," and he sighed, as if somehow he knew a better way.

He bade her farewell and told her to call him if she needed anything. She heard the now familiar sound of the Bel Aire starting up and leaving the parking lot.

Once again, she was alone in the space. She knew that the remaining part of the process, although simple, would take her awhile to complete to have a finished loom ready for the next day. So, she sighed and went back to work.

Chapter 3: Warp and Weft and...

(Jenny found herself totally engaged in Lizzie's account of her encounter with the professor and the offer of an "apprenticeship." This was by no means what she expected to find. Obviously, this was connected somehow to Lizzie's further adventures, and she had her suspicions about Professor Cormier. She took another sip of lemonade and kept reading.)

The next morning, Lizzie awoke with a kind of buzzing in her head. It wasn't a sound, really. It was as if there was something just beyond her hearing, like a radio signal not quite tuned in. She almost felt as if she could turn a little knob just slightly and it would come in clearly.

Per her instructions, she had thought about the questions she needed answers to before turning out the lights to go to sleep. She decided to go eat breakfast and get right to work. Perhaps it would resolve itself when she got into the rhythm of weaving. She had heard that weaving was a relaxing activity, once someone was familiar with the process.

The night before, she had completed the persnickety task of carefully hammering the finishing nails into the spaces she had precisely marked off on the top and bottom of the frame. She carefully staggered them above and below the line so they wouldn't create a crack in the grain of the frame. When it was done, she was pretty proud of the neat rows of nails. A simple thing, but absolutely necessary to the proper use of the loom.

Something about that thought tweaked at the thing still humming inside her head, but she ignored it. She went to the cupboard Professor Cormier had told her held the choice of fibers available to her for her project. She had already considered what might make a good first design. She wasn't really an artsy or crafty person, so she concluded that perhaps a dresser scarf would be fun to make and would be easily accommodated on her new loom.

She found some cotton carpet warp thread that looked like a good color and decided to match it as nearly as possible to the same color with the weft yarn, and then she realized she had no idea how to calculate how much she would need for her project. She needed to watch the film before she would be able to proceed at all.

She had a good idea how to put the warp on the loom, but she didn't know how wide she would have to make it to get the desired width for her project. It was obvious to her that there would be some width-wise shrinkage in the weaving process. But how much and what the proportions needed to be, she had no idea.

Again, the little background hum that persisted in her mind surged and receded. She shook her head and took her notebook into the screening room. The film was already in place, so she turned the projector on and started the film. She took notes assiduously and stopped the film often, being careful to turn the lamp off each time so as not to melt the film while she jotted down her thoughts.

By the time the film was done, she had several pages of notes. It had all seemed so simple on the surface. Just weave the weft in and out across the warp enough times and you came out with a finished product. She'd had no idea how many calculations were necessary to know how much yarn would be needed and how wide to make the warp or the technique necessary to create a finished piece that wouldn't look like a kindergartner had done it. She also discovered she had been missing a piece of equipment.

After shutting down the projector and then rewinding the film and replacing it on its proper place on the film rack, she ran up the outside stairs to her little flat and got a dinner fork out of the utensil drawer. Turns out she would need it for batting down the yarn after pulling it through the warp threads.

When she got to her worktable, she consulted her notes and made the necessary calculations to know how much warp and weft material she would need. Fortunately, she had plenty of both. Also, the film had given her the idea of creating a colorful border on either end of the scarf. The warp and weft of the main body of the scarf was a cream color, and she would use a royal blue for the border.

Now she had to string the warp; back and forth and back and forth she strung. Before she had watched the tutorial, she would have immediately started the weaving process. But now, armed with that knowledge, she carefully went back through the warp threads, individually tightening them until they didn't have so much give. This was a bit painstaking, but it would allow her to create a superior end product. By the time she was finished, she was shaking her head. This was a lot more complex than she had ever suspected. She was beginning to have an inkling of some of the lessons she was going to learn from this, and the humming in her head softened a bit more.

When she glanced up at the clock when the warp was finally tied off, she was shocked to realize it was past lunchtime. Where had the time gone? She put the remaining warp thread to the side and decided she would take the next steps after lunch.

As she ate, she contemplated how badly she would have messed this project up after having made a good loom if she had not taken the time to watch the film. Suddenly she realized she had developed a sense of respect for this seemingly simple process that she had not even considered before.

She hardly noticed eating her meal; she was so absorbed in jotting down her observations. As quickly as she could, she cleaned up her lunch mess and headed down the stairs eagerly. Her attitude towards the project had definitely changed. She still wasn't completely sure how this applied to physics and science, but it had taken on an importance of its own. It was now a challenge, and Lizzie never let a challenge stand in her way of learning something new.

When she got to her workbench, she grabbed the dowel and some more warp thread and began threading the heddle. It worked like puppet strings. When she had threaded the heddle and raised it, every other warp string was pulled up at once, creating a tunnel to send the yarn shuttle through.

Now she took the shed stick and wove it through the warp opposite to the threads the heddle was attached to. Now, when she turned the shed stick on its side, it made a new tunnel for the opposite weave of the warp.

She wound some yarn around the shuttle, enough for several passes back and forth of the loom.

But she wasn't ready to start yet. The final step was to create a special padding that would keep the yarn straight while she was weaving. She took two very straight pieces of cardboard, an inch wide and as long as the loom was wide, and wove them into the warp, pushing them flush along the nails the warp was strung on. This would keep the bottom of the weave straight as she wove and would stabilize the warp as the shuttle passed back and forth.

Whew! All of this and she hadn't woven a single strand. But if she had left out a single step or forgotten a single one of the tools, she would have been able to weave only something that would have fallen apart as soon as she removed it from the loom or soon afterward.

Before she began to finally weave, she consulted her notes one more time, just to be sure she hadn't left anything out, and realized there was something she hadn't taken into consideration. The loom was too tall and wide to weave with it on her lap. She needed some way to stand it up at a decent height so she could weave from a seated position. She considered. This hadn't been in any of the instructions she had seen.

It occurred to her that there was a presentation stand folded in one corner of her work area. Had it been put there intentionally? Whether it had or not, she shortened the legs so the ledge the presentation pad would have rested upon was located about knee height and set the loom on it. The ledge of the stand was wide enough to support the bottom of the loom, and the lip on the edge of it would hold the loom securely in place. She positioned everything so the light from the skylights above her shone on her work. This would be fine. She also had the ceiling lights when the sunlight ran out, but she knew that real sunlight was much better for seeing details. She let out the breath she didn't realize she was holding. Even if she had only a few hours before supper, she could get a good start on it now.

She let her thoughts drift as she fell into the rhythm of weaving. At first it felt a bit awkward, and she realized that even knowing the process didn't actually mean it would be easy to do. Push the shuttle through the opening made by the shed stick. Turn the shed stick flat. Bubble the yarn across the warp. Use the fork to batten down the row of weaving. Then raise the heddle while guiding the shuttle through the new tunnel made across the warp. Bubble the yarn across the warp. Batten it down with the fork. Again, and again. Over and over.

By the time she had a couple of inches of the royal blue weave above the spacer strips that would form the border of her project, she realized she needed a break. To her shock once again, the hands of the clock seemed to have moved way too far while she had been absorbed in her work, and the natural light was beginning to fade.

It would take some time to change thread color, which was a process in and of itself. For now, she would get some supper and she would spend the evening with a good book. She felt she had earned that much.

She made herself some canned vegetable soup and some bread and butter and went to her bookshelf. Professor Cormier had added some of his favorites. One of the titles intrigued her, *The Hobbit*. What was a hobbit, and what did *that* have to do with science?

She took the slim volume off the shelf and began. "In a hole in the ground there lived a hobbit. "

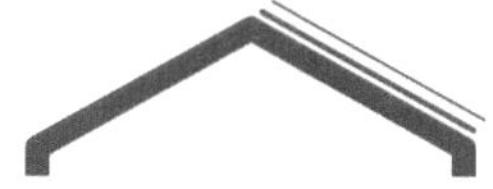

Chapter 4: The Threads of a Pattern

(Jenny found herself intrigued. Of all of the adventures she had expected to find in Lizzie's journals, building a loom and weaving a dresser scarf was never considered. She knew enough about her aunt to know that Lizzie always had a reason for everything she did. It surprised her to find her aunt pursuing something so mundane, but something about the account made her wonder about this professor and what in the world he could possibly have meant by putting Lizzie to this task.

Chidwi had evidently decided to follow Tidbit out into the garden to observe the koi or perhaps to chase butterflies, something they both enjoyed. Of course, they never even tried to actually catch them. They would have been horrified at the idea of harming such an ethereal little creature, but nevertheless, they both seemed to enjoy them.

Jenny knew they would be happily occupied. For now, she just wanted to find out where Lizzie was going with her narrative.)

After two days at the loom, Lizzie woke with pain in her shoulders and lower back. She wasn't used to this particular activity, and her body was telling her about it. As she entered the office, before she entered the lab, she noticed a note on the desk. In Professor Cormier's bold, striding script, it simply said, "Call me," with the phone number inscribed below the words.

Lizzie promptly sat at the desk, picked up the heavy receiver of the black telephone, and dialed the number. The process of dialing had always been an irritant to Lizzie, especially when there were nines and zeroes in the number. It seemed to take forever for the wheel on the dialer to make its slow progress back to the starting point to dial the next digit in the sequence. Finally, the phone rang, and in two rings the professor answered the phone.

"Professor, you asked me to call you," she said before he could say more than his usual professional greeting.

"Ah, Lizzie. You are prompt and at it early, as usual. I'll be dropping by to see your progress at the weaving later today. Please have your notes ready. Although I will want you to continue with your weaving project, I want to hear your early thoughts about it, as I may have something more for you at that point. Also, have you been away from the lab at all since last we spoke?"

"No professor. I have been focused on getting this project done so we can move forward."

"As I thought. Okay, we'll also discuss that when I get there. I'll bring us some lunch. How do you feel about hamburgers and some fries?"

"Sounds like a treat, professor."

As she hung up, she realized that the dividing line between professor and student was changing. She remembered as a child being surprised to find a teacher in a grocery store, as if they didn't have a life outside of teaching students. It was almost as if they just magically appeared to teach every morning and then disappeared each evening when they were no longer needed. Of course, she no longer thought that way, but it was interesting to realize that she still felt teachers were somewhat outside of the realm of everyday life, like they stood apart somehow.

Eating meals with the professor was both disconcerting and enjoyable, and she found herself looking forward to the meal with him.

As she sat down to the loom moments later, she groaned quietly when she raised her arms to begin the process. The project was only about half finished after several days of constant effort, due partially to her own perfectionism. More than once, she had painstakingly unwoven several rows of threads when she had discovered a flaw in the weaving. And now it seemed that her body was rebelling at the posture she had to assume at the loom. She hoped that in time her body would accustom itself to the action with arms raised, leaning slightly forward, but for now it was not at all comfortable.

By the time the professor arrived with a bag full of burgers and fries and (surprise!) two strawberry milkshakes, she was in considerable pain. She generally didn't take any kind of medicine, preferring for her body to repair itself, but this time she was beginning to be tempted to take some aspirin at least.

She sat down carefully across the office desk from the professor and couldn't repress a small groan when she leaned forward to grab her burger. He arched a brow. "You appear to be in pain," he commented, before biting into his burger.

"It's okay. Just a little sore from sitting at the loom."

"Ah, yes, one of the things I wanted to talk to you about. I don't believe you have budged from the lab since you started the project. Am I right?"

"No, I wanted to get the first project done."

"Well, then, I will add a new requirement for you. Every day you will take a full one-hour break. You will leave the premises and not return until the full hour has passed. During that time, you will either walk or ride your bike to someplace that is not a library. You will move during that time either on foot or pedal. I do not want you used up and burned out. Your continuing health is vital to the endgame of our association. You will do this every weekday. On Saturday and Sunday, you will pursue other avocations of your choice that are not related to your lab work, even if that is just resting and reading a book. This means a complete break from working in the lab. Are we clear?"

Lizzie wanted to object, but she knew she had made a commitment to follow his rules and she wasn't one to go back on her word, so she nodded, chewing thoughtfully on a mouthful of burger.

"Over time, the reasons for this will become increasingly clear, but for now I hope you trust me enough to continue until you understand more fully what is at stake."

Once again, she nodded. She wasn't sure why, but she actually did trust him.

"Good," he said between bites. "As soon as we finish this fine repast, we'll head into the lab and discuss your project and its ramifications so far."

So, they ate in companionable silence. Lizzie finished quickly and the professor wasn't far behind, so they cleaned up their lunch mess and donned lab coats.

The professor pulled up a stool to the worktable beside the loom and solemnly inspected her work for a few minutes.

"Nicely done so far. I see you mastered the joining of the two colors, a somewhat finicky part of the process."

"Professor, are you a weaver? I was wondering, as you seem to know a lot about it."

"Actually, no, but my wife was. She left behind a lot of her materials, and I decided not to waste them. I learned a lot by watching her and listening to her discuss it with her weaving friends."

"And your wife is passed?"

"About a year ago. I miss her, but I look forward to crossing paths again in a future time," he replied softly.

"I'm so sorry " Lizzie replied, one hand to her cheek, feeling awkward. "I shouldn't have brought it up."

"It isn't a problem, Lizzie. Thinking of her is always a joyful thing to me. I believe our parting is temporary. Don't fret yourself about it. As I was saying, I learned a lot about weaving from an observer's point of view. You, on the other hand, are learning it from a start-from-scratch experience. I would like to hear your thoughts. I notice you have made copious notes. Have you answered any of your questions yet?"

Lizzie thought about where to start, turning the pages of her notebook.

"One of my observations is that apparently simple things are not always as simple as they appear. The loom, even this simple one, is not just the sum of its parts. It made me consider how anyone even decided this was a possible or desirable thing to try. When did we go from animal skins to weaving cloth? What person was just sitting around one day and decided they could knot a bunch of strings together and make cloth? Where did the first strings come from? Who decided they could take the fiber from a sheep or a cotton plant and turn it into strings that they would use on a loom that probably wasn't invented yet?

"My mother loves to crochet and knit. I know those arts originally came from net-making by fishermen, or so it is said, but there seems to be so much more to this than just weaving string in and out, over and over and over again, to make a piece of cloth.

"I have gained a great deal of respect for those early pioneers of the weaving craft. Even a simple loom like this one with good tools at hand takes time to build and master. My results so far seem inadequate, although I intend to finish the project.

"It never ceases to amaze me the inventiveness of the human mind and the diversity of its applications. My frustration now becomes, if this one simple thing that isn't as simple as it appears is actually this complex, how will I ever learn enough? What is this path you are leading me along?"

"Ah yes," he said with a sparkle in those bright eyes. "As I had suspected and hoped. Curiosity is a driving factor. I had wondered if you would see beyond the mundane into the nearly arcane world of true science. So, let's see if you can answer the first question you asked me. Why did I set you this task and what does it have to do with science?"

"Well, I think there is more than one answer to that question, professor."

He raised his hand to stop her. "Lizzie, let's make this whole thing a little easier. Call me Gaston. Our work together does not require such formality. Please continue."

"Erm, uh, okay. Well, it seems to me the first thing is that you were testing to see if I would follow instructions carefully and take care in my work to do my best, not discounting the simplicity of the task and the apparent lack of connection to the high science I aspire to. I admit I wasn't exactly thrilled at the assignment, and it took a lot of pondering to decide there was some sort of 'method' to your 'madness,' as you say.

"Secondly, I realized that maybe there was a broader point to it. Upon consideration, I also realized it was a simple way to introduce me to protocols in the lab and to test my work ethic.

"On a deeper level, I also realized that this ended up being a study in the scientific process on a very basic level that turned out not to be so basic after all. I kept asking myself the question you asked in your office last week: why am I here? The answer is both complex and simple, but it boils down to what you just said. Curiosity drives me. I always have more questions than I have answers, and I would really like to jump ahead. But I can see you have a specific course charted for this journey, and I will only learn where it will lead me one step at a time.

"This requires me to trust you to lead me right. I learned some things about the mechanics and interaction of separate parts to make a machine that is functional and was able to ponder in the process the whys and hows of what drives the creativity of the brain. I found myself wondering if, had I lived back in the time when this simple tool was high-level innovation,

I would have had the insight to put all of these pieces together in such a workable format."

"Such deep thoughts," Gaston said as Lizzie paused. "Exactly why I chose you for this project! The loom is a metaphor, which I hope you will continue to ponder. Even when we go on to other projects, I hope you will continue to use it and master the craft. Weaving definitely lends itself to contemplation, the rhythm of the process is soothing.

"Tell me, Lizzie. What is your least favorite branch of the sciences?"

"Biology and medicine. Hands down. They are messy and more unpredictable than their practitioners are willing to admit, most of the time. Organic creatures tend to have too many variables. I prefer things that are more quantifiable."

"Hmm. I think I understand. We tend to separate the sciences into categories, which includes levels of logic and what we think of as 'hard fact.' We scientists, as a whole, are often much too sure of ourselves. We fail to remember that almost all science is theoretical in one sense or another. Whether it is physics or mathematics, we often find that things we had thought were immutable turn out to have a lot more to them than we had previously believed. We must be careful not to confuse science with truth. Although they often coincide, they are not necessarily synonymous."

Lizzie nodded thoughtfully. This sounded very much like what she had been trying to say in many of the papers she had turned in to her science professors. Not all of them had appreciated her attitude in this regard.

"I think," she said, treading carefully, "that one of the reasons you started me with this project was to allow me to teach myself that science is a lot more than supposed 'facts and figures' and that there is a lot more to any of it than we generally think. I think I have learned that I may have bitten off more than I can chew. Making the loom taught me not to assume and not to underestimate your cunning. What have I gotten myself into?"

Gaston laughed. "Always another question with you. Good!

"I really can't tell you. This is a journey that needs to be taken carefully. It's like the difference between taking a walk in the forest or driving through one in a vehicle. Details, often important and amazing ones, are lost when you speed through. Likely, looking back, you will think that it has all flown by too fast, regardless of our current pace. But when you do, I hope you will have at least gotten the answer to *some* of your questions.

"I think we will be ready to start your next project tomorrow. Take a break today. Get away from the lab and give yourself some time to think. No libraries or museums. Get out to the beach or a park and just *be* for a bit."

"Thank you, Gaston," Lizzie replied, still somewhat uncomfortable using his given name. "I will do as you say. Thank you for the burger and the food for thought. Both were delicious."

Chapter 5: Messy and Unpredictable

(Jenny found herself wondering who this professor really was and where he was going with this line of thought. She could feel the conflict of emotions within her aunt. Of course, she had an inkling of where Lizzie's journey would eventually take her, but she was beginning to understand why Lizzie had made a point to ask Jenny to read the journals.

Neither she nor her aunt could have expected Jenny's own journey to have been so precarious. Jenny was sure that if she had been given the luxury of taking her own training step by step, she would have taken the time to read these before now. She found herself grateful for the break she was getting to finally read the journals and get this insight into her aunt and the chance to fill in some of the gaps in her training so far.)

Lizzie found herself impatient when she followed Gaston's direction to take a break between assignments. She was ready to plow forward and see what new surprises the professor had in store for her. Even the request to call him by his first name had made her wonder. It was as if he was trying to put them on an equal footing, and she wasn't sure if she qualified for that.

She decided to head out to the beach. It was in the middle of the work week for most people, so the beach would be uncrowded, especially since the day was a bit overcast. She hopped on a "Red Line" bus, making connections that eventually took her out to Long Beach. She walked onto the Pike, a favorite stop for her, especially when it wasn't crowded with the usual weekend mobs.

High above towered the Cyclone Racer, the second largest roller coaster in the United States. Thrilling and even dangerous (there had been some loss of life among riders over the years), it was a focal point among the shops, carnival games, and other attractions along the pier. She decided the risk was worth it and paid the fifteen cents for a ticket. She needed some perspective.

The ride was exhilarating and, although it only took a couple of minutes, she loved the elevated view at the tallest of the steep climbs of the little car. From that vantage point she could see far out to sea, if only for a moment, like one of the seagulls that swooped and circled along the beach. As she dismounted from her car, she realized she hadn't done anything like this in an age.

As a kid she had sometimes come out to the pier with her family. Of course, in between there had been the Second World War, six years of uncertainty and incredible sadness. Her father had volunteered in the navy, and her mother had worked as a seamstress. Lizzie and her siblings had necessarily had to take care of themselves a large part of the time. The boys had done a number of things to bring in money. Her family had barely survived through the Great Depression, and the war had been yet another blow to them and their neighbors.

Now, five years after the treaty was officially signed, people were mostly thriving. Her father had come home from the war, more serious than before and intent on moving forward. Her mom had returned gladly to being a homemaker, and her siblings had all moved on to their various occupations. As the youngest, Lizzie was just now exploring her options.

Leaving the Pike to stroll along the beach, she found herself deep in thought. What was she really doing? It was all well and good to think she was flouting the educational system, and Professor Cormier's offer did seem generous on the surface. But what was he getting out of all of this? And in the final analysis, what would she get out of it? He kept asking that question: why *was* she here? Why was she making the choices she was making, and where would it all lead?

She knew herself well enough to know that curiosity was her constantly driving force. At the age of four, she had taken her father's alarm clock apart while her parents were occupied elsewhere. Her father had been surprisingly calm when he asked her why she would do such a thing. The only answer she could give was, "I wanted to see why it worked."

He had made her promise to ask before she took something apart again and didn't punish her. He went out and bought a new alarm clock and had given her the parts of the old one, which she did finally assemble into a working clock (with a few parts left over).

Was she ever going to get the answers she was looking for? Was she kidding herself that she could ever find an occupation that would pay her to live while still allowing her to satisfy her urges to disassemble everything that intrigued her? Obviously she couldn't continue as an apprentice forever.

What she had said to the professor was true. She really didn't aspire to wealth. As long as she had her basic needs met, and she could continue to study what she wished, she was quite content. But there was always a cost to education in one form or another.

As she watched the breakers crash against the shore and looked out to the horizon which appeared to be endless, her thoughts seemed to swirl in an equally endless vortex. As she often did, she pictured in her mind the spiral arms of the Milky Way reaching out into extended space, spaces so large as to overwhelm the human mind. And yet, she knew there was so much more out there, far beyond where any telescope could reach. Inversely, she also pictured endless iterations of smaller and smaller bits of matter. No end in either direction was both soothing and disturbing to contemplate.

However, this did mean that her search for ultimate knowledge was beyond her ability to fathom or complete. Was she being foolish to want to soak up every bit of knowledge she could find? Or was she really searching for understanding and meaning to it all?

She leaned down and picked up a still-living starfish from the sand in front of her and tossed it as far as she could out into the waves. It might have a fraction of a chance of surviving even then. It might just wash up onto the shore again to die. A small thing. A miniscule thing. But wasn't she a miniscule thing in the great pattern, one single thread in the warp of an enormous weaving?

She sighed and sat on the sand just above the tide mark and stayed there for a long time, just letting sand sift through her fingers. Ultimately, she decided her time with the professor would be a tiny fraction of her time on the Earth, if all worked out as she hoped. In the final analysis, it was like all investments, potentially worth the risk. Regardless, she had signed a commitment, and she wouldn't renege on her promise.

It startled her when she noticed the sun was descending towards the horizon when she came out of her reverie. She hadn't eaten since her meal with Gaston. She hurried back to the pier, picked up some fish and chips from a vendor, and consumed her meal on her way back to the Red Line stop. She noticed her back was no longer hurting, and she actually looked forward to sitting down at the loom in the morning. Tonight, she would finish *The Hobbit*, and tomorrow she would see what the professor had for her when he checked in on her at lunchtime.

Sure enough, it was close to noon when he showed up the next day, once again with a burger and fries and a lumpy grocery bag. They ate their lunch chatting about her thoughts on the beach the previous day.

Gaston listened thoughtfully, simply nodding and making polite "hmms" and "reallys?" as she went along. When she wound down, he blotted his lips with his napkin and said, "This leads us nicely into our next project. Are you finished? Good. Come into the lab."

They cleared up the detritus of their meal, donned lab coats, and went to a new workspace, separate from the woodworking area. He set a bag on the table. "I'll be right back," he said. "Don't peek."

She heard him leave the office and go out to his car. He returned quickly. He had two boxes, one, which was covered with a cloth, he put on the desk in the office. He practically bounced on his way back over to the worktable with the other box under his arm. With a flourish he emptied about five pounds of small oranges from the lumpy grocery bag onto the table. They went everywhere. Some of them rolled off onto the floor. He laughed, and she helped him retrieve them and set them back on the table.

What in the world? she thought.

He laughed again at her perplexed expression. "You should see your face!" he said, wiping tears from the corners of his eyes. "Come now, your eyes will pop out of your head if you continue like that!"

Lizzie shook her head, not sure what to think.

"Okay! Okay! Let's begin a new adventure. Are you familiar with the 'Kissing Number' problem in geometry? It's also known as the 'stacking problem.'"

"Hmm. Isn't that something to do with the number of touch points created by any multiple of geometric structures, usually spheres, when placed next to one another? I can't see why it is a big deal, actually. It should be a simple calculation based on the number of sides or number of potential contact points and how you decide to stack them. What does this have to do with anything?"

"Ah, Lizzie. It has *everything* to do with, well, pretty much everything. As we speak, physicists all over the world are puzzling on this. For now, I want you to practice stacking these oranges as many different ways as you can to get the maximum number of kissing points. It may seem basic and even obvious, but, like the weaving project, upon further contemplation you may begin to see new possibilities.

"I'm not necessarily looking for a quantitative answer or a formula. There are plenty of those in abundance in the math and physics community. I am more interested in your observations as you proceed. Once again, you will write these down in your work journal. Leave a few extra pages between projects as you go, as you may discover that, in retrospect, you will continue to have new insights into previous projects."

Lizzie just nodded. He smiled and then opened the box and pulled out a cube-shaped aquarium and set it on the worktable. "I will leave it up to you how you use this in your project. You may choose to ignore it, but I believe it may spark something if you decide to include it. At the very least it will contain the oranges in some kind of visual and organized way."

Lizzie shook her head and barely prevented herself from rolling her eyes. Based on her earlier experience with the loom, she decided she needed to withhold judgment.

"Any questions?" he asked, ignoring her reaction as if he had expected it and maybe even had been looking forward to it.

"Is this about the math or physics, or something else? The equations are already out there."

"Hmm. I would prefer you to not consult any of your geometry or physics textbooks in regard to this project. This is more about your observations than anything. Pretend you are Newton, or Pythagoras just starting out. Observation and curiosity are always where the math begins. Math is just one way of expressing the results of your observations."

"Okay. I'll do my best."

"One thing I have observed about you, Lizzie, is when you are fully engaged, you always do your best. It's one of the many reasons I chose you for this apprenticeship."

Lizzie blushed. She hadn't expected such effusive praise, especially since she still wasn't completely sure what this was all about. In classwork, she was always used to dealing with clear expectations of the outcome. And this was all so far from clear, that she couldn't help but suspect she might be missing the point. Or was there a point?

Gaston held up one hand as she began to ask him again about the point of these exercises. He turned and went back out to the desk in the office and carried the cloth-covered box into the work area and set it on the worktable next to the cubed aquarium.

"This is a big space," he said, pointedly looking around the perimeter of the lab. "And one of the things I first noticed, working alone in here, is that after a while the very size of the space is not only distracting but sometimes disconcerting. I tried just playing the radio when I worked, but it was also a distraction; commercials and all of the announcements. Records didn't work because I had to keep stopping to change the record. I finally decided I needed some companionship.

"I'm pretty sure you will come to these conclusions yourself, so, I got you a lab partner."

He pulled the cloth off of what she had assumed was a box, but it wasn't. Under the cloth was something like a small rectangular bird cage made out of wicker. The inside appeared to have a little loft instead of a perch for a bird. On the loft was a tiny cushion and a little blanket. Curled up on the blanket was something...

"Professor, what is that?"

"Lizzie Japhet, meet Thumble, a friend from far away."

The tiny creature was about seven inches from head to tail, covered in curly dark brown fur. It lifted its tiny round head topped with two bumps, which might have been ears, and opened dark brown oval eyes and blinked at her and the professor. It stretched and arched its back like a cat, except it had *six* legs! Its front paws seemed hand-like; three stubby little fingers and an opposable thumb. It had a button-like tail, much like a sheep whose tail had been docked. Standing on all six feet, it probably was about five inches tall at the shoulder.

Thumble cocked its head to one side, examining Lizzie curiously without any apparent fear.

"It's cute, professor, but do you really think I have time to care for a pet along with everything else?"

She had noticed he hadn't really answered her question as to what she was looking at. Everything she had ever learned in biology told her that a creature with six legs must be an insect, but this little thing was covered with curly fur and looked every inch a mammal.

"Thumble can care for himself," he replied. "He's very independent. He knows where his food is, although he wouldn't say no to an occasional piece of fruit, especially pineapple. He likes rock and roll music and is usually given free reign of the lab. He has his own 'necessary' and uses it. He also keeps his little house as neat as any innkeeper. He doesn't generally make loud noises, and he's a good listener."

He unlatched the little wicker door. "Come on out, Thumble. Lizzie, lay your hand out on the table, palm up."

Lizzie did so, and Thumble ambled out of the little wicker house and onto her palm. His tiny feet were warm and soft on her hand. By settling on his rear haunches, Thumble fit nicely on her palm. She lifted him so she could see him close up. Thumble regarded her calmly, his big dark brown eyes with large black pupils fastened on hers as if he could see what she was thinking.

"Hi, Thumble. Gaston seems to think we can be friends. What do you think?" She wasn't about to do the whole cooing and baby-talk thing people tended to do with cute animals. And this one definitely was cute, the big eyes and curly fur, tiny nose, and bowed mouth made for classical cuteness. But if she were going to spend time with the little animal, she wouldn't fawn on it.

To her surprise, Thumble nodded his little head and appeared to grin, showing tiny, squared teeth (obviously not a carnivore).

"Do you understand me?" she asked in surprise.

"He has a surprisingly agile mind," Gaston replied for him. "He is his own little person, with his own ideas about things. I think he will surprise you."

"He already has, Gaston. I'll ask again. What is he?"

"Ah, well, he's not from around here and kind of a hush-hush subject. I promise to fill you in at some point. As you recall, I told you that *everything* in this lab is covered under your nondisclosure agreement. Thumble is one of those things. He can come upstairs with you, but always either in his wicker home or in a small carry bag."

He reached back into the box that had housed the aquarium and pulled out a small cloth bag with a square reinforced bottom and a zipper opening. One side of the bag was mesh that you could see through.

"When you carry him in his travel bag, always make sure the mesh is toward your body, so no one outside can see him. The mesh allows him to breathe and have light. It also has a flap you can put down when it is raining. The flap doesn't fasten at the bottom, so it still lets in a modicum of light and air."

He handed the bag to Lizzie.

"Now that I've told you the essence of your project and introduced you to Thumble, I have to leave. I have a student conference in just a bit. I'll just make it on time if the traffic isn't terrible."

And with that and a wave of his hand, he scooted out the door. In a minute she heard the purr of his car as he pulled out of the parking lot.

Lizzie turned to Thumble, still sitting on her outstretched palm. "So, what do you think about that? He just makes his introductions and skedaddles. I'll say this much about this mess I've gotten myself into: I'm not going to be bored. Would you like me to set you down? You can help me figure out this puzzle."

Thumble rubbed his head against her thumb, which she took for assent. She put him gently down on the worktable and then considered something. "Would you prefer I put you on the floor? And the professor neglected to tell me where your house goes."

Thumble made a very soft sort of *mrrr* in his throat and proceeded to jump lightly to the floor on his own and then turned and sprang back up onto the table.

"I see. So, you can get around on your own quite nicely. How about we set your house on the bench back here for now, and I'll get to work?"

She suited words to action and Thumble scampered off. Apparently, he already had his own things to attend to.

Turning to the worktable, she examined what Gaston had given her to work with. Scattered over the tabletop were two dozen small oranges and a cube-shaped glass aquarium with no top, and she sighed. It was going to be a *very* long day.

And it began. Week in and week out, every week a new challenge. Instead of answering all her questions, each new project seemed to generate new queries, and the idea intensified that this was heading in a direction that was beyond anything she had imagined.

Gaston was easy to work with and work for. She enjoyed their twice-weekly lunches where they discussed her findings and thoughts about the various projects. The orange stacking problem had been followed by nightly stargazing, looking for anomalies in the night sky.

For that project, Gaston had revealed a platform at the top of the lab where the roof retracted, and the platform rose level to the peak of the roof, where an observatory-quality telescope was revealed.

From the street below, an observer would notice the housing of the telescope only if it was being used. Lizzie didn't go up to the roof except after most people were sleeping, so the likelihood anyone would notice in this industrial park area were minimal. Also, by that time of the evening, the light pollution was greatly reduced.

After that project, she was set to studying the sciences of plastic molding, glassmaking, silver refining, and even herbology. The projects were so diverse and so seemingly disconnected that Lizzie was having a hard time fathoming where this would all lead.

Thumble had become a rather nice lab companion. He mostly kept to himself. Gaston had created a little gym and playground for Thumble in his own tiny lab apartment towards the back of the lab.

These days, however, they had also constructed a smaller version of his space up in Lizzie's apartment. Each evening she would carry Thumble up the stairs in a sturdy basket-like wicker purse she had purchased specifically for this purpose, which she considered a better option than the cloth bag Gaston had provided for her originally.

She had carefully removed the lining from the sides of the purse, so light would filter in through the slats, and padded the bottom with a scrap of an old blanket for Thumble's comfort. He happily would hop inside anytime she invited him.

During the day, as she worked on her projects, she could hear him puttering around in his lab area, humming to himself. He never seemed to be bored with watching, as if he were supervising, as Lizzie worked. She found herself talking to him as if he could understand her, explaining in detail her thought processes in her current project. It actually helped to be able to vocalize her thoughts and didn't feel as odd as when she talked aloud to herself.

She discovered that Thumble really *did* like rock and roll music. During their break times for lunch or occasional breaks to stretch and move, they would put his favorites on the worn record player in the break area, and he would dance for her. After a while, when she found her toe tapping, she would join in, to his seeming delight and her own surprise.

Day in and day out, she did as Gaston had instructed and went out to exercise, either walking or riding her bike. As she did so, she found she could think deeply about whatever she was working on at the time. She continued to spend time every day at the loom in the evening after she had cleared and washed the supper dishes. Over time she had gotten good enough at it that she could allow her mind to wander, and it did. Surprisingly, she found herself thinking about how she could have taken each of Gaston's assignments farther and could have gone into more depth.

None of her projects seemed to have a point in and of themselves, but they were definitely stretching her mind. All of them were so disparate that it made no logical sense to her how this would ever connect over time. She had to admit, though, that she was never bored, and it was much better than sitting listening to lectures in a classroom. She had to hold her biggest question back, however. He had warned her from the beginning she might not understand it until he was ready to connect all of the dots for her.

As she continued, she found herself falling into a rhythm. The tasks began to be harder and last longer. What had been fairly consistently weeklong projects began to be two- or three-week investigations into new and different types of crafts, processes, or research.

The research projects were her favorites. They always began with a question she needed to answer and a trip to the library. Gaston had arranged her to have free access to the university library, which made things easier. She would come back to the lab with three-foot stacks of research materials and a couple of fresh notebooks and sit for hours in the study, alternating between the comfortable reading chairs and the cast-iron typewriter at the desk.

By the end of the assignment, she would hand Gaston a large stack of typed pages with her conclusions, which he would take home with him, and the following day their lunch together would include discussing her thesis and her conclusions and theories. There was no grading here, and there were no written tests or formal evaluations.

During this time, just as she had while at the university, she stayed in loose contact with her parents and siblings via mail, with an occasional long distance phone call. There had been no major emergencies that required her presence at home. She and Gaston observed Thanksgiving together at a local restaurant that featured "good old-fashioned home cooking."

As the weather got colder—not that it ever got very cold in Los Angeles—Lizzie realized that the time had passed without her even noticing the holiday decorations that had sprung up everywhere, even in the industrial park. She wondered what Thumble would look like dressed as a little elf.

By this time, she realized that Thumble was no longer this furry little guy who happened to also live in the lab and up in her apartment. He was now a companion. In the apartment, he had taken to sleeping on a pillow next to hers on her bed. He was always around, and most of the time they lived in harmony. She did have to occasionally ask him to stop humming, especially when she was working on a complex research assignment.

At times like that, she noticed he seemed to understand her when she spoke. He would immediately stop the humming, which she knew he didn't often realize he was doing until she pointed it out. It was kind of like an uncle of hers who would whistle as he went about his chores. He had told her it helped him think. She couldn't imagine how that would be helpful, but she was beginning to realize that everyone had a different way of doing things.

In the various projects she had worked on for Gaston, she noticed how different scientists and inventors functioned with their own processes and eccentricities. One of her assigned projects had been to read the biographies and autobiographies of many of the prominent scientists and inventors in history. They each had not only different skillsets but completely different approaches to their study and application of what they observed. The common theme, however, seemed to be intense curiosity that always led to some kind of action on their part.

Chapter 6: Holiday Cheer

(Jenny realized that she and her aunt had something in common. She found it amusing that the passage of time seemed to go unnoticed by her aunt as long as she was thoroughly engaged in a project. She knew that feeling. When she was in the middle of a writing project, she would actually go hours without remembering to eat. And even now, she noticed the time had flown by as she read.

Chidwi had once again draped herself on the back of Jenny's chair, and she hadn't even noticed. She stretched, patted Chidwi's hand extended by her neck, and carefully turned another page.)

Lizzie hardly noticed how the time had flown by when Gaston came into the lab around the time of their usual end-of-week lunch. However, this time he did not come bearing the typical covered basket full of either homemade or fast-food goodies. Instead, he sang out cheerfully from the office door, "Merry Christmas, Lizzie and Thumble!"

Lizzie had been reading *Relativity: The Special and The General Theory* by Albert Einstein, and she looked up with a start. "Christmas, Gaston? Really? I thought that was next week!"

She had known it was coming, of course. Up in her apartment she had several of what she had thought were early Christmas cards sitting on the end table of her sofa, but she had not realized the time had come already. Her parents had gone off visiting family on the East Coast, and she didn't feel like making the long flight and trying to sleep on some cousin's couch somewhere or go through the hassle of getting a motel room.

She had sent off early Christmas cards and gifts for her parents and siblings a couple of weeks past and then set thoughts of the coming holiday to the back of her mind, out of the way of her studies.

"Yes, Christmas! Earth to Lizzie! You can't possibly be that absorbed, can you?" he asked, his head cocked to one side, birdlike. "Oh my, perhaps you can. Well, mark your place. You're done for the next few days. Run upstairs and pack some things for an overnighter. I won't have you spending Christmas with no company besides Thumble. You're both coming to my house. My housekeeper will be there as a chaperone, so, nothing untoward. Come on! Chop, chop!" he finished waving his hands at her to shoo her out of the lab.

Confused, Lizzie looked at the page number and memorized it. She wouldn't potentially damage a book by using a bookmark or dog-earing a page. Her mother had taught her to simply memorize the page number and come back to that place later. Other students had thought this behavior some kind of superpower or something, but it had never occurred to her that it was anything out of the ordinary.

"Don't worry about preparing Thumble. I have his traveling case in my car. I'll take care of him. You just bring everything you'll need for the day, as well as your sleeping things. You and Nita will be staying in the guest room," he called after her as she rushed out the door.

It didn't take her long to pack her pajamas, a change of clothes, a hairbrush, and her toothbrush and toothpaste. Lizzie had never been much of what her father used to call "a girlie girl," so she could put everything into a small overnight bag with room to spare.

Downstairs, she noticed Gaston had doused the lab lights with the exception of the normal security lights and was busily locking the outer door. "You didn't need anything from the lab, did you?" he asked, glancing over his shoulder. "No work allowed; you know. This is a holiday, something you haven't done since we started."

Lizzie shook her head and Gaston opened the passenger door for her, a gesture that made her feel somewhat awkward. This was different from usual. He was treating her like a guest, instead of a comrade. She nodded as she got into the passenger side, and he closed the door and got in the driver's side. Like his lab, it was pristine and well cared for. It was a new model, and he kept it shiny and polished on the outside and just as well taken care of on the inside.

She knew several male students had earned some regular pocket money washing and polishing the car every week. Evidently, they also cleaned the inside.

As they moved onto the freeway, she realized she had no idea where he lived. She vaguely knew he lived somewhere in the foothills of Los Angeles, but she had never been to his house. Because it was Christmas Eve Day, the freeway wasn't as crowded as it often was at noontime any other weekday. Lizzie could picture people all over the city occupied with wrapping gifts, preparing Christmas dinners, and greeting relatives and guests for a special holiday dinner.

At the university, students who had stayed over for the holidays were preparing for the various Christmas parties and events hosted by the school. It was odd. This was truly the very first Christmas she had ever been completely on her own, and she found herself grateful for Gaston's thoughtful invitation. She probably wouldn't have noticed she had missed Christmas until after the fact, but it would have saddened her that she had spent it alone.

By the time they pulled off of the freeway, commercial buildings had become fewer and farther between, and most of the structures they saw were neighborhoods of various sizes. Then even these became sparse, and they only passed an occasional house. The road twisted and wound its way around the hills as they climbed high enough to begin to view Los Angeles from above, here and there, as they would come around a bend.

Once again, homes began to edge the road, most of them facing out from the hill to take advantage of the view.

They had driven along in companionable silence for the most part, occasionally commenting on unusual Christmas decorations or shops or restaurants that Gaston had frequented.

"Almost there," he finally remarked, "just ahead," as they rounded a particularly sharp bend in the road. He stopped at the stop sign. The green street sign read, "Infinity Loop." Sure enough, on the other side of the four-way stop was a bending street lined on either side with hacienda-style homes. As in most well-to-do neighborhoods, the houses were spaced well apart with generous front yards and what appeared to be well-kept redwood-fenced back yards. The cars in the driveways were late models and all as shiny as Gaston's.

Finally, he pulled into the drive of a nice little home in the same style as the rest of the neighborhood. The landscaping was mostly desert plants such as yucca, aloe, and other succulents, but the vibrant magenta bougainvillea around the wrought iron archway that led into the entry of the house set the white stucco and red-tiled roof off beautifully.

"I love the hacienda style," said Lizzie conversationally. "It really fits Southern California. I had no idea this neighborhood existed."

"It is rather secluded, and the commute to pretty much everything is more than most people are willing to make," he said, leading her under the archway. He opened the red front door and gestured for her to precede him.

She entered and was greeted by a large sunny living room that looked out on the front garden through a large window framed by a window seat. On the window seat was curled a large black cat that appeared to be napping in the sunshine. The room was white stucco, with a mantled brick fireplace and red ceramic-tiled flooring. You could see directly into a large dining room that exited into the backyard via four white French doors. To the left of the dining room appeared to be the door to a small kitchen, and to the right was a hallway that led to the bedrooms and bath. Not a large house, but roomy enough for a couple of people. From what she could see, the backyard was larger than the entire house, with a large lawn and well-manicured landscaping that contrasted with the desert theme in the front.

"Wow, Gaston, this is really nice!"

"Thank you, Lizzie. Just a moment and I will get Nita. I think she is out in the backyard hanging out some clothes."

Lizzie stood there taking in the subtle holiday decorations in the bright living room. The mantle was trimmed with holly, and red and green candles on brass candlesticks stood on either end, with a small worn nativity in the center. On the coffee table in front of a dark maroon sofa were displayed several Christmas cards, and Christmas lights were strung around the entrance into the dining room. There was no Christmas tree, but Christmas ornaments decorated a red and green table runner that ran down the center of the dining room table.

Since she believed the professor lived alone, she was surprised that there was even that much decoration. The house was tidy, but perhaps this was because of his housekeeper. She knew few bachelors who kept a tidy house.

Gaston and a short Native American woman with greying braids dressed in slacks and a red smocked-gingham blouse came back in through the French doors. "Lizzie, this is Nita. She keeps house for me. Generally, she stays in the little attic apartment we built into the garage, but tonight she will be sleeping in the guest room with you."

Nita smiled a wide white smile. "Welcome, Lizzie! The professor has told me so much about you. He says you have been helping him in the Los Angeles laboratory. Glad to finally meet you. Come with me, and I'll show you the guest room."

She led Lizzie down the *L*-shaped hallway. On the left, at the corner of the *L* was what was probably the master bedroom. In the center of the hallway was a bathroom, and to the right at the end of the *L* was the door that opened into a roomy guest bedroom with a twin bed on either side of the room, each with a small end table. At the head of the beds was a large, curtained window. Currently, the curtains were drawn back to let in the light.

Lizzie could see that some of Nita's things, a hairbrush and a water glass and a paperback book, were on the table next to the bed on her right, so she took the bed on the left. She simply laid her overnight case on the bed, not caring to unpack anything at the moment.

"How long have you worked for Professor Gaston?" Lizzie had noticed that Nita used the word "professor" as if it were in all capital letters, so she decided that using the honorific was a good idea with her.

Nita didn't seem taken aback by what might have been considered a personal question. "I've been with the professor since his boys were in junior high school," she answered with a reminiscent smile. "After his wife got ill and needed help, he hired me to take care of her and the boys. Gladys passed about five years later, and I stayed on. His wife insisted he make a nice little apartment in the attic of the garage so I wouldn't have to commute a long distance. My children were grown at the time and my husband had passed, so I had been living alone."

Lizzie was a bit taken aback by her forthright answer. She had only realized after she asked the question that it probably was none of her business. Nita must have understood this by the look of concern on Lizzie's face.

"It is good to work for the professor, yes? I have noticed he treats everyone with respect and kindness, and he is very generous with his employees. He has told me how much he respected your attitude towards learning and how very glad he is that he chose you for your position. Are you enjoying working for him?" Nita asked.

"Of course. I'm still not entirely sure what the end result will be, but the work is interesting, and he is an easy person to work with. I'm learning a lot, and it's very different from classes at school. It was very kind of him to invite me for Christmas."

She and Nita left the little bedroom and went to the living room. From the kitchen, Lizzie could hear Gaston humming happily to himself. "Is he cooking the meal for us tonight?"

"Oh, yes!" replied Nita. "The professor loves to cook, and he is quite good at it. While his wife was sick, he always did the cooking when he wasn't at work. He says it is calming and allows his mind to wander the multiverse."

This was a side of Gaston that Lizzie hadn't thought about before. She tended to think of him as a rational scientist and teacher, not a person with hobbies that had nothing to do with his profession. She also noted the use of the word *multiverse*. It wasn't a term bandied about often by physicists, and she was surprised to hear that Gaston used it so casually, as if it was a known and understood concept.

She settled onto the couch and looked around her. She wondered if she should go and volunteer to help in the kitchen, but Nita also sat down in an overstuffed chair in one corner of the room and pulled some embroidery out of a basket next to the chair. Lizzie remembered her mother saying that needlework was not just about creating something beautiful, but it also centered the mind and allowed her to pay better attention to the conversations around her.

Lizzie looked around. There, on the window seat were the big black cat and, to her surprise, Thumble. The cat was curled up in a loose ball and snuggled happily between his paws Thumble had also curled up in a little ball, his eyes closed.

"They seem to know one another," Lizzie commented to Nita. "Does Thumble usually live here then?"

"Off and on," Nita said with a fond smile. "The professor generally took him back and forth between here and the lab until he decided to let him stay on with you as some company. I think he was worried that you would become antisocial without some kind of interaction with someone. Thumble can be very good company without being terribly distracting. I think Tidbit has been missing him," she added, glancing at the pair with a motherly smile.

"Gaston named that big black cat 'Tidbit'? Really? He's huge."

Nita laughed. "Most people are surprised by his name. I have a friend with a chihuahua named 'Ogre.' The professor is funny like that. Sometimes it's hard to tell whether he is kidding or not. But I suppose the cat was a kitten at some point. Maybe he was truly a tidbit then. He's an old cat, but very spry for his age. He pretty much rules the neighborhood, or at least I think he thinks he does. But he and Thumble took to one another right away. Odd that. I would have thought Tidbit might have considered him a likely snack, cats being cats."

Lizzie realized she really liked Nita. She was open and kindly. The little crinkly lines around her eyes and mouth indicated that she smiled more than she frowned. She could see how she must have been a great comfort for Gaston after the passing of his wife.

Gaston popped out of the kitchen, an apron that looked like a Santa suit around his middle. In each hand he held a frosty glass filled with what was obviously eggnog.

"Not to worry about drinking too much of this stuff," he said with a grin as Lizzie eyed the drink somewhat suspiciously. "Alcohol free. We don't need any of that sort of thing to have a fun time. The closest thing to a euphoric is the nutmeg sprinkled on top, and not enough of that to do more than enhance the flavor. Just a second and I'll get mine, and we'll toast the season."

He bounced out of the room and returned with his own brimming glass. He raised his glass with a nod, and they did the same.

"To the many gifts of the season and the hope of peace on Earth and goodwill towards all men... and women, of course," he toasted with a broad wink and a grin.

The eggnog was a perfect balance of sweet, creamy, and a tiny bit spicy. He plunked himself down in what was obviously "his" chair, an overstuffed comfortable-looking chair with clawed feet and damask upholstery.

As they sat in companionable silence, something came to Lizzie. When they had toasted, Gaston had mentioned "gifts of the season." *Oh no!* She realized she hadn't gotten a gift for him and, since she hadn't known about Nita, she didn't have a gift for her either! Now she sat there feeling embarrassed and wondering what to do if there were gifts for her here and now.

Evidently Gaston recognized her consternation. "Are you okay, Lizzie? The eggnog not to your taste?"

Lizzie hung her head and replied in a soft voice, "No, Gaston. I just realized I came without a single gift for you or Nita... not even a kitty treat for Tidbit. You must think me a terrible guest."

Gaston let out a loud guffaw. "Oh, my dear. Not all of us celebrate Christmas for the presents, don't you know? Now, don't be embarrassed or concerned. We will be gifting, but not to anyone in this room. After supper we will be heading to a local orphanage with a large red sack. Not a single gift has any of our names on it. You'll see. It truly is better to give than to receive."

Lizzie let out the sigh she had been holding in and took another sip of the eggnog as her stomach muscles relaxed.

"Oh dear! It's awfully quiet in here. I plumb forgot!" Gaston said, setting his cup on the end table by his chair. He hopped up and rushed over to the large stereo system in the dining room, and all of a sudden, the house was full of Christmas music.

"I set up the stack of Christmas albums before I came to get you and forgot to turn it on when we came in," he explained, as he returned to his chair.

Lizzie turned to Nita, who had resumed her embroidery. "What are you making?" she asked.

"I'm embroidering pillowcases for a niece of mine who is getting married in February on Valentine's Day. I tried to tell her to pick a different date as she will only get one gift on Valentine's Day and her anniversaries, but she said she didn't care as long as she had lots and lots of anniversaries." She shook her head as if to say, "Young people and their notions."

Lizzie laughed and said, "Well it sounds like she has her priorities straight, for sure. I noticed a lot of my fellow students in school seem to be of the impression that, 'It's just as easy to marry a rich man as a poor one,' as if wealth or position makes for a 'good match.' Personally, I don't get it, and I'm in no rush to find a rich or a poor man. I've got too many things on my to-do list to devote time to being a wife and/or mother."

Gaston raised an eyebrow. "Really, Lizzie? I know you are very focused with your studies, but I would have imagined an intelligent and comely young woman like yourself would have had many dating opportunities in school."

Lizzie blushed, but simply said, "It isn't lack of 'opportunities' so much as a lack of interest. There'll be plenty of time for that later."

Nita simply smiled over her embroidery and Gaston drained the last of his eggnog. "You hinted from the beginning you had some large but vague plans for your future. Anything coming into focus yet?"

Lizzie shook her head. "I'm still trying to figure where this 'apprenticeship' is heading, Gaston. We've been all over the map with these projects, and I'm struggling to connect the dots. I can see that each project in and of itself is interesting, and I learn something new every time, but I can't help but wonder if this is as random as it seems.

"Something tells me you aren't someone who does things without having a specific reason for it, but, if there is a point, it's gone way over my head.

"Don't get me wrong," she hastened to add at Gaston's raised eyebrows. "I'm loving it. School seemed so restrictive, and I couldn't see how it would all fit into that gut feeling that there had to be something much more than what a formal education claims to offer. That being said, I tell myself at the end of each of your projects, 'Okay, that's done. Next time he'll finally tell me where we're going with all of this.'"

Gaston grinned a somewhat mischievous grin. "Ah, Lizzie. I knew I picked the right person when I brought you on. You have the necessary spirit and curiosity to be an incredible success in whatever field you decide to embark on. I'm actually encouraged that you still haven't settled on a specific tack in your journey. You won't have to wait much longer. This isn't the time, really, to talk about work, but I promise you that your patience will pay off.

"In the meantime, I guessed I fibbed a bit when I said I had no gifts for you today, but it isn't a Christmas present, strictly speaking. I want you to know that in my opinion you have passed your first tests admirably. After the first of the year, I'll also be taking a sabbatical from the university and taking you along with me on an adventure of exploration. How does that suit you?"

"Really, Gaston? Where will we be going?" Lizzie asked, leaning forward expectantly on the edge of the little couch.

"Well, like most gifts and rewards, it won't be any fun if I don't allow you the joy of unenlightened anticipation, will it?" he said, now positively glowing with mischievousness.

Lizzie shook her head. "I guess the new year is only a week and a half away. I can wait that long."

A soft "ding" sounded from the kitchen. "And the good news is that you don't have to wait any longer for our Christmas Eve feast," he chuckled. "Supper is ready. Let us retire to the dining room."

The table was already laid with plates, cups, and silverware.

"Have a seat, both of you," he called over his shoulder jovially as he strode into the kitchen. "Tonight, it is my delight to serve you."

He came out with a tray of dishes: squash, stuffing, applesauce, and cranberry sauce. He set each of them on the table and returned to the kitchen to fetch the main dishes: a beautiful Christmas ham and a large bowl of mashed potatoes.

"There we go," he said, and reached beside his chair to the stereo and turned the sound down. He turned to Nita. "Would you care to offer a prayer on the food?"

She nodded, and they all folded their hands and bowed heads reverently. She thanked heaven for the bounty of the feast and the purpose of the celebration and asked help for the needy and downtrodden.

At her soft, "Amen," Lizzie looked up at Nita and said, "Thank you, that was beautiful. I should do that myself more often."

Nita just smiled at her and reached for the mashed potatoes. Gaston turned the volume back up on the stereo. They all filled their plates and for a few minutes there was no chatter, just the familiar sounds of holiday music, plates being filled, and "pass the cranberry sauce" or whatever they needed.

Plates loaded, Lizzie basked in the quiet companionship, the tasty food, and the beautiful Christmas music. She hadn't felt this much "at home" anywhere for a very long time.

After the meal, despite Gaston's protests, she and Nita helped clear the table, put the leftovers away, and washed and dried the dishes, occasionally singing along with the carols issuing from the stereo in the dining room.

"Okay, grab your jackets, girls. There are orphans waiting for Santa's elves to arrive." He handed each of them a traditional elf's hat and escorted them out to the Bel Aire. Evidently, he had already stowed the huge red bag of gifts in the trunk of the car. They cruised down the now festively lit street, and several twisty turns of the hilly road later they arrived at a large building that looked a lot like a school.

The large brightly lit curtained windows of the two-story building showed the shadows of children and adults moving around inside. Nita and Lizzie helped Gaston lift the large red cloth bag full of lumpy parcels and went up the steps to the entrance. Inside, they were greeted by someone Lizzie assumed must be the administrator of the orphanage. She was a middle-aged woman with gray streaks highlighting her dark hair.

"Welcome! Stay here for just a moment while I get everyone assembled in the dining room."

A few minutes later she bustled back in and beckoned cheerfully to them. "This is as close to Santa as most of these children may ever get. Finding adoptive families is an ongoing challenge and some of these children have lived here most of their lives. Thank you so much for doing this."

They entered the large dining hall to enthusiastic applause, hoots, and joyful laughter. They escorted Gaston to a large, overstuffed chair at the front of the hall and gestured for Lizzie and Nita to flank him on either side.

Lizzie discovered that these weren't just random gifts. Evidently Gaston had researched the names, ages, and needs of each child. For each one, starting with the youngest among them, there was a package and a stocking filled with goodies. Each child was called up as a gift came out of the bag. Lizzie was handing him packages, and Nita was giving out stockings. He called out each name with gusto and cheerfully shook each hand and said something kind and encouraging to each child.

There were about thirty children in those assembled. Once every child had a package, three gifts remained. These were for the Administrator and her two assistants. He also gave her gift certificates for a meal at a favorite local restaurant to give to other helpers who weren't there this evening.

Finally, he handed the administrator a sealed envelope. "To help with other things," he whispered quietly to her, barely heard over the excited cries of children opening packages and treats.

She bent over and hugged him where he sat. "Thank you, professor. This means more to these children than I can express."

Lizzie saw to her surprise that Gaston was blushing. "Just doing my bit," he replied quietly. "I look forward to it every year. It is the highlight of my Christmas celebration. Of course, as you know, it was Gladys who began it."

"We miss her too, you know," she said, hugging him again.

As they drove back to Infinity Loop, Lizzie couldn't help but think that this was the best Christmas she could remember. Gaston had risen even higher in her estimation. None of the gifts they had given those children had been cheap or low quality. He had taken each child's needs and desires into consideration. She was pretty sure the envelope had contained a generous check to support ongoing expenses and needs at the orphanage.

She felt now that she had made the right choice in accepting this position. Gaston was more than knowledgeable. He was a good person, and she realized now that she could trust her future to him.

Chapter 7: Field Trip

Lizzie never knew a week to pass by so slowly before. Gaston had given her a list of tasks to make sure the lab was clean, organized, and prepared to be unused for an undetermined amount of time. He also had her check to be sure her passport was in good order and that she was up to date on all her immunizations.

He had purchased her a nice set of luggage and had given her a line of credit at a favorite clothing store. He advised her that she wouldn't need anything very formal, but good solid clothing for "adventuring," as he called it, would be needed.

Unlike most of her female peers, she generally wore pants rather than skirts, so she already had a fairly good collection of serviceable clothes, but she was female enough to enjoy picking out a few new outfits. He had told her to be prepared for different climates, so she also picked up some Bermuda shorts and a decent sun hat. She already owned a good pair of sunglasses. She kept the colors neutral, staying away from whites and bright colors.

By the end of the week, a couple days before New Year's Day, she felt like she was pretty well prepared.

She was surprised to discover that the professor expected to take both the cat and Thumble with them in their journeys, whatever those were going to be. Evidently, the carrier he had brought Thumble to the lab in was fine for traveling wherever they would be going, and Tidbit had his own cat carrier as well. Gaston explained that they wouldn't be carrying that. It had its own wheels.

She made a last inspection of the facility. Gaston would be picking her up in an hour or so. She had double-checked to be sure that all deliveries had been stopped to the lab and she had her newly packed things waiting in the office by the door. Thumble had obediently hopped into his carrier and was now humming cheerfully to himself.

"You're such a happy little guy," she remarked to him, as she latched the door to his traveling domicile. "I kind of wish you could talk. You're good company, and I'd love to know what is going on in your head. Maybe then I could solve the mystery of where you come from. I've yet to find anything like you in the zoological records, and I've never heard of anything like you in any of the lists of mythological or extinct creatures."

Thumble didn't reply, of course. Finally, she heard the purr of the Bel Aire as it pulled up in the parking space outside the door. At last, she would maybe find out what Gaston had put her up to, or so she hoped.

"Passport in your pocket?" Gaston asked, in the way of greeting as he grabbed her suitcase by the door.

"Yep," she replied, lifting Thumble's travel cage. "By the way, I was wondering how Thumble and Tidbit are traveling; won't they question his, um, unusual appearance? Aren't there rules about traveling with pets?"

"Indeed, which is why Thumble will be doing most of his traveling in Tidbit's travel crate. Every pet should have a stuffed toy to comfort them on a long journey. It will never occur to them that Thumble is alive if he is snuggled between the feet of a large predator like Tidbit. They would assume, if he were alive, Tidbit would be eating him." His eyes twinkled.

"Sounds like you've done this before. Do you often travel with your cat? I mean couldn't he just stay home with Nita?"

"I suppose, but, as you may not yet realize, as you don't know him well, Tidbit is a very special cat."

"All pet owners think that about their pets, I suppose," Lizzie agreed. "I don't guess I have much experience with that. My family don't seem to go in for owning pets much. I think I have an uncle with a Yorkshire terrier, but he lives out East, so I don't know a lot about it."

Gaston only chuckled. "You may be wondering where we are headed."

Lizzie rolled her eyes. "Are you finally going to tell me, then?"

"Couldn't keep it a secret much longer since you might notice our destination at the ticket counter. Have you ever been to Switzerland?"

"No! What will we do there?"

"There is a remote observatory in the Alps. Most people don't know it exists. It's privately funded, and the research there is very hush-hush. This week a number of the, shall we say, um, stockholders will be gathering, and I would like to introduce you. They are of various disciplines. I have been reporting the results of your projects to them from the beginning of your apprenticeship, and they wish to meet you. They are my associates in many fields of research. I have told them I think you show promise. Much of what we do going forward will depend on how well we all get along."

"Then, do you work for some hush-hush private corporation?"

"Something like that. Nondisclosure agreements and covenants don't allow me to discuss it further than that until you're vetted. This meeting is part of that process."

"What if they don't vet me?"

"Not to worry, Lizzie. You will still have several options, all of which are potentially attractive. Or, when our contract is complete when your year is up, you can go your own way, with my recommendations, to any of your future endeavors. Okay?"

"Fair enough. It sounds like it will be interesting. So, if you are able to tell me this much, is Switzerland your company headquarters?"

"No. It was just a central, very private place for all of us to gather. Did you notify your family you would be away for a while?"

"I did. My mother was a bit taken aback that I would be traveling with a man they didn't know to a mysterious destination with no particular agenda. As to whether or when I would be back, however, I'm not fussed about it. I just told her that I trust you and that you are a respected professor at the university. That calmed her down a bit. I told her it was a part of a special internship, and that part of my test was my ability to keep confidences. I'm sincerely hoping that was an accurate, if not somewhat vague, summary of our venture?"

Gaston nodded, exiting the freeway toward the Los Angeles International Airport. He pulled into the area reserved for long-term space rental, found a spot, and pulled Thumble out of his travel carrier and handed him into Tidbit's crate where he happily curled up between Tidbit's protective legs and appeared to promptly go to sleep. Tidbit looked up at Lizzie and Gaston with those amber eyes and curled around the little creature with a rumbling purr.

Gaston then waved over a porter to help stack their luggage on a cart, and off they went to the ticketing gate. Standing in line, Lizzie found that her stomach was agitated. She wasn't often nervous or anxious, but she did feel a surge of adrenalin at the thought that she was now committed to go into the unknown.

She was used to planning everything in her life, step by careful step. This throwing-caution-to-the-winds situation was completely outside of her comfortable routine and habits. True, she had always longed for adventure and out-of-the-ordinary experiences, but so far, she had lived a fairly mundane and somewhat predictable life.

She showed her passport and identification at the ticketing counter, was handed her boarding passes, and watched as the ticket agent tagged their luggage, including Tidbit's crate, and placed them all on the conveyor belt that slid it all out of sight.

"Upward and onward!" said Gaston cheerily, pulling her out of her reverie. She shook herself mentally and followed him towards their gate.

She found herself contemplating the other travelers around her, coming and going, and wondered where they were going and what prompted their journey. She was surprised at how many there were. Along the way there were shoeshine stands, with young men working vigorously on the dress shoes of men in suits and ties as they read a newspaper or a book. There were several shops hawking snacks, books, magazines, and other handy things for travelers, and there were several food vendors. There was even a small stall where travel-weary adventurers were receiving neck and shoulder massages.

They got to their gate and presented their boarding passes and once again showed their identification. The gate attendant motioned for them to be seated with assorted other passengers. Lizzie was curious to find that her nervousness was receding as she observed the other travelers, a mixture of obviously bored regulars and excited travelers new to air travel. She also noticed more than one who looked anxious and a trifle sick.

This would be only Lizzie's second time on an airplane. Her family were somewhat in awe of her for that. Most people traveled on buses and trains, but Lizzie could see that the time would come when more and more people would begin to prefer the speed of air travel to the hassles of other types. Normally, an overseas destination like this would require a train or bus to a cruise ship and then a long ocean voyage followed by more buses or trains to get to your final destination.

Gaston had explained as they sat there waiting to board the plane that there were several stages to their journey. First, they would fly across the United States to an airport in New York. The second stage would be across the Atlantic to Germany, where they would be met at the airport by a member of the company to transport them via car across Germany into a heliport in Switzerland. The man, who was also a pilot, would take them by helicopter to the top of a mountain in the Swiss Alps, where the observatory was perched.

When the boarding call came, they proceeded to their assigned seats. Gaston had warned Lizzie that, since the trip would be a long one, she should be prepared with at least one good book and perhaps a few light snacks. Of course, they would be served light meals aboard the plane, but he told her that in his experience it was always good to have a little extra for the in-between times.

She settled in and watched the stewardess bustling from seat to seat, checking that seatbelts were properly fastened, taking drink orders, and the like. The last time she had flown, it had been in what her dad called "the cheap seats," but Gaston had gotten them seating in the first-class section, with much more leg room and dedicated stewardesses waiting on their every whim.

"It's not about luxury," he had told her. "It's a practical matter when you are traveling as far as we will travel in the next 24 hours. I promise you; you will appreciate the little extras by the time we have been in the air for a while."

Gaston had given her the window seat, which she appreciated. She had always been slightly claustrophobic and being able to see out the window definitely helped that. Besides which, she really enjoyed the view from a plane in flight.

As they taxied down the runway, she impulsively reached out and grabbed Gaston's hand, which surprised him, but he didn't draw away. "Thank you so much for this, Gaston. I have no idea what is about to happen next, but I trust it will be more than worth my time and commitment. I am not sure why I got chosen for this, but I want you to know that despite my sometimes-thorny attitude, I really do appreciate the opportunity you're offering me here, and I'll do my best to make you proud. I know you're taking as much of a chance on me as I'm taking on you."

Gaston actually blushed! "Why Lizzie, I'm not sure how to reply to that. You are an able and bright student, but I am hoping that in the near future you will also be a colleague and a friend. Upward and onward!" he said as the plane lifted from the ground and the nose of the plane pointed toward the wispy clouds in the east.

Two plane rides later, in the which they had been pampered and waited on, hand and foot, they exited the plane in Germany. The trip had been uneventful. On the trip over the ocean, they had slept peacefully, with only slight turbulence at one point, and Lizzie actually felt rested and ready for the next leg of their journey.

It was very early in the morning in Germany, and dawn hadn't completely shown itself.

The fellow who met them at the baggage claim area was short and stocky, with sun-darkened skin and curly black hair. Obviously, Gaston knew him well. He rushed up to him and extended his arms in an enthusiastic hug. "Manawa, my friend! So good to see you! Allow me to introduce you to

Lizzie Japhet, my apprentice. Lizzie, Manawa is from the outback of Australia."

"G'day, Lizzie!" Manawa said extending his hand with a flash of white perfect teeth. "Glad ta meetcha!"

Bemused, Lizzie shook his hands and realized that now her adventure had well and truly begun. "Nice to meet you too. I understand you are a pilot?"

"Righto. You'll be flyin' in me bird in a few hours. I have a van outside. Let's get your bags and collect Tidbit, shall we?"

"You know Tidbit?" Lizzie asked, a bit surprised.

"Aye, he's me big old black furry mate, he is. Always good to have a cat around, isn't it?"

Lizzie wasn't sure what to say to that, so she nodded.

They rolled the luggage cart to the parking lot and then up to a large, eight-passenger van, and loaded the luggage into the van. But before Manawa could close the doors, Gaston held up a finger. "Just a minute," he said, and reached into Tidbit's crate to lift Thumble out and hand him to Lizzie.

"He could probably use some fresh air and space," he said, with a wry smile. "It's been a very long trip to stay put without an opportunity to stretch You coming, cat?" he called out. And Tidbit, after a massive stretch like only a cat can make, hopped over the back of the back seat and settled himself in an upright sitting position, apparently waiting patiently for the humans to get their act together.

Lizzie laughed in spite of herself. "He can almost talk, you know," she remarked. "I think he pays a lot more attention to what's going on than any of us expect."

For some reason both Manawa and Gaston found this funnier than the remark seemed to require.

In the van, Lizzie was seated comfortably in the middle seat in the back. It had large windows throughout, potentially the type used to show tourists the sights. Thumble seemed content to perch on the back of the seat behind her, humming happily to himself.

Manawa explained as they drove along that they had about a four-hour drive ahead of them, not counting a stop for breakfast and any necessary stops along the way. His expectation was to lunch at the top of the mountain after about a forty-five-minute flight.

They stopped at a little restaurant a few minutes later, where Gaston ordered for them in German. "It's good to eat the local traditional food. I seem to remember you don't have any known food allergies?"

"No, I'm good," she said, wondering how many languages Gaston spoke. She never remembered having a conversation about languages with him. Lizzie had some very basic French from her high school language courses, but she never got a chance to practice it, so it was very spotty indeed. She found herself wondering if speaking a second or, heaven forbid, a third language was going to be a necessary job qualification.

Their breakfast came soon after, before she had much time to worry herself about it. It looked and smelled marvelous. Dark rye bread, still warm, a few different kinds of cheese, a generous slice of ham, a slice of cooked spiced pear, and a large glass of juice and a cup of hot cocoa completed the meal. "Looks and smells great!" she said.

Pots of marmalade and some kind of berry jam were also set on the table. Lizzie watched to see the proper way to eat these things. Gaston immediately reached for the marmalade, spread some onto his rye bread, added a slice of white cheese and the ham, and ate the sandwich open-faced.

Manawa followed suit and Lizzie did the same, choosing the berry jam instead. It was delicious and very filling. The hot cocoa was creamy and rich-looking, but as Lizzie reached for it, Gaston put a hand on her arm. "Wait a second," he said, digging into his coat pocket and bringing out a wrapped peppermint stick. "Try stirring your chocolate with this," he said. "A great way to end a great breakfast."

Lizzie grinned and unwrapped the peppermint stick. Now the aroma coming up from her hot chocolate was even more heavenly. After tasting it, she vowed to always keep a peppermint stick with her. They walked out of the restaurant with full and happy tummies, Lizzie sucking on the remainder of the peppermint stick.

Gaston had asked the waiter to wrap up the remaining meat and cheese and asked for a piece of the spiced fruit to be included.

Out in the van, he unwrapped the meat and cheese for Tidbit and laid the piece of fruit on a small plate (where had he gotten that?) on the seat beside Lizzie for Thumble, who happily munched on it. "I'll get you both some water at our first rest stop," he said to Tidbit, as if the cat would understand. Tidbit simply looked into his eyes solemnly as if in answer to the remark.

The trip that followed was amazing. Lizzie had been up in the mountains that surrounded Los Angeles, of course, and she loved to visit Yosemite, but these mountain ranges were breathtaking. The little villages and towns, as well as some cities that nestled in valleys and nooks as the road wound itself higher and higher, were charming. Although the sun was bright and the sky was as blue as a robin's egg, it had snowed recently and the houses in the villages they passed were like large gingerbread houses with thick white frosting.

The roads were clear, and in about three hours with only one stop to water "the critters," as Manawa called Tidbit and Thumble, and allow the humans to take care of their urgent needs, they approached the Swiss border. Lizzie had expected some kind of border stop to check passports and such, but Manawa drove past the border station with a happy wave to some people standing in front of the building there. Evidently, they recognized either him or the van, for they waved back.

The elevation was definitely increasing. As they passed one little town after another, Lizzie noticed how clean everything was and remarked on it.

"The Swiss people put a high priority on cleanliness and order," Gaston explained. "Each day the Swiss sweep not only the sidewalks, but the street in front of their homes. Traditionally, each family takes responsibility for the appearance of their property and consider it highly disrespectful and even criminal to drop even so much as a gum wrapper on the street."

Lizzie was impressed. "I wonder what it would take to start that up in Los Angeles?" she mused wistfully. "I can't imagine making laws about it would work. There are way too many of us for policemen to enforce such laws, especially since they are already understaffed to keep crime under control."

"It's all a matter of the attitude of a culture. Different cultures have different priorities, as you will discover as we continue with your apprenticeship," Gaston explained. "Other than the basic laws that protect people's rights and property, most governments haven't been successful in going against cultural norms. Generally speaking, I have noticed that the most effective way to persuade people to change is to show by example the benefits of certain actions and attitudes."

Lizzie thought about this. She had often heard the term "teaching by example" but hadn't actually considered what that really meant.

"So, if I started sweeping the street in front of my house in Los Angeles, do you think it would catch on?"

"Like many experiments, it probably wouldn't hurt to try, but most people would be worried about being hit by a car," Gaston said with a smile. "However, you could try it on Infinity Loop. Not much traffic there."

Lizzie laughed in spite of herself. She was never quite sure when Gaston was teasing, but she felt this time he probably was.

Manawa had been mostly quiet during the trip, speaking up only to point out a particular landmark or scene as they drove along. Now he piped up, "In the outback, the human population is pretty sparse, and we don't use a lot of disposable things, so litter is virtually unknown. We consider ourselves stewards of the resources available to us and seldom throw anything away if it has any potential to be useful."

Lizzie nodded. "My mom used to tell us, 'Use it up. Wear it out. Make it do or do without,' which I think is similar to what you mean."

"It is certainly one aspect," Manawa agreed. "Of course, it is also important to create things in such a way to get the best use out of it from the beginning. Things that are well built or carefully crafted of the best materials available means you're less likely to throw it away. It's also about the attitude of cherishing the part of the planet you have been given stewardship for."

He turned off of the main road onto a narrow, paved road without a street sign. The road was surrounded by stately conifers so tall that the sun was mostly blocked from view. In about a mile, the road widened out into a paved area about the size of a football field. There was no sign announcing the purpose of the property, but there were two large hangars, and out on the tarmac was a small helicopter that would hold only four people.

"Welcome to Dragonfly Air," Manawa announced with a grin over his shoulder at Lizzie. "Hold on while I get the luggage. It's a bit brisk out here."

He hopped out of the van and sprinted over to where a metal luggage cart sat waiting. He ran it over to the van and opened the back doors.

Lizzie picked up Thumble and sat him on her shoulder. "Coming Tidbit?" she queried. He stretched luxuriously and ignored her outstretched arms, jumping out the van door with feline grace. He sauntered towards the helicopter as if he knew exactly where he was going.

"He's been this route before," Gaston explained. "He even has his own spot in the 'copter. Let's get you situated."

Now Lizzie began to feel nervous again. She wasn't worried about the helicopter ride, but more and more this was feeling like a turning point in her life. She knew she wasn't all that good with people. Most people she met tolerated her, but she knew they thought her a bit odd. Normally, this didn't bother her all that much. But this was different. This could affect her professional life and was an opportunity she hadn't expected to have this early on in her studies.

She still wasn't sure where this was taking her, but she had a gut feeling that a lot of her future depended on the success of this "meet and greet."

As she strapped into the seat behind Gaston, she noted that Tidbit did indeed have his own space, complete with blanket and pillow. Thumble climbed off of her shoulder and once again settled himself between the curled legs of his cat friend.

The rotor blades began to whirl above them, and Lizzie felt a slight lurch in her middle as the skids of the 'copter lifted from the ground. Over the course of the trip so far, she had felt altitude pressure in her ears change several times, so she knew they were already at quite an altitude, but now once again her ears began to pop.

The doors on either side of her were solid, so she could only look ahead through the bubble-like windshield over the shoulders of Gaston and Manawa. Her stomach and her mind were both churning. The questions that swirled in her brain would be answered eventually, and she didn't want to have to shout over the roar of the engines and beating whirl of the rotors above her head.

The trip was surprisingly short. In forty-five minutes, she noticed that they were slowing slightly and beginning their descent into a wide meadow. The scene before her took her breath. A huge multistoried building loomed ahead. It looked like it had been built into the granite side of the peak of the mountain. Its domed roof dwarfed any dome on any building she had ever seen.

"Wow! What is this place?" She asked Gaston, when the rotor blades of the copter had stopped.

"Come and see," he replied, his eyes twinkling, and his head cocked in his typically questioning manner.

Chapter 8: Introductions and Insights

(Now it begins...

Jenny realized the journal had drifted closer and closer to her face in anticipation. She was certain she knew what was coming next. She felt like one of the conspirators in a surprise party.)

The front of the building had an arched doorway covered by an accordion-style roll-up metal door. In front of the door stood several people waiting with welcoming smiles. A very short man with wispy white hair and rosy cheeks stepped forward as they approached. "Welcome! We wanted to be here to welcome you properly, but it is cold out here and nice and warm inside. Come! Come! Let's get you all inside, and we can make introductions!"

Lizzie couldn't help but grin at the welcome. Gaston nodded toward the door and gestured for her to precede him.

In the entry hall, Lizzie couldn't help but gasp. She had expected this huge edifice, seemingly carved into a rock to be dark and forbidding like some ancient castle, but it was bright and roomy inside, sparkling clean, with white walls and high ceilings. The entryway was furnished with comfortable looking overstuffed chairs and adorned with antique tables upon which were artistically arranged fresh flowers. In the wintertime? Lizzie wondered. Impressive and beautiful.

The rest of the group had filed in and now stood in a circle. Lizzie counted a dozen of them and all so very different. Gaston had mentioned that this research group was international, but she could see that this was a bit of an understatement.

"Again, welcome, Lizzie Japhet, to Sternlicht. That translates as 'Starlight' in English. I am Ernst, the administrator of this facility. This observatory is known only to a chosen few, and as such its existence is included in your nondisclosure agreement. We have gathered here today at Gaston's request to potentially vet you for future assignments and projects with our international team. I apologize, but for security reasons we don't have a title or designation for this group.

"And now I would like to introduce you to my associates."

He nodded to the first person to his left. "Let's just do this the easy way. Going clockwise around the circle, each of you tell Lizzie your name and a little bit about yourself. Keep in mind that they have had a long journey and probably the next things on their list are food and sleep."

He turned to look up at Lizzie. She realized he was about six inches shorter than herself and yet, somehow, she didn't feel like she was looking down at him.

"My name is Grenheim Stormfinder. I live in a little valley in Sweden, and I am a trainer and the team leader there. My interests are physical sciences, traditional folk music from all cultures, and ice-fishing." He nodded to the person on his left.

She had long brown hair with auburn highlights, was about the same height as Lizzie, and wore a green smocked tunic shirt with soft brown breeches, knee-high leggings, and calf-high moccasin-like shoes. Her beautiful green eyes sparkled as she nodded to Lizzie. "My name is Miriha, and without disclosing my location, we can just say that I'm not from around here. I am a teacher and administrator. I oversee all of the projects of this team, and I am the primary decision maker for the workings of this cooperative."

It was strange. Miriha had a very calm and welcoming air about her, and yet Lizzie felt she would not want to challenge her on anything important.

After smiling warmly at Lizzie, she turned and nodded to the stocky, dark-skinned helicopter pilot who stood on her left.

"I am Manawa, and my home is the outback of Australia. As you know, I like to fly, and I love to prowl the rough places that surround my home. I have a fascination for interesting creatures and consider myself a steward of the land."

"I am Lela," the petit redhead next to him broke in. "I originate from the Emerald Isle, don'tcha know. I am a biologist and don't get much time to spend at me home. I am fascinated by the complexity of life, and I love to dance when given the opportunity."

Lela winked at her and nudged the man next to her. He had straight dark hair streaked with silver and wore a deep-gold brocaded tunic with a high collar. "My name is Atul. I hail from the land of India, the land of wonders," he began in a soft melodious voice. "My research is the origins of ancient myths and legends of Earth. I play the sitar in quiet moments when I can find them."

Next to Atul stood a very tall black man with broad shoulders and a shiny bald head. "I am Yaw," he intoned in a deep bass voice. "In my home of Ghana, I am a primatologist. I study primates and work to preserve their habitat and protect them from human predators."

Lizzie could imagine that no one who valued their personal safety would ever mess with this man, and she expected he was very good at his job. She was beginning to understand what Gaston meant when he had told her that their fields of expertise were diverse. What in the world could they all possibly be working on together?

Next to him stood a woman with golden brown skin. She was dwarfed by Yaw, but Lizzie didn't think she would want to mess with her either. The common thread among these people seemed to be that they radiated power and confidence. She wouldn't want to find herself in the middle of a disagreement between any of them.

The woman piped up in a soft melodious voice with a slight Hispanic accent. "I am Idoya. I come from the Land of Enchantment, Puerto Rico. I own a mango plantation, I am a student of exotic self-defense practices, and I love to cook."

The tiny black-haired man beside her stepped forward somewhat importantly, but Lizzie noticed the amused looks on the faces around her and realized he was known for this, and that few took his pompous stance seriously. "I am Wang Xiu Ying of China. My interests are world history, calligraphy, and archaeology. I greet you, Lizzie Japhet of Los Angeles," he said, with a haughty lift to his chin followed by a shallow bow, and he stepped back.

A petit woman in a blue, long-sleeved, floor-length dress and a matching hijab looked at Lizzie with kindly eyes. "Greetings, Lizzie, from my home in

Pakistan. I am Tahira. I am a spinner, weaver, and dyer of fabric. I live in the verges of a forest at the foot of a mountain where we raise goats and sheep for their wool."

She nodded solemnly to Lizzie and then to the tall, wiry blond man who stood next to her, his startling blue eyes crinkled in a welcoming grin.

"I am Alexej of Czechoslovakia, but most call me Alex. My current project is solar energy, although I am working on the generation of thermal energy as well. I also created the aquaponic system used in this facility. I'll be happy to show it to you, once you are settled in."

Finally, a middle-aged man with dark curly hair spoke up. "I guess they saved the best for last," he said with a mischievous chuckle. "I guess you could say we are neighbors. I live in Canada. My name is Shepherd. My specialty is ecosystems and habitats and the balance of nature. I'd love to have you come and visit the forest where I live with my wife and our critters."

Gaston grinned at her. "I guess you have now been well and thoroughly introduced." He turned to Miriha. "What's for lunch? We're starving!"

Miriha laughed and gestured for them to follow her. The entryway led into a large high-ceilinged room that reminded Lizzie of nothing so much as a very spacious hotel lobby. Lizzie couldn't see exactly where the light was coming from, but it was as bright and welcoming as the entryway, with intermittent conversation areas defined by comfortable looking chairs and loveseats, surrounding occasional tables with brass lamps on them. Currently, none of the lamps were turned on, but she could imagine it made for a very nice atmosphere in the evenings as night came on.

There were doors spaced around the lobby area. Miriha led them through double doors to the left of the room into a spacious dining hall. The large table down the center of the room was surrounded by over a dozen chairs, and to the right side of the hall was a large buffet, laden with salads, soups, and the makings for sandwiches. Lizzie's stomach growled. Miriha led the way to the end of the buffet, where they picked up trays, silverware, and plates.

Lizzie realized that gatherings like this must not be all that unusual in this place, as they were well prepared for a dozen or so people to all sit down together for a nice meal. Lizzie selected a bowl and helped herself to what appeared to be a beef and vegetable soup and the makings of a meat and cheese sandwich. Miriha had sat at the end of the table and gestured for Lizzie to sit beside her.

In a very short time, they were all seated and eating. It was obvious from the conversations that buzzed around her that these people knew each other very well. The usual teasing and joking and also some earnest conversations went on while Lizzie and Gaston chatted with Miriha, mostly about the nice luncheon and Lizzie's background and interests. It was small talk, to be sure, something Lizzie wasn't particularly good at.

When everyone had finished their meal, Miriha stood and said, "Let me show you to your room, and we'll get your things settled. Then Ernst and I would be happy to give you a tour of the facility. From there, how we will proceed is that each of the associates will take some time to discuss their various specialties with you, which may take a few days. As you know, you have been invited here to see if you might be a good fit to work with us. This will work best if you are just yourself.

"This team has been working together for a long time on highly specialized and important projects. We have discovered that the ability to get along and create a congenial atmosphere is important to our success. If it turns out you aren't a fit for us, we each have influence in various scientific fields to recommend you to a program that might work better for you."

"I'm just excited to be here," replied Lizzie as she stood to follow Miriha. "This is my first foray into practical application of my education. Professor Cormier has been very generous, but I admit that the eclectic direction of my apprenticeship with him had me a little baffled. I begin to see where he was headed with it, and I look forward to getting to meet people who are doing science in real life."

Miriha led her back into the lobby, where a curving staircase extended up to another level. "We do have elevators that we use at need, but the life of science and study is often sedentary, and most of us prefer to take the stairs. We have four levels in the observatory, as you will see when we do the full tour, but the living suites are just up here."

"I don't mind," agreed Lizzie. My apartment over Gaston's lab is on the second floor, so I am up and down stairs several times a day. Speaking of the lab, I just realized... where are Tidbit and Thumble? I'm embarrassed to admit I haven't thought of them since I arrived. It's all a bit overwhelming."

Miriha laughed. "They have their own space, as you will see. They've been well fed and are currently pursuing their own interests. Ah, here we are." She paused in front of a door in the long hallway at the top of the stairs. She handed Lizzie a key on a key ring with a number on it that corresponded to the number on the door.

Lizzie unlocked the door and entered ahead of Miriha. The room was larger than any of the dorm rooms at the college, more like a nice hotel. Curtained windows looked out on the valley below, and from here she could see some outbuildings. One looked a lot like a large barn, and there were what were probably corrals outside of it. Inside the room was a queen-sized bed, dresser, closet, and the door to what was probably a bathroom. A desk with a cushioned chair sat next to the dresser. The colors were beiges and greens, so that the room reminded her of a mountain lodge she had visited in Yosemite as a girl.

"This is really nice," she enthused. She noticed her luggage was sitting on a luggage rack next to the closet. "I don't know what I was expecting, but this certainly wasn't it. Thank you for your kind hospitality."

"Don't get used to it," Miriha retorted, a twinkle in her eyes. "If you end up working with us, I can't guarantee it will always be this way. We travel a lot in our work, and the environment differs from assignment to assignment."

"That's okay, I know how to rough it when I need to," Lizzie assured her.

She noticed someone had already hung up her jacket, which had been taken from her as she sat at lunch. She felt like she was getting the VIP treatment. She hoped she could measure up. This was turning out to be a bigger deal than she had imagined. She also realized there must be some people working here she hadn't met yet.

"Okay, Lizzie, do you need some time to rest, or would you like to get the grand tour?"

"Oh, the tour, please. The room looks comfy enough, but I doubt I would sleep. My brain is in adventure mode, and I have a feeling I may not even sleep tonight. Even with the time difference, I'm feeling too antsy."

Miriha laughed her tinkling laugh again. "I like your enthusiasm, Lizzie. Just don't wear yourself out too soon. We have a lot to cover over the week you will be here."

"A week? Really? Gaston never told me how long we would be staying. That's amazing. Lead on! Uh, I mean, let's get started, please, Miriha."

Lizzie realized with a blush that she was probably behaving a little immaturely and was concerned she wasn't showing a very professional attitude, but Miriha just smiled and reached out two hands to Lizzie. Lizzie took them and, looking into those green eyes, suddenly felt calm and accepted.

"It is refreshing to see such passion for new experiences, Lizzie. I am afraid some of us get a bit jaded, the longer we spend at our common tasks. As I said previously, just be yourself. Grab your lab coat, as we will be touring the labs as well. Shall we go then?"

Lizzie nodded happily. She grabbed her lab coat from the top layer in her suitcase and they left her room, headed down the hallway, pausing at what was obviously an elevator. It was larger than the usual passenger elevator, which made Lizzie suspect they often used it to move supplies and equipment as well as passengers.

"We're going to take a shortcut to the basement to start our tour, but then we'll use the stairs as we proceed upwards," Miriha said, pushing a button labeled "B."

The doors opened soon after, and they exited to one of the most interesting rooms Lizzie had ever seen. In a space the size of a small warehouse were rows and rows of glass-walled tanks with fish of different species swimming around, and at the top of these aquariums were trays filled with plants that Lizzie recognized at once as vegetables and herbs. She had spent too many hot days in her family vegetable garden on her knees weeding in the rows not to know what she was seeing. Lights like nothing Lizzie had ever seen were suspended over each of the tanks, evidently supplying artificial sunlight for the plants that looked healthy and green.

But the combination of the aquariums and the vegetables were new to her. "What is this?" she asked, wondering if it was a stupid question.

"These are the aquaponics systems," replied Miriha. "These supply much of the food for the facility here. The fish are all edible species. Whatever we don't consume is either frozen, canned, or dehydrated for future use. Come and see. The special plant lighting is not yet available anywhere else on Earth, one of the private projects of our organization covered by your nondisclosure agreement."

She led Lizzie farther back into the room, beyond the last tank, to a door that led into what appeared to be a large commercial kitchen. Lining the walls on one side were freezer cases with glass doors, and along the wall facing that were shelves and cupboards. Down the center of the room were what appeared to be granite countertops, and there were more cupboards underneath. At the far end were a couple of stoves with large ovens, and several cabinets with glass doors showed racks of trays laden with various foodstuffs.

"This is the preparation room I was telling you about. Most of this is probably recognizable to you. Those glass cabinets down at the end, however, are not very common in most kitchens. They are dehydrators. We maintain about a year's supply of preserved food of various types, and the excess is distributed among the less fortunate down in the villages at the foot of the mountain.

"Most of the hired hands who work for Ernst in this facility are housed in a barracks near the barn, but they are fed from these stores as well. Each of the workers who manage the various aspects of the observatory have been vetted for security's sake and are restricted to specific areas on the property."

"Wow. I can see that it makes sense to have a year-round supply of fresh food available, since it isn't like you can just run to the grocery store for a carton of milk and a loaf of bread. Tell me more about the aquaponics. I've never seen anything quite like it before. I imagine one of the benefits is you don't have to battle weeds and garden pests."

At that moment, Ernst strode into the kitchen. "Absolutely," he said. "We get a much larger and more consistent yield, and the plants are healthier, as they aren't subjected to adverse weather, drought or pestilence. We also don't have to use pesticides or artificial fertilizers. The plants are fed organically by the waste created by the fish, and we grow the food for the fish as part of the organic cycle, so the system is completely self-sustaining.

"We raise tilapia, koi, and catfish, as well as freshwater prawns and other shellfish. We often serve an amazing fish stew for the supper meal. We also grow medicinal and culinary herbs in addition to the vegetables.

"It's nice to see you are interested in our little system," he added jovially.

"Why don't they do this everywhere?" Lizzie asked incredulously. "It seems that this would be a logical answer to areas where conditions aren't ideal for farming or raising cattle for food."

"Ah, Lizzie, it's still somewhat experimental, and humans are slow to accept change. I hope to see a time when this will be the norm rather than the exception, but we will see. How would things change if every basement to every building also provided the food for its occupants, yes?"

Lizzie nodded thoughtfully. "Is this system expensive to maintain? I see that electric power is necessary to run the lights, and the tanks look like they might be expensive to manufacture."

"Actually, that brings us to another topic entirely. You'll want to have a conversation with Alex about that. He is working on some power sources that may be much easier to tap than our current use of coal and oil, for instance. He would love to show you the special enhancements of this particular facility. You've probably noticed that there were no power lines anywhere, as you came in. We provide all of our own power needs, which, as you can imagine, are rather large."

They wandered out of the kitchen, and Lizzie realized something. Every room they had entered in this space was lighted, and no one was turning lights on or off.

"I can see even just the tour of this place is going to be a major education for me," she remarked to no one in particular. "Will I get to come back here later and talk more about this?" She asked Ernst.

"Yes, of course. You'll be spending a portion of a day with each of us while you're here. In the meantime, let's go up to the laboratories and check in with some other projects, shall we?"

Lizzie felt like a kid at a carnival with a pocketful of cash. She nodded, and they went to a stairwell that led up to doors that opened into the lobby area. They walked across the room to another set of double doors across from the dining room entrance. It opened onto a long hallway with doors spaced about 50 feet apart. Lizzie realized that this must be part of the facility carved deep into the rock; and yet, once again, the hallways were brightly lit. As she looked for the source of the light, she realized it was coming from the ceiling, but not from any light fixtures she could discern.

It was almost as if the light were painted onto the ceiling, but that was silly. Most glow-in-the-dark objects had to be regularly recharged by sunlight, so it couldn't be that. How were they doing it? She guessed this must be part of Alex's work, so she held her questions until she would be able to speak with him. They walked to the end of the hallway to another set of double doors and entered a large room about half the size of the lab in Los Angeles, except the ceiling, instead of being a roof, was rough-hewn rock also coated in whatever was giving off the light in the hallway they had just left.

In the center of the lab on tall stools at a worktable sat Grenheim next to Shepherd, a study in contrasts. On the worktable was Thumble, and both men appeared to be examining him carefully.

"Ah, Lizzie, welcome. Pull up a stool. We wanted to talk to you about Thumble," Shepherd said.

"What about him?" Lizzie asked suspiciously as she pulled up a stool. "I really don't know much except that he's been hanging out with me in the L.A. lab for a while."

"Yes, of course. But what do you know about him?"

"Actually, not very much. He doesn't look like any species I've ever read about. I wasn't aware of any mammal with six legs, for instance, and I haven't been able to find a description of him in any of the biology books I have found. Not to say that there isn't something about him somewhere. I am beginning to think he's the last of some extinct mythical beastie from far, far away. I've never seen anything like him before.

"I guess I assumed, since he belongs to Gaston, that you folks would be able to tell me what he is."

"Well, I think that your nondisclosure agreement doesn't necessarily yet extend to telling you what we know about him. We were hoping, however, to hear about your observations; behaviors, food requirements, peculiarities, and so forth."

"Oh, so this is a test? Okay, then."

And she pulled out her little notebook out of the pocket of her lab coat. It was such a normal thing for her that when she had folded her lab coat to put into her suitcase, she hadn't bothered to remove it from the pocket she carried it in.

The eyebrows of both of the men shot up in surprise. "It's a thing we do in Professor Cormier's lab," she said. I now have several of these filled with notes in my desk at the office. I have a specific one for each new project, and then my general one for everyday observations and thoughts as they come to me," she explained, as she flipped to the section about Thumble.

As she read aloud from her notes, they would interrupt from time to time to ask clarifying questions about her observations. By the time she was finished, Grenheim whistled softly.

"Were you assigned to take notes on Thumble's activities?" he asked.

When Lizzie shook her head, he said, "You are thorough. Very interesting. What did you say your scientific course of study was?"

"I'm actually pretty eclectic there," she said. "One of the problems I had in college was settling on a specific scientific discipline."

"Not to worry. Curiosity is the evidence of intelligence. You will eventually find a branch that will spark you. In the meantime, I encourage you to continue to explore," Shepherd said. "But for now, perhaps we should consider taking our little friend into the dining room. I don't know if he's hungry, but I sure am."

They pushed their stools back under the edge of the worktable and they all left with Miriha, who had been quiet during the interview, observing them all with calm interest.

In the dining room they were once again greeted with a buffet nearly groaning with the weight of the food that had been prepared for the group. Grenheim sat Thumble on the table and brought him a little bowl of fresh fruit that had evidently been prepared especially for him.

"Where's Tidbit?" Lizzie asked Gaston, when he sat down across from her at the table.

"Catting around, I expect. He knows where his food is. I don't expect you'll see much of him while you're here. He's a cat. He has his own agenda. For the nonce, my agenda is to eat this creamy bowl of fresh fish stew and one of these magnificent black rye rolls with some of this amazing marmalade." And he suited action to his words.

As Lizzie watched Thumble daintily nibble on an apple slice, she decided to ask. "How intelligent do you think Thumble actually is? He seems curious about his surroundings, and he sings to himself, not so much like a bird warbling, but more intentional and tuneful; and he is very quick to respond to requests, like to stop humming. Is that just really skilled training?"

Shepherd grinned at Gaston. "You have a 'noticer' on your hands, professor. Lizzie, it is obvious to me that you pay attention to small details, and you are good at drawing logical conclusions. To answer your question as well as I can without giving away things I shouldn't," he said, with a significant glance at Gaston, "you are correct in your theory that Thumble is smarter than we might think a furry little creature might be. Although, to be honest, human beings are often overly surprised at the intelligent actions of most creatures." He concluded this with a wry wink, as if he had just let Lizzie in on a great secret.

"After supper, most of us will return to our labs. Your next appointment is with Lela and Yaw. They have developed an interesting relationship that will actually segue nicely from our current conversation. I think you will find their study both interesting and entertaining."

Miriha, Gaston, and Lizzie said goodbye to Shepherd and proceeded back down the long hallway of labs, pausing before a door to the right of the hall. Gaston turned to Lizzie before opening the door. "We need to be quiet for a moment and move slowly until we are instructed otherwise. I never quite know what to expect from these two and their companions."

He opened the door slowly and led the way inside what appeared to be an indoor jungle, complete with a pond with a waterfall. Perched in a tree overhanging the pond was a brightly colored parrot. Yaw and Lela sat on the rock edge of the pool. Lela looked up and smiled a warm welcoming smile. She nudged Yaw, who looked up and also smiled, his white teeth brilliant against his nearly blue-black skin.

The two of them were such a contrast, the large, muscular black man and the tiny, pale redheaded woman. Lizzie continued to be amazed at the diversity of cultures and races all gathered here for some common purpose, all of whom were also seemingly distinct in their scientific disciplines.

Lela stood and moved forward, both hands outstretched in a welcoming gesture similar to Miriha's. "Welcome, Lizzie! Gaston has told us so much about you, and we have been looking forward to finally getting to meet you. Come, come! Have a seat with us on the edge of our indoor tiny lagoon. Your timing is perfect, as we hadn't started yet with Bobo and Laia."

Lizzie took a seat between Lela and Yaw and waited expectantly. She felt a little shy next to the large man. She was tall for a woman and normally didn't feel intimidated by tall men, but Yaw stood a good six and a half feet tall and was obviously highly muscular, even through his white lab coat. The uniform at the observatory seemed to be jeans and a t-shirt covered by a knee-length white lab coat. Lizzie actually found herself wondering if he had to have his specially made.

Gaston sat on the opposite side of Lela, who nodded to Yaw. "Assemble!" Yaw called out, seemingly to the apparently empty space in front of them.

To Lizzie's surprise and delight, several primates of varying sizes and types moved into view and faced them. Lizzie always pictured most monkeys to be a bit fidgety, but these all stood calmly facing them.

"Begin," Yaw said quietly, nodding to the large greyback gorilla at the far right of the group.

The gorilla nodded and, taking a small drum he had been holding behind his back, began to beat a slow rhythm. At once, the others began to dance! Lizzie blinked in amazement. There was no doubting it. The dance appeared to be deliberate and choreographed. Two chimpanzees partnered with one another as if in a ballroom. An orangutan stomped to the rhythm, clapping his hands in time, and several spider monkeys took up a circling pattern, turning and stepping in a bouncing strut around the chimps in the center of the display.

"Wow!" Lizzie exclaimed under her breath. "What are we looking at here?" she asked Lela in a whisper.

"When they have completed their performance, we will tell you," Lela whispered back.

The two chimpanzees turned in a classic underarm twirl, and as they did this, the drum did a rapid tattoo, and all the dancers froze where they were. Lizzie immediately broke into applause and was joined by the others. The little troupe all faced forward and bowed together.

"Bravo!" exclaimed Lizzie, continuing to applaud. "That was amazing!"

"Well done," agreed Yaw, addressing the monkeys directly. "Come meet Lizzie, our new friend."

At that, the primates, starting with the spider monkeys, came forward one at a time and proffered a hand to shake. Some of them hooted gently and nodded as Lizzie was given their name by Lela, and Lizzie said, "Nice to meet you."

The two chimpanzees came up to her as a couple. "These are Bobo and Laia," Lela said. "They were born in Ghana, brother and sister, and traveled here specifically to meet you, as did their spider monkey friends. They are part of a preserve colony assembled by Yaw."

"It is good to meet you, Bobo and Laia," Lizzie said in an awed tone. "Thank you for traveling all this way to meet me." She felt a little foolish with this little speech, sure that a monkey didn't require such formality. To her surprise, Bobo looked straight into her eyes and began to sign to her, his fingers moving rapidly.

"I'm sorry, I didn't catch that," she said with a sideways glance to Lela.

"He says that the trip was fun, and they hope to travel more often. He especially liked the plane ride, but Laia was afraid to look out the window."

Lizzie's jaw dropped. "He actually said that? Really?"

Yaw laughed a rich bass laugh, holding his stomach. "You see? You have impressed her," he said, directing the comment to the assembled primates.

The large greyback moved next to Bobo and Laia and also signed, his hands moving rapidly. "He says, 'that was the point. And it isn't surprising, as all humans are surprised and impressed to see the true nature of *the people*.'" Yaw interpreted. "They call themselves 'the people,' a loose translation. It's as close as I have been able to get to the exact meaning. This is Haran, Lizzie, also from Ghana," he added, nodding to the greyback. "He is very opinionated, but also very kind."

Lizzie offered her hand and was surprised when Haran pulled her into a gentle hug, and she surprised herself by hugging him back. This was far from anything she ever expected to do in her lifetime. When he pulled back from the hug, he looked directly into her eyes for what seemed to be a long time.

He began to sign vigorously. "He says you are not at all what he expected," translated Lela with a grin, and they all laughed, including all of the primate troupe.

"Naturally, I have about three thousand questions," Lizzie said to Yaw and Lela. "I don't think my visit will be long enough to ask them all. But my observation is that these are not just well-trained animals. These are thinking and feeling beings with something to contribute. How is it that we don't know this?"

Yaw guffawed again. "You've got a good one here, professor," he said wiping a tear from one eye. "You weren't kidding when you said she was quick." To Lizzie, he said, "Young lady, you are a great find. After you have completed this first part of your orientation, Lela and I would be happy to sit down with you and have discussions about the unknowns of so-called 'animal behavior.' Lela, like you, has a curious mind, and we are investigating how our two disciplines can take us further in my research. You see, this is one of the important things this cooperative is about, exploring the unknown and supporting the advancement of Earthly sciences. My personal assessment of your 'find,' Gaston, is that she has the heart of an explorer."

Lizzie had no idea what to say to this, but Gaston simply said, "I agree, Yaw. Which is why we're here. She is the most promising candidate I have found in all my time at the University. I was beginning to believe I might need to search elsewhere."

Lela, seeing Lizzie's confused expression, said, "Don't mind them, Lizzie. Needless to say, you have impressed us, but you needn't feel any pressure. The whole point of this meeting is to allow you to be your genuine self among us. Nothing else will serve our purpose if we are to discover what will work best for you and for us in a future working relationship. We are very particular about who joins our little confab. Be assured that this evaluation goes both ways. You are also here to determine if you even wish to be a part of this group of disparate and often eccentric individuals."

Encouraged by Lela's kind smile, Lizzie said, "I really have no idea why I am here. I have learned to trust Gaston in the past several months, but I am mystified as to where this is all leading. Will I know more by the time the week is out?"

"Assuredly, Lizzie," Gaston said, patting her hand. "By the end of the week you will have several options, all of which will be clearly laid out for you. Will that work for you?"

"If you say so, Gaston. I wouldn't have missed any of this for the world, and I look forward to learning about the various projects represented here. Do I understand that you are all gathered here specifically for my benefit, that you normally work in other places? I get the feeling that these gatherings are fairly infrequent and that each of you follow your various disciplines at your own facilities."

"You are correct," Yaw replied. "This opportunity to network and catch up where all of us are here at the same time is rare. We look forward to it, but we do exchange time and visits throughout our network as time permits and when projects overlap.

"In the meantime, when we get the opportunity to get together, it's like old classmates at a reunion. We can relax and exchange ideas and outrageous stories, and you might even see a certain amount of one-upmanship amongst us. The competition is friendly, for the most part, but like siblings in a large family, we do have a wide range of dispositions and interests. It keeps things interesting."

Lizzie nodded. This was already turning out to be an eye-opening experience. She couldn't even begin to anticipate what the coming week would be like, but she knew she wouldn't have missed it for anything.

The troupe of primates had stood in a loose half circle before them as if avidly following the conversation. Lizzie turned to Haran. "I wanted to thank you for your demonstration. It made me think more carefully about drawing conclusions without all the facts before me. Can I come to visit you again later this week? I would like to learn more about you and your people."

Haran hooted once softly and nodded. She recognized the sign for "you're welcome" and then a series of rapid gestures. Lela translated, "he says he would be happy to do that at any time. He was impressed that you did not laugh at their demonstration and says you might be all right for a 'furless one.'"

Lizzie smiled when Haran once again held out a hand and this time shook hers vigorously. His hand was very large and muscled and warm as hers disappeared into it well past her wrist, but he didn't squeeze it as hard as she guessed he might have.

"And now," Gaston said, standing up, "we should retire for a cup of hot cocoa and enjoy some much-deserved rest and relaxation. Lizzie has a very long day tomorrow as she gets to know the remainder of our little tribe. Thank you for your welcome, Yaw, Lela, and friends. Fascinating, as usual."

"Yes, thank you so much," Lizzie said, also standing and holding out a hand for Yaw and then Lela to shake. "I am awed by the generosity you have all showed me here."

Waving at the primates, who waved back, Lizzie and Gaston turned and headed for that hot cocoa, which happened to be accompanied by some sugar cookies sprinkled with cinnamon and Gaston's peppermint swizzle stick.

Chapter 9: Revelations

(As she had expected might happen, Jenny didn't even notice when Lizziebot removed the plates from her supper meal. She found herself wishing her introduction to the Alliance had been more like Lizzie's.

She knew where this was heading at this point, of course. Nevertheless, she felt a building anticipation. She was learning things about the Alliance she had not expected. Obviously, she, Jenny, was the exception rather than the rule. She began to see why so many of her fellow guardians and agents had been so shocked by her unusual and abrupt progression from ghost-writer to guardian to gatekeeper.

She wandered back into the living room and curled up in her chair. She realized reading this journal had taken an entire day so far.

"I'll just read until bedtime," she told herself.)

After Lizzie had spent a peaceful evening mostly listening to interesting conversations around her, Gaston remarked to her that she was dozing in her chair, and Miriha offered to escort her back up to her room. Lizzie gratefully agreed and was happy to settle herself into the cozy bed with a warm comforter over her as she drifted into a dreamless sleep.

Next morning, she awoke to a soft knock on her door. "Wake-up call," said Miriha with a smile, when Lizzie threw on her bathrobe and answered the door. "Here's today's schedule, more or less. You have a lot to look forward to. Breakfast in about an hour. See you then." And without waiting for a reply, with a smile she turned and headed out the door.

Lizzie yawned and stretched, went through her morning routine—making her bed, bathing, dressing, and brushing her teeth and hair—and headed down the stairs to find others also heading to the dining hall. They smiled and uttered bright and sometimes sleepy "Good morning" greetings as they all made their way towards the smells of breakfast.

Many were already seated and eating when Lizzie entered to find Gaston and Miriha in earnest conversation in their usual places at the end of the long dining table.

"Good morning, Lizzie. Sleep well?" Gaston asked as Lizzie brought her filled plate to the table and sat.

"Very well, thank you. I thought I wouldn't sleep with all the thoughts chasing around in my head, but I guess the trip tired me more than I realized. I am ready to go now, however. I see my schedule is pretty full."

"Yes, indeed. Today your guide will be Miriha. I have other pursuits this morning. I'll see you at lunch." And with that, he nodded to Miriha, picked up his plate and utensils, and, leaving them on the sideboard provided for dirty dishes, proceeded out of the dining hall.

"So, how was your first day?" Miriha asked just as Lizzie had taken a bite of the breakfast sandwich she had gotten from the buffet.

Lizzie chewed hurriedly and gulped. "It was great—well, 'great' isn't adequate, but I don't think I know any words that could describe it. I feel like my eyes are just beginning to open, if that makes any sense."

Miriha laughed, an almost tinkling sound, her eyes crinkling. "Every person in this gathering has gone through a similar experience before they joined us. That makes perfect sense, Lizzie. I still find it enlightening to spend time with this elect group of curious minds."

This time she waited for Lizzie to take another bite and chew it before asking, "I was wondering if you had decided to pursue a specific scientific discipline yet?"

Lizzie noticed this was a common question at almost every interview so far. "Actually, that is one of my biggest failings, Miriha. My curiosity is never satisfied, and I find all of it—" and she gestured with wide open arms as if to encompass everything she could see— "intensely fascinating. I want to know how it all works, how it all came to be, and what the future holds in store. " She sighed, feeling like she didn't completely express what she really felt, but not feeling up to the task of explaining more clearly.

"Gaston says I will eventually get over my impatience with my process, but I don't know how. It's an itch I am unable to thoroughly scratch."

Miriha didn't laugh. She reached out a gentle hand to take Lizzie's. "It is exactly these qualities that make you a prime candidate to participate in our program. And, over time, you will eventually become more focused. Assuming you come on board with us, you will be given specific assignments, and each one will take you farther along your path."

"Part of the reason Professor Gaston took you through such varied projects was to see if you could focus clearly on the task at hand and still migrate to new and dissimilar tasks without becoming bored or distracted. He tells me you passed this part of your evaluation brilliantly."

Lizzie wasn't quite sure what to say to this, so instead she took another large bite of her sandwich and chewed slowly and thoughtfully.

"The next few days will be an extension of what Gaston already began with you. After the remainder of your introductions today, you will work on a short project with each of our company. There won't be any breaks for recreation, I'm afraid, except for a brisk walk around the grounds twice a day after your lunch and supper meals. On the seventh day of your stay here, we will all get together and report, in your presence, regarding your performance and any significant factors we have noticed."

"Assuming we agree that you are able to continue to full fellowship, we will at that time make you a couple of offers of opportunities that may or may not interest you. The final decision at that point will, of course, be yours. Do you have any questions?"

Lizzie shook her head. "I think I understand. I want to tell you up front how much I appreciate the opportunity to apply for this position, even though I don't yet know the details. I can already see, based on my first day here, that I can learn much more working with this group than any degree program I could possibly pursue with the university. I'm ready. Let's get to work."

She completed the rounds of the remainder of the group that first day and then worked from early morning in the dark to late at night, every night. Each new person and each new project were revelations to her.

Her favorite was her time with Ernst and Alex regarding the observatory itself. The huge facility was completely self-sufficient, due to the many ways they had found to create power, light, and food.

Ernst explained the unusual lighting system was such an advanced secret that, until she signed her second nondisclosure agreement, he couldn't teach her the science behind it, but the rest was absolutely fascinating.

"Soon after this site was chosen for the observatory due to many unique properties of the land, which you will discover later in your training when you officially come into our little group, we also discovered fumaroles on the property. The heat and steam generated by the fumaroles are trapped by a special system I've developed to generate electricity. It's clean energy and the power is consistent, regardless of the time of year or time of day."

Alex clarified. "These fumaroles provide all of the power for every building on the property. Not enough power to fulfill the needs of a city, for sure, but more than adequate for our use. I can see potential that geothermal power could perhaps provide most of the electric power on the planet at some point, but for now, my little experiment gives us all of the electric power, heat, and hot water we can possibly use, without the fumes and pollutions created by traditional power sources."

He explained the aquaponics system in more detail, allowing her to accompany them as he and Ernst did the simple maintenance of the system. "We also grow outdoor crops and keep some cattle, poultry, and sheep on the property. At necessity, we could be completely sustainable here, even with no contact with the outside world. I don't know that there is another place I can name that has better internal resources than we do." Ernst said proudly. Lizzie had to agree. The thought, planning, and ingenuity that had gone into all this was unique in her experience.

Of course, there was the observatory itself. Her first full day of projects was capped off with an evening in the observatory. Gaston told her that this was the second largest telescope in the world; the largest telescope actually resided in California. The difference was that here, in the high reaches of this remote area of the Swiss alps, there was as close to zero light pollution as you could get nearly anywhere on Earth.

Lizzie took great delight in the opportunity to directly study the stars and planets via the huge telescope, as the study of space excited her. She dreamed of a time when humans would finally break the bounds of the Earth and be able to travel to the stars as easily as taking a plane to another continent on Earth. Although many scientists pooh-poohed the idea, she was certain that the time would come when humans would venture into space, and she hoped with all her heart it would happen while she was alive.

Of course, she knew that the science of her time didn't extend to the point where the challenges of interplanetary or intergalactic travel was remotely possible, but the idea of it fired her imagination and was one of the things she had hoped to have a part of at some point of her scientific career.

Regardless of the magnificent view afforded her by the telescope, however, she knew that somehow even that wouldn't completely satisfy her curiosity about the workings of the wonders of nature and science. She realized she was being somewhat silly. After all, what could possibly be bigger than the universe?

Just as fascinating, however, was her time with Tahira. Gaston had brought her initial weaving projects, to Lizzie's embarrassment, to show to her. He handed the piece to Tahira and excused himself for another appointment.

Tahira examined the simple dresser scarf with interest and, to Lizzie's surprise, did not laugh at or scorn her effort.

"And you built the loom yourself and did this without instruction by a weaver? Impressive. The uniformity of the weave is unusual for your first try-piece. And I am also impressed that you chose such a simple pattern. Too often beginners get over-enthusiastic and attempt something beyond their ability and get discouraged as a result. A simple design is an elegant solution and a wise choice, any time you are learning something new."

She sat Lizzie down in front of a more intricate table loom than the frame loom she had built, that was obviously meant for an experienced weaver. She showed her the moving parts that took the place of a hand-operated heddle and shed stick and demonstrated how these small advances made the work so much easier. She showed Lizzie the simplicity of creating a houndstooth pattern and set her to it, speaking as Lizzie worked about the entire process of producing usable woven items from raising the sheep to the shearing and processing of the wool into usable thread and yarn.

Lizzie began to appreciate how each craft, each bit of technology, and each bit of new insight gave way to more advancements, and how understanding the workings of apparently simple things could lead to greater discoveries.

At the end of their session together, Tahira presented her with a beautiful intricately woven shawl, soft as a breath of warm air and exactly the right length to drape elegantly while wrapping her warmly. The gift touched Lizzie so much that tears threatened to dribble out of the corners of her eyes.

Tahira noticed this and told her, "Lizzie, those of us who are so blessed as to share this week with you have gotten so many great reports from Gaston that, admittedly, we have been slightly skeptical. It is a joy to see that his reports were not only accurate but understated. It would be natural for you to be a bit overwhelmed by this opportunity, but I have a feeling that you will soon find yourself at home in such company. Based on our observations so far, you have a spark of greatness in you that you don't begin to understand yourself.

"I had heard you were a bit on the arrogant side, but I begin to see that you are simply confident in your abilities and perhaps a bit introspective, not particularly outgoing mainly because you spend so much time in your head. Time and experience will perhaps change that, as you continue to develop. You are young, and I have a feeling you will round out socially over time, when exposed to the right people and circumstances.

"I gave you this scarf to remind you that what you focus on over time becomes your own art. You will potentially always enjoy weaving as a pastime, but probably not as an art. However, understanding the principles of one kind of art often leads to the spark that will lead you to the unique art form that becomes your life."

Lizzie was surprised that something as basic as the skill of weaving could produce such deep thought and insight. But then, she did find it easy to think deep thoughts when she spent time with the peaceful rhythm of the loom. She was beginning to see the method in Gaston's madness and what all of the disparate projects were preparing her for.

She didn't know what she had been expecting, but she always thought of scientists as being somber, critical, and demanding. What she was finding here was that this wasn't necessarily the case or even the norm. Instead of the competitive environment she was used to in collegiate circles, these people were all open, helpful, and eager to share their thoughts and ideas with her and to accept her on equal terms, despite her age and lack of practical experience.

None surprised her more than her time with Idoya, the tiny lady from Puerto Rico. She met her in a small gymnasium. Idoya was dressed in a simple karate gi, her hair tied back in a ponytail and her feet bare. Lizzie had been warned ahead of time to dress in something loose-fitting and casual, so she entered wearing a t-shirt and sweatpants.

Idoya got straight to the point. "Okay, Lizzie, this will be quite different than anything we have put you through so far," she said, by way of introduction. "One of the things Gaston may have neglected to tell you is that your role in our group might be more than intellectual. A fit mind in a fit body is important. You are obviously not overweight or flabby, despite your focus on intellectual things, but we need to go beyond simple fitness, so it is my job to determine what will be needed to bring you up to our standards. Let's put you through some paces and see what we have to work with, shall we?"

And so, she began. For two solid hours Lizzie not only engaged in basic calisthenics but also walked on a balance beam, did yoga posturing and stretches, threw balls, threw darts, built towers from unusually shaped blocks, and even did some dance moves.

By the time they were done, Lizzie was ready for a shower, but then she was directed to sit on a mat in front of Idoya, as Idoya tested her ability to relax every muscle in her body and then to tighten one area of her body while simultaneously relaxing other muscles. This was harder than it should have been, as Lizzie tended more toward active tension than relaxation.

"I didn't actually expect you to do as well as you did. People from academia usually come to us pretty deficient in the physical area. You will definitely require some instruction and building up, but you have a pretty good base to begin with. I also appreciate the lack of whining and complaining."

Lizzie wasn't quite sure how to reply to this. She had hoped that spending time with all of these people would help her to puzzle out what they were actually looking for and how or why they would want her to be involved. However, the more time she spent with this diverse and often eccentric gathering of intellects, the more confused she became. There seemed to be no specific focus or goal. She was obviously missing something because this was no ragtag bunch of "mad scientists." No group that could afford and create a facility like this one could be purposeless.

By the evening before her final day, Lizzie was both exhilarated and increasingly confused. From the beginning, she had been honest with Professor Gaston about her desire to explore beyond the restrictions of academia, but this was so much more than she imagined might come of that. If she thought the eclectic projects he had assigned her were random, she was sure she had missed something important along the way. She thought of herself as really good at discerning patterns, but the boundaries of this seemed to be beyond her.

As she listened to the buzzing of conversation around her in the dining hall, she found no hint about what was coming next, so she ate quietly, finishing her strawberry-filled crepes with a sigh.

At that point, Miriha stood; and when she did, the room fell silent.

"Well, Lizzie," she began, her eyes wide and eyebrows raised in a question, "we've put you through your paces. And I must say, the reports from every single participant have been glowing. Gaston's instincts are generally good, but I think he has outdone himself. Of course, you likely feel no more enlightened than you did when you arrived.

"You have been exposed to a number of challenges, all so different as to seem unconnected. So, I am guessing your analytical mind is expectant as to what happens next.

"After conferring extensively with one another and in view of our needs, I believe we are in agreement?" At this, she paused and looked pointedly at each of her colleagues around the long table. As she paused momentarily gazing into each face there was a solemn nod. When she came back to Gaston, who was seated across from Lizzie, he also gave his nod with a confident smile directed at Lizzie.

"It is unanimous, then. Lizzie, what I am about to tell you is held in strictest confidence, but you must be informed of it before we can proceed. We have observed that you are not a close-minded person, but also that you are not gullible nor likely to swallow a wild tale without proof. Therefore, we need to give you some background on two of our number who have been somewhat absent from your program."

She followed Miriha's glance toward the back of the hall, and in came Tidbit with Thumble riding on his back, humming joyfully. Lizzie couldn't help but smile. It was true. During the previous week, they had been conspicuously absent from the proceedings.

"Lizzie, we would like to introduce you to Tarafau." Thumble hopped from Tidbit's back, and Miriha gestured toward Tidbit, who seemed to fade out for a moment and in his place suddenly stood a very tall black man wearing colorful robes similar to African or Polynesian people's native costumes. He was bald, his pate shiny as if polished, and he had pointed ears, but not like those she had seen depicted on classic elf or fairy pictures—the points hung from his earlobes. He smiled, and as he did, she saw his teeth were fanglike, very similar to the cat.

"So good to meet you, Lizzie," he said in a soft baritone voice. "You already know me as Tidbit. Outside of certain protected areas, on your Earth, I can only appear as a cat. I am a Daringi from a planet outside of your universe or, in other words, your dimension. I have the ability to change my physical nature. Your legends would call me a shape-changer."

He walked over to her and put out his hand for her to shake.

She timidly extended her own hand. His hand was large, strong, and very warm. The pupils in his large amber eyes were open and black. His skin was about the same shade of black as Tidbit's fur.

"Good to meet you, Tidbit, er, um, I mean, Tarafau," she said, continuing to look into those big amber eyes.

He laughed gently. "It's okay, Lizzie. I don't bite, at least not in this form."

Lizzie gazed around at the group seated around the table, all of whom watched her with avid concentration.

"What is this? Is this real or is this another test?"

"Probably a little bit of both, Lizzie," Miriha replied, amusement clear in her tone. "It's okay. We've all had a similar experience in our own introductions. Come and meet Lizzie formally, Thumble."

To her astonishment, Thumble leapt from the floor onto the table and, standing on his hind legs, he chirped, "Surprise!"

Lizzie nearly fell off of her chair. "You can talk? What?"

"I speak little Englishes. I like Lizzie. You still like me too?"

In answer, she stroked his head with one finger, as she usually did as he sat on her lap while she read up in her little apartment above the lab in Los Angeles. "Yes, of course. You just surprised me, is all. And where are you from?"

"Planet in distant dimension, far, far away. You come and visit my home someday?"

"Visit?" She turned to Miriha. "Okay! Enough. What is this really about?"

"Sorry, but we know your analytical and somewhat cynical mind by now, Lizzie. We thought some concrete evidence was the best way to introduce you to our offer. Relax for a moment while I explain some things to you. For now, just listen. There will be time for questions later."

Lizzie nodded her head, her expression dubious and her mind racing.

"The first thing you should know," Miriha continued with a smile, "is that I am also not of your Earth. My planet is in an entirely different dimension or what you might call a 'universe.' I am what is known as 'The Gatekeeper.' I have a very specific position in our organization, which I shall explain.

"The twelve people in this room, with the exception of Tarafau and Thumble, are what are known as 'Gate Guardians,' which denotes a position of authority beyond any held by any government entity on your world, but they do not influence or interfere in any political or other organization on your planet, due to strictures they are bound by oath to obey.

"Beginning at as close to the beginning as we are able to see, there is more than one universe 'out there,' and they are interconnected by naturally occurring dimensional portals. For reasons we do not fully yet understand, and as far as our understanding extends, this network of portals only seems to occur in any particular universe at or around a single planet. Our scientists are at a loss to explain how a particular planet is 'chosen' by the phenomenon, although there are theories. Nor do they have a clear understanding of how, when, or why these portals were formed.

"A person can step through a portal and be transported from their home universe and planet to a totally different universe and planet in an instant. On Earth, to our knowledge, there are twelve of these portals. There may be more, but some of them may be in places yet unexplored by humans to any degree. In ancient times, these portals were wide open, and it was not unusual for them to be discovered by a being from a distant dimension stepping through them, either by accident or intent.

"For many who discovered this, it became a way to study other species, cultures, and universes. For others, planets with less technology or understanding became hunting grounds for them. Some decided to experiment with colonization or even domination of cultures they discovered beyond the portals. And in some cases, cultural exchanges and trade began to take hold.

"When the groups who had banded together to trade ideas and goods conferred, it became apparent that there were predators out there, who, if left to their own devices, would use these portals to enslave, pillage, and take advantage to satisfy their desires of greed and power over others.

"That was of grave concern to the loose association of dimensions. They decided that perhaps there might be a way to control traffic through the portals; and by so doing, it would allow them to protect the weak from the strong and allow those less able to defend themselves to grow and develop without fear of predators or interference from more advanced cultures.

"Thus, the Dimensional Alliance was formed. They combined technologies and sciences to create a system to detect gates throughout the multiverse and set up a network of controlled gates that would bar non-Alliance cultures from using the gates to prey on others.

"To prevent eventual incursion by those who might have the technology to infiltrate the system, they also set up a structure that meant each known gate was guarded by a being who became responsible for monitoring the comings and goings through those gates. Thus, were the Gate Guardians of the Alliance recruited from each planet where it was possible to use native guardians. Not all universes are active members in the Dimensional Alliance, as not all of the cultures or intelligent beings on a planet are technologically advanced to the point that we can afford to introduce this information to the populace at large.

"In the beginning, the Alliance made the error of not taking this into account. As a result, some cultures were changed radically and ultimately destroyed themselves with technology they weren't ready for. Earth is not an active member for that reason. It is not and never has been the intent of the Alliance to alter the destiny of any culture. On the contrary, one of the primary concerns of the Alliance is allowing the freedom of a culture to choose their own destiny and develop as a unique and treasured asset in the multiverse, not a clone of another culture.

"An example of this was the huge world wars your Earth has been experiencing. We have the technology to have put a complete stop to those wars and all of those around the globe that seem to plague humankind. However, no culture is truly at peace if they are forced into it, and in our experience an enforced peace never lasts. Eventually, if the necessary lessons are not learned, a culture will regress to their earlier state. It is our firm belief that every culture should have the right to choose their ultimate destiny, and the diversity of the multiverse is one of its most valuable treasures."

As she listened to this, Lizzie realized her mouth was hanging open, and she shut it. Miriha had paused and was looking at Lizzie expectantly, so Lizzie said the first thing that popped into her head.

"Okay, so assuming that all of this is more than an extremely elaborate and unnecessary practical joke, what does it all have to do with me?"

"Good!" said Miriha with a delighted grin. "So glad to see you using your head. Of course, with the tech available to us in this facility, as you have seen, we could have created an illusion to deceive you. This was well thought out and well said. Would you be averse to one more quick demonstration before I answer your question?"

"I suppose not," she said, squirming a bit in her chair, painfully aware that all eyes were fixed on her and her reactions.

"Then please stand," said Tarafau's soft low voice behind her. She stood hesitantly.

"This won't hurt. I am going to take you to my home planet for a few moments and we'll be back to get the rest of your questions answered. Simply stand still."

Before she could reply or react, Tarafau put a large hand on her shoulder, and suddenly the room faded from sight. In an instant she was standing in a meadow surrounded by what looked like large military tanks. In the top of the arc formed by the tanks was a very large statue of a woman standing with her arm outstretched as if pleading. The sky was more violet than what she was used to. There were flowers growing between the wheels of the war machines like none she had ever seen before.

He reached down, plucked a blue flower that was growing at their feet, and handed it to her.

"This is a special place on my planet, in walking distance from my home. It is a memorial to a woman who changed the history of our planet from a war-stricken place of greed, intrigue, and violence, to a peaceful community where each being is valued and peace reigns," he said, gesturing around the meadow. "Someday, assuming you join us, I will take you down the road that leads to my home and introduce you to my family, but time is short and there is much more for you to discuss about your future choices, so we will return to the observatory."

Before she could answer, he placed his hand once again on her shoulder and once again the dining hall faded into her view. She felt shaken and more than a little overwhelmed, to put it mildly. She looked down at the exotic flower still clutched in her hand.

"Was that a gateway?" was all she could think to ask.

"No. It is a talent of my race to be able to transport through the dimensions without a gate. The purpose of this trip was to lend some reality to this discussion and give you more understanding as you are called to make some important choices in the next twenty-four hours."

She plopped back down into her chair and looked wide-eyed at Miriha. "Can you do that too?"

Miriha laughed. "No. As far as I know, the beings on Tarafau's planet are the only ones in the multiverse with that talent, but the multiverse is a big place, so I imagine there may be others. My race is not among them. So, now we come to the point of this entire week.

"When Gaston started watching your progress in his university and learned more about you, he became aware of an opening we would have in the near future for what you might call an apprenticeship. We are looking for a few candidates to become agents for the Dimensional Alliance. Agents, unlike Gate Guardians, have a much wider role in the Alliance and often are groomed to eventually become Gate Guardians.

"Gaston chose you because of certain qualities that are necessary for this position, including honesty, kindness, a sincere desire to do good, a curious and intelligent mind, and the ability to learn and adapt quickly to unusual circumstances. We need those who are advanced in their thinking and wouldn't be corrupted by access to advanced technology and the knowledge of the gate system.

"It involves and requires intensive training in body and mind, as well as the ability to stick to a task and follow very specific and involved directions. The professor designed that apprenticeship course in his lab to test you for these qualities. Even Thumble and your visit to Gaston's home at the holiday was a sort of test.

"The second phase was the week you spent with us here. It is easy for a teacher to become blinded to the shortcomings of a student when they grow to like and care about them. We needed to expose you to people who didn't know you well, to see if Gaston's observations were accurate or slanted in any way.

"The consensus from the guardians is that you meet the qualifications. Otherwise, we would simply have found you an internship in a worthy research facility somewhere on Earth, where you could advance your career and get on with your life; and you would never have heard or experienced what you have this evening."

"So, I passed the test, and now what are you asking me?" Lizzie asked.

"We would like to formally extend an invitation for you to join the Dimensional Alliance agent training program. It will be challenging physically, mentally, and perhaps somewhat emotionally. At no time would you be required to change any of your personal beliefs. And if, at any time, you choose to opt out, you can do so with the caveat that your memories of everything you have experienced up to that point that concern the Alliance in any way will be wiped, and new memories will replace them.

"You would be placed in a highly favored position in a good company, and you would have no idea any of this had ever happened. None of your previous memories would be erased, of course. You would just think of Gaston as Professor Cormier, a nice instructor at your former college. The degree you had been shooting for would be awarded to you, and all of the school records would reflect that you completed your coursework with honors.

"On the other hand, the 'coursework' for the Alliance training program is extensive and grueling. No textbooks and limited library time. You will be exposed to technology beyond anything you've ever seen before and will be expected to master its use. You will be held to high physical standards as well.

"It will also mean there will be much of what you do that you will not be allowed to share with even your closest friends or family. You will be provided a feasible cover story, which you will be drilled in thoroughly. The first six-week section of your training will isolate you from family and friends. You will tell them you have been accepted into a six-week internship that will take place in an area inaccessible to mail or phone.

"From time to time, you will return to Earth to allow you to make contact with family and friends. You will be studying off world and out of your dimension during most of your training, with occasional breaks to continue to nurture family relationships and enhance your cover story.

"After that, assuming you pass or exceed expectations, you will become an agent intern of the Dimensional Alliance. Following the completion of formal training and your internship, you will be doing a lot of traveling throughout the dimensions, depending on your assignments. Some of these may be extended amounts of time, as long as a year, with few breaks for intermingling with your friends and family on Earth.

"The benefit to you will be the opportunity to expand your learning in the sciences and much more. We are of the agreed opinion that you have the qualities that would allow you to be successful and valuable as an Alliance agent. During the course of your internship and your term as an agent, you will be exposed to and get hands-on experience in science beyond anything you may ever find here on Earth. Your efforts will benefit all beings on your planet and in your universe."

She paused and looked meaningfully at Lizzie. "Do you have any questions?"

Lizzie shook her head and then nodded, realizing she had just contradicted herself. "Well, yes. Of course, I have about a million questions. However, I realize all of them would easily be answered over time by simply accepting your offer. Therefore, I will ask only one: how soon can I start?"

The room was silent for a moment that seemed to last forever. Miriha cocked her head to one side, much like Gaston when he was puzzling something out or was surprised by one of her retorts. "We generally give an applicant a full twenty-four hours to make this decision. If you agree, arrangements must be made. Are you sure you are ready to accept that responsibility with full integrity?"

Lizzie looked directly into those intense green eyes. "Miriha, I swear to you and in front of this quorum of witnesses, that I will do this and give it every effort I am able to make. I finally see what Gaston was preparing me for, and I am overwhelmed and gratified that he chose me. The sooner we can get started, the sooner I can finally find out what I am fully capable of. Do I need to sign anything?"

Once again, Miriha paused, searching Lizzie's face. She took Lizzie by both hands. "So shall it be," she intoned solemnly.

"So shall it be," repeated the assembled guardians. It sounded very formal and very final to Lizzie, like a ritual of some kind.

"Lizzie Japhet, do you covenant to uphold the laws and ideals of the Dimensional Alliance; to defend the rights of choice and liberty of the downtrodden and vulnerable of the multiverse under the direction of the Dimensional Alliance Council, to fulfill all assignments with integrity and diligence, and to always do your best in every assignment you are given by those in authority over you, as far as it is within your power to do so?"

Lizzie nodded her head. "I do so covenant."

"So shall it be," Miriha repeated.

"So shall it be," the assembly echoed.

Miriha drew Lizzie into a warm embrace. "Welcome, little sister, to your new family. There are now new doors open to you. There will be some formalities to deal with. Gaston and I will meet with you in a few minutes, but for now, rejoice with us!"

Suddenly music sprang up from seemingly nowhere, the usual bright lights softened, and the room burst into applause. Thumble ran up the table to throw himself at Lizzie, little arms open wide. Lizzie barely caught him in one hand as he chirruped, "Lizzie is ours now! We can keep Lizzie!"

She perched him on one shoulder while the others gathered around, each shaking her hand and congratulating her and some bringing her into warm, enthusiastic hugs. She was surprised to realize there were tears streaming down her cheeks. "I'm home," she whispered to herself. "I'm finally home."

Chapter 10: The Journey Begins

(Jenny looked up from the page with tears in her eyes. Even though she had known this would be the outcome, she could feel deeply the emotion Lizzie felt. She often felt the same way herself, although her induction had been much less formal or involved. Now she would get to the part she had hoped for.

Having never received the full formal training of an agent or guardian, much less a gatekeeper, she was excited to compare her experience to her aunt. She turned a page.)

After a fairly carefree celebration the evening before, the following day was devoted entirely to getting Lizzie set up to begin her training in a week's time. She would be returning to Los Angeles to make a number of interesting arrangements that would satisfy her family that nothing was amiss and pretty much cover her tracks legally.

Miriha had knocked on her bedroom door without her usual sheet of schedule notes in hand. Instead, she said, "Hold out your right hand. Lizzie complied, and Miriha pressed something that looked like a rubber stamp to the back of her hand. She didn't notice it left an imprint, but her hand tingled slightly. "This is a temporary measure to give you access to today's activities," she explained.

"We have a lot to do today. Had you not passed this week's evaluation, right now we would be sitting you down to show you several potential vocational options; and during that time, much of your memory of this trip would have been wiped of all of your experiences with us and they would have been replaced with a more typical corporate head-hunting experience. You would have received multiple job offers upon return to your apartment, which would have been relocated to a place you would have 'remembered' as your own.

"However, those complications aside, we would have made sure you were happily redirected to something that might have led you to fulfill some of your ideals and vocational hopes.

"As it is, however, now we have a completely different agenda. Today you will be doing some traveling that doesn't require a helicopter or other Earthly transport. You won't need your luggage," she added, as she noticed Lizzie's eyes stray to her suitcase.

"You won't be gone for more than the day, and everything you need will be provided. You appear to be ready to work," she said, noting that Lizzie was already dressed and had donned a lab coat. "But you won't need the lab coat. We will be a little less formal in that regard today. Gaston and Tarafau are waiting downstairs. Shall we go?"

Lizzie didn't have to be asked twice.

As a group, they initially went down into the basement, past the aquaponic units into the preparation room with its many shelves, refrigeration units, and dehydrators. Ernst was waiting there with a big grin on his cherubic face. Where he was standing, to her surprise there between two sets of shelves, instead of the shelf that had been there before was a door that hadn't been there last time.

"Welcome, Lizzie. This was previously omitted from your initial tour. Allow me to welcome you through what is known among us as the Switzerland Gate. He opened the door and led the way into an office-like area, with a couple of desks, shelves with various curious sculptures, rocks, and books. It was roomy and felt like a really nice home library. At the other end was another door that Lizzie thought must be a closet, but no. Ernst walked across the room and opened the second door which led to a long lighted hallway, so long that Lizzie couldn't quite seem to make out the end of it. On either side of the carpeted hallway, much like a large hotel, were ranged a number of doors, each a different color with different symbols on them that she didn't recognize.

"How far into the rock did you have to dig to do this?" Lizzie asked in amazement.

"Technically we aren't in Switzerland anymore," Miriha said, amusement plain in her voice. "When you stepped across the threshold into this little office, you entered a space between dimensions that I am unable to adequately explain to you. We are about to step through one of those doors onto my home planet that does not exist in your universe. As you exit the door onto my planet, there will be creatures there to greet you that may be surprising to you. Do not fear. They will not harm you."

Lizzie was speechless. She simply nodded and followed Miriha, Gaston, and Tarafau into the hallway, and Ernst waved a happy goodbye and closed the door to the little office behind them.

As Miriha opened the first door to her right, bright sunlight spilled into the hallway, and Lizzie felt a warm, light tropical breeze and heard the crashing of ocean breakers. They exited onto what appeared to be the porch of a little hut on a sandy beach.

Speeding down the beach toward them were two creatures, as Miriha had predicted. They were similar to overblown dragonflies, with a good three-foot wingspan, iridescent bodies, and glittering eyes.

"Not to worry," Gaston said quietly beside her. "These are gem-eyes. They are a simple security measure. They scan both for potential weapons and ill intent. They are good at their job and completely harmless, at least to all who come unarmed and in friendship."

They hovered in front of each of them in turn, their wings moving so quickly as to be nearly invisible. They started their motion just above each head and then gradually moved downward until just before they might have touched the sand. Then they turned simultaneously and sped back off in the direction they had come from.

Miriha beckoned them down the beach toward a stand of tropical looking trees with reddish leaves instead of green. As they neared the trees, Lizzie noticed two things: first a wide path between the trees heading inland, and also a soft crooning sound that wasn't the wind through the trees. She looked up and, to her surprise, she saw peering from between the leafy branches, large blue eyes surrounded by white circles peering down at them curiously.

Some of them edged from behind their leafy shields, tiny hands gesturing towards the party walking on the path beneath. The creatures were covered with pale green fur, but their eyebrows, which trailed down their faces to mix with long moustaches, were dark green. They reminded Lizzie much of a tamarin monkey, and she wondered if Yaw knew about these.

"What are they?" she asked Miriha. "They are charming."

"Those are linklings," Miriha replied with fondness. "They are protectors of this place and are dearly beloved of my people. They are very curious about you. You will have an opportunity to meet them closer up as you complete your training."

As she spoke, they emerged from the copse of trees into the verge of what appeared to be a large town square like Lizzie had seen in paintings in a historical museum. In the center of the square, surrounded by stylized buildings, was a conglomeration of booths of various sizes, selling many different types of goods and foodstuffs. People were wandering the aisles between booths, perusing the goods around them. Many were gesturing to one another, seemingly in conversation, but to Lizzie's shock she realized they were not speaking, not moving their mouths at all.

It was quiet, with only the occasional rustling of goods being moved or soft footsteps on the grassy paths between booths. Lizzie noticed Miriha watching her carefully.

"Am I missing something?" Lizzie whispered to her, not willing to stand out in the silence of the scene.

"All will be made clear, and all is well. Let us continue," Miriha replied softly. They turned to the walkway that skirted the square in front of the whimsical buildings. They seemed almost distorted, but in a nice way. There were few corners or hard lines in their design. Even the windows were rounded. Corners seemed to be a foreign concept to this culture. Lizzie noted that many of these more permanent structures also seemed to be shops of various types.

She recalled from history that ancient cultures had a similar system of commerce, both established merchants and those who lived in farms outside the city limits or traveling merchants and craftsmen who made their living with goods and services who lived outside the community. She supposed this was somewhat like the farmer's market in Los Angeles, a place for many people to gather and sell their wares without the permanency or overhead of a brick-and-mortar shop.

They suddenly stopped in front of a large green building at the top of the square. It appeared to be several stories, but it was hard to tell with the difference in architecture. At the wide entrance were large carved doors, and at either side stood two folks in matching outfits that Lizzie assumed were some kind of uniform. Unlike the people in the square who were dressed in tunics similar to peasants in medieval time, except that the women wore breeches like the men and the men all wore their hair in long braids, these doormen looked much more formal in dark green suits of what might have been some kind of linen fabric with matching carved wooden buttons down the front of the jackets.

They bowed cheerfully in greeting and opened the double doors for Miriha's company. Next to the door were a couple of racks on which sat several pairs of shoes. Copying Miriha, Gaston, and Tarafau, Lizzie took off her sneakers. Miriha indicated instead of putting her shoes on the rack she should carry them. She was feeling a little underdressed, compared to the colorful dress of the townsfolk and the crisp well-tailored doormen, but at least she knew her socks were clean and there were no holes in them.

Miriha gestured for the group to follow her as Lizzie looked around in awe. The great lobby-like area was like being in the inside of a large, well-lit egg. Around the far edge there was a long curved carpeted staircase. They climbed to the top, where there was a balcony in front of a simple round door, much like Lizzie had pictured the door of a hobbit hole.

At Miriha's approach, the door opened by itself, unaided by anyone or anything Lizzie could see.

Inside was another round, high-ceilinged room on a smaller scale that looked like a combination library and sitting room. Miriha gestured them all to comfortable looking, three-legged chairs, once again rounded in every way, including the padded backs of the chairs. Miriha remained standing, gazing at each of them in turn in the way she had that always made Lizzie feel like she could see everything about her, including whether she had donned clean underwear that morning. Despite that, it wasn't a judgmental look, but somewhat measuring and always kindly.

"Welcome to my home, Lizzie. Now we have the privacy and security to be able to complete your induction. Today you will be traveling to three more places in a manner you never considered possible. Before we begin, however, there are a few things we must do here to prepare you. Your thoughts so far? You have been unusually quiet."

Lizzie ducked her head for a moment and then looked up at Miriha. "There aren't any words big enough," she replied softly. "When I told the professor I felt limited by my educational opportunities, I had no idea how true those words were and where they would eventually take me. I can see now that I am about to embark on something that is huger than anything I had considered. Are you sure you want me for this? I spent most of my academic career feeling pretty smug and superior to my classmates, and now I have a feeling I am about to find myself at the other end of the stick, so to speak."

"Yes, Lizzie, we do want you. I am sure you will measure up in ways you do not fully even imagine. That being said, please stand."

Lizzie stood, and Miriha drew her over to stand in front of the large oval desk in one area of the room. She took a small box from the top of the desk, and from it she withdrew a small necklace on a golden chain. The center of the piece was a golden "8" on its side that Lizzie recognized as the symbol for infinity, "∞."

"Please turn around, Lizzie."

Lizzie complied, and Miriha hung the necklace around her neck and fastened it. As she did so, Lizzie felt a brief tingling and realized the necklace had shortened to fit her neck as perfectly as the string of pearls her mother had given her on her sixteenth birthday.

"I don't wear jewelry much," Lizzie demurred.

"Don't consider this jewelry," Miriha replied, gently turning Lizzie to face her. "The majority of people won't even notice you have this on. It is, however, a badge of office that identifies you as a Dimensional Alliance agent. It is programmed, or perhaps a better word is 'enabled' with certain identifying attributes that allow gateway security systems to know who you are and what privileges you are allowed. At this point, your privileges are limited by your status as a trainee. I promise that you will learn more about it as we continue.

"Now, to confuse you even more, I will give you another gift." She touched a tiny gold key that hung around her neck on a similar gold chain. With a start Lizzie realized she hadn't noticed it before. While touching the tiny key, Miriha reached out and touched the infinity symbol that now hung around Lizzie's neck.

"Lizzie, can you hear me?"

Lizzie jumped. Miriha had been looking directly into her face, but although Lizzie heard her question, Miriha never moved her mouth.

"What was that?"

"Simply think my name and then think what you would like to say. Try it now."

"Miriha? What is this?" Lizzie asked incredulously.

"This is mindspeech. Try it now with Tarafau or Gaston. They can't hear our conversation unless we intend for them specifically to hear, or we broadcast to the entire room. For all they know, we are telling each other silly jokes about them," Miriha sent with a mischievous grin.

"Gaston? Tarafau? Can you hear me?"

Both of them grinned joyfully at her.

"Indeed," sent Tarafau, in a lovely mental imitation of his normal deep voice.

"Coming through loud and clear," mentally intoned Gaston.

"You will need to be able to use this gift in your future duties. It is the common speech of the dimensions, as otherwise communications between so many beings of so many races would be untenable. You will be using it exclusively in your training. I recommend, if you are worrying about your voice suffering from disuse, singing in the shower." As she sent this, her eyes crinkled in amusement.

"That would be a bad idea, if there is anyone around to hear," Lizzie replied ruefully. *"My singing voice generally makes people cringe."*

They all chuckled about that, and Miriha sent, *"Oh, wait a minute! I almost forgot!"*

Out of her pocket she pulled a small circle of what appeared to be a wide black rubber band. *"Hold out your off-hand, the one you usually don't write with."*

"I'm ambidextrous," sent Lizzie, somewhat perplexed. *"But I guess I use my left hand more than my right."* She held out her right hand tentatively, wondering how many more surprises they had for her today.

Miriha laughed and slipped the rubber band around her wrist. On one side was a small emblem of some sort embossed in gold. *"This is an MDP, which stands for Miniature Dimensional Portal,"* she said, stepping back. *"It is *standard issue for a new agent or guardian. It is a storage device you will learn more about in your training. However, as The Gatekeeper, I am only one of a handful within the Dimensional Alliance who is authorized to issue them.*

"Keep it on your body, even when you shower or go into the water. Being in that habit may save your life someday."

Lizzie didn't reply but simply nodded her head, which was spinning with ideas and questions. She realized this was probably not the time, and she began to wonder if there would ever be enough time to answer all of the questions she already had. She knew, based on her own habits and experience, that many new questions would be generated as she continued her training. *Not enough hours in any given day or lifetime*, she thought, with a sigh.

"At this point there is nothing left but to wish you good journey and send you on your way. Tarafau will accompany you through the gate to Sanglarka, the first stage of your training. Now is the time to put that great brain of yours into action and learn to see the multiverse through new eyes. I have great hope for your future, Lizzie Japhet."

Miriha extended both hands and squeezed hers warmly.

"I will miss you, Lizzie," sent Gaston. *"I may drop in to Sanglarka from time to time to see how you're doing, but for the most part you will now start the great learning adventure you have been craving for so long. I have to get back to the Los Angeles gate for now."*

He reached out to her to shake her hand, but Lizzie surprised both of them by pulling him in for a warm hug. *"I will miss you too, Gaston. I owe you so much. I will try to do justice to your mentorship."*

Gaston nodded and turned away. Were those tears welling up in his eyes? Lizzie took a step in his direction, but Tarafau put one hand on her arm. *"He will be all right,"* he sent. *"He is a bit sentimental. You will do him the most good by excelling in your training. You should put on your shoes. Shall we go?"*

He gestured toward a door on the other side of the office. Lizzie nodded, slipped into her shoes, and followed him through, giving one last look towards Miriha, who nodded encouragingly.

Chapter 11: Hands On

(Finally, something Jenny recognized. She had looked back on her time in Sanglarka as some of her best and most treasured memories of her journey to become a guardian and eventually a gatekeeper.

She knew Lizzie's experience would be slightly different, as most of the people who ran Sanglarka in her own time were yet children, but Sanglarka felt like a home-away-from-home for her.

She could picture it clearly, and the images sharpened in her mind as she read.)

As they stepped through the door in the long hallway, they were greeted by a dark sky sprinkled lavishly with diamond points of light and a sliver of a moon.

They exited into a meadow from under an archway covered with climbing roses. Around them, shimmering in the dim light of the moon and stars, were towering white mountain peaks.

Before them, holding a lantern, stood a tall blond man in a vibrant blue and white sweater and what were probably jeans. His bright blue eyes twinkled with welcome. *"We meet again, Lizzie Japhet,"* sent Grenheim. *"Hello, Tarafau, my friend. It is cold. Come along to the lodge. There are many who are eager to meet you before we adjourn to our beds for the night."*

They followed along behind him towards the large, brightly lit lodge on the well-worn, stone-lined path. The windows in the lodge were large, with shutters on either side and flower boxes under each. Lizzie imagined that in spring and summer the bright flowers against the wood exterior would have been a cheery accent to the simple lines of the three-story building.

They entered the double doors to a large lobby area, much like you would see in a very nice hotel, with conversation areas scattered around the room that was dominated by a huge stone fireplace. A fire burned merrily in the hearth and, all in all, it gave off a feeling of warmth and welcome.

Standing expectantly in a semicircle just beyond the double doors were a half dozen people Lizzie didn't recognize. Somehow, she had expected to see some of the people she had met in Switzerland, but of course, they had probably all gone back to tend their various gates all over the world.

"Allow me to introduce the training staff of Sanglarka," Grenheim said, a note of pride in his mind voice. *"You will be working and living with one and all during the first six weeks of your training. We all use mindspeech as a general rule, to accustom you in its use and to eliminate misunderstandings, as not all here speak English natively."*

Lizzie found herself nodding a bit apprehensively. She had spent more time interacting with people over the past couple of weeks than she had ever done, even in school. She was a loner by nature. This would definitely take some getting used to.

He gestured first at a dark-haired, medium-height, stocky man on the left of the group wearing a dark-red turtleneck sweater and black corduroy pants. *"Meet Oak. For now, I suggest you call him that, as his real name is difficult for Earthlings to pronounce. Even in mindspeech."*

Lizzie started slightly at the word "Earthlings" but held her peace. She was sure explanations would come later, or so she hoped.

"Oak does all of the physical training, as well as orientation, so you will begin with him first thing in the morning after breakfast.

"Moving on, next to Oak is Livia, my wife and the mainstay of the lodge. She supervises meals, makes sure the staff keeps everything clean and orderly, is a sympathetic listening ear or mind, if you will. She also will be training you in certain mind disciplines that will be crucial to your duties as an agent."

The petite, strawberry-blond woman bobbed what could have been an ironic curtsy and beamed at Lizzie. She was dressed casually in jeans and a blue gingham shirt, over which extended a long denim vest with deep front pockets.

"Next is our groundskeeper, tracker, and all-around handyman, Gustav. He also is our medic, so if you feel ill or are injured, he is the fixer upper."

Gustav was short and wiry in build, dressed in grey sweatpants and a matching sweatshirt with curly, tousled dark hair and brown eyes. His dark eyebrows were his most distinctive feature, bushy and a bit wild, but his smile was cheerful, and his round cheeks were rosy and hairless.

"And now we come to your tech instructor. She will be introducing you to Alliance technology and instructing you in its proper use, as well as safety and security protocols. This is Meta. As you can probably tell, she isn't from around here. "

The person he pointed to had a slight blue tinge to her skin, as though she had been caught out in the cold longer than was prudent. Her long silvery hair was caught up in an elaborate braid that held it close to the contours of her head. Her eyes were large and violet, and she had no eyebrows. She wore a snug silver bodysuit which Lizzie's mother would have thought scandalous, but it extended modestly up to her neck, down her wrists to very long dexterous fingers, and to the tops of what appeared more to be delicate silver slippers than shoes.

"My people are called 'Liliophytes,' Lizzie," she said in a chiming, nearly sing-song mind voice.

This startled Lizzie, as she began to realize that mind voices were as unique as any person's regular voice was, and she found herself wondering how her mind voice sounded to the others around her.

"And last, but certainly not least," Grenheim continued, *"Randall, our communications expert. He will be teaching you the ins and outs of the Alliance communications network. "*

After Meta, Lizzie had to admit, Randall looked pretty ordinary. Almost too ordinary to be honest. Light brown hair, brown eyes, medium height, medium build, wearing a t-shirt and jeans and tennis shoes, he could have been anyone passing you on any city street in Los Angeles.

"It is good to meet you all," was all Lizzie could think to say. She had to be honest with herself; this was more than a little disconcerting. The rapidity of the transport and the complete difference in her surroundings with no opportunity to orient herself was definitely going to take some getting used to.

Grenheim said, *"I'm sure we could all use some rest, as we have a lot to do tomorrow to get you settled into your routine and start you properly. Livia will see you to your room and get you settled in. You have a lot of work ahead of you. Goodnight, one and all."* And with a nod of his head, he dismissed them.

Livia gestured towards a long, wide, wooden staircase leading to the second floor. *"Your things have already been taken up to your room from the Switzerland gate,"* she sent to Lizzie, leading her up the stairs. *"If there is anything you need beyond what you have brought with you, please let us know. A large part of the function of Sanglarka is to support, supply, and provide initial training for new agents and gate guardians."*

From a long balcony that led the entire length of the lodge, they could look down into the lobby area. Livia led Lizzie to the second door and opened it, gesturing for Lizzie to precede her.

Lizzie had expected some sort of small room like her dorm room at the college, but the room was a generous size with a queen-sized bed, a dresser, and a large desk that looked out of a picture window. There were also two doors on either side of the room. She assumed that one was a closet and the other a bathroom, although, based on her experiences today, she wasn't so sure she would ever look at a door in the same way again. The gauze curtains were drawn at the moment, but Lizzie could imagine that during the day the view looking out onto the valley and into the surrounding mountain peaks would be glorious.

Her suitcase laid on top of the dresser. On the desk was a leather book and a fountain pen.

Livia noticed her glance at the book. *"We generally gift each trainee with a blank journal to allow you to preserve your memories of this time of your training. It is a great way to look back and understand how far you have come and how you can avoid pitfalls in the future."*

"Thank you, Livia," Lizzie sent. *"This is amazing. I don't see an alarm clock, and I failed to bring one. When should I get up in the morning?"*

"You will not have any trouble getting up in time, I promise." Livia said, her eyes twinkling with some secret amusement. *"Now, if there isn't anything else, I'll leave you to it. Your bathroom is fully stocked with towels and a bathrobe that should fit."*

"Thank you again, Livia. Goodnight."

Once Lizzie had showered and dressed for bed, she remembered thinking there was no way she would sleep with all the ideas, observations, and questions that were buzzing in her mind. But the next thing she knew, her dreams were interrupted by what was definitely an alarm. Instead of hearing it with her ears, though, it was in her head.

She shot up out of bed. The light filtering through the gauze curtains was bright and warm. She practically jumped into the clothes she had laid out the night before, a long-sleeved t-shirt and jeans, gave her short cap of auburn hair what her mother would have called "a lick and a promise," and rushed down the stairs, anxious not to be late her first day.

In the lobby, Livia was speaking to Gustav, a clipboard in her hand. Since she was not broadcasting but mindspeaking to him specifically, Lizzie couldn't overhear what they were saying. It occurred to Lizzie that mindspeech was potentially a much more effective means of communication than verbal speech and saw how it would make many things much easier in the long run. However, the quiet while they obviously were nodding and gesturing during their conversation was admittedly a bit unnerving.

Livia looked up as Lizzie was halfway down the stairs. *"Lizzie, good morning! I hope you slept well?"*

"Better than I expected, actually. I guess I was more tired than I had thought. The bed was comfy, and the nice hot shower definitely helped. I hope I am dressed correctly. I wasn't sure what to expect today."

"Actually, you look like you are dressed to work, and that is a good thing. Breakfast is through the double doors in the dining room. We should be sitting down in the next few minutes." And she turned back to Gustav, evidently to finish their conversation.

Lizzie crossed the shiny wood floors of the lobby area and, as instructed, went through the double doors into a long room with doors along one side and a long trestle style table with seating for over a dozen people down the center. On a long, brightly patterned linen runner were spaced many covered dishes, as well as condiments and serving utensils.

Everyone but Lizzie, Livia, and Gustav was already seated, mental conversations already going on, based on lively expressions and occasional nods or chuckles.

Lizzie took a seat on one side next to Oak, who nodded to her. *"Good morning, Lizzie,"* he sent. *"Lots to do today. Eat a good breakfast, you'll need the energy."* And he grinned at her in what Lizzie hoped wasn't intended as an evil grin but felt very much like it.

At that moment, Livia and Gustav entered and Grenheim stood. *"Ah, good. Now that we're all here, let us be thankful for this good meal that has been provided by Providence and for the comfort of good company to enjoy as we eat. At the end of your meal, please remain seated, as we need to do a short orientation for Lizzie before we each go about our respective tasks for the day."*

And with that, the covers were removed from the various dishes. There were peeled hard boiled eggs, yellow and white cheese, some sort of dark thick rye crackers, and jam and butter. Livia got up from her chair beside Grenheim and went through a set of swinging doors and returned in a few moments with a tray of steaming mugs of hot chocolate topped with cream.

Lizzie watched the others as they went through their morning routine and decided to copy them, since this was very different than the breakfast she typically made for herself when dining alone: oatmeal, with brown sugar and raisins, and a glass of milk.

As she saw the others do, she laid slices of cheese on a large cracker and cut the hardboiled egg into slices and laid them on top of the cheese. It was actually quite good. Most of them also followed their cheese and crackers with an additional cracker with butter and jam. Lizzie also tried it. She decided she could easily get used to this.

The hot cocoa was rich and made a great accompaniment to the crackers and jam. However, she wished she had a peppermint stick to finish it off. She pushed her plate back with a happy sigh. About that time, Grenheim stood up at the head of the long table and began.

"Friends, one of the best and most satisfying things we do as part of our service to our planet and the Dimensional Alliance is the training of Alliance agents and gate guardians. Our new friend, Lizzie, embarks today on a both marvelous and potentially perilous journey. Our key purpose in her training is to prepare her for her final training at Dimensional Alliance headquarters, in a dimension far away.

"Lizzie, it behooves you, as you have made this commitment to serve, to pay strict attention to the instruction you will receive. Much of it will perhaps be perplexing to you at this point, but I promise you that you will be grateful for it down the road.

"Today you will begin a strict schedule with each of your trainers. They will be pushing you hard. Several things that will help you get through this: Get

plenty of sleep when you can. Eat well, as I promise you will burn every calorie you take in. Be sure to use your break time for true relaxation. Write in your journal every night before retiring. Can you do this? Of course, you can.

"You will begin every day in the workout room with Livia and Oak, Livia in mental training and Oak in physical disciplines.

"After time to shower and change, you will take training with Meta. She will be teaching you how to use alien tech. I cannot emphasize to you enough that this information is strictly confidential. Our Earth, although advancing faster than you might realize in many areas, is far behind the advancements we have access to in the Alliance. Revealing anything you learn in your training to anyone outside the Alliance could have devastating consequences.

"Then you will break for lunch.

"After lunch, you will head outside with Gustav, who will teach you how to navigate in unknown areas, how to track, and, of course, additional physical conditioning to increase your levels of stamina and strength.

"Finally, you will study with Randall, who will instruct you both in the history and culture of the Dimensional Alliance and the Alliance communications network, vital to your work going forward."

As he paused, Lizzie had to check to be sure her mouth wasn't hanging open. She wasn't sure what she had expected, but this certainly wasn't it. She had promised Gaston that she would be patient with the process. It was hard, however, not to have words spill out of her mouth. Instead, she nodded and waited.

Grenheim smacked his hands together with a loud *clap!* and the rest stood. Lizzie rose and Grenheim sent, *"Let's get to it, then! Good success to you, Lizzie. Please follow Livia and Oak to the workout room. The rest of us will clear up."*

And, suiting words to action, each of them began to reach for plates and utensils and serving bowls to take to the kitchen.

Oak led out, followed by Livia and Lizzie. They passed several doors spaced about eight feet apart to the final door on the wall of the dining area. Another set of double swinging doors led into a spacious room. It was about half the size of a basketball court and had a polished wooden floor. Large picture windows lined one side of the room, letting in bright sunlight. From this vantage point, the valley spread before them, and the peaks of the mountains rose majestically surrounding it like sparkling sentinels tipped with snow.

Half of the room was covered with padded mats. There were also various types of gymnastic equipment lined along the far wall. On another wall were two more glass doors. Through one was a small swimming pool, and through the other what appeared to be a sauna.

Livia and Oak each seated themselves cross-legged on the mat and Livia patted the mat beside her. *"Come,"* she sent. *"Let us begin with some breathing exercises. It may seem silly to you, but we will be learning 'intentional' breathing and relaxation, techniques intended to allow you to focus your mind as well as nourish your brain and body. These exercises are taught to every agent and gate guardian. You may find yourself amazed at how helpful this will be, going forward.*

"I am aware that you began this journey to learn about science and how things work. This is science. The human body is an amazing machine. Medical science has only begun to scratch the surface in it quest to discover how we function.

"Breathing is foundational. You already know that if you stop breathing you die, but it is so much more than that. Learning to breathe intentionally allows you to control much of your mental and physical functions.

"We will begin by learning some basic controlled breathing techniques. It will require you to concentrate very intimately on your body and the timing or spacing of your breathing as well as the depth and length of your breaths. Let us begin."

By the time they had been at it for about forty-five minutes, Lizzie felt like she would have after a long run on the beach. It had never occurred to her that simply breathing could be so much work.

"That will be enough for now," Livia sent at last. *"You will practice these techniques for at least thirty minutes every night before bed, and we will continue instruction in more advanced patterns every morning immediately following breakfast."*

She and Oak rose, Lizzie following their example. Then she realized she wasn't done. Oak hadn't said a word during their breathing session, merely breathing with his eyes closed the entire time.

Now he looked her up and down somewhat critically. *"Tall for an Earthling female, not flabby or overweight. What do you generally do to keep fit?"*

Once again Lizzie was a bit taken aback by the word "Earthling." Was Oak also alien? She hesitated to ask, hoping all would be revealed in time. She admitted that Oak was physically a bit intimidating. Especially now with that carefully evaluating look he was aiming at her, as if she were a laboratory rat.

"I ride my bike and I like to run on the beach when I get a chance," she replied, looking him directly in the eyes. She wasn't going to allow herself to show how disconcerted she was.

"That will do for now. Do you have any weapons training?"

"Weapons? No, not really. I've fired a gun before on a shooting range, and I learned the basics of archery at girls camp when I was about fourteen years old. Haven't handled a bow since. I don't remember anyone saying anything about weapons training before now—"

"One of my assignments is to teach you methods of defense and how to handle yourself in, shall we say, difficult circumstances "

He walked over to a basket against the wall with all of the gymnastic equipment and pulled out a long stick slightly longer than Lizzie was tall and tossed it to Livia. He took one himself. The stick almost looked tiny in his large hands.

"Observe," he said, and launched himself at Livia, swinging the long stick at her head. Livia blocked it with her own with a loud *crack!* and pivoted on one foot, reversing her swing towards his middle, which he blocked with his stick upright in two hands.

Back and forth they went, the sticks clacking rhythmically while they pivoted, side-stepped, and ducked in what looked like a choreographed dance.

Finally, Livia got in a tap on Oak's thigh, upon which he held his stick horizontally across his chest. *"Score to Livia!"* he sent, and they both faced Lizzie, panting lightly.

"These," he said, gesturing to the sticks, *"are quarterstaffs. You will be learning to use them as part of your training. I will explain the whys and wherefores at another time. For now, we will do some stretching and calisthenics*

to get a proper picture of where you are now and what we need to do to get you up to standard before you head to Dimensional Alliance headquarters for official agent training. Do you have any questions?"

Lizzie actually had lots of questions, but she decided to hold her tongue for now. Both Gaston and Miriha, knowing her inquisitive and often obstinate nature, had advised her to do more listening than questioning until she knew enough to ask the right questions. So, she shook her head, not trusting herself to answer otherwise.

Oak didn't take her quiet amiss. He simply ran her through a series of stretches and exercises, many of which she recognized from P.E. in school and some that were new to her. As she did each exercise, he would stop her after a few seconds and reposition her, correct her posture, and re-demonstrate the proper execution of the exercise.

By the time they were finished, she was tired, and she expected she wouldn't feel the real impact until the next morning. Livia reminded her that after her shower she would want to go to Meta in the lab next to the library. She pointed out the doors leading to each of these as they exited the workout room.

Lizzie was so excited about the opportunity to learn tech and science from an actual alien that she rushed through her preparations and was soon heading down the stairs towards the dining room.

She was delighted when she saw Meta standing in front of the door, a plate of fruit and cheese in one hand and a pitcher of what appeared to be lemonade in the other. *"Come, Lizzie. I'll bet you could use a snack after your workout. I know Oak doesn't believe in going easy on his students."* She chuckled, and Lizzie observed that the musical sound of her voice was very similar to her natural voice. She then realized that this had been similar with all of those with whom she had mindspeech conversations.

She found herself wondering: is the mental voice you project based on your own idea of what your voice is supposed to sound like? A question for Livia at their next mental exercise session.

She followed Meta through the door to the lab and was interested to note that, although there were aspects of any lab she had ever encountered in her studies, this was arranged in an interesting way. There were the standard worktables equipped with what she thought of as standard lab equipment, but there was also an area sectioned off with a circle of comfortable chairs interspersed with small low tables surrounding a very low round table, much like a large coffee table.

Meta led the way to the circle of chairs and gestured for Lizzie to sit.

"Make yourself comfortable," she said, seating herself in a chair next to Lizzie and setting the plate of snacks on one of the small tables between them. *"You may be surprised to know that as many scientific advancements happen in this little circle of chairs as do any of the time we spend actively working with the equipment in the lab. Please feel free to munch on the fruit and cheese as we talk. One of the advantages of mindspeech is that we can eat and converse at the same time without worrying about speaking with a full mouth."*

At this she smiled, and Lizzie couldn't help but smile back. Meta had small white, even teeth, and her lips were a dark teal color.

Meta continued. *"Your species' current level of technology is somewhat primitive in comparison to that which is available in the Dimensional Alliance, although you have progressed remarkably over the last several centuries. What you will be learning to use over the next several weeks is vital to your ongoing training at the Dimensional Alliance training unit. We don't want you to be at a disadvantage with the other agents in training."*

"Then, this isn't the actual agent training?" Lizzie said, remembering only belatedly her resolve not to ask questions before she was ready.

"No, Lizzie. This is a preparatory class to bring you up to speed before you are subjected to the training to become a certified agent. That course would be the equivalent in Earth time to gaining an Associate degree in your Earth colleges. The first section of that training will be coursework with classes and labs. The second section will pair you up with a 'Guide,' where you will do field work, as you would call it. What we do here is simply prepare you, so you don't begin at a disadvantage."

"Thank you for clarifying that, Meta. I will try to do Sanglarka credit."

"That is a great way to begin, Lizzie. So, today I will simply explain our coursework and how we will proceed. Starting tomorrow, we will delve deep into what most of your Earthling associates call 'alien tech.'

"The first thing I must emphasize and will continue to reiterate is that all of this information is to be held secret to anyone outside of the Alliance. This includes as you go to other worlds throughout the dimensions. Not all of the

worlds you will visit will be at the same technical level as the Alliance. By agreement, the agents and representatives in the Alliance have access to tech from all over the multiverse, but only because they do not share this technology with species or beings of a lower technological development, including those on their home planets.

"Revealing any of this is a serious infraction and can be punished severely. It often results in a wiping of the memory and resettling the perpetrator back into their original culture with a feasible cover story for their extended absence and no further contact with the Dimensional Alliance.

"Is this very clear to you? I know you may get tired of the many reminders of this, but it is vital to uphold this as part of the interdimensional agreements that allow the Dimensional Alliance to do its work. You will learn more about the culture and history of the Alliance with each of your instructors and in much more detail in your training at the agent training unit."

Lizzie found that this was actually very helpful in calming the racing questions in her head. Now they were finally getting to some useful information.

By this time, the fruit and cheese plate was empty, and they wiped their hands on the napkins beside the plate. Lizzie also realized that she had unconsciously drained her lemonade.

Meta reached out onto the round table in the center of the circle of chairs and picked up what looked like a very shiny slate, like the kind small children use to learn their letters. To her surprise, when Meta touched the side of the slate, a light came on from underneath and small pictures were revealed.

"This is a tablet, a small computing device used for training, communications, and recording important data. Tomorrow you will be receiving your own, but for now, I will instruct you in its use."

Thus began Lizzie's first introduction to alien technology. She was instantly smitten with delight and satisfaction. At last, she would get her questions answered and she would put every effort to keeping track of her questions and checking them off as they were answered until the time was right.

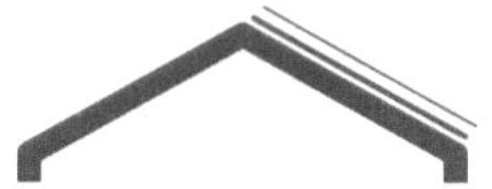

Chapter 12: Be Careful What You Ask For

Jenny was delighted to see Burt step into the living room from the hallway where the gateway lay hidden from anyone without a key or infinity symbol around their neck.

"Honey, I'm home!" He called as he emerged. His hair was as wild as ever, and his eyes twinkled with the joy of seeing her.

"Reading the journals? I was wondering what you would do with all of the time you have on your hands for the next few weeks. Anything good in there? Have you gotten to me yet?"

"No, silly, I'm just at the beginning. At last, I'll get to see what I missed out on. Lizzie has just started agent training in Sanglarka."

"I'll bet there's more than a little culture shock going on then. I remember how it was with me, and we were a lot more advanced then than she would have been. Well, don't mind me. I'm only stopping in to check on you, and I'm off again. Shall I bring you some lunch?" he asked, kissing her on the top of her short curls.

"Thank you, Burt! I'll admit I'm feeling almost guilty about taking time off at this point, but it feels good to connect with Lizzie and what might have happened for me if things had been different."

Burt knelt down to give her an enthusiastic hug then got up and rambled out to the kitchen whistling a merry, albeit unrecognizable tune. It was fun to hear him puttering around in their little kitchen. So many of the homes and facilities that housed gates were large and impressive, but Jenny loved her roomy little house on Infinity Loop with its large well-manicured back yard and welcoming living space. After having had it trashed by minions of the Fleistians, it had been not only restored but refurnished, and it looked and felt like home.

In short order, Burt popped back in with a little tray with a sandwich, a small salad and some lemonade, Jenny's favorite lunch. He knelt again, kissed her thoroughly, and hopped up.

"Back to it," he said. "I'll be back in to check in on you in a day or so. I'm working with the planning team right now, prioritizing targets for liberating dimensions from the Fleistians. We have a little breathing space for now, but not much. We'll all be glad when your little 'vacation' is over. Lolly wants you to know she will be happy to see you when you are better. She's been hanging out with BaaGah, mostly at headquarters, helping Merv's team to learn about 'the spaces.'"

He chuckled. "All because I picked a fight with a bully. Goes to show, you never know where something will lead."

And with that he headed back down the hallway and Jenny heard the door close behind him.

"Now where was I? Oh yes," and she opened the journal again...)

Lizzie lay panting, looking up into Gustav's brown eyes, which were crinkled in amusement. His face was haloed by the sun streaming from above him. *"Are you okay, Lizzie?"* he inquired, not all that sympathetically. *"I don't suppose you noticed the small pile of earth on that part of the trail. Gophers and other burrowers inhabit this wood, as is their right. Let's take a look at your ankle."*

He squatted down beside her and gently unlaced her tennis shoe on the right foot. It hurt, but not as much as it had when she had stepped into the hole in the trail that had been hidden by a covering of snow. She winced as he carefully pulled the sock down and ran one hand along the ankle while supporting it with the other.

"Hmm, not broken, but it may smart for a while. Just a moment." His eyes went unfocused. *"Oak will be here in a few minutes to help you back to the lodge. This is a good lesson as we move on. I won't fuss at you about it, but you will learn as you go to focus more on what is around you instead of all of the questions and possibilities running around in that brilliant mind of yours."*

He picked up a handful of snow and applied it to the ankle and chuckled as Lizzie winced. He was absolutely right. She had been thinking of all of the possibilities for the new tech Meta had showed her today. After nearly a week of study, each time she thought her brain would burst from it all, she found that she had only scratched the tiniest bit of the surface of all she needed to know and understand.

Oak arrived, and instead of the stretcher Lizzie had expected, he simply bent over and lifted her into his arms and immediately strode at a quick pace towards the lodge, his long legs eating up the distance so fast without actually running that within fifteen minutes they got back to the lodge. The trip out had taken them twice that.

Meanwhile, Gustav followed behind, arriving about five minutes after Oak had deposited her on one of the window seats in the lobby area. *"I'll be right back,"* he sent to Lizzie and returned in a few minutes with a first aid kit. He double-checked the ankle and wrapped it carefully in an elastic bandage. In the meantime, Livia arrived with an ice pack and a set of crutches in her hands.

Lizzie was horribly embarrassed to be causing such a stir and said so.

"You wouldn't be the first trainee and won't be the last to sustain an unintended injury during training. You'll need to stay off of the ankle for a few days and then you'll be right back in the middle of all of the physical training. In the meantime, you needn't slow your other training at all," Livia said, her hands on her hips.

Lizzie winced again. It wasn't fair that they were all being so nice and understanding when she felt she deserved more of a tongue lashing at the very least.

"Help her stand," sent Gustav. *"I need to adjust these. She's a bit taller than the last person to use them."*

Livia helped Lizzie up, supporting her so she could stand on one leg while Gustav measured one crutch. *"Sit her down and I'll get her some of that medicinal tea to help with the inflammation and then apply the ice pack. It's going to hurt more before it hurts less."*

Livia hurried off and Gustav finished adjusting the other crutch. *"Now, take it easy on the ankle for the next few days and I'll look in on you in the morning to rewrap it after you've given yourself a sponge bath and dressed. Livia will see to it that you have a chair in your bathroom to make that process a little easier.*

"Oak will be your transport up and down the stairs, so don't be surprised when he knocks at your door in the morning."

"Thank you, Gustav. I promise to be more attentive to what I'm doing in the future. I haven't had much of a need to pay attention when I'm outdoors in the past. I'm mostly used to sidewalks and paved streets, other than the beach. This whole outdoorsy thing is admittedly pretty new to me. I went camping when I was a kid, but I usually took a book or two and hung out under a tree somewhere while everyone else was exploring and things."

"I am sure you are probably wondering why going out in the wilderness around the lodge is important, but you've just learned a great lesson. You will find yourself in many strange and unexpected environments as you complete your training in other dimensions and finally begin your work as an agent. If I could sum up for you one of the most crucial things you will learn from me, I would say, 'Pay attention.'"

Lizzie didn't reply, just bobbed her head, which also hurt since she had hit the ground pretty solidly when her foot had gone into the hole.

Livia arrived with the tea. Lizzie sniffed it and grimaced. It smelled as she had imagined a "medicinal tea" might smell.

"It has turmeric and willow bark in it, among a few other things that will help relax the muscles, reduce inflammation, and stay calm," Livia remarked with a grin. *"You* will *drink every drop before you leave this area. Then you will go to Randall for your communications lesson. There is nothing in the tea that will inhibit your ability to think."*

Lizzie drank it down as Livia applied the ice pack, trying not to make too much of a face. It was drinking temperature, not too hot. When she had sat for about twenty minutes under Livia's attentive gaze, she grabbed her crutches and swung her way to the library room, where they had their communications lessons.

The library was more than just a large study lined with books. At the far end was a corner dedicated to various types of communications equipment ranging from short wave radio to some other things that at first were puzzling to Lizzie.

For one thing, there was a much larger version of the tablet Meta had given her and a qwerty keyboard, but not like any typewriter Lizzie had ever seen. Instead of actual keys you push down with your fingers, it was flat with the letters embossed on the flat surface. Simply touch a letter and it showed up on the writing area of the screen. But, wonder of wonders, you could simply talk to the screen, and it would type out what you said as fast as you could speak!

Randall called it a computer. Lizzie's only reference for that word related to the Standards Western Automatic Computer, otherwise known as SWAC, she had heard of at a lecture by a professor from the Institute for Numerical Analysis at UCLA. But that device was huge, compared to this device that consisted only of a screen and a keyboard, and the SWAC could only calculate numbers, outputting results via a printer onto paper.

This device, on the other hand, with no vacuum tubes or even any discernable wires, could store more information than was contained in all of the books of most libraries, communicate with the Alliance into another dimension, and even create complex, three-dimensional visual models from a flat image at the touch of a button. It could do much more than that, according to Randall, but it was all so far beyond anything Lizzie had ever imagined.

Randall looked up as she entered on the crutches, and she could tell by the twist of his mouth he was trying really hard not to laugh, which irritated her all the more. She not only didn't think it was something to laugh about, she was terribly embarrassed about the whole incident.

He didn't laugh, however, but instead turned to the screen once she had awkwardly seated herself in the rolling office chair next to him.

"The good news is that there are no hidden potholes to deal with here," he sent with a quiet chortle.

Lizzie rolled her eyes. It was clear she would not live this down anytime soon. *"So, what are we doing today?"* she asked, instead of acknowledging the jest any further.

"I thought we would discuss your MDP and its uses. By now you have learned how to store things in there and how to remove them. There are other features you should be aware of. For one, although no one besides yourself can currently get access to anything inside your MDP, there is an option to have it keyed to another person. In order to do that, you need to designate someone you trust to receive permission, and they need to have those permissions registered with the Alliance Council, a simple matter, but necessary.

"You can't designate just any person or being to access your MDP. They must be either a registered agent, a guide, or a guardian to qualify. As you begin

the internship part of your training, you will be assigned a mentor known as a "guide." Guides are registered agents of the Alliance and are especially trained for that position after years of agent-level experience.

"It is traditional that this person will be the first person to have emergency access to your MDP. Later, as you become certified, you can change that by notifying the Alliance. You can also rescind those permissions as you need to by the command, 'lock.' The lock command means that no one besides yourself, under any circumstances, can get into your MDP. There is no override for this, unless you give the command, 'unlock' with your keyword. Clear?"

"Of course. Why would I want to give someone permission to enter my MDP?"

"One of the reasons would be to allow them to enable the emergency beacon. Every MDP is equipped with a beacon that can issue a continuous signal that can be picked up by the Alliance when they are in range. The beacon isn't inter-dimensional, but most agents carry a device that can detect the MDP beacon as long as you are on or around the same planet as the beacon.

"If you were unconscious and you needed to be left where you were for some reason, your companion could activate your beacon and could go for help."

"That's pretty handy, but what is the likelihood I would find myself in such a situation?"

"It isn't an everyday occurrence, but it can happen." Randall shook his head. *"Not every mission you go on for the Alliance will necessarily be public to the area or a simple in-and-out situation. Sometimes you will encounter the unexpected, and it pays for us to prepare you in every way that is possible. However, much of your agent training will teach you how to handle difficult, challenging, or emergency situations effectively."*

"It seems like every time I think I have this all figured out, I find out something I didn't count on in the beginning," Lizzie sent with an audible sigh.

Randall puckered his brows in concern. *"Are you having second thoughts then?"*

"Oh, heavens no!" Lizzie replied sincerely. *"It's just so much to learn and assimilate. I certainly didn't count on how physical this would all be. But I wouldn't trade this experience for any amount of money."* She shifted her weight in the chair and winced as she inadvertently touched her foot to the floor. *"I know I have a lot to learn, and I get impatient with myself sometimes.*

I understand my attitudes can be a bit off-putting." And she shrugged her shoulders as if to say, "Nothing I can do about it."

"Give yourself some time. None of us learned what we know in a few weeks or even a year. This is why we take all this in stages. We won't be doing much beyond scratching the surface here at Sanglarka. Even after your more advanced agent training, you will still be a babe in the woods. Like any discipline, especially in the sciences, learning is a lifetime pursuit.

"You have a good mind, Lizzie, and in many circumstances your self-sufficient attitude and your craving for solving every mystery science can provide will stand you in good stead. But patience is probably the most desirable quality you can pursue along with everything else. Over time, if you don't learn this, you will find you will move slower rather than faster, as many doors will remain closed to you.

"I don't mean to lecture you, and you always get to choose your path, but as one of your instructors, it is my job to highlight the best possible path for you. Whether you take it or not, in the final analysis, will be completely in your own hands. One final caution, however. Although we each have the right to choose our paths and our actions, none of us get to choose the consequences of them."

Lizzie nodded solemnly. *"Thank you for your honesty, Randall. I know impatience is a failing of mine. And I tend to hammer at the things that stand in my way instead of learning to understand why the barrier is there so I can fix it, go around it, or maybe learn from it. I'll continue to work on that."*

And so it went for the remainder of the six weeks she spent at Sanglarka. Her ankle healed fairly quickly with the ministrations of Livia and Gustav. She advanced in all of her classes to the satisfaction of her instructors, with no additional injuries worth thinking about.

She even found herself warming to the quarterstaff. It had begun to feel natural in her hand. Her balance and timing were improving, and she had mastered some of the more complex breathing and relaxation techniques.

She still felt in awe of the technology she had been exposed to and was having a difficult time imagining going back to where every telephone was attached to a wire and the smallest calculator took up an entire desk. The tiny black and white television screen in the big wooden box that dominated her parents' living room seemed incredibly archaic, and yet it was the finest one on the market.

Her instructors had assured her that humankind was on a path that was rapidly taking them far beyond their current level of science and technology, but she could definitely understand why she was under such an obligation to see to it that none of this would leak out to the world in its current state. In the wrong hands at this time, it could cause some serious upheaval.

It was amazing to her how fast the time passed. Before she realized it, she was seated across from Livia at a special feast to celebrate her departure for her training at the Alliance Agent Training Unit on an alien world.

As she looked around at the faces that were now so familiar to her, she felt a bit sad and even a little afraid. She would miss them all. And now she was truly launching into the unknown.

She had been acquainted with the concept of alien life, and through Meta she had learned to be careful not to judge by sight alone. Meta and she had become not only teacher and student, but good friends, often spending time together outside of the formal classes. However, as she understood it, the majority of the beings she would be associating with in the next stage of her adventure would not be humanoid at all.

Grenheim stood at the end of the meal, and all heads turned towards him. *"Lizzie, it has been a pleasure to have you here and watch your progress in your studies. But now you leave us. Not forever. You will find yourself returning regularly over time. The room you have occupied during your stay here will be reserved for you and will always be available at any time you come back to us.*

"It is customary to give a parting gift to our students. Livia?"

Livia bent beneath the table and stood with a quarterstaff in her hands. Unlike the practice staves, it was metal shod on top and bottom, and the top of the staff had an "L" etched into it, with a tree embossed over the planet Earth.

"This is your staff of office," Livia sent. *"Many in the dimension recognize it as giving you some authority in the Alliance, not to mention its being a handy weapon when the need arises. It is my hope that it never does. That being said, it will be helpful to have your own, as your training in its use will continue over your time at the training unit."*

"Thank you," Lizzie said, and for a moment her eyes teared up. *"I will miss you all so much. I'll send you a postcard."* And they all laughed. They knew she would have to do any messaging to them via her tablet. They had assured

her that they would be apprised of her progress via the Alliance Council, but they would all enjoy getting an occasional personal message from her.

"It will be early morning when you arrive at Alliance headquarters, and their days are 32 hours long, so it will be a long day for you. Meta will escort you and see that you are properly introduced to the three high councilors and then conducted to the training unit. Install your staff into your MDP. Are you fully packed otherwise?"

"I am," Lizzie returned, looking one last time into each face.

Chapter 13: The Gamut

(Jenny found herself getting excited. Sanglarka was something she was familiar with; and so far, Lizzie's training, though somewhat modified based on her particular needs and the difference in the level of technology she was familiar with, had been very similar to her own.

However, now she would come to the part that Jenny had missed. She had never gone through the agent training and had never actually even gone through the gate guardian or gatekeeper training, circumstances being what they were at the time. Now was her chance to experience through her Aunt Lizzie what she had missed. She turned the page...)

Lizzie stepped under the rose arch at the end of the path from the lodge, Meta at her side. Meta had warned her about the scanner on the other side, a silvery shield that looked a lot as if she were going to step into a vertical pool of water. She felt nothing as they stepped through.

Looking around her, she admitted she had somehow thought it would look more alien. And although there were differences, a violet tint in the sky and trees that were not quite the same as Earth but still green and leafy, it was somewhat comforting that her first assay into an alien dimension was not too bizarre.

A well-worn path led down the gentle slope. From this height, between the leaves she could see what was obviously a city below. The buildings weren't all that different from other cities, windows sparkling in the sun. Many of them were multiple stories, and some kind of vehicular traffic was evident from this elevation.

Meta's encouraging smile helped to calm her heart. She considered herself a logical and unexcitable person in general, but she had to admit that taking this next step was more than a little intimidating.

They got to the bottom of the hill in what seemed like no time and forever at the same time, as it often does when you are heading towards something anticipated, but yet unknown.

At the end of the path stood two tall guards in uniform. They each had three eyes, one centered and two above it on either side, with fuzzy yellow hair and hands with seven fingers on arms that reached nearly to the ground. Nearby was a vehicle with no wheels, floating quietly in place. *"Lizzie Japhet reporting for agent training,"* Meta sent.

"She is expected," the guard replied, nodding formally. *"Welcome, trainee Japhet. They are waiting for you in the private council chamber."*

He opened the door on one side of the vehicle for Lizzie, and Meta got in on the other side. Without a sound, as soon as the doors were closed, it took off.

"Who's driving this thing?" Lizzie asked Meta, slightly alarmed.

"It is autonomous, pre-programmed to take us to a specific place. The guards would have seen to that before we arrived."

Lizzie was feeling a bit shaky, trying with all her might not to show it. She wanted to appear calm and unaffected by the strangeness she knew she was about to encounter. She wasn't sure if she would be able to carry it off, as she had never been much of an actor or pretender, but she didn't want their first impression of her to be that of a goggle-eyed tourist.

As they entered the city and pulled out into traffic, she noticed something else that was concerning, at least to her. There seemed to be no stop lights or any other traffic-directing devices or signs in evidence. Nevertheless, the other wheelless vehicles moved along efficiently, occasionally stopping or turning without even a near miss. Along the walkways various beings, many humanoids but not all, strolled along like any other foot traffic in a large city, occasionally stopping to chat or look into what might have been shop windows. At corners, the walkways ascended on bridges above the traffic in place of crosswalks, so pedestrians and vehicles interacted in peaceful and safe coexistence.

"This is impressive, Meta. I wish more thought had been given to street traffic in my world."

"They'll get there, Lizzie. Be patient. This society is much older than your own, and yet the beings on your world are progressing much faster in their

learning curve than many. Comparatively, your culture is advancing at a rapid pace. I predict that in twenty years you won't recognize the technological landscape of your world, and in fifty years you will be much closer to what you see here than you can imagine. Patience."

Lizzie just caught herself before rolling her eyes. She was getting really tired of that word.

At that moment, they pulled up in front of a tall glass building fronted by huge double glass doors. On either side of the doors stood two more uniformed guards. These were a bit more Earth-like, with the exception of their mouths, which spread from ear to ear as if they wore a constant grin.

"Welcome, Lizzie Japhet and Meta," one of them sent as they stepped from the car to the walkway. *"Meta, you know the way."*

Meta nodded, and the huge glass doors opened silently. They stepped into a room that much resembled a cathedral she had once visited on the East Coast, only much larger. The oval stained-glass windows about two stories up made beautiful patterns on the white marble floor. Ahead of them was another set of huge doors.

These evidently were the entrance to an exceptionally large elevator. You could have driven a delivery truck into it with room to spare. *"Council Chamber,"* Meta sent.

The elevator didn't seem to move. Lizzie jumped slightly when moments later a soft female voice said aloud, "Council Chamber," and the doors slid silently open.

They opened into an ample reception area much like most she had seen in pretty much every office building she had ever visited on Earth, with one exception. Facing the elevator was a desk, and behind the desk sat a bird-like being, feathers and a beak, but with arms. Her feathers were shaded from a deep teal to dark green, and her wings were tucked neatly behind her shoulder blades.

"They await you. Please enter," was all she said. Or at least Lizzie assumed it to be female, as the mental voice was soft and melodious. She realized with a mental shake that she should probably get out of the habit of assuming anything based on past experience.

They went through another large set of double doors, which slid open at their approach. The council chamber was about the size of half a tennis court, with a high ceiling and a raised dais at one end. On the dais were three beings, all of whom were what any Earthling would have described as alien.

One of them stood. Tall, with four arms and two heads, one of which had a short crest of brilliant red hair much like a mohawk and the other with long blue wavy hair and both with bright green eyes (two of them each). *"Greetings, Lizzie Japhet of Earth. We hear good things about you. We are Gleph and Linaa of planet Ning of the Acleasias dimension. We are the Chief Councilor of the Dimensional Alliance.*

"Allow us to introduce our first and second councilors. Khol of the planet TKZ in the Invi dimension, and Benviniarcusa, whom you can call 'Ben,' from the planet Liftzi in the dimension of Gul."

Each stood as they were mentioned. Khol was much like an octopus who had escaped the water, but with more than a dozen tentacles that Lizzie could see. His body was taller than those of the other council members, and he had a large single golden eye but no mouth or nostrils that Lizzie could discern.

Ben, on the other hand, reminded Lizzie of an extremely fuzzy oversized orange beach ball with four arms that appeared to also serve as feet. If there were eyes or ears, she couldn't see them.

Kohl's mental voice had a bit of a buzz to it, as a bumblebee might sound if it could talk. *"It izzz pleazzant to greet you, Lizzzzie,"* it sent. *"We look forward to making your acauaintanzzze."*

Another very soft warm mental voice added, *"Indeed, Lizzie Japhet. We welcome you. Reports of your progress have been interesting. We anticipate great things from you."*

"Thank you," was all Lizzie could think to say. She didn't feel afraid. The mindspeech voices of these beings communicated kind intentions, which was one of the benefits of mindspeech. It communicated emotions attached to the words that were 'spoken.'

"Lizzie has performed well at everything we have set before her, and we believe her to be ready to access the next level of training as an agent of the Alliance," Meta sent.

The words sounded formal to Lizzie, which was confirmed when Gleph (or was it Linaa?) replied with, *"So it shall be. Lizzie Japhet, do you agree to this assignment of your own free will?"*

"I do."

"Then, be true, Lizzie Japhet, and persist in doing good and giving with a full heart and a willing mind. Your escort has arrived." Gleph pointed to someone behind her, and Lizzie turned. There stood a humanoid, not much different than some of the linebackers she had known in college. His muscles were obvious even in the loose-fitting white linen tunic and black trousers he wore. Part of Lizzie was relieved, until she noticed he had no discernable ears and only three fingers and a thumb on either hand.

"Welcome, trainee Japhet. I am Lall, and I am the instructor for your training pod. I assume you have all of your worldly goods in your MDP and that you are ready to begin training."

It was not a question. *"Yes, sir,"* she replied.

"No honorifics are required, trainee. I am Lall, and you will address me as such. Say goodbye to your escort and follow me."

Lizzie turned to Meta, who sent, *"Farewell for now, Lizzie Japhet. I know you will make us all proud,"* and she gave her a quick one-armed hug.

"Thanks for everything. I'll stay in touch," Lizzie said. Meta smiled knowingly.

And with that she turned and followed Lall out of the council chamber, for the first time feeling more than a little lost.

Once they got out of the elevator on the main floor, he took her to a large door to one side of the lobby, which led to what could only be described as a parking garage. Rows upon rows of hovercars were neatly arranged before them. Several rows over, he opened the door to one of them and sent to what appeared to be no one in particular, *"Training unit, 3rd Pod."*

As soon as they were seated and the doors closed, the car levitated up from the parked position and silently took itself out of the garage and blended seamlessly into the street traffic.

Lizzie was bursting with questions but thought that, considering Lall was the equivalent of her drill sergeant, showing her ignorance probably wouldn't be the best way to begin that relationship. Instead, she sat silently, trying not to gawk as she looked around to take in her new surroundings.

Finally, he sent, *"You are from Earth? I've often thought I'd like to visit there, but I doubt that would be politic, under the circumstances."* He chuckled. *"In any case, you will get many opportunities to tell us about where you are from.*

"I imagine Earth to be different than anything any of our trainees have experienced. We often spend any downtime we have after drills and training trading information about our native planets and dimensions. It really is just another aspect of the training. Many of our trainees might fit in well in the Earth population and may actually find themselves on assignment there at some point."

"You have sent Alliance agents to Earth? I mean agents that aren't from there?"

"Of course. I know that there are many myths of Earth that describe beings from 'outer space,' but I speculate that some of them may have simply been an agent that made a cultural error."

"So, the whole alien invasion thing isn't just fiction?"

"I wouldn't necessarily call it 'an invasion,'" he countered wryly. *"Non-interference is part of the Dimensional Alliance pact. Any being from another dimension that attempted to forcefully invade your boundaries would be immediately taken care of by the Alliance, preferably without any of your fellow beings catching on that there had ever been a problem.*

"Now, look smart. We're here, and I'm about to introduce you to the administrators of the Agent Training Center after I show you your quarters. Your fellow trainees are only about a week ahead of you, so you should be able to catch up quickly, based on our reports from Sanglarka."

Lizzie sat up a bit straighter and looked back out of the window. She had been so involved with listening to Lall that she hadn't even noticed that the nearly silent hovercar had slowed down.

They had arrived at what appeared to be much like any military base she had ever seen in her dad's photographs of his war days.

Neat rows of what she assumed were barracks to house the trainees faced inward to a large grassy rectangular area about the size of a football field. For now, the area was empty, and there seemed to be no one about.

"All trainees are currently at classes. You'll meet them after we've had a chance to introduce you to the school staff. But for now, let's take a look at your living quarters."

He led the way to the second building on the right of the hovercar through the door into an area with a dozen single-person beds. There were no footlockers. Lizzie decided this must be because of the MDPs provided to each trainee for their personal property and equipment.

At the end of the large room was a roomy area with eleven chairs of various styles in a half circle facing a twelfth chair. It appeared to be a discussion or training area. Obviously, training wasn't restricted to the classrooms.

Lizzie assumed there would be times when the team leader or other officials would be addressing them as a team, or what Lall had called a 'pod,' away from the general population in addition to their classwork. Behind the training area were a few doors, which she discovered led to private bathing facilities, several small rooms with shower heads on a wall and a drain in the floor. Each of the small rooms contained a small, curtained area with a bench on the opposite wall and something resembling a toilet resided in one corner beside the bench.

"You won't be spending a lot of time in the pod unit: some private training, sleeping, personal hygiene, and preparing for the day. You will notice that the hygiene facilities are very general and simple, and you will understand why when you meet your pod members."

He walked over and stood next to the closest bed to the door. *"This will be yours. Keep it neat. You may, if you wish, add or subtract blankets or a different pillow, but keep these in your MDP unless you are actively using them. You will also notice that the pod area is clean and tidy. Each pod member is responsible for their own things. Each day, tasks will be assigned to you, and you will be on a rotation as far as cleaning and maintaining the pod area is concerned.*

"This is part of your training since part of your assignment as an agent is to be an ambassador and representative of the Alliance. Learning to keep your area clean and observe proper courtesy as a guest is more vital than many realize, and the Alliance will be judged by your behavior and civility."

Lizzie had no answer or comment to any of this. It was logical and thus appealed to that side of her personality.

"I am sure you will have questions going forward, but for now, let me take you to meet some of the staff and prepare to introduce you to your podmates."

He turned and strode out and she followed, her stomach fluttering slightly in anticipation. She was having a hard time believing she was actually doing this. But here she was, and it was all too real. Then, standing in the sunlight she suddenly noticed she had two shadows. Looking up, she saw there seemed to be a second sun in the sky, the first one bright and close and the second pale, small, and distant-looking.

"Two suns?" she queried.

"Our planet is circumbinary. It is not as common as planetary systems orbiting a single star, but it happens. We only see both suns certain times during a year, which for us is several of your Earth years, as I understand it. It does, however, make for long spaces between seasonal changes, and we only experience "night" as darkness a short time of any given day. Some seasons it is light all day long for long stretches. You'll get used to it eventually."

They walked to the end of the rectangular field until they came to a large, long, official looking multistory building, which appeared to be made of reddish stone.

"This building houses the classrooms and administration offices for the training center. Most of the time you will spend here will be strictly for instruction, but from time to time you may find yourself working here as part of your training; and hopefully even rarer, you may find yourself here for discipline or correction."

They entered the large double doors and a question occurred to Lizzie.

"What is the reason for all of the huge doors and doorways in all of the buildings I have been in so far today? Even the doors in shops on the street in the city were huge. Is this a style or tradition thing? It probably has nothing to do with anything, but I am curious."

"Yes, you are," chuckled Lall, *"or so your previous instructors have reported. The reason will soon become apparent. Come, you are about to meet the Chief Administrator and her assistants."*

He led Lizzie down a long hallway into another set of large doors. The room was bright, with ample windows looking out over the grounds. Just outside one window was a huge tree with pale foliage that created a stained-glass effect in the room of greenish-yellow light. In one corner, instead of a desk, there was a long chaise. And on the chaise—

Lizzie caught her breath. A dragon! There was no other thing it could possibly be. And in the dragon's large, clawed hands was a book!

The dragon was blues and greens of various shades from light to dark. Lounging as it was, it took up the entire over-twelve-foot-long chaise. When not reclining, its head would nearly brush the fourteen-foot-high ceiling.

"Chief Administrator Liliath, please allow me to introduce our newest trainee, Lizzie Japhet of Earth."

The answering mind voice as Liliath looked up from her book was soft and low pitched but felt definitely feminine.

"Welcome, Lizzie Japhet. We hear good things of you from your instructors of Sanglarka. The guardians of Earth agree, as does Mirihah. You are a prime candidate for agent training and perhaps more."

"Thank you, Administrator."

"You may call me Liliath. We don't stand on titles here. It has been a while since we had a trainee from Earth. They always add a great deal of spice to the stew, as one might say," and she bared her teeth in what Lizzie fervently hoped was a smile.

"I will have a hand in your training in addition to the other staff whom you will meet momentarily. One of my specialties is the disciplines of the mind, and I hear you have potential if you can ever bring down the barriers you have created. We shall see."

At that point, five beings came into the room from a side door that appeared to lead to a conference room. Lizzie could see a long table and chairs of various configurations through the open door.

"Lizzie, allow me to introduce your instructors.

"First, you have already met Lall. He will be in charge of seeing to it that you are as fit as you are able to be. Recognize that we have attempted to put you into a unit of mostly humanoids, but each of you has different strengths and weaknesses.

"None of you will be required to go beyond the specific strengths of your various cultures and physical attributes. Lall is an expert in defensive arts training and will take you as far as you are able to go in that discipline for your own safety. His job is to help you discover your strengths and how to capitalize on them."

Lall nodded to Lizzie, and she nodded back, not sure what else to do.

"Next, we have Lulindu, who will be instructing you in the history, political structure, and ethics of the Dimensional Alliance. This will be vital to guide

you as you represent the Alliance in many different cultures and environments. Knowing what you represent and what we stand for is crucial to your success in every assignment you will receive."

Lulindu was as tall as Lizzie, but there the resemblance ended. She had no hair of any kind that Lizzie could discern. Her huge, deep-green eyes were a darker reflection of her pale green skin. Lizzie almost expected her to have scales, but instead her skin was very smooth and unlined. She had a small dark blue mouth and only two slits instead of a nose. Her hands were squarish and looked strong. Her feet were covered by a long teal robe that extended also to her wrists and close around her neck. She did something that resembled a short bow in Lizzie's direction.

Lizzie copied the gesture, hoping she was doing it right.

"And this is Fin. He will be teaching you etiquette. Being an agent ambassador is a heavy responsibility and understanding how to quickly size-up a culture to avoid unnecessary misunderstandings will be important as you continue. You won't always know ahead of time the best practices in the cultures you encounter. Fin is an experienced agent with an impeccable record, and he will hone your intuition and reflexes in difficult circumstances."

Fin nodded. He appeared, at least as far as she could see, to be a somewhat short human, almost dwarfish. His brown eyes and expression were so calm that Lizzie almost thought he would go to sleep where he stood, but she suspected that, based on Liliath's description of him, there was more to him than appeared. She nodded back, and he actually smiled at her.

"Next is your science and technology instructor."

And to her happy surprise, Meta stepped forward from behind Lulindu.

"You already know Meta, and she will continue your program of study but with more detail and with more work in alien tech, as well as dimensional science as far as we understand it, including physics. She took a break from instructing for us to give you a better start at Sanglarka."

Meta grinned at Lizzie's delighted surprise. Her look said, "I'll bet you didn't expect this." And Lizzie had to agree.

"And finally, your presentation coach, Baird O'Flaherty, of Ireland, Earth. He will teach you how to blend in with any culture, how to read the actions and deeper meaning of the words and expressions of the beings you will come in contact with. He will also be honing your skills in controlling emotions and

reactions in intense situations. He is well known for his cunning and the ability to be inconspicuous at need and in plain sight. It may surprise you how often you will bless The Creator of All Things for his instruction."

Baird was nearly spindly, tall and quite thin with auburn hair, bright blue eyes, freckles, and a dazzling smile. He reached to shake Lizzie's hand.

"Welcome, Lizzie," he sent. *"Happy to see someone from me old stompin' grounds, I am indeed."*

Lizzie shook his long fingered slender hand, happily returning his smile.

"These will be your main instructors, although you will also learn much from your podmates and the other instruction assistants. At one point you will be assigned a 'Guide' during your internship to take you on your first assignments. Upon certification, you will be assigned to various missions or posts as need arises. Are you ready?"

Lizzie considered this. Was she ready? Really? She nodded seriously to Liliath. *"I am, Liliath. I think I have been preparing for this all of my life."*

"Then go with Lall. Classes are about to break in a few minutes, and he will introduce you to your podmates. You will receive a schedule of your classes and activities on your tablet later today."

Lall put a hand on her shoulder and nodded towards the door. They had been dismissed. Lizzie took a look around the pleasant, if unusual, faces of the gathered instructors and turned and left with Lall at her side. It had begun.

Chapter 14: Answers

(Jenny looked up from the journal with a start when she realized Lizziebot was turning on lights and closing the curtains in the living room and dining room.

She was almost surprised to find herself here, as absorbed as she had been in the beginning of the Alliance training that she had missed out on. It almost felt as if she were experiencing it alongside her aunt. If it hadn't been for the death of Lizzie, followed swiftly by Miriha's death and the drastic circumstances of the invasion of Earth, Jenny would have had podmates and training in these same Alliance training facilities.

"You haven't eaten," Lizziebot chided gently. "May I fix you something so you can continue to read?"

"Yes, please," Jenny said. "I'm just starting to get to the good stuff." And she read on...)

Lizzie walked next to Lall in a daze amidst a torrent of questions racing through her head. She suddenly felt like a freshman, unprepared and somewhat overwhelmed by the magnitude of what she had just committed to.

Even entering the university (what now seemed like eons ago instead of only a couple of years), she had not felt like this. She tended to be confident of her abilities to meet any challenge, but she was no longer quite so sure.

Lall stopped beside the door to the pod quarters and turned to face the administration building. Lizzie copied him and soon realized why he was facing this way and why they hadn't gone inside. A musical tone sounded from the building, somewhat like a chord on a xylophone. Nearly immediately after came the sound of hundreds of feet and a stream of beings of various sizes and descriptions pouring from the building onto the walks surrounding the large field.

Lizzie worked hard at keeping her expression neutral. Even meeting the staff had not prepared her for the sheer number of varying shapes, sizes, and colors of the students of the agent training center. Some of the colors she couldn't even put a name to, and only a relatively small number of them appeared to be even remotely humanoid.

Lall stood calmly by her side, seemingly unaffected. *"You will notice that this school accommodates beings that some of us would have never imagined ourselves if we had not had the opportunity to be a part of the Alliance. Individual species and cultures often imagine themselves as the ultimate expression of intelligent life, but what you see represented here is only a small fraction of the beings you may ultimately interact with.*

"I find it helpful for students to get over some of the shock of it before meeting their podmates. At that point, the differences don't seem quite so insurmountable." There was a humorous tone to this sending, although his face remained inscrutable.

Lizzie didn't reply. She watched while the various beings sorted themselves into the barracks surrounding the field. Hers was at the far end of the compound, so she was able to see this from a curious perspective. She noticed that similar types of beings were grouped in pods, which ultimately made sense, as she assumed they all had differing needs where useful facilities for sleeping, bathing, and other hygiene requirements were concerned.

She found herself wondering about food. Her stomach reminded her that she hadn't eaten since breakfast. Since the days here were quite a bit longer than those on Earth, she realized that meal schedules must be different also. Obviously, becoming an agent for the Dimensional Alliance would mean adapting to more than just different foods and how people looked and acted. Things like gravity, length of day, and seasons would also potentially take some getting used to.

Now coming closer and closer was a group of humanoids who appeared to be in mindspeech conversations, based on changing facial expressions and body language as they walked along.

There were ten of them. They halted just short of Lizzie and Lall and waited expectantly.

"Pod, I wish to introduce you to the final member of your pod for this term. This is Lizzie Japhet from the planet Earth in the Terran dimension. She has

just come from her initial preparatory course at the Earth training center. Agent training is her first opportunity to meet beings from different dimensions. You all remember how that felt, so please help her to adapt.

"Lizzie, these are your podmates. Pods work as a team to aid one another in excelling in the coursework that will prepare you all to be agents of the Alliance. Let us retire to the training area inside so you can introduce yourselves."

He nodded to Lizzie, gesturing for her to follow him into the barracks. He led her up to the front of the training area and pulled one of the chairs up to the front, aligning it with the chair that already faced the half circle of chairs, and motioned for her to sit.

The others took the facing chairs. She could now see why the chairs were varying types and sizes. Three of her podmates were very similar to overgrown linebackers, so large and muscular that one of the other chairs would not have supported them and would have been very uncomfortable.

Lall instructed, *"Let's go from left to right, starting with Negoth."*

Lizzie wouldn't have been able to pick Negoth out of any crowd on Earth. He was tall, about six feet, but had no unusual features that she could discern: brown hair worn longer than most men would have in current cultures on Earth, brown eyes, large hands, and tanned skin.

"I am Negoth of Elarna," he began in a soft, deep mind voice. *"You look a lot like a cousin of mine, so I would guess we are very similar in many ways, although I am learning that outward appearances can be very deceptive."* He smiled and sat down.

Lall nodded to the next in line, who looked a lot like the receptionist at Alliance headquarters, also winged, but feathered in intense reds, oranges, and bright yellow, with a beak, and with slender, humanoid arms and delicate hands. Lizzie's best guess was that this was female, which seemed to be confirmed by her soprano mind voice.

"Hello, Lizzie. I am Reanni, a Calyx from the planet Langtrey in the dimension, Alluvia. Our culture has long been a full member of the Alliance, and I have met other Earthlings. I am sure we can work well together."

She nodded at Lizzie and sat down.

One by one the rest stood and introduced themselves:

Linlin was about the same height as Lizzie, equipped with four arms and long green hair that wiggled and squirmed Medusa-like. She designated herself as female from Glang of the Fleuvali dimension. Her mind voice was somewhat bland and unemotional, as was her facial expression. Her hair seemed to be the most expressive part of her.

Mang was from Gligingamandixx. Evidently, Mang was a nickname, as none of the others could pronounce his full name. He seemed okay with it. He looked a lot like what might have been called an elf on Earth, pointed ears and all, but his skin was a deep magenta in color and his eyes were catlike and green.

Feth was as dwarflike as Mang was elflike, with very pale, almost translucent skin and no beard. His head was bald, and both ears sported begemmed earrings that hung to the base of his square jaw. He was from the planet En from the Slysian dimension. His stalwart appearance was belied, however, by his somewhat squeaky mind voice and a humorous twist to his mouth.

Minth didn't appear to be out of the ordinary, except he seemed to have rubber gloves on his hands, which he held up as he introduced himself. *"I wear rubber gloves and shoes for your protection and mine. My species have a much more intense electrical charge than most other lifeforms, and we can be somewhat dangerous, especially when aroused with strong emotions, including humor, anger, and friendship. This works well on our planet, Wyle, but in other places we need to be careful. So, you will excuse me ahead of time for not shaking hands or engaging in any of the other touch-related gestures that are common among various cultures.*

"My studies here are to prepare me to be an ambassador strictly to dimensions already enrolled as members of the Alliance. Obviously, I would have a difficult time camouflaging my true nature in an alien culture outside the Alliance. I will eventually serve as a liaison between the Alliance and my people."

This was the longest introduction so far, but Lizzie could see why it was necessary.

Next came Gi. She explained that her name wasn't short for anything. It was just Gi. Her appearance would have been pretty Earthlike, if it weren't for the light green tint to her skin and her bright blue and yellow hair that stood out spikily from her head. She claimed the planet Finque from the dimension of Il with pride, and the tone of her mind voice was deep and silky.

Then, surprisingly, all three of the large beefy beings stood in unison. In a single mind voice that felt like a chorus, they sent, *"Lizzie, we are Geln. We are a joined-mind entity with the convenience of three physical presences. You address us as a single being. We have the capability of acting individually but are directed by a single consciousness. We come from the planet Krix in the Bevial dimension."*

They sat down again and Lall stood. *"I imagine you are probably hungry, Lizzie. I have set up a special meal for you and your podmates so you can get to know one another better. Normally we have four mealtimes daily, one at break of day, two what you would call lunches, and finally an evening meal.*

"You will be dining with your podmates exclusively until the second stage of your training. By that time, you will have completed the first half of your ambassador etiquette training, and you will get the opportunity to practice what you have learned by dining with and mingling with fellow trainees in other pods from many different dimensions.

"After you have eaten, your podmates will escort you to your Alliance history class. You have about a week of catching up to do, so before bed each night one of your podmates, on a rotating schedule, will help you get up to speed for the next few weeks. Your lesson materials have been translated to your language and will load to your tablet the next time you open it.

"After classes today, Reanni will take you to the outfitter station, where they will add some essentials to your MDP, tools, clothing and other things you may decide you need.

"For now, just follow your podmates and do what they do. Any questions?"

Lizzie shook her head, her brain spinning. Always before, she was ahead of every one of her classmates in every subject. She didn't know how to respond to not only being behind but feeling more than a little awed by the seeming vastness of the task in front of her.

"Then let's go get some food and relax for a bit."

As they all stood, Lall put a hand on Lizzie's shoulder. *"Lizzie, I know this may be a bit overwhelming at first, and we're going to work you hard. Morning and evening physical workouts on top of all of the information and mental exercises you will be getting in all of your classes, not to mention self-defense training at midday. If at any time it seems a little too much, you can count on any of your instructors, including me, to help you reorganize and take any necessary steps to get you back on track.*

"Eventually, you and your podmates will also discover you can count on one another, as if they were a part of your family. Much of your evaluation at the end of the certification process will depend on not only your personal achievements but how well you work with a team."

Lizzie nodded once again. She had never found herself tongue-tied like this before. She always had an opinion and often annoyed both her instructors and the other students in her classes by her outspokenness, constant questions, and generally always having an answer when a professor asked a question of the class.

They headed for a path between the barracks units to a street of single-story buildings. They were plain, painted white with the now familiar huge doors in different colors. Lizzie had to assume this was so you could tell them apart.

"The green door is the dining hall," Lall continued. *"The red door is the outfitter station. I will leave you and your podmates to your meal."* And he walked away past the other buildings and disappeared around a corner.

"Come on, Lizzie," sent Gi. *"I imagine they have starved you since you came through the gate. I know by the time I went through my orientation I was ready to eat a full grown Glark."*

In mindspeech the concept of "Glark" came across as something large like an elephant with spines and six legs. She laughed, and that broke the tension that had been building up since she had walked through the Sanglarka gate.

The dining hall was set up in sections. She had expected this to be similar to the cafeteria at every school she had attended, but this was very different. It was a lot more like a restaurant, and she began to understand why as the meal progressed.

There was a long table at their section with appropriate seating all around it. She noticed there were twelve chairs. She assumed that was because Lall would join them from time to time for meals.

A humanoid being, tall, willowy, and gray-skinned, greeted them and one at a time asked for their orders. Lizzie didn't recognize any of the dishes requested by her podmates. When the being turned to Lizzie, she introduced herself as Maun and explained that Earth dishes had been programmed into the menu at this point and appropriate foodstuffs had been imported to the pantry to allow her a wide selection. She asked Lizzie to pull her tablet out of her MDP to see the selection of dishes. Lizzie did so and asked for a peanut butter and jelly sandwich and a glass of lemonade, which felt like the safest choice for now.

When the food was served from a rolling cart to each of them, they didn't immediately begin to eat, so Lizzie waited as well. Negoth sent, *"We begin each meal with a moment of silence to allow each of us to address the Creator of All Things in thanks in their own way. If this is not your custom, simply wait until all are finished, if you please."*

They each bowed their head, and it was quiet for a minute. Lizzie had been taught to say a blessing on her food, since she was very young, but was somewhat surprised to see that this practice was observed in this very alien environment.

One of her favorite aspects of mindspeech was that one could eat and talk at the same time. Lizzie ate without talking much, listening to the conversations going on around her with great interest.

"I hope the D.A. lesson today is a review," sent LinLin, her hair waving softly around her face. *"Lulindu seems to be bent on finishing the entire course in the first month. I'm having a hard time keeping up."*

"I'm sure this past week was just an overview," assured Feth in his squeaky voice. *"I had an apprentice master who was wont to do that with each new task. He would rapid fire information at you until you were overwhelmed and then go back through, step by step."*

"We think it will all be fine, but it's etiquette that has us wondering," Geln said, all three heads nodding. *"So many things to remember, and how are we to know the customs of every culture we encounter? So far, we can't even begin to understand how that works. Even on our planet there are so many cultures with so many different ways of doing things, and that is hard enough. Boggles our mind."*

"We've already had mental training this morning, with Liliath's assistant," Minth remarked to Lizzie. *"You really haven't missed as much as you might fear. And the Presentation professor is from your own planet, so that might*

make things a bit easier, although his line of thought has me more than a little concerned. Unpredictable."

"I also know Meta," Lizzie replied. *"She began my tech training in Sanglarka before I came here. Evidently, she was doing double duty, gating back and forth between dimensions to see that I got my initial training. I can say I was surprised to see her here in my initial briefing at the admin building."*

And so, it went on, each putting in an opinion about their schoolwork. It was obvious to Lizzie that they had already begun to bond as a group, and they seemed welcoming enough to be going on with. This was a new way of thinking about education for her. It had always been mostly a solitary pursuit. It would all take some getting used to, notwithstanding the interesting differences in her podmates.

Mealtime seemed to fly by. In almost no time, there was nothing but crumbs on her plate and the lemonade was empty. Her podmates had also cleaned their various-sized plates. The server had rolled the cart back to the table and began to clear the plates and utensils.

They trooped out and headed back along the path between barracks to the main assembly area and into the school.

They went up three floors to the Dimensional Alliance Studies classroom. Professor Lulindu stood at the front. The room was lined with large windows on one side and surprisingly Earthlike desks and chairs in various sizes in a semicircle facing the instructor.

Located at the far right was a single seat that wasn't taken by the other students. As Lizzie seated herself there, Professor Lulindu sent to her, *"Please take your tablet out of your MDP and click on my face to access your course materials."*

Lizzie did so, still in awe of the technology that allowed such a thing. She remembered hauling a bag of heavy books from class to class at the university and was grateful to get beyond that.

Inside the digital folder for the class were a number of books, as well as a notes section and a folder with instructional videos and charts. In addition, there was a place for her to create and submit reports and essays to the instructor.

As it turned out, Feth had been right about the preceding week's being an overview. Lulindu began at the beginning of the founding of the Dimensional Alliance today.

"The actual beginnings of the Alliance are not well documented, as any original records were lost over eons of time. Tradition tells us it began as the result of a multidimensional war that lasted thousands of years. One of the dimensions had taken to raiding other dimensions for resources. It wasn't until the affected dimensions banded together to face their foe that they were successful in ending the threat.

"Once they had contained the offending dimension, it occurred to them that the naturally occurring gateways continued to be a threat as other dimensions discovered that they could be used in such a way. They combined their resources, and their scientists discovered a way to control access to incoming and outgoing traffic through the gates.

"We don't know a lot about the science behind this, but once they had created monitored gates between the allied dimensions, it occurred to them that other dimensions without the benefit of this science were still at risk. Could they in any conscience continue in safety, knowing that others didn't have that luxury?

"Also, they realized that there needed to be a central controller to the gate system, and that had to be done by agreement amongst the Alliance members.

"So, they took on a daunting, almost impossible task, on the one hand, seeking out naturally occurring dimensional portals in other dimensions and, on the other hand, developing a system of governance for the existing gate system to prevent corruption of the use of the gates.

"They decided that the guiding principle in all of this needed to be the guardianship of the right of each culture in each dimension to pursue their own destiny without interference from any other dimension.

"As long as no dimension interfered with any other dimension, they could choose their own path, whether others agreed with it or not.

"The temptation to meddle in the affairs of dimensions that might be pursuing a path to their own destruction was great, however. It was often argued that the Alliance could interfere if it was for the dimension's 'own good.' But the few times that the Alliance did that, it ended in disaster, regardless of their best intentions. They discovered you cannot force a culture to do what is best for them.

"They also discovered to their horror that exposing cultures who were not advanced enough to receive technology beyond their normal development was also intrinsically a flawed concept. Thus, we developed a policy of non-interference; this meant that, although we protect every portal we discover with carefully selected native gate guardians, we do not offer Alliance membership to every dimension that has known gateways.

"These are the basics and foundational principles of what we will now learn by specific examples. This course of history is intended to reinforce the reasoning behind the whys and wherefores of our policies.

"We will begin by having each of you research the gate history of your own dimension and its connection to the Alliance. You will find those reference materials in folders labeled with the name of your own dimension. In two weeks, each of you will do a presentation of your personal dimensional history. Understood?"

There were nods of assent from each of the students. Mang asked, *"Does this mean that students will be teaching the class?"*

"Indeed. You will find that this is a standard teaching method during your agent training. We want the students to be invested in their education, and we want you to be able to relate strongly and personally to the principles we teach. In addition, research has shown that one of the best ways to internalize something is to teach it to someone else.

"For the coming few weeks, we will meet here in the classroom where you can ask questions and discuss what you are learning from your personal studies while you prepare your reports. After that, we will be taking some field trips to demonstrate more clearly what you are learning. For now, you are dismissed."

There was a scraping of chairs as they rose.

"Now where?" Lizzie inquired of the group in general.

"Science," sent Gi in her soft, deep, almost musical mind voice.

The laboratories took up the entire basement, segmented into the various disciplines of scientific study. Today, Meta would be teaching an overview of the background of gate science and some of the history of advances over the past couple thousand years. They would be exploring other Alliance technology over time, but this was the basis of everything they did.

As they proceeded through the lesson, Lizzie felt comforted by the fact that most of her podmates weren't much better informed than she was, and that was actually quite common among the general populace of even the longest standing member dimensions throughout the Alliance.

It was a lot like the fact that most people on Earth had no idea how the lightbulb worked and only thought about it when it didn't work. As long as the light went on every time you flipped the switch, why did you have to know the whys and wherefores?

In this class they would also be taking multiple field trips to gates around the Alliance planet, including to one that hovered in space not far from the star base that orbited the planet.

By the time they finished with the science class, Lizzie's stomach was rumbling again. But evidently it wasn't time for the second lunch break yet. The elongated days were definitely going to take some getting used to.

As they left the classroom, Negoth piped up with, *"Etiquette next. Get ready for some eye-opening revelations. No reports or presentations to prepare here. It's all hands-on labs and performance-based examination. Fin is easy going unless you decide to sluff off or fall asleep during one of his lectures."*

Lizzie smiled at him, and he smiled back. Then, as she entered the classroom at the top of the basement stairs, she stopped smiling, admittedly a bit confused.

The classroom was large, square, and divided into four areas. There were no desks. Instead, one area looked like the back room of a tailor's shop. Another appeared to be a formal dining room. In the corner next to that was a cleared space with a shining marble floor. In the fourth corner was what might have been the inside of a tropical hut.

Fin greeted them at the door, waving them towards the dining area. There were placards in front of each of the chairs, and at each place was set a variety of different foods.

It was interesting to see the various characters written on each of the placards. Lizzie's name was inscribed in calligraphy in English, but evidently each of them recognized their names and went straight to their places at the table, which sat a dozen people comfortably. Fin stood at the head of the table behind an ornate chair with gold scrollwork on the seat back.

"As you can see, we will be learning best practices when eating in a formal dining situation. As those of you know who have attended my classes this past week, the areas of this room change from time to time. We will be doing the

eating etiquette module all this week. At the end of this section of your course, we will be presented with a feast, at which time your performance will be evaluated to determine if you will need any remedial instruction.

"On each of your place settings you will notice that there are foods you recognize and many you do not. I can assure you that all of the food choices presented are appropriate to your own constitution, and none of them will harm you in any way.

"In future modules, we will be learning how to test unknown foods and the most congenial way to refuse something that might harm you. In addition, we will be covering the supplies in your MDP of antidotes and medicines to rescue you if there are ever any delayed symptoms or reactions to something you have eaten.

"Most of the time, but not always, there will already have been research on the edibility of the native foods in any area you are assigned.

"But for today, we will be exploring the basics of common etiquette practices in your own planets, to demonstrate clearly what you are up against. Each of you will demonstrate as much as you know about common practices of formal dining where you live, with foods you are familiar with.

"The second half of the class will be devoted to having each of you try at least two foods you are unfamiliar with.

"So, let us begin."

Lizzie felt a little panicked at this. She was used to trying new foods; her parents had insisted on their children having a wide variety of eating experiences from various cultures. But the idea of teaching the etiquette of Earth to her podmates was daunting. She had only had a very few experiences with formal dining and wasn't at all confident about teaching it to anyone else.

However, it soon became evident that she wasn't the only one who wasn't confident about her prowess in this area. From the stricken looks on Gi's and Feth's faces, she could tell they were trying to figure out what they could possibly say on this topic.

Placed before her was a meal typical of what she would have been served in Sanglarka. A dinner salad, a hearty stew, a roll with a pat of butter on a bread plate, a glass of water, and a piece of apple pie. The setting included an array of silverware, a cloth napkin, and a small tray of what looked like hors d'oeuvres.

She paid strict attention as each of her podmates explained the meal that was set in front of them as well as the varying utensils. These ranged from variations on spoons and forks and chopsticks, as well as eating knives that served as forks as well. In some cases, the only utensils were their fingers.

Some of the dishes were meat heavy, and some were strictly various vegetables and fungi. In any case, by the time they got to Lizzie, who was extremely grateful she was saved for last, she had organized her thoughts and explained the various spoons and knives and the use of the napkin.

She had noticed that none of her podmates had mentioned the plate with bite-sized bits of food that evidently were not appetizers.

When she finished her explanation, Fin told them to go ahead and eat their meal, observing one another as they went. He also instructed that the little plates were "samples" of some foods they had probably never tasted before, assuring them once again that they were perfectly safe for them to try.

As they ate, Fin explained some of the different types of eating experiences they might have over their time as an agent, including everything from eating outside sitting on rock benches or the ground, to eating in the equivalent of restaurants and pubs or dining in banquets in palaces.

Lizzie found that as hungry as she had thought she had been before they started, she would probably not be able to finish the ample servings placed before her and felt she needed to place a priority on the sampler tray.

She picked up what looked like a slice of fruit. It was incredibly sour, but she tried hard not to pull a face or to pucker in response. Once the shock of its bitterness wore off, she realized that it might be nice if the juice was added to something else to dilute it down, but not for casual eating, as one would eat an apple or orange.

Some of the things she tried were extremely salty or sweet, but many had flavors she didn't quite know how to describe. In all cases, she realized that sitting in a formal setting and showing distaste for what was set in front of you probably wouldn't be considered good manners. If this was so complicated just dealing with something as simple as eating a meal, how was she ever going to master the rest?

Fin didn't give any sign that he was evaluating their performance. He did, however, tell them that tomorrow they would get their first opportunity to eat in a completely foreign setting and promptly departed the class, not giving any indication whether they had done well or not.

They trooped out of the admin building to assemble on the turf in front of the pod. Lall was waiting there, feet planted shoulder width apart, arms folded across his burly chest.

"Staffs out!" he called out in the mental equivalent of what her dad would have called "parade ground voice."

Lizzie surprised herself with her own immediate response to this command. Without her stopping to think, her staff had appeared in her hand from her MDP in guard position, almost like magic. She had groaned at the many times Oak had made her practice this. Like a swordsman sheathing and unsheathing a sword, Oak had explained that the ability to have the staff at hand in an unexpected attack could mean the difference between defeat and survival.

"Your new podmate makes your number uneven, so for now I shall pair with her, and we will switch off each day, rotating through until each of you have had the dubious opportunity to be my partner. For the next week we will be practicing the forms. Face your partner. On my count: one, two, three, and begin!"

At a measured pace they worked the forms that had become so familiar to Lizzie. She was now very grateful for the opportunity she had been given in Sanglarka to work with Oak. Although she was fairly sure she would never be a brilliant staff fighter, she could generally hold her own with only a few bruises to show for it.

The forms were much like a choreographed dance that moved forward and back, one on defense and one on the attack; the rhythmic "clack, clack, clack" of the staffs striking one another echoed off the walls of the facing pod buildings. It was almost hypnotic, and when the echoes of the final clack reverberated and faded, Lizzie almost felt bereft.

She realized she was sweating. How long had they been working? She hadn't noticed the passage of time.

"Well done, one and all. You are dismissed until the stretching run. Second lunch now, and more classes on your schedule. See you this evening." The dismissal was genial, and Lizzie felt she had acquitted herself well enough.

Ironically, it was now time for second lunch. Despite their workout, they all agreed that going to the dining hall after the meal in Fin's class was unnecessary at this point, so they went to their pod instead.

Geln immediately collectively laid down on their individual beds with a choral sigh. The rest settled into the training area, tablets in hand, to go through their notes and begin on their report for Lulindu. Each of the chairs in the training area was equipped with a slide-out stand that could be adjusted to hold their tablets at the best optimum level for their individual use.

Instead of a physical keyboard, the tablet utilized a holographic keyboard, each designed for the individual being who used it. Meta had helped Lizzie customize hers to look a lot like the keyboard on her old typewriter at home. It was a little odd getting used to not having the feeling of touching the keys, and it was awkward in the beginning; but over time she was getting used to it. She had taken a "touch typing" course in college, so once she became accustomed to not having to feel the actual keys under her fingers, she had gained speed and accuracy.

Lizzie was beginning to relax somewhat in the company of her podmates. What she had observed in the first three classes and having dined with them twice so far was that they weren't so far ahead that she couldn't catch up, and none of them seemed to expect her to be any more than what she was.

"We have one more inside class today," sent Linlin in her nearly monotone mind voice as she adjusted her tablet stand. *"Baird is an interesting person. His instruction style is a bit flamboyant, but the information is well thought out, and he has the advantage of many years' experience."*

"Thanks for the heads up," Lizzie replied. *"I find it interesting, the various teaching styles and the subjects they have chosen for us. Very different from anything in the universities on Earth. Is it the same for you?"*

"Indeed. Sometimes some of the classes almost feel frivolous, but over time I think we will see the reasoning behind them. I admit I find myself poorly prepared for the scope of it all."

"Really? I'm so glad I'm not the only one who feels that way. Is your planet an Alliance member?"

"Yes, but only for about the last hundred years. And you?"

"Earth is not a member of the Alliance, but we are a gateway planet for our dimension, so although there are Alliance Gate Guardians and, from time to time, agents are recruited from among us, the existence of the Alliance and the gateways is strictly guarded from the general populace."

"Then I suppose this is even more daunting for you than for those of us from Alliance member dimensions. If you need any help, please let me know. I'm not as outgoing as many of our colleagues, but I am very interested in other cultures and societal structures."

"Thank you," Lizzie replied wholeheartedly. *"I appreciate the support and look forward to exchanging information with all of you. It also helps a lot to know I'm not terribly behind everyone else."*

As Linlin had said, Baird was as unique as the other instructors had been in methodology as well as in energy and enthusiasm for his subject. As they entered the classroom, the layout once again was very different from the other classrooms.

Instead of the semicircle of chairs and desks or chairs sitting around a table, the desks in this room were laid out in a circle. Outside the circle facing inward were mirrors, so that one could see their own face reflected as well as the two sitting on either side of them. At any given time, individual trainees could see their own face, the faces of those facing them in the circle, and those sitting on either side of them.

It was a bit disconcerting at first, and Lizzie wasn't the only one in the circle who tended to look down at their desk rather than out into the mirrors and the faces of those across the circle from them.

"It's a habit you will lose over the course of this class," Baird intoned with a chuckle, noting their downcast eyes. *"Nearly every being has a hard time with the mirrors and a class where you are constantly looking into one another's faces. But, over time, you will learn how to look yourself in the eye and all those you meet, with a very few culturally warranted exceptions.*

"In this class you will learn to be honest with yourself and to govern your facial expressions and body language and to alter it at need. Diplomacy is not very effective when your body language and facial expressions belie your words. And it is much harder to blend in with others in an alien environment when you don't know how to recognize common social behaviors. So, noticing and remembering what you see will be of prime importance.

"After this class, you will be put under the tender mercies of Lall, where you will no doubt face pain and fatigue of the body. But in this class, you will face pain and fatigue on a mental level. This is different from your mental discipline classes, as we are more concerned about what you show to those around you and not so much about what goes on inside.

"Lizzie, we welcome you to the class. I wish you to notice that although your podmates have been exposed to this discipline for a week now, they still struggle with the mirror exercise. Knowing what I know about the denizens of Earth, however, I have a feeling you will catch up soon enough.

"Now, on with it…

"Each of you please look up and into the mirror facing you. Although you will be able to also see your classmates, I wish you to look directly into your own eyes and note what you see."

Lizzie looked up as instructed, but without enthusiasm. She didn't care much for mirrors. She only ever looked into one when it was absolutely necessary. She kept her hair short for a reason. The less time spent in front of a mirror trying to get her hair to behave, the better she liked it.

So, she looked carefully and critically at her own face. At first it was all about the fact that her short auburn hair had been tousled by the slight breeze on the compound that day around her tanned face, and she looked more than a little tired. Her day had started early on Sanglarka; and since the days on this planet were so much longer than the usual 24 hours of Earth, she found her eyes to be a bit droopy, as her mom would have said.

She had never thought of herself as vain or absorbed with her appearance, but she had to admit to herself that she was somewhat plain; deliberately so, if she was honest. But as they continued to sit there staring uncomfortably at themselves, she began to notice some other things.

Looking into her own blue eyes that almost appeared violet was difficult. Especially since she could see beyond the face into her thoughts of insecurity and self-criticism. She never quite thought she was as capable or smart as she would have liked to have been. She put a good face on it to the outside world, but something inside her drove her to become more, to excel beyond her own perceived abilities, and she was generally harsh with herself when she fell short.

Now she asked herself, in context with Professor Baird's remarks, what others saw when they looked at her. Did she come off as confident, or just arrogant? Did her lack of attention to her appearance show a lack of consideration for others' opinions? Did she need to overhaul her attitude? Could it be that Miriha was mistaken in her confidence in her abilities?

She shook her head, losing confidence moment by moment. She risked a look out of the corner of her eye at her podmates. None of them appeared to be happy with this exercise. Gi actually had a tear glimmering in the corner of one eye. Evidently, Lizzie wasn't alone in her personal assessment.

Then, Professor Baird interrupted her chain of thought with, *"Very well. I can see you are all squirming. This is good. Now, I want each of you to look at one another. Not now. But throughout the coming day. Tomorrow we will be examining our thoughts and will be reporting on what we see in each other. I know none of you have known each other long,"* he continued, holding up a hand to prevent comments or questions. *"This exercise is about judgment, not criticism. Being able to judge a situation by observing those around you is an important skill. You are dismissed to the tender mercies of Lall."*

And at that, he strode out through the door.

For a moment, the entire pod sat there, somewhat stunned.

Then, with sheepish looks at one another, they rose and followed him out of the classroom door.

No one spoke as they trooped out to the commons. Sure enough, Lall was waiting at the edge of the large grassy training area between the rows of pod buildings. They halted before him, quietly awaiting his orders.

"After undergoing all of that intense stimulation of your brains, it is time to recharge your system. Today we will be running the aerobics course. In the morning we will run the stretching course. We will continue this pattern until I am confident you are ready to do both the morning and night exercises without stress.

"Your requirement as an Alliance Agent is to be fit physically as well as mentally. Not all of you will find yourself in situations that will require extreme physical exertion, but this also addresses your ongoing health and usefulness. A sick agent is not effective or useful. In your role as an Alliance Agent, strengthening the body is as vital to your success as strengthening your mind.

Now, follow me. Mang, please bring up the rear of the group and aid any who are having difficulty."

Mang nodded curtly, almost as if he expected this.

And so, they ran. The aerobics course consisted of segments of about a five-minute run interspersed with various calisthenics intended to bring the heart rate up and strengthen various parts of the body.

Lizzie found she was now very glad for the initial training in Sanglarka. She was not the least capable of the pod, at any rate. Feth seemed to struggle the most with the various exercises due to his short legs, but he never complained. And as Lizzie had suspected, Mang didn't even seem to be short of breath or sweating when they were done.

Geln, as bulky as they were, was her biggest surprise. They were more light-footed than she would have expected. Indeed, they were probably second only to Mang in making the run seem almost beneath their abilities.

For the rest of them it was a workout, to be sure, but not beyond any of their abilities. By the end of the course, all but Mang and Lall were panting, but none collapsed or complained. Lizzie knew they would all be grateful for a shower and bed, however.

Chapter 15: Intensity Cubed

(Jenny was intrigued by the Alliance training process. It amused her that her aunt had struggled with many of the opposite issues that would have been difficult for her in the training. She flipped forward in the journal in anticipation.)

As the days stretched on, things began to fall into a routine, but it was never boring.

Lizzie's curiosity had led her to this point, she knew. But, as she continued to pursue this unusual course, she realized that she had gotten more than she had asked for. The classes and instructors were unique, and the expectations were so much different than her experiences in Earth academia.

For one thing, there were no grades. You either passed or didn't. There were no formal exams and no written tests. Each student was evaluated by their performance and participation and, as needed, they were given extra assignments on an individual basis, either because they were struggling with a concept or because they were ahead of the class and were ready for more advanced instruction.

And the classes! There were no lectures after the first week. Assignments were given in advance of the class, and then practical application or discussions followed based on the study of the day before. It wasn't even unusual for students to be called on extemporaneously to teach sections of the lessons.

All in all, Lizzie was both fascinated and frustrated by the process. She had been so used to being top of the class and ahead of her classmates that this new paradigm made her realize that she wasn't as unique or advanced as she had always considered herself. Her podmates had been chosen for the same qualities she had. For the first time in her life, she was working with her equals, and in some cases, her superiors.

Nevertheless, as time went on and she got to know her podmates, she found that she was actually making friends. This in and of itself was a new experience for her. She had never really related much with her fellow students on Earth, especially in her college years. She had been so wrapped up in her studies that she had not set aside much time for socializing. Even in the cafeteria she had generally eaten alone, with only a textbook for company.

Now, however, she felt a part of something so completely different and in an environment so alien that she knew she would never make it without the help and support of her podmates.

Not only did they study together, but they also spent time getting to know one another and relating experiences in their differing cultures and backgrounds as part of their classwork. As a result, by the second week, Lizzie was feeling more at home than she had ever been before.

By far, her two closest friends were Minth and Gi. Minth was humble and earnest and so willing to help his other podmates. Gi, although she had come across as somewhat arrogant at their first meeting, turned out to be cheerful and kind, with an energetic enthusiasm for their studies.

"I'm looking forward to today's lesson in Professor Baird's class. He hinted it might be fun, and there were no preparatory assignments to go with today's lesson. I wonder what it might be? He did say that we were progressing in our ability to look at the mirrors and that lessons would be shifting," Gi said, as they left the etiquette class well into the third week.

"I don't know. His lessons are always so strange. How long have we been staring into those mirrors now? It seems like he has reasons for what he does that I don't fully understand. Usually, course aims coincide with some kind of logical coursework. This method of teaching is far beyond my experience," Lizzie replied, shaking her head.

"I hear you. I know, based on our conversations, that our cultures are very different from one another, but I don't think any of us have encountered anything quite like this before. Every time I think I have things figured out, I find I was mistaken. I know they have been training new agents more or less successfully for a very long time, but I honestly don't understand the point of many of the lessons or the method of instruction.

"I mean, with the exception of the history of the Alliance and the science and tech classes, what does all of this have to do with representing The Alliance?" agreed Minth.

When they arrived at the classroom, it had been rearranged. Instead of the circle of chairs and mirrors, there were now three long tables, the obligatory mirrors behind each of twelve chairs facing one another across from each other, four chairs at each table.

In front of each chair was a nametag. They immediately found the tag with their name on it and sat, each directly across the table from the other facing the mirror image of themselves. Lizzie was seated across from Linlin, who smiled her wan smile as she sat, her hair waving complacently around her face.

Lizzie noticed that Geln had been separated to face three different people: Feth, Reanni, and Negoth.

Mang found himself facing an empty chair, which seemed to worry him, one eyebrow cocked and his mouth a thin line across his face.

Soon after they had all found their seats, Baird entered the room. He was wheeling a small cart, like they used in the cafeteria, upon which sat six small packages.

"Today we will be beginning an exercise we will be pursuing for the next 4 weeks of training. This exercise has more than one purpose.

"You will notice the mirrors remain, and for good reason. As you face what has now become your opponent, you will be able to see both your facial expressions and those of your opponent simultaneously. This will be instructive, as you will discover shortly.

"We are about to play an ancient game that has been passed down within the Alliance for centuries. This game is strategic. It teaches logic and tactics. Adding the mirrors to it, also teaches us how to school our expressions, to either choose to give no signals or to potentially give false signals as part of the strategy necessary to win the game.

"One of the interesting outcomes that may surprise us is how Geln, a joined consciousness, functions against three separate opponents in three different games.

"There is an element of chance in the game, which mirrors the element of chance you will experience as you encounter different cultures, political systems, and personalities in your ventures as an agent."

He then began to set one package on the tables between each pair. No one reached for the packages, simply awaiting instructions. They had already learned that they could take nothing for granted in these classes, as surprises and subtle tricks abounded.

Professor Baird sat himself in front of Mang and continued, *"In each of these packages you will find all of the components for the game."*

He unwrapped the fabric around the package in front of him. The wrapping laid out in a rectangle with symbols on it and in the center was what appeared to be a multicolored cube, four squares across and four squares tall. He removed what Lizzie now realized was a separate individual cube from the stack and held it up for them to see, revolving it in his fingers so each side was exposed in turn.

"Each of the large cubes is made up of 64 smaller cubes. As you can see, the opposite sides of each cube are inscribed with matching symbols and colors. There are three symbols on each cube... the loop," and he showed the blue side with a gold infinity symbol on it, *"the chain,"* and he showed the red side with a gold circle on it, *"and the gate,"* and he showed the yellow side with a silver rectangle in the center of it.

"This game is essentially a matching game. The goal is to match as many sets of three as you can. The opponent with the most matches at the end of the game wins. This sounds simple—and it would be, except that there are other factors in the game."

"You may have noticed that each of these symbols relates to something you have already seen in the Alliance culture. The agent gate pass, the chain it hangs on, and the gate itself. And this," he said as he lifted a small key, similar to the keys Lizzie had noticed hanging around the necks of the Earth Gate Guardians, except this one was not on a chain. *"Of course, it represents the Gate Guardian key. You will also notice a coin. It has no value except in the game,"* and he held it up, flipping it to show each side, one with the chain symbol and the other with an infinity symbol.

He had everyone's riveted attention. This was even more bizarre than any of the lessons they had been given so far.

"You may be wondering, at this time, what this has to do with becoming an Alliance Agent. I assure you; it is an essential tool to teach you skills that will benefit you throughout your agent experience. I will explain the rules of the game in a moment, but the game is simply a tool to teach much deeper concepts, the first of which is that things are seldom as simple or obvious as they seem to be.

"Please unwrap your packages so we may proceed to learn the game."

Each group complied, revealing their own cubes, the small key-like tokens, a coin, and the curiously marked game board. On the board facing each player, between them and the cube in the center of the board, were two squares next to one another. Each of the squares was marked with a three-by-three lattice. In addition, on the square to the player's left was a pocket shape, and above the same square was what looked like a swirling vortex.

"Each of you take one of the key tokens and place it in the pocket below the square on your left. To begin the game, you will also need the coin, which can be placed next to the main cube."

They each placed a key in the pocket-shaped space and the coin next to the cube.

"For this first game, for the purposes of brevity, your cubes are pre-shuffled. I will demonstrate how to shuffle them for future games before we start the next game. I thought perhaps you would prefer to get directly into game play as quickly as possible." And he smiled, a mischievous twinkle lighting his eyes.

He removed the little key from his "pocket" and replaced it with an ornate green stone surrounded by Celtic knots sculpted in gold.

"Avid players of the game tend to keep their own unique key tokens. This one, carved from the national gemstone of Ireland, Connemara marble, is mine. Not all are as elaborate as this one, but for each player a personal key token generally has some significance to them. Assuming you develop a liking for the game, you may eventually acquire your own. For now, the key tokens that come in the game set, resembling the Guardian or Gatekeeper's keys, have enough significance to go on with.

"To begin, we must first determine who takes the first turn."

He pulled a coin from his pocket. On one side was a stylized harp and on the other was a bird in flight. *"We will designate the harp as 'heads' and the woodcock 'tails.' I will flip the coin into the air. Whilst it's still in the air, Mang will call out either 'heads' or 'tails.' If he calls correctly, he will start the game. If not, I will begin it. Ready?"*

He tossed the coin and Mang called *"heads."*

The coin landed harp side up.

"You will proceed first, then. Would you wish to represent the loop or the chain?"

"The loop."

"Very well. As the first move of the game, you must remove any cube from the cube stack that has at least two exposed sides. The goal of the game is to match sets of three, transferring completed sets to the scoring area of the board to the player's right.

"To begin, after choosing a cube from the center cube stack, you will place it on your board. That move is considered one turn. Please proceed."

Mang chose a cube with a loop symbol on the top. He placed it dutifully, without turning it, on one corner of his game play area and waited.

"In each turn, every player can choose to do one of three things. They can remove a cube from the cube stack, turn a cube on the playing board of their opponent, or move a cube either on their own board or on their opponent's. Any of those actions in and of itself counts as a turn."

He turned towards the rest of the class. *"Are we clear so far? Everyone determine which player goes first, and the first player may take and place a cube. Then we will proceed. For our purposes today, the chain symbol on the coin is 'heads,' and the player on the same side of the tables as me will flip the coin."*

There was a ringing sound as coins hit the tables. Linlin tossed the coin and Lizzie called *"heads."* She won the toss and pulled a blue cube with the loop on it and placed it on the right-hand corner of the board.

They all made their moves and paused, waiting for instruction.

"Now you will each take turns, making as many matches as you can as you go. At some point you will run across a cube that looks like this." He held up a cube, with the yellow gate side up. Inscribed on the rectangular gate symbol was a keyhole. *"This is what is called a 'locked gate.' Its purpose is to pause play and create the necessity of strategy, planning, and tactics. It is also one of the two ways your key token comes into play. There are two situations where the locked gate is found, and each has its own strategy.*

"The first possibility is that it may be found face up at the top layer of a column of cubes in the cube stack. When that happens, that entire column is taken out of play and placed in the vortex." He indicated an area on the game board that looked like a small cyclone. *"None of those cubes are accessible for the remainder of the game.*

"The second possibility is when it is found on an exposed side of a cube during play. When that happens, the one who takes the cube can instantly turn the locked side up or may leave it hidden until ready to play it.

"At any point during their turn, they can rotate the cube lock side up and place it on another's game board either on a cube or space on that board during their next turn. This effectively locks that space or cube until the player uses their key to unlock it. Unlocked gates are placed onto the vortex and cannot be used again. Once you use your key to unlock a gate, it cannot be used again and will also be placed in the vortex.

"You can also use your key as if it was a locked gate to lock another player's cube. If you have already used your key and someone locks your cube either with a locked gate or their key, that cube remains locked for the entire game.

"As you can see, there are strategic options built into the game.

"For purposes of this class, you have two goals. One is to do your best to win the game as often as possible. The second is to learn to 'read' your opponent's while either hiding your own or appearing to express opposite or different emotions than you are feeling during play.

"In diplomacy, both of these skills are often necessary. Learning to either give no clue or present false clues to your intentions may be vital to your success as an agent.

"Please begin."

Immediately every pair became focused entirely on the task at hand, and it became evident, even though everyone was communicating with mind speech, that this was not as easy a task as it first appeared to be. Lizzie was beginning to suspect that this was a theme in her new educational challenges. Every time she thought she had figured out where they were heading, her instructors came up with something new and perplexing.

But she couldn't complain. She had asked for this.

In her early school years, she had been challenged only in physical education but decided that this was unacceptable, so she had started to put real effort into physical conditioning. She never became anything like a star athlete, as that wasn't her goal, but she never got picked last for teams, and that was enough for her.

Now, here she was in the middle of a matching game that looked so simple on the surface and proved to be a bigger challenge than any of them had expected.

On the one hand, it took a while to learn to play the game, even in its basic form. On the other, trying to figure out strategies and pay attention to the facial expressions and body language of the other player while trying to control their own seemed nearly impossible to do.

In the exertion of doing so many things at once, the expressions on faces vacillated from intense concentration to utter immobility to sometimes bizarre contortions. Even using mindspeech, there were often muffled sounds of frustration interspersed with some verbal expressions which Lizzie could only assume might have been cursing in their various languages.

Each round of the game took about fifteen to twenty minutes to play, and they rotated around the table, each facing Professor Baird at one point or another. By the time it was Lizzie's turn to play against him, she was feeling a little less stressed about the game play and more engaged in changing her view from the mirror behind her opponent, glancing at her own expression, and the face of the player in front of her.

Professor Baird grinned at her and addressed her in mindspeech.

"Well, me lass, how do you think this is going?"

"For me, or in general?"

"Either one," he replied, as he flipped a coin to begin the game. *"I am guessing you are getting about a 50/50 success rate, and that isn't pleasing you much."*

Lizzie found herself wondering how much of that he had gotten from her own facial expressions and body language.

"I don't like to lose, professor. And I'm not much for playing games."

"Ah, me fine lass, I'm not so surprised at this. I marked you from the beginning as focused to the point that it might not be healthy. Gaston tells me you are very exact and not very compromising when it comes to success or failure."

"Is that a bad thing?"

"Perhaps not, if you don't ever want to get any real joy out of life." And he turned one of her cubes to unmatch the one next to it.

Lizzie realized that the conversation had been intended as a distraction from the game. She should have expected it. He wasn't the only one using this tactic. She didn't answer but gave him what she hoped was the expression he had been looking for.

She lost by a considerable margin to him, which was no surprise. As he finished with her, he called out to the group in mindspeech, *"Time's up. Please reset the games to the starting point and leave them there for tomorrow. I'm sure you'll be looking forward to a nice hard work out with Lall. We'll give it another try tomorrow, shall we?"*

They complied and, unless they were continuing to try to hide their emotions, she guessed that most of them were relieved to be done with this game for the day.

Chapter 16: Holiday

(Jenny marveled that something as simple as a game could have so many layers of meaning and application. Somehow, in all the things she imagined the agent trainees being taught, this was definitely not in it. However, it made sense.

Thinking back, she remembered seeing the troopers play the game during their break time, when they had been preparing for the Groga assault, although at the time she had no idea it might be significant.

Obviously, the skills needed to do what Burt and other agents did required a different approach. She could even see why she could have found this kind of instruction useful in more than one situation.

She flipped through the journal. Much of it was daily notes on Lizzie's progress and self-evaluation. Jenny had always thought of her aunt as being very confident, but remembering the stories others had told her, and now seeing into Lizzie's personal thoughts, made her realize that she had learned her lessons of projecting emotions well, even though she seemed to think herself deficient. Jenny read on...)

Classes, workouts, and daily challenges to what Lizzie thought she knew and understood about science, life, and the various personalities she dealt with continue to challenge her.

Slowly but surely, she was beginning to think of her podmates as friends, rather than simply people she worked with. She began to recognize the quirks and talents that differed so much from one to another and yet seemed to enhance the overall experience for everyone. However, she could not have honestly said she felt particularly close to them. She was used to thinking of herself as an outsider, and the feelings persisted.

She didn't want to admit it to herself, but she found herself homesick from time to time, especially at the end of the day when things got quiet in the pod as various ones were settling into their beds for a well-deserved rest.

As she lay in her bed, she drifted into remembrances of walking along the beach near the pier, shopping in the farmer's market, or even hanging out with Thumble in the lab as she had worked Gaston's assignments. She was beginning to realize that the diverse types of assignments were to see if she would be fit for this crazy patchwork of learning experiences in the Alliance Agent Training Center.

Therefore, just over two months into the training, she had been excited to hear that it was "holiday time." Lall explained to the trainees during their evening formation that starting the next day there would be periodic opportunities to go home and communicate with friends and family and take a short break. Evidently, Gaston would be picking her up and escorting her through the gate for a weeklong leave and would return her to the next stage of her training after it had passed.

The next morning, her things packed conveniently into her MDP, she watched Gaston stride across the training ground to greet her happily. *"Do you have anything in mind for your time off?"* he asked her. As usual, his bird bright eyes were dancing with just the slightest bit of mischief.

"I thought I'd spend some time on the beach, and of course I'll want to phone my family. Don't fancy a visit, not really. And I think I might buy a gift or two for some of my podmates. Don't know if they celebrate birthdays here or not, but it can't hurt to have something on hand that comes from Earth."

"They'd probably like that, I'll bet. So, connecting with family, some shopping, feeding up on Earth food, and just relaxing? Sounds like a good plan," Gaston agreed.

They entered through the gate on the hill above the Alliance headquarters city and came out through the Sanglarka gate. Lizzie was surprised by this. She had expected to exit into the Los Angeles gateroom.

"The Earth guardians and the training staff wanted to treat you to a little celebration before we head home," Gaston said, with a twinkle in his voice and a mischievous grin on his face.

There in front of them were the entire Sanglarka crew and all the other gate guardians, all smiling like kids caught with their hands in the cookie jar.

"Welcome home," said Grenheim, gesturing around him. To his right and left, every face was smiling welcomingly. Miriha stepped forward. *"We hear good things about you from your trainers,"* she sent, gesturing to Meta, whom Lizzie hadn't noticed standing slightly behind Miriha.

Meta beamed. *"I think it is safe to say that Lizzie isn't disappointing any of us. Our hopes for her seem well merited."*

Grenheim gestured to all of them to follow him up the path to the lodge, and Lizzie felt very welcome and warm even before they stepped into the inviting lobby. He led the way into the now familiar dining room. He pointed to the seat next to his at the head of the table, and everyone immediately found seats and waited expectantly.

Livia had not joined them but had gone through the swinging kitchen doors and returned with a cart laden with the standard Sanglarka fare. Fluffy home-baked rolls and all of the condiments anyone might care to add, including Livia's famous lingonberry jam and fresh churned butter, were placed along the center length of the large table. Tureens filled with soup and stew, sitting on a warming tray, stayed on the cart.

They sat quietly for a moment, as was their custom, heads bowed. When everyone had looked up, Grenheim passed a basket of rolls to Lizzie. *"Enjoy!"* he sent, as he ladled a large helping of stew into his own bowl from one of the tureens on the cart next to him. Livia pushed the cart around the table, and each ladled their choice of soup or stew into their bowls and began to eat.

It was so delicious, and such a delightful change from the more mundane food at the training center. Each of the guardians took it in turn to congratulate her on getting this far in the program. They had their own stories to tell.

Many went back for extra helpings, and by the time more and more of them were pushing their plates and bowls back and leaning back in their chairs, Lizzie was feeling very warm and at home.

Miriha finally stood and addressed the group, smiling warmly at each of them. *"It is always such a treat to spend time with the Earth guardians on occasions like this. When Gaston first introduced me to Lizzie, I had a strong feeling that she would be a perfect fit for the agent position and potentially more, over time. Lizzie, we are all very pleased at the effort you consistently put into everything you do. Your instructors—including Professor Baird, if you would like to know—report that you have the makings of one of the best Earth agents we have had in a long time.*

"The next stage of your journey will be much more exciting as you begin to get some hands-on opportunities to meet many more beings from the vast starscape of the multiverse. On the opposite side of that training, you will discover things, hidden within your own depths, that you never suspected. Each of us looks forward to following your adventures on this journey.

"When things get difficult—and they will—please remember there are many of us who are rooting for you. We carry you in our thoughts and hearts."

She walked around the end of the table to stand next to Lizzie's chair and gestured for her to stand. Lizzie did, and Miriha enfolded Lizzie in a gentle hug.

Lizzie had never been a "hugger," but coming from Miriha, this was so encouraging and so natural that she didn't even feel embarrassed by it.

And before she knew it, every single one of them had stood and each took a turn giving her hugs.

"Now," Gaston said, *"You are properly launched into your holiday. You can sleep here tonight or go directly to the L.A. gate. Which would you prefer?"*

"I would like to spend the day here, as there seems to be only a little daylight left, and then leave for L.A. in the morning," Lizzie replied, realizing it would be good to catch up with all of these people. She looked forward to hearing more of their own stories about the training process.

The remaining afternoon passed genially in the lobby area on the big squishy chairs ranged around the fireplace. Supper was a casual affair, as Livia had prepared a buffet with both a chilled area for a salad bar and a steam-tray area for several different heated dishes that seemed to hail from all over the globe. Lizzie, now used to eating exotic dishes, tried a taste of just about everything.

Before bed, some of them got out various musical instruments and performed some native music for the rest. Lizzie had never learned to play an instrument, but she loved music. She was especially impressed with a small wooden box with a range of steel prongs sticking out from a fret-type board played by Yaw.

"It is an mbira," Yaw explained, when Lizzie asked him about it. *"This one has three octaves, but there are simpler ones. You can play pretty much anything*

on it from classical..." and he plucked the opening stanza of "Ode to Joy" "*... to rock and roll,*" and he played a quick version of "Sh-boom."

"That's amazing. I wish I had some kind of musical talent. I've never had any music lessons in my life, but that doesn't look very hard, and it has a lovely sound."

Yaw chuckled, and out of his MDP he invoked a second box, this one with only seventeen keys on it.

"A gift," he said simply. *"I learned to play on one very similar to this. We've taught our primates to play them, so I'm pretty sure it is within your reach."* And he handed it to her.

"I don't know what to say," she began, but he cut her off with a wave and a smile.

"Just play it. You don't even need to play a recognizable tune to have it soothe you and give joy to those around you."

Lizzie timidly plucked a key with her thumb as she had seen Yaw do and was delighted at the quiet ringing note. It was a peaceful sound. She continued to randomly pluck various keys, delighting in the round tone of the notes.

"Thank you so much. I will gladly use it during break times to calm my nerves. I may even learn to play a song or two."

"That would make me very happy. Next time you come back to join us, you and I can play together."

Lizzie pulled the beautiful shawl out of her MDP that she had been given in Switzerland what seemed an age ago and carefully wrapped the mbira in it and returned them both into her MDP.

It seemed no time before the lights came on in the lobby, and many began to yawn and stretch. Lizzie remembered that they all came from various time zones on the planet, and for some of them it was very far past their bedtime.

She bade them all goodnight, as she assumed they were all politely waiting for her to retire before doing so themselves. The chorus of goodnights sent her up the stairs to her room feeling the warm delight of welcome and realizing that she had done much more than become an agent for the Alliance. She had acquired a new family.

The next morning, they celebrated with a traditional Sanglarka breakfast of rye crackers, eggs, and cheese and one by one they departed for their various gate responsibilities across the Earth. Miriha had gone in the night to receive them, as all of them had to travel through the Gatekeeper's gate to get to another Earth gate.

"Gates within a planetary gate system cannot connect directly with one another," Miriha had explained to her. *"You can travel from any Earth guardian's gate to just about anywhere else in the multiverse, but for some reason none of a planet's gates connect with one another. This means, to get from Sanglarka to any other gate on Earth, you must come through my gateroom first."*

Finally, Grenheim and the Sanglarka staff saw her and Gaston through the gate. They didn't come out through the beach gate, but instead were transported directly to the gateroom outside Miriha's office, where they walked down the hallway to another door.

When they walked through the door from the gateroom through the gate office and into the hall of the little house on Infinity Loop, Gaston called out, "Nita, we're home!"

Nita came out of the kitchen, wiping her hands on her apron, apparently unsurprised. Of course, she would have had to know something of what Gaston did, Lizzie mused. After all, she had been with him for a very long time.

"Lizzie! So good to see you. I'm pretty sure you've already had breakfast. What do you have planned for today?"

"Planned? Hmm. I hadn't really thought much about it."

At that point, Tidbit wandered into the living room, Thumble riding delightedly on his back.

"Lizzie home? Thumble glad. Missed you," he said in his soft mind voice.

"I missed you too, Thumble. I'll be here for a few days, though, before I go back to training."

"Lizzie will be brilliant in training. Lizzie will win all the prizes!" Thumble enthused.

"We're glad to see you back," Tidbit intoned. *"Training as an agent is challenging, to say the least. I hear you are doing well."*

Lizzie had a hard time, looking at Tidbit and recalling how large and imposing he was in his native shape. The cat, although he had the obvious cat-like attitude, especially with those large golden eyes, was only a little less intimidating. She wondered how he managed that.

"Thank you, Tidbit. I'm trying to do my best."

"It's all anyone would expect of you, Lizzie." Tidbit replied, a bit stiffly, Lizzie thought.

"Well, I suppose I'd like to go back to the lab for a few days. Would it be all right while I'm there if I make a few long-distance calls?"

"Of course," Gaston said, grinning at her. "You've earned it, for sure. Do you want alone time, or would it be all right for me to stop in for our usual lunches?"

"I would love that, Gaston. But, yes, I think I need some thinking time. I'll probably run out to the beach a few times before the week is out, as I miss it a lot. Your policy of my taking regular time out had me looking forward to beach time, and the closest body of water to the training center is several miles away—some kind of river, or so I hear."

"Ah, yes... I remember. So, you've already have had a great breakfast, but here it is late afternoon. I doubt you're tired, as I know your body clock has gotten used to a much longer rhythm. Is there somewhere you would like to go or something you would like to do before I take you to your place?"

"No, I think I'm good. If Thumble wanted to come along, that would be fine. I've kind of missed him."

Thumble nodded his tiny fuzzy head enthusiastically.

"So, Nita, I'll be back around suppertime. Let's keep it light. I'm afraid those rye crackers fill me up, especially when I add Livia's famous lingonberry jam to them," Gaston said, patting his stomach.

Nita nodded happily, hugged Lizzie, and turned back to the kitchen, humming as she went.

Lizzie realized she felt very at home in this little house and hoped that, once she started her agent duties, she would still get the opportunity to visit here often.

When they arrived at the lab after a long commute due to freeway traffic, Lizzie thanked Gaston, who waved to her as he backed out of the parking lot.

She climbed the stairs, fished her keys out of the MDP, and opened the door to her little apartment with a satisfied sigh.

She let Thumble out of his basket. He was humming the same tune that Nita had been back at the house. All in the apartment was as she had left it, but surprisingly there wasn't a coating of dust, as she had expected might be the case. Evidently Gaston or perhaps Nita had been in, from time to time, to clean.

There wasn't really anything to do, at the moment, as she had already read the books on her bookshelf, so she got her mbira out of the MDP and decided to see what she could do with it. She had been wanting to try it since Yaw had given it to her, but so far had not had any quiet time to do so. She really hadn't wanted to fumble around with it in front of anyone. That would have been embarrassing.

She plucked some of the keys tentatively with her thumb and enjoyed the lovely ringing tones she remembered. She tried doing some scales, alternating from side to side from one thumb to another. Even simple scales made calming music from this tiny instrument. It was hardly bigger than both of her hands laid flat side by side and yet the tones that came from it were rich and almost haunting.

Lizzie really didn't know much about music. She did enjoy listening to a very eclectic mix of styles and types but had never really had the energy or the time to really study it. She decided that one of the errands she would undertake during her break was to see if any of the music stores in the area might have an instructional manual to help her on her way. In the meantime, she decided to see if she could pluck out a few simple tunes.

After about an hour she had figured out "Mary Had a Little Lamb" and "Three Blind Mice" and could play them haltingly from memory. Surprisingly, Thumble found this very interesting and began to hum with her delightedly as she played. She felt like she could get to like this, and for some reason it reminded her of all of the strange assignments Gaston had given her while she served her initial apprenticeship in the lab.

She had a niggling theory that was beginning to take shape, but it was still in embryo. Her curiosity had launched her into something that she was beginning to feel was way over her head, and that this break time, with no assignments to worry about, might help her to begin to put those ideas together somehow.

By the time she had tired of efforts on the mbira, she realized that it was twilight. She decided on a peanut butter and jelly sandwich and some hot cocoa, to get some early sleep. She was going to make an early day of it tomorrow.

She surprised herself by falling asleep quickly, with Thumble happily resting on the pillow next to hers.

"Would you like to come with me on my errands in your wicker carrier or would you rather I let you loose in the lab today?" she asked Thumble as soon as she arose in the morning.

"Let's go, Lizzie. Thumble will be good and peek out from inside the basket. Not make noise or scare anybodies," he piped up cheerfully. *"Will we go shopping?"*

"Probably. I'll pack us a lunch and we can eat on the beach. Does that sound good?"

Thumble nodded his little head enthusiastically.

Off they went on her bicycle, first to a music store, which just happened to have the book she needed. It turned out that the mbira was also known as a kalimba or "thumb piano," and there was quite a bit of music and instruction on how to play it. The store owner had been delighted to hear that she was learning.

"It's nice because it is even more portable than a guitar. And unlike a flute or recorder, it doesn't require breath control. Let me know if you ever need it tuned. They can go off tune by tiny increments. I can even show you how to do it yourself, if you'd like," she said with a grin. "I don't often get people in here who even know it exists."

From the music store, she stopped in at the farmer's market, one of Thumble's favorite places. True to his word, he didn't hum or make any noises when they were out, but from time to time, he would comment in mindspeech about the people he saw around him and the various displays at the market, especially the areas where they were selling fresh fruit.

Lizzie bought a pineapple to share with him, and some really sweet-tasting green grapes the stall-keeper had let her try. She also found some of her favorite homestyle strawberry jam that she resolved to store in her MDP for use at the training center. Now that she had sampled the food there, she realized that her MDP would allow her to take along some home comforts that weren't otherwise available.

She carried a netted cloth shopping bag, deciding that trying to put her purchases furtively into her MDP might be problematic, and she wasn't planning on really loading up this time. She would save it for the day before her holiday was over.

Thumble kept up rambling mindspeech chatter about all of the people and things they passed on their journey. It was entertaining, to say the least, to hear his opinions about what he saw, or thought he was seeing. Occasionally, he would ask questions about what something was or how it was used.

"What that does?" he asked about a refrigerator holding various meats. Lizzie patiently explained the need for refrigeration. *"Why not just eat it when it is fresh?"* he queried, puzzlement obvious in his voice. *"Meat eaters kill and then eat. That's what they do. Why wait?"*

He had a hard time grasping the idea that the meat eaters, specifically humans, on this planet didn't kill their own meat generally, and the whole idea of storage was definitely foreign to him. He confessed he had wondered about the refrigerator in Gaston's house and Lizzie's apartment but had never gotten around to asking about it.

Evidently, where he had come from, there were few meat eaters, and his kind avoided them as much as possible, for fear they might be on the menu.

As far as Lizzie could discern from Thumble's stories from his past, his species were gatherers, as they lived in a climate and ecological system where fruit and edible plants were abundant year-round. The idea of farming had been a revelation when Gaston had explained it to him, and he had been fascinated when Nita would go out into the garden to tend the herbs and other plants there.

Evidently, Gaston had obtained Thumble during one of his training trips as an Alliance agent. While on Thumble's home planet, Thumble had hitchhiked to Earth in Gaston's backpack. When Gaston had offered to take him back, Thumble had demurred. He liked Gaston and found Earth fascinating. *"Earthers are funny. Fruit here is good, and my home has no 'rocking roll,'"* he had explained.

Lizzie enjoyed his company, especially now that they could communicate.

After the farmer's market, Lizzie decided to take the bus to Belmont Pier. During the work week and on a cloudy day like today, it wouldn't be crowded, and she could have the quiet she needed. There were still so many unanswered questions, and she was beginning to realize that she had to answer the most important ones for herself.

As she stepped off the bus, she inhaled deeply. There was something immediately soothing about the clean salt air of a beach. As she strolled down the paved path down to the beach, she was delighted to find it almost deserted. Most other people would be hard at work.

At the end of the path, she paused to take off her shoes. She needed to feel the sand under her feet.

The surf on this beach was gentle, due to the breakwaters that had been created to protect the navy's Pacific fleet during the war, so the surf was not so loud as on many beaches on either side. Nevertheless, the sounds of the water lapping the shore, the seabirds wheeling and crying, and the feel of the gentle breeze was so very soothing.

She looked around and noticed no one close enough to see what she was doing. She installed her net shopping bag into her MDP and pulled a large beach towel out to sit on and a small picnic basket. She sat the wicker travel basket on the towel next to her. The picnic basket shaded the small wicker basket without blocking the view of the beach for Thumble.

"I need to think for a bit," she told Thumble. *"I will be sitting here quietly. If you have questions, please wait for a bit. We'll have some lunch later, but before then, would you like a snack? I brought an apple and some crackers."*

Thumble agreed that a snack would be nice and didn't speak or hum as he ate happily.

Looking around again to be sure there was no one within sight, she took her mbira out of the MDP and settled herself, plucking the keys randomly. She had learned to play a few simple tunes so far, but she found the random tones soothing. She had discovered that interacting with the mbira helped her to think. She noticed that Thumble was humming happily along, as if he recognized a melody in her tuneful doodling.

As her mind calmed, she found herself returning to the question that continued to plague her waking hours and even her dreams. Without thought she stopped playing the instrument in her lap. What was she really doing? She had made a commitment to a very specific course of action without knowing all of the facts, which was very unlike her. She didn't think of herself as an impulsive person.

People with ordered minds didn't just jump at new opportunities. And yet she had. Why was that? She didn't feel the fervor she had noticed in her podmates. The more she learned in the agent training program, the more she wondered if she would ever really be as urgently committed as they seemed to be.

She remembered back when her dad had joined the navy, and the light of determination and energy that was in his eyes. He was committed, signing a blank check to his country up to and including his life, if necessary. He hadn't hesitated and had never once indicated he doubted his decision.

Her mother had been in total sync with that decision and proudly displayed the small, red-edged flag with the blue star in her window, announcing to all passersby that her husband was serving her country.

But this wasn't like that... or was it?

She would have given anything to have the fire in her eyes she had seen in her parents during that time, but she wasn't feeling it. She still felt, as she always had, distant and aloof from her fellow beings, human and alien, as if she were observing their lives from far away. She had never actually had a close friend; and although she loved her family members, it was almost as if someone had turned the volume down on her ability to feel deeply.

Was this how it was always going to be? Am I doomed to see, to analyze, but never to feel the deep connection I observe in the people around me? Even though she had been warmly welcomed by the Earth guardians and others in the Alliance, she still didn't feel as connected to them as she thought she ought to.

She did feel a loose link, but nothing that she would mourn for long if it should be severed for any reason. And her studies in the Alliance were not driven by any intense feelings of loyalty to their cause, only by the commitment she had made. Regardless of her feelings, she would keep her word.

As she considered, she continuously ran the grains of sand on the beach next to her through one hand. The action was soothing, almost mesmerizing. As she did so, she found herself focusing on the individual grains. Although on the surface the beach appeared to be made of white sand, she noticed that many of the miniscule grains were actually of various shades of yellow, orange, and even red, not enough to dilute the overall coloring of the beach.

Am I like one of these little colored grains? So different and yet mixed into the background of the billions of pale grains that surround me? So many questions. It's like an addictive drug, this need to know. Why can't I feel the same way about the people around me?

She sighed heavily, and to her surprise she felt Thumble's tiny warm hand on her arm. She looked over to see the little fellow looking at her intently with those huge dark eyes.

"Lizzie is okay? Lizzie is hurting on the inside? Thumble feels your hurting." The soft mind voice was tender, and she felt his intention, one of the valuable things about this particular method of communication. She could tell that Thumble actually cared about what she was feeling and had identified more clearly what she was feeling than she had herself.

"I'm going to be okay, Thumble. I just am worried that maybe I'm not doing what I should. I know I need to keep my promise to the Alliance, but I don't know if it is the right thing for me."

"Maybe it will be the right thing for you when your whole heart decides to do it?" he sent, still patting her arm softly.

"Oh, Thumble," she replied, realizing as she did so that tears were coursing down her cheeks, *"Do I really have a heart?"*

Thumble crept over to her and touched one of the tears on her cheek. *"Lizzie's heart is on her face,"* he said simply.

At this Lizzie broke down and sobbed, Thumble continuing to gently pat her arm. She cried for a long time.

Then, straightening, she looked around her. The beach was still mostly deserted. Far down the beach an elderly man in a broad sun hat was strolling along the water line away from her, but other than that, in either direction there was nothing but her, Thumble, and the wheeling gulls.

What's gotten into me? she wondered. She replaced the mbira into her MDP and fished out a sandwich and some chips from the picnic basket, along with some of the sweet grapes she had bought at the farmer's market for Thumble. There was also a bottle of somewhat warm lemonade, as the ice had melted, but it was good, nevertheless, to sit and eat in silence, absorbing the calmness that waterscapes always gave her. She remembered days at Lake Cachuma with her family.

Probably her favorite activity in those days was to sit out on the pier, a fishing line dangling into the water. She didn't generally care much whether she caught anything or not. It was the environment she craved.

She did actually catch a turtle on her line once, however. The poor thing had been injured as the hook had caught between the shell and its front leg. She had taken it home to nurse it back to health and had dubbed it Snag. It had lived a happy life hiding out in the ivy along the back fence, emerging to eat fallen hibiscus flowers or various veggies they left out for it.

Lizzie and Thumble finished their lunch, and she decided it was time to head back home. "What did I accomplish here today?" she asked herself as she put the remains of their lunch back into the picnic basket and settled Thumble back into his wicker transport. She didn't have any answers... yet.

Chapter 17: Linked

(Jenny had known that her aunt had a very different personality from her own, but she always had thought of her as so confident. And those who had known her, like Bob, Burt, Liliath, and Miriha, had all thought of her as kind and optimistic.

To be let behind the veil to see Lizzie in this way made her realize how much people changed and grew over time. She knew that she, herself, had definitely changed since she had first picked up the keys to the house on Infinity Loop and had unknowingly connected herself to the Alliance via the tiny key that still hung around her neck.

She touched the key unconsciously. She didn't think about it much anymore; but, like Lizzie, everything had changed from the moment she put it on. Although in many ways their journey had been decidedly different, they both learned more about themselves than anything else.

It was as if her aunt had reached across time and space to give her a gift worth more than anything Jenny could imagine. She stretched and turned another time-weathered page.)

Lizzie couldn't believe how quickly the time had passed. Her holiday seemed to be over almost before it really began. She had spent nearly an entire day catching up with family on phone call after phone call. Then she had gone shopping with Gaston tagging along as she looked for things she wished to take back with her to the training center.

She had eaten lunch most days with Gaston, their usual lunch date in the office, and had caught up with mundane things like answering mail and finishing up some of the interrupted projects she had been doing for Gaston before she had been recruited into the agent training program.

Gaston had said she didn't need to complete them, but there was something in her that just couldn't let them go.

When she wasn't working on projects, she spent time continuing to learn to play her mbira. She liked the logic of the way the keys were laid out; and before she knew it, she was playing harmonies in the songs she was learning.

She also picked up, wrapped, and addressed packages to various family members, dating them so Gaston would know when to send them out for birthdays and other holidays. He would send them from various places around the world to coincide with her cover story. She hadn't intended to do that originally but realized that this might be one careful step towards getting closer to them.

The entire time, her mind was whirling in circles trying to discover that spark she so wanted to kindle. She was committed, without a doubt, to the course she had chosen, but it was not that deep commitment, that intense fervor she had seen in others under similar situations. Over and over, she found herself wondering what was wrong with her.

When Gaston picked her up on her last day to take her back to his house to go through the gate to see Miriha before going back to training, she couldn't shake the feeling that this holiday had only been a dream and she would awake in her bed in the pod, as if none of it had ever really happened.

On the drive back to the house, Gaston had said, "Lizzie, are you all right? You seem almost melancholy."

"I'm really not sure. I got plenty of rest and did all the things I had planned to do. All the boxes are checked off. And yet, I really don't know what's going on with me. I'm looking forward to getting back into training, as it was just beginning to get interesting. It's almost like I don't really have a life here on Earth anymore. I don't know how to explain it."

"Ah, yes, it does feel a little unreal after being exposed to how big it all is," Gaston agreed. "Somehow, when I first went through the training, I felt like the Earth was very, very small and I was the smallest speck of matter in the multiverse. It can be so overwhelming."

Lizzie nodded. That was close to what she was feeling, yet still not beginning to touch the edge of it. She sighed.

"I'll figure it out eventually. It's what I do. I think I really hate to see a challenge without an answer, and I'm afraid the answer to this one will be a long time coming. And I'm not at all sure I will like it when it does." She sighed. "I'm not a very patient person."

Gaston chuckled. "I noticed that."

After that, they chatted about Lizzie's conversations with her family members and friends, and by the time silence had fallen once again, they were pulling into the driveway of the little house on Infinity Loop.

Lizzie let Thumble loose from his travel carrier as soon as they got inside, and he scampered off to visit with Tidbit, who was sprawled lazily on the bright sunny window seat in the living room.

Nita greeted her warmly and ushered them into the dining room, where a simple lunch of soup and salad was laid out.

"Can't let you leave on an empty stomach," she said with a grin.

Lizzie knew that Nita was well aware of Gaston's activities and seemed to take it all in stride.

While they ate, Nita entertained them with stories about the various neighbors on the loop and their activities, and before Lizzie knew it, they were sitting back in their chairs full and satisfied.

"We'll be saying goodbye, Nita," Gaston said, cheerfully patting his stomach. "Lizzie still has a long day ahead of her."

Nita nodded and stood and gave Lizzie a motherly hug.

"Thank you, Nita. I hope to see you again soon."

"I look forward to it, Lizzie. Thumble and I will be happy to see you when you return."

Gaston led her through the gate office into the gateroom, Tidbit trailing behind them. They emerged onto the beach, and the gem eyes scanned the three of them. They moved on through the little grove of trees, with the crooning linklings humming in concert above them.

It was somewhat disconcerting to see Tarafau striding along beside them. He dwarfed them both, in bulk and in height. He seemed very much at his ease, not even glancing up at the little faces peering down at them as they made their way under the shady palm-like trees that lined the path.

Lizzie, on the other hand, couldn't help but look up. The little creatures seemed to emanate a peaceful and cheerful feeling that was somewhat infectious. To her surprise, as she continued to watch them, one of them scampered lightly down the trunk of one of the trees ahead of them and stood in the path directly in front of them, as if waiting.

Evidently, Lizzie wasn't the only one surprised by this behavior. Both Tarafau and Gaston halted and waited quietly to see what the little creature would do next.

The linkling was tiny, only a couple of feet tall, and covered with pale green fur, with the exception of the tufts on her little ears and the eyebrows that blended into long mustaches that hung halfway down her chest; these were dark green, the color of an evergreen tree of Earth. Her large blue eyes were surrounded by white circles that only emphasized the deep blue irises and wide dark pupils. The nose on her short snout was wrinkled in what Lizzie guessed might be a smile—or at least she hoped so, as the little square teeth were bared.

"This one is Lizzie, yes?" came a soft melodious mind voice that made Lizzie jump in surprise.

"I am Lizzie. May I ask your name?" was the only reply that came to Lizzie's mind.

"I am called Ynni, and your mind shines like a bright star to me."

Lizzie looked from side to side at Gaston and Tarafau. Both appeared to be as shocked as she was at this pronouncement.

"Can I do something for you?" Lizzie asked, not knowing what else to say.

"You are mine," Ynni replied simply, and then added mysteriously, *"You have finally come."*

"Yours? What does that mean?"

"Mine. Our link is complete. I am also yours. We are us. We are now one." And Ynni reached out a tiny hand toward Lizzie.

As she did so, Lizzie found herself mimicking the motion unconsciously and took a step towards the little creature. Their hands touched, and Lizzie felt a tingling warmth spread from their hands to her heart. It was like being wrapped in a warm blanket by a mother's hand.

Ynni leapt from the ground to Lizzie's shoulder, but this time Lizzie wasn't surprised. She knew in the split second before that this was Ynni's intent. How she knew, she couldn't have explained, but a connection had been made that could not be denied. Ynni's tiny hand was warm on Lizzie's cheek as she gently turned Lizzie's face to hers. Looking into those deep blue eyes was like looking into the vastness of space on a night with no moon.

"We go now?" Ynni asked. *"Miriha waits, and we have things to do."*

Lizzie nodded. Looking at Tarafau and Gaston she asked, "Did either of you hear any of that?" They were both looking at her with raised eyebrows.

"What does the linkling want?" asked Gaston. "I've never seen one of them behave like that before."

"I'm not sure. She says we are linked, and I believe her, even though I have no idea what just happened. She's coming with us to see Miriha. Maybe she will be able to explain this to us?"

Tarafau sent in his deep baritone. *"I believe you have just been offered a great honor, Lizzie. It appears that there is much more to you than any of us expected."* The tone was thoughtful and a little wry. *"Few can say they have ever been honored so."*

They continued down the path, but before they got to the end that opened out onto the village square ahead, Lizzie realized the little creature had disappeared. She could still feel the slight weight and warmth of the little body on her shoulder, but she could see Tarafau striding along beside her through the space where Ynni had just been.

"What just happened, Ynni? Where are you?"

"Ynni has turned her reflection off. No one can see me when my reflection does not stop light. Light can pass through me. At any time, Lizzie can tell me to turn my reflection off or on, and I will obey."

"Turn your reflection on," Lizzie told her tentatively. Immediately Ynni was sitting on her shoulder again looking into her eyes. *"Why did you turn it off?"*

"I did not wish to attract attention in the village. They all know about linklings, of course, but I guessed Lizzie might not want them all staring at her or gathering around her as she proceeds to Miriha's home."

"Good thinking. Then, please turn your reflection off." Once again, her little companion disappeared from view.

The path opened out onto the village square, the marketing of the day in full swing.

As they walked down the street by the permanent shops that lined the square, people nodded as they passed one another or gathered in small groups of two or three, gesturing and smiling to one another, apparently engaged in interesting conversations.

No one remarked at the three of them passing along the edge of the square.

At the far end of the square was the large, dark-green building, the only one of more than two stories on the square.

When they finally got there, they were once again met by the two uniformed townsfolk in green.

"Welcome," they said, greeting the travelers. *"You are expected."*

They all removed their shoes and as she did so, Lizzie noticed how well Ynni balanced on her shoulder without wobbling as she performed this task. She guessed the long silky tail helped her in this, but Ynni didn't try to grab Lizzie to support herself. It was strange to feel her there and not be able to see her. So many strange things in such a short time....

Tarafau led the group up the winding staircase to stand in front of the door at the top. Although he didn't knock, the door swung open quietly and he went inside, followed by Lizzie and finally Gaston.

Miriha stood in the center of the room and held out both hands in her usual gesture of welcome. In turn, Tarafau, Gaston, and finally Lizzie took her hands in theirs. She gestured for them to sit in the comfortable chairs circling the room, and she sat as well, folding her hands gracefully in her lap.

"I notice we have an additional visitor with us today," she sent to Lizzie's surprise. Suddenly Ynni appeared on Lizzie's shoulder, nodding in agreement.

"Miriha is wise and sees deeply," Ynni remarked. *"Lizzie should always listen to Miriha."*

"How did you know? She hadn't turned her reflection on and even I can't see her when it is off."

"My Amni told me." And with that another linkling appeared on Miriha's shoulder. *"He says he is happy for you on your linking day."*

"Thank you, Amni. I am still trying to understand what has just happened. I am glad Ynni chose me, but I really don't know what it means."

"It means, that Lizzie will never be alone. It means that Lizzie has a forever friend," Amni replied.

"You have been accorded a significant honor, Lizzie. Few are ever chosen by a linkling. You have become a part of Ynni and her family. It is like being sisters, but more intense than any sibling relationship you may ever have. For one thing, linklings have no secrets from one another. And you will never have any secrets from her, since, unlike the rest of us, they can accurately see the minds and hearts of those around them." Miriha clarified.

"They read minds?" Lizzie asked, realizing she wasn't doing a very good job of controlling her facial expression and she tried to smooth the look of shock from her face, *"Really?"*

"Yes, but it is more than that. They see deeply into parts of your mind you may have even hidden from yourself. They are empathic and feel your joys and pain and sorrows. They are completely nonjudgmental, but they are very careful to link only to those who are true of heart and spirit. It is a signal honor to have been chosen by one who knows all of your shortcomings, as well as your accomplishments and talents, and still wants to spend forever with you."

Lizzie looked once again into Ynni's deep blue eyes. *"Are you sure about this?"* she asked timidly.

"Ynni is sure."

"But what about my training; what about all of the traveling and schooling I need to do? And what will the Alliance have to say about this?" Lizzie asked Miriha.

"As for that, allowances will be made. If anything, this strengthens your position as an agent. It verifies our analysis of your character. It doesn't mean you don't have a lot of growing to do, and you still will make mistakes. Nor will you always be successful in all of your challenges, but being linked will give you an edge beyond your podmates.

"However, this will work only if you continue to put out the same effort you have shown in the first stages of your training. In the meantime, the purpose of our meeting today, beyond a celebration of your link, is to advise you of what to expect in your next stage of training.

"You are about to be exposed to cultures and beings very different from anything you have ever seen so far in your training. You are going to get to know much more about those of your podmates whose dimensions are members of the Alliance. Under controlled circumstances, probably in Switzerland, you will play host to some of them as well.

"You will also be starting mental training with Liliath herself. This will challenge you in ways you cannot imagine. The same mental mechanisms that allow you to do mindspeech grant you so much more, depending on your natural gifts and the work you are willing to put into it.

"In another eight weeks, you will return to us for another break and will be able to once again spend some time catching up with friends and family. In the meantime, your tablet has gotten an upgrade. You can now call home directly from your tablet and send what will appear to your family as regular physical mail, as often as you wish.

"Keep in mind the cover story we have given you. You are doing an internship with a high-level international corporation with a strict nondisclosure agreement and will be away from your apartment for long stretches. All physical mail will be collected from your mailbox at the lab apartment by Gaston and transmitted to you via your tablet.

"Any questions?"

Lizzie was getting really tired of people asking her if she had any questions, as if she ever ran out of questions to ask, but she asked only one.

"In the meantime, what do I do with Ynni?"

"Ynni goes with you for now. You will find she will be an asset in this stage of your training. At any point that your training requires you to leave her, we will make arrangements. Simply tap my face in the messaging area on your tablet and I will take care of everything."

Lizzie nodded. The rest of her questions would be best answered by her instructors and podmates at the agent training base.

Gaston stood. *"Then I will be off, Lizzie. Congratulations on your little surprise today. None of us were expecting that. I never even realized that this was why they call them 'linklings.'"*

He patted her back and turned to Tarafau. *"Coming?"*

"I'm sure we'll see each other again soon enough, Lizzie. In the meantime, give my greetings to Liliath." And with those mysterious words, he followed Gaston through the door to the gateroom.

"I'll be escorting you to the training base today, Lizzie. I have some business with Liliath, and I need to get things settled for Ynni to accompany you in your training," Mirihah said, as they departed.

She led the way through to the gateroom, and they departed for the next stage of training.

Chapter 18: Stretching

(Jenny sat back, stunned. She had known that Ynni would probably come into the picture at some point, but she had not expected it to be so soon in Lizzie's journey. This meant that it was likely that the first photo Lizzie had sent her of the two of them, Lizzie and Tarafau, had probably also included Ynni with her reflection turned off.

Knowing how close her own relationship with Chidwi had become, almost instantaneously, she could relate to the awe and wonder Lizzie was experiencing at this time in the journal pages. However, she couldn't begin to imagine how this would affect her ongoing training.

It was late, and she had hardly budged from the chair all day. It was in keeping with her Alliance doctor's orders to rest for the coming weeks, but she felt somewhat guilty. She had been so incredibly active during all of the upheaval of the past year that it felt almost indecent to be just sitting and reading when she knew so many in the Alliance were tirelessly working to free dimensions from the tyranny of the Insenium empire.

Nevertheless, she might as well do this as any other restful activity, and she was learning so much from her aunt's journey through the Alliance training program.

Maybe just another hour or so before she went to bed. After all, she could sleep in tomorrow morning...)

Lizzie didn't really much care for being the center of attention, but there was no help for it. Even with Ynni riding quietly on her shoulder with her reflection turned off, she knew rumors about her incredible new companion had already spread.

For one thing, in the dining hall special arrangements for Ynni's dietary needs had to be made, and Ynni couldn't eat with her reflection turned off, so other diners had been very attentive to the little linkling's activities, watching her antics with delight and more than a little speculation about what this meant.

Liliath had been delighted when Miriha presented Ynni to her upon their return to the training administration building the day before. She had greeted Ynni with warmth and respect and had immediately assigned a staff member to see to her needs, whatever they might be.

Rather than objecting to Lizzie's keeping Ynni with her at all times, she encouraged them to become a partnership, intimating that this might qualify Lizzie for some special assignments, later on.

"It is a rare thing, but not unheard of," she explained. *"In addition to linklings, there have been other symbiotic companionships within the Alliance agents' admissions. Ynni will be welcomed at most places. Of course, her ability to hide herself when necessary is also a great asset, especially with her particular talent for reading the minds of those around her.*

"Linklings are known to be very discreet about this, however, and she will only ever use this talent in cases where you might otherwise be in danger. You will learn the best way to leverage this as you go, and your instructors will be happy to help you work it out over time."

Lall had met them in Liliath's office and was obviously excited but not disconcerted by this addition to his pod.

"This won't be the first time we've had a symbiote amongst us. Your podmates will adjust over time, but don't be surprised or concerned by the different reactions to Ynni. Part of your training is to encounter and adjust to unusual circumstances and individuals in your assignments. This will be a good test at how well your podmates, and the other trainees have been paying attention in Fin's classes."

Lizzie had chuckled at that. Fin was continually stressing the importance of leaving cultural judgments behind and adopting an attitude of acceptance, or at least tolerance, for the quirks and mores of other beings.

So, off they had marched to the pod, with Ynni sitting on her shoulder with her reflection turned off. Most of her podmates had returned from their holiday and were sitting around chatting in mindspeech when they had entered the pod building.

"Welcome back," Lall called out to the group as they entered. *"I hope you had a good break, because we're about to work you harder than ever."* This was sent with a good-natured tone, and they all chuckled. Lizzie was pretty sure Lall wasn't joking, however.

"I expect Mang and Negoth will be along in a few minutes. There will be more than a few changes in your schedules and assignments over this section of your training. All of this is building up, of course, to the time when you will begin to have guided assignments in the last half of your training. You will be getting to know much more about your podmates in this section and we will be moving more towards evaluation as opposed to pure training over the next six weeks."

At this point, Negoth and Mang came through the door to the pod, obviously in the midst of a mindspeech conversation.

"Come in you two," Lall greeted them with a wave of his hand, indicating they all seat themselves in the training area.

"Now we can begin. As I was saying, we have a lot more in store for you this section of training. Besides Lizzie, how many of you are from non-member dimensions?"

Feth and Geln raised their hands.

Lall nodded. *"You all come from special circumstances, but it still comes down to this. Each of you will have the opportunity to both visit other dimensions and host agent trainees in your own dimension at the end of this term, after which you will have your next break. Professor Baird will be pairing you up for these excursions.*

"During this term, you will be doing many gate travels to different environments to acquaint you with some, but not all, of the conditions you may face as an agent. Understand that there is no possible way for us to allow you to experience every possible situation you may be placed in, so over this term we will be exposing you to a lot of different and sometimes stressful situations to allow you to test your mettle.

"During this time, you will learn more about teamwork and test the extremes of your stamina and endurance."

He gestured for Lizzie to stand. *"And now for the first of many surprises of this term: you now have a new podmate. Lizzie, please introduce us."*

"Um, yes, of course, Lall. Everyone, this is Ynni." And without any coaching by Lizzie, Ynni turned her reflection on.

A few gasped, and some leaned forward in their chairs to get a better look. Ynni sat up straight and looked each of them in the eye, one by one.

"Ynni is a being known as a linkling. She has bonded with me in a way I don't yet completely understand. She is not a native of my planet. She connected to me while I was on my way to visit the Gatekeeper, Miriha. She can turn her reflection on and off, so even though you may not see her, most of the time she will be with me, either on my shoulder or nearby. Say hello, Ynni."

"Hello, podmates," Ynni sent immediately. *"It is nice to meet you all. Ynni is linked to Lizzie and will always be here for her. Lizzie's friends are my friends also."*

"Well said, Ynni. Welcome to the pod." Gi sent warmly, at which point the others chimed in, their various mind voices blending into a chaotic chorus of the sentiment.

They had a celebration of sorts at the dining hall during which Ynni had been admired as she daintily ate the fresh greens, fruits, and vegetables that Miriha had evidently provided from her own planet. The dining staff member had happily assured Lizzie that an adequate supply for Ynni's needs had been provided and in future would be delivered via gateway on a regular basis.

Geln had been somewhat quiet during most of the meal and finally piped up with this: *"Lizzie is linked. How does that compare to a joined mind?"*

Lizzie was somewhat startled by the question, but Ynni answered, *"Your mind is one and not one. For us it is more a joining of hearts. Our minds remain separate, but we can speak via the link in different ways than just mindspeech. But our link is new, and much must be learned before it has grown beyond the need to speak."*

Geln had turned all three of his heads to focus on Ynni as she answered his/their question. They frowned slightly, as if trying to take it all in, and then nodded in chorus.

This was as much news to Lizzie as it had been to Geln. She hadn't considered the exact nature and deeper meaning of the word "link" to describe this new relationship. She had assumed it was much like the imprinting of a baby bird on its mother or a very strong bond of friendship. This would require further consideration, and Ynni was right. Lizzie still had a lot to learn.

After a good meal and some catching up, listening to each relate how they had spent their holiday, they retired to bed. Lizzie lay there a long time, Ynni curled up next to her on her pillow.

The invisible sound barriers between the beds, another technological marvel she would have given anything to understand, made the silence around her absolute. She didn't think she snored, since Thumble would have probably gleefully informed her back on Earth, but she hoped her nightly stirrings would not affect Ynni's sleep.

She had asked Ynni if she needed special sleeping arrangements, but evidently Ynni was used to sleeping in a pile of linklings and was fine with sleeping with "my Lizzie," as she often called her. Lizzie's mind went round and round as it often did before she could settle enough to sleep. Finally, the incredible happenings of the day calmed to whispers and she drifted off to dreamless sleep.

She awoke to tiny warm hands gently patting her cheeks. *"Lizzie slept well?"*

"Good morning, Ynni. Yes, I did. And this is good, as we have a long day ahead of us."

Her other podmates were stirring, and it was obvious that the sound shields had been lifted. Lizzie had determined her first week that there was some kind of autonomous timing mechanism turning them on and off, as none of them had any idea how they worked.

With nervous anticipation, she was looking forward to her first day back. There had already been a bit of angst about what was coming next, and adding Ynni to the mix seemed a little much at this point.

Nevertheless, she had determined, as she reflected on her holiday experience, that she would attempt a more positive attitude this term. Unlike a new term at the college, she had no idea what to expect next, and this was a mixed blessing. The one thing she knew absolutely: she would not be bored.

The morning run was longer today. Lall had added new obstacles that required them to work together to make it over, under, or around them. By the end, they were all sweating and panting, many holding stitches in their sides.

"In this stage of your training, stamina is the focus of our morning run; and, like every other course you will begin today, working together as a team will be

vital. Over the next six weeks, you will find yourselves faced with challenges you may have only imagined until now," Lall told them as they nearly staggered to the pod to shower and change for breakfast.

Ynni had stayed in a tree near the pod while Lizzie had worked out. *"Lizzie needs to focus on her work, not on Ynni, this morning. I will be waiting when you are ready for breakfast."*

True to her word, when Lizzie had emerged from the pod Ynni had leapt happily onto Lizzie's shoulder. Already this was beginning to feel normal to her. She admitted to herself that during the run, Ynni's absence had felt somewhat uncomfortable, almost like a shoe on the wrong foot.

Breakfast was a quiet affair, little conversation going back and forth as they fueled up for the day. They had all been more than a little stunned by the intensity of today's workout, and each was deep in their own thoughts. Lizzie guessed that they were probably thinking, like her, that if this was just the physical part of the new term, what were the rest of the classes going to be like?

Her fears were confirmed with each class. In Lulindu's class, they would be studying the Alliance Interdimensional Trade and Warfare Agreement, a complex document that laid out the governing principles of The Dimensional Alliance. Unlike the United States Constitution, this document was ancient and, as such, about as long as *War and Peace* which Lizzie recalled was over a thousand pages.

In Fin's class, they would be meeting various Alliance council members from different dimensions who would be explaining their cultures and giving practical demonstrations of the correct way to do various things from how to dress, to behavior at formal events, and even sporting practices.

Meta's class wouldn't be held in the lab but would consist of using the gateroom in the basement of the admin building to transport to different dimensional environments to acquaint the agents with the various pieces of equipment in their MDPs and the science behind them.

Evidently, the presence of that particular gate had been the reason for putting the agent training compound in this area in the first place. With only a few exceptions, this gate was not for general use, but for training purposes.

In Baird's class, they would begin a new stage in presentation. They would be given an assignment to approach a delegation (played by various training staff members) from another dimension on one of several topics: trade, military aid, or various cooperative philanthropic projects. The aim was to train them in diplomacy skills and hone their ability to act rationally under pressure.

In addition, besides defense practice that would be branching out to hand-to-hand fighting, each of them would be spending private time with Liliath several times a week for the mental disciplines.

There would be little time for much of anything but working out with Lall, studying, and taking care of basic needs. Every fifth day would be a rest day, with two rest days per ten-day week. Considering the thirty-seven-hour days, Lizzie wasn't sure how they would have survived otherwise.

Rest days implied, they could use their time as they wished on an individual or group basis, but Lizzie knew that more than a little of that time would be spent in studying and preparing for the next four days. If Lizzie had thought the ten-day week of thirty-seven-hour days was intense before, she realized she had very much underestimated how much could be packed into that time frame.

For perhaps the first time in her life, Lizzie felt real pressure in her studies. The first term had only been a warmup. In every class they moved from theory to application, and in every class they noticed a renewed passion in the attitude of their instructors.

Lizzie was grateful for Ynni, perched happily on her shoulder. The bond between them was a conduit for energy and encouragement. From time to time, Ynni also provided a new perspective on the increasingly complex situations the students were exposed to.

When they did their sparring matches in the afternoon, Ynni sat on the sidelines, not only cheering Lizzie on, but also warning her about oncoming attacks that Lizzie might not have otherwise noticed. This was a good thing, as Lizzie had still not come into her own where staff fighting and hand to hand were concerned.

She was only adequate at defending herself from the attacks of her podmates and had never developed the enthusiasm or intensity necessary for effective attacks. She had the physical strength and agility, but this was her least favorite part of the physical training. The morning and evening runs were becoming easier for her, but she just couldn't stay motivated where the defense lessons were concerned.

She was doing well in the technology classes with Meta and was becoming more competent with controlling her facial expressions in Baird's classes. With Ynni's help, she found that Fin's classes were her least difficult. It was like having an extra brain. Ynni easily remembered names and details that sometimes slipped past Lizzie.

She was encouraged to know that she wasn't the only one who was challenged by the increase in the pace of their instruction. By the end of the day most days, as they prepared for bed, none of them lingered long before "hitting the sack," as her dad would have put it.

Chapter 19: The Dragon in Her Head

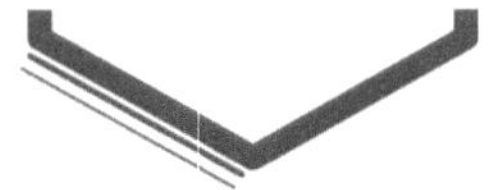

(Jenny woke the next morning to a kiss on the forehead. Burt was bent over her, his eyes sparkling with that look he reserved only for her.

"Hey, sleepyhead, Chidwi, BaaGah, Lolly, and Tidbit are already chasing butterflies in the garden, and Lizziebot fixed you breakfast in bed." He gestured to a tray sitting on the bedside table. Sitting beside it was the journal Jenny had been reading the night before, her place carefully marked.

"At the rate you're going, you'll have all of those journals read by the time your break is over. Learn anything new?"

"I'm beginning to realize maybe I got the easy path. Agent training is even more intense than I thought it would be. And she hasn't even gotten to the part where she is trained as a gate guardian. But I'm beginning to get a real feel for who she was and what the Alliance is about. I think I'm getting to the good part now."

Burt grinned as he propped her up with pillows and got the breakfast tray settled across her lap.

"I remember it being pretty intense, all right. When you're finished reading the journals, we can swap stories sometime. That being said, I wouldn't have wanted to be trained the way you were, Jenny.

Do you need anything else? I just popped in for a few minutes, to check in on you. I have to run. Enjoy your day, and don't think I won't know if you aren't following doctor's orders. Be sure to take a short walk today and be seen by the neighbors, but you might want to change out of your jammies before then," and he winked, "even if you are adorable in them."

She laughed, and he kissed her again before leaving her to her breakfast and her reading.)

Lizzie approached her first lesson with Liliath with foreboding. She knew, or at least hoped, that Liliath didn't bite, but the only thing she was less proficient in than mind training was the physical defense exercises. Reining in the constant ebb and flow of thoughts in her mind was nearly impossible for her. She could focus well enough at a given task, as long as she needed to, but when left without something solid to direct her thoughts at, she found herself easily drifting into endless branches and side paths of inquiry and speculation.

So, when she entered Liliath's office in the admin building at the end of her lessons for the day, she was more than a little anxious. Liliath wasn't inclined on her chaise, but stood in the center of the large room, her head turning at Lizzie's entrance.

"Welcome, Lizzie and Ynni. Follow me."

Liliath turned and exited through another door on the far side of the room. It led into a large space similar to the gym in Sanglarka, only about twice as large. Considering it was in use by a dragon, Lizzie supposed this wasn't all that surprising.

Liliath stretched out on the mat and indicated that Lizzie should sit. *"Assume your usual thought training position,"* she instructed. *"Today we will be adding Ynni to your usual breathing exercises and will practice going into a modified REM state, similar to sleep. Once you can do this without coaching, we will use this to learn control over various physical responses to stimulus such as pain and to help you defend your mind against potential incursion by beings who have the ability to use their minds to control others.*

All agents and gate guardians are trained in this particular discipline. That being said, like any other skill, some take to it easier than others, and some never get past rudimentary application. You, I think, with Ynni's help, may find you can accomplish more than you might otherwise expect."

Lizzie was skeptical about this. She often puzzled about why mindspeech was even possible, and the other applications of mental training baffled her. To her, it seemed a lot more metaphysical than scientific and therefore suspect. She couldn't, however, discount the practice, as she had seen evidence with her own eyes that some people, even on Earth, seemed to have a lot more control over autonomic body functions than others, which they claimed was due to these same mental disciplines.

So, she settled into the routine of careful, mindful breathing, as she had been taught in Sanglarka. Lall had always required them to do the exercise before both their morning and evening runs, so she had become relatively skilled in this part of the task. However, the only thing that kept her mind from wandering or simply falling asleep due to the relaxation of it, was painstakingly counting her breaths and concentrating on the rhythm of it.

Once she had fallen into the final stage of the exercise, Liliath's mind voice blended into the count, *"Now, Lizzie, I need you to give me permission to enter your mind at this point. Picture a locked door, and turn the key. I promise I will not be able to view anything you don't wish me to see, but it is necessary for the next steps."*

Lizzie squirmed a little at the idea of allowing a dragon into her mind, but she realized that she desperately needed to succeed in this if she was ever going to get all of her questions answered. She complied, picturing the door to a bank vault. Surprised, she didn't have to wonder what the combination was. She saw herself carefully dial the combination to her old high school locker and heard the lock click.

In her mind, she opened the vault door, which was appropriately sized to allow the entrance of the dragon and stepped aside to watch Liliath step into the room beyond. She followed her and was surprised to see the vault was a lot like Gaston's lab, but larger. She couldn't see the farthest walls in the distance.

"Very good. Now, Lizzie, I need you to form a picture in your mind of a peaceful place where you feel safe and relaxed."

Obligingly, Lizzie pictured an alcove in the university library where no one ever intruded. The little desk in an obscure corner of the research section had been her favorite retreat at school when she really wanted to focus on her continued inquiries into the mysteries of science not yet covered by her professors in her classes. It was hemmed in on three sides by tall shelves of worn, thick leather books, often inscribed in gilt lettering in old fashioned typefaces.

"Interesting, that you should choose such a place," Liliath remarked dryly.

Lizzie was surprised to hear the voice so close behind her and realized that this was no longer mindspeech. In her mind she turned to see Liliath standing behind her, her head bent to keep from brushing the library ceiling.

"Why can I hear your voice? And how are we here together? I assume this is just a place in my mind and we haven't somehow traveled to a library in my dimension."

"Since you allowed me through the door to the world you have created in your mind, and as you deliberately picture your surroundings, I can travel with you through the world you create in your mind. In this place, mindspeech is the common language, so you 'hear' my mind voice as if I were speaking vocally."

"Ynni sees too; Ynni will guard what Lizzie would keep safe." And to her surprise, Ynni stood beside Liliath, nearly as tall as Liliath was, dressed in mail armor and holding a spear.

This made Lizzie laugh; and abruptly, Ynni shrank to her normal size, armor no longer covering her silky green fur. Ynni laughed with Lizzie and, shockingly, so did Liliath, or at least Lizzie hoped it was laughter. The baring of Liliath's mouth full of sharp teeth was a bit alarming, otherwise.

"As Ynni said, because it is the talent of her race to read any mind, she is aware of any who are close by or who have ill intent. She also has the ability to guard your thoughts to a certain extent. This will be helpful moving forward.

"This place we are in now is a haven you can come to on command. You will want to decide on a key phrase we will call a 'trigger.' When you deliberately think this phrase, you will immediately be able to find this place in your mind, and it will become a mental shelter for you. As we move farther into mental defense, you will learn to use such visualizations to strengthen your mental responses. What key phrase will you use?"

Lizzie considered this. Something that would call this peaceful place to her mind should be something that would be easy to remember in a stressful situation, but not necessarily easy for someone else to guess. To her own surprise, the word that came to her mind was "campfire."

She remembered one of her most cherished memories from her younger years. Her family had loved going to a campground in Monterey during Easter vacation. Her favorite part of the several days they spent there together was in the evening, sitting around the campfire, toasting marshmallows while her parents told and retold stories from their own youth. It was a peaceful time when Lizzie had felt connected to her family and safe from whatever else life dealt out.

"Now let us return to your vault," Lizzie said. "We need to explore and determine future mental expeditions there."

Lizzie pictured the vault, and they were immediately all there, standing in the area that contained the loom she had made for Gaston, that seemed ages ago and which had set her on this new path.

"The things you will encounter here may surprise you, and they will change over time," Liliath instructed, looking around her. "Each thing in this space lives in your mind, but not all of them are literal. They are symbolic representations of thoughts and experiences. Sometimes we find ourselves puzzled by what they mean.

"The fact you are here right now says something for your potential. It means you at least have access. Some struggle to get even this far in their mental exercise."

"I was only following your instructions," Lizzie protested. "No real effort on my part."

"Ah, there is where you are mistaken, Lizzie. You just displayed unusual trust in your own mind. For many, even getting to the locked door, much less getting past it, takes weeks.

"We will return to this place frequently over the coming weeks. It will be important, moving forward, for you to do your breathing exercises every night before sleep. I know you, like your podmates, go to your bed thoroughly weary at the end of the day, but you will progress much faster in our lessons if this becomes a habit. Eventually you will do it without thinking. But for now, be consistent in your nightly practice.

"Let us return to the practice room."

And with that, Lizzie came to herself, sitting on the mat across from the dragon, Ynni seated beside her, one small warm hand resting on Lizzie's knee.

"That was a good session, Lizzie. Do you have any questions?"

"Not really. I'm still taking it all in. Can I do that without you guiding me?"

"Not for now, at least not intentionally or easily. Going in with a guide is the best way to begin this. We are entering the place where all of your night dreams come from, and not all areas are pleasant. Until we have put your defenses

firmly in place, you should content yourself with your breathing and relaxation exercises. I will see you tomorrow. For this first week, we will be doing this every day at the same time. Until tomorrow then, enjoy your workout."

Lizzie heard the kind but obvious dismissal in her tone and nodded, got up, and left for her evening workout. She knew she would be extra hungry for supper tonight.

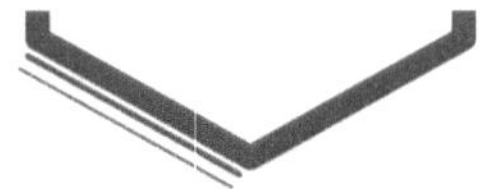

Chapter 20: Music to Her Ears

(True to her promise to Burt, Jenny had taken a walk in the neighborhood. As she walked, her mind was fully engaged with Lizzie's first venture into mental training. She found it interesting that Lizzie's mental guard was a vault. Hers had been a medieval fortress with an armored guard at the drawbridge and portcullis.

Since she had met Burt, her place of safety had been outdoors at a small eddy pool on the Merced River. However, Lizzie's was a quiet place in a library. This obviously said a great deal about their differences. It was fascinating to her to see how different their experiences had been, and yet, how much she identified with Lizzie.

She was eager to continue the story, finding it more engaging than any fiction book she had read. This wasn't fiction. It was the life she would have had if fate had not intervened. Their struggles had been different and yet parallel, each leading to heavy responsibilities.

Entering her bright living room, she noticed that Lizziebot had put a favorite snack of peanut butter spread on celery sticks next to the little table by her overstuffed reading chair. Tidbit was stretched out in the sunshine on the window seat, and Chidwi was perched on the back of her chair, knowing that Jenny would be avidly continuing her reading in Lizzie's journals.

Her relationship with the little linkling had grown to the point that they seldom had to use mindspeech, except when having actual conversations.

With a contented sigh for the peace of the moment, knowing that this respite was only temporary, Jenny sat, opened the journal to the bookmark and reentered Lizzie's world.)

Lizzie parried another blow from Negoth. She grinned at him, and he scowled. Negoth was one of the few sparring partners she actually felt competent around. She could let her mind drift a bit with him because he was so predictable.

They had long since advanced from simply doing forms to regular sparring matches with the quarterstaff, followed by hand-to-hand martial arts. Now, although they still warmed up with the forms at every session, the sparring matches had become more and more intense as they learned new tactics and techniques. This was still the least favorite part of her training.

However, Lizzie was enjoying the stepped-up pace of her other lessons, which, with the exception of studying the Dimensional Alliance charter documents, were almost all hands on. It was what she had wished college to be: no lectures, just labs of exploration and experimentation.

Not all of her podmates had exhibited the same enthusiasm, however. It turned out that first impressions were not necessarily accurate.

Geln, for instance, despite their apparent bulk and size, were more cerebral than she had expected and had struggled even more than Lizzie with the sparring matches. Evidently Geln's race was extremely pacific. They participated willingly in the runs, morning and evening, but it was soon obvious to everyone that they didn't like even the defensive measures they were being taught, much less practicing attacks on their podmates.

Linlin, Mang, and Feth had been extremely proficient in all of the martial arts they were studying, and over time Lall entrusted them to ordering the drills and often paired them with those who were struggling the most, namely Geln, Lizzie, Negoth, and Minth.

Minth, with his heavily charged body, was an issue as far as the metal shod staffs and other metal weapons such as a sword were concerned. Unless they had wooden handles, these were problematical for him, as even with his rubber gloves and shoes, he still exuded a static force around himself that would make people's hair rise on their heads when he got closer than a foot away.

Physical hand to hand was even more of an issue, and he had to be taught special techniques and wear additional protective clothing, which was more for his opponents' benefit than his. He would never be a proficient fighter in these forms because he was hesitant to injure another person and very aware of the damage he could cause, without all of the precautions they had to take with him.

However, regardless of the electric barrier between him and his podmates, Minth was kind and attentive, and his gentle sense of humor made them want to be around him. He was easy to talk to and was popular, even among beings from other pods, and was often greeted by beings Lizzie didn't recognize.

Reanni appeared to be fragile on the surface, with her bright plumage, wings, and slender legs. However, she proved to be not only strong, agile, and resilient, but fierce in her attacks. She handled the quarterstaff with such speed and dexterity that it was often only an indistinct blur. She could also leap higher, with the aid of her wings, than any of her podmates, and her attack from above was indefensible.

Negoth was a scholar but fared well during workouts, even with his stolid and uninventive approach to defense. He almost never went on the offensive. He was serious and inwardly focused. Although he didn't shun the others in the pod, he preferred to sit quietly by himself at the end of the day, not entering into the bantering and good-natured teasing of his podmates.

Gi was on par with Lizzie physically and mentally. They often had long mind conversations discussing theory and application of what they were learning in their lessons. Lizzie's first impression had been that she was a bit arrogant, but, as it turned out, Gi had confessed she had thought the same of Lizzie. Neither of them was what anyone would have called a "social butterfly."

They found they had a lot in common, mainly their intense curiosity about pretty much everything and their ambivalence about their defense practices.

"Ouch!" Lizzie had let her mind drift too far. Negoth had gotten in a good rap on her thigh. Unlike Lizzie had done, he didn't grin in triumph, just grunted and bowed, victorious but not excited about it.

"Thank you for the match," Lizzie said, also bowing in the traditional courtesy.

"You were a little off today," Negoth replied bluntly. *"What were you thinking about?"*

"Just how much my life has changed. I'm still not entirely sure how I got myself into all of this, especially when my dimension isn't even in the Alliance. I mean, what were the odds when only a small handful of Earthlings even

know there is such a thing as another dimension? Earth scientists all work on the assumption that our universe is unique and that we are alone amongst the vastness of space."

"Deep thoughts," he nodded approvingly. *"I believe I grew up taking the idea of dimensional interaction for granted. Your dimension has much to look forward to. It will be exciting for you to be one of the pioneers who eventually bring your people into understanding."*

By this time the others had concluded their matches, with the exception of Mang and Feth, who were moving like a couple of dancers in a complex choreography of pivots, whirls, and rapid connections between their staves.

When at last Feth got in a tap on Mang's elbow, they bowed and exchanged courtesies.

"Good workout, all. Go to your well-deserved clean-up and lunch. I understand Baird has something special for you all today," Lall commented as they dispersed.

After cleaning up, they trooped off to the cafeteria. They had begun taking the shortcut between buildings, which was lined with tall shady trees. Light from the two suns filtered lazily through the red leaves edged in green. With the buildings bordering on either side, it was a quiet and somewhat private area in a place where there was little privacy to be had.

At the table, the conversation was lively. Most engaged in speculation about what Professor Baird might have in store for them. They had long since stopped routinely playing the cubes game, although many of them had purchased their own game sets and often spent their few leisure hours playing it. Lizzie noticed it was also played routinely in the cafeteria by some pods during meals.

Baird had hinted they might have a special guest, but none of them had a clue as to who that might be.

Minth was querying Lizzie about her holiday. He found the idea of an ocean to be fanciful. On his planet, all water was underground, pumped to the surface or accessed by wells or succulent plant life. The idea of anyone deliberately immersing themselves into a body of water that was over their head was incredible to him.

Gi, had laughed. The one thing about laughter is that unlike mindspeech, it had a physical sound and was different for each species. In Gi's case, her laugh was low and round tones nearly like an oboe. Lizzie couldn't help but laugh with her if nothing else but for the pure joy of laughing in harmony with Gi.

Of her podmates, Gi and Minth continued to be the ones she felt closest to. Oddly enough, it was their differences that Lizzie found most attractive. Minth was handsome enough with his dark pool-like eyes that always seemed somewhat surprised at life, but it was his honest sincerity that she found most appealing. He never was deliberately unkind, but he always spoke his mind, including honest assessments of his podmates when it was appropriate.

Gi was lighthearted, despite her seemingly arrogant appearance. This first impression had a lot to do with her posture. Gi tended to sit very upright, her chin slightly raised, but it turned out that this was a physical characteristic of her people. As far as her personality was concerned, she was very much the opposite her appearance.

She had one of the most positive outlooks of anyone Lizzie had ever met. Not in the airy-fairy way that many people seemed to put on, but a sincere belief that even difficult challenges and even painful experiences had a purpose and were designed to give a being the opportunity to grow and meet their true potential.

She looked upon mistakes and outright failures as an opportunity to improve; and instead of complaining or murmuring at the exigencies of fate, she stopped, looked at the experience, and decided what she needed to do to learn an important life lesson from it. She was constantly encouraging and uplifting the rest of the team without being condescending or making anyone feel stupid.

Lizzie realized she wasn't the only one in the pod who looked up to these two, but she was so glad they were part of it and that they seemed to enjoy Lizzie's company as well. The bonus was that Ynni also liked them and cheerfully joined in their conversations.

The pod had accepted Ynni without exception as simply another member. Lizzie had been somewhat surprised to see how quickly they adopted her as one of them, with no special favors or any sign that they found it unusual for Lizzie to have this extra help.

Professor Baird greeted the pod as they filed into his classroom later with a cheery *"Come in and be seated!"* The chairs were set in a semicircle facing the back of the room and there were no nametags designating where they were to sit, so they sat and waited while he bustled to face them.

"Today we have the privilege of meeting one of our most successful agents in the past hundred years. Her exploits are somewhat of a legend among us. She has some interesting abilities that admittedly give her a bit of an edge. But that being said, there is much you will learn from her today, and for the next few weeks she will be leading us through various member dimensions.

"I know you are currently doing a lot of exploring, and it is well you get used to it. Over the next few weeks, we will be meeting in the gateroom for classes. Today, after a short introduction, we will be going to the outfitters to get you set up and prepared for the coming excursions.

"May I then introduce you to Galena of the Utolian dimension of the planet Lutia."

From behind the curtain at his back, a short, dark green woman stepped next to Professor Baird. She nodded at the assembled pod. She was definitely only partially humanoid. Her long black hair was plaited into multiple braids that were woven together to create a curtain of hair on either side of her face. Her eyes were huge and also dark green, framed by lashless eyelids and no eyebrows that Lizzie could see.

Her arms were longer than her slim torso and had six almost spidery fingers alongside an opposable thumb. When she smiled at the group, it was obvious by her pointed teeth that those of her race were carnivores.

"It is good to see the next generation of agents coming up." Her mind voice was almost a whisper. *"You are probably at that stage in your training where all of this feels more than a little overwhelming. I am about to make it worse if that's possible. However, based on reports received from your instructors, you will all be up to the task."*

With that astounding introduction, it was as if she faded, physically blending her features, stretching and becoming tall, pale and multi-limbed. She reminded Lizzie starkly of those stone statues of Durga, the Hindu goddess she had seen depicted in her world studies books. Her hair was nearly transparent and straight, hanging like a shimmering waterfall to her waist.

Once again, she smiled, this time without the pointed teeth, her vividly red lips only barely parted. *"As you can see, I am not what I seem to be."*

Once again, she faded and merged and blended, now looking a lot like what her friends in the Northwest United States would have called a "Sasquatch." She shook her huge furry head at many raised eyebrows and even a gasp or two.

"I think Professor Baird was correct in his assessment that you continue to need practice in schooling your expressions. This is part of the reason I am here. My ability to change my appearance at will is native to my species, but even I had to go through this training. Even with my abilities, controlling my reactions only came after years of experience and practice."

She scanned their faces, her furry brows knit in a frown of focus on each of them. As she did that, Lizzie had the uncomfortable feeling that she was seeing much deeper than the mere surface of their features. She shivered slightly under that intense gaze but tried to keep her face placid.

"Better, I see. It is easier to handle these types of shocks in a comfortable environment and under no stress. We will be beginning, therefore, to expose you to more complex and intense situations as we go."

As she said the last few words she began again to change. This time it was as if all of her mass was sucked into a tiny space not much bigger than Lizzie's hand. To her delight and awe, she now saw before her the classical lines of a pixie, including iridescent wings that fluttered like a hummingbird.

"Ah, yes, Lizzie." Galena sent in an amused tone," *Professor Baird told me you were of Earth. You would recognize this form, as well as some of my previous morphs. My ancestors frequented your planet before the gates were controlled by the Alliance. As I think you will discover, many of the current Alliance members considered Earth to be a prime place for exploration and adventuring.*

"I know the last time I visited there, I found much in the way of art and literature referring to our antics over centuries. Perhaps at some time we can discuss some of your legends?

"And Geln," and with this she triplicated into what could have easily been Geln's younger sister(s). *"I have also had the opportunity to visit your dimension and experience the joined mind."*

Lizzie couldn't help herself. Her hand shot into the air. *"Please, Galena. Are there many of your kind, and do they visit Earth and other planets frequently? There are many on Earth who insist that we have been visited by beings from other worlds, even now, when the gates are in place."*

She blushed, realizing she might have spoken out of turn, but she couldn't help herself. Before the Second World War had broken out, the public had panicked due to a radio broadcast version of the book *War of the Worlds*, by H.G. Wells, and many continued to insist that the fiction was not all that far away from possibility.

Until her exposure to the Alliance, Lizzie had been skeptical about the idea that aliens, if they existed, might have any interest in Earth, although she had repeatedly insisted that imagination was as important to science as investigation, experimentation, and theorizing based on established principles of math and physics. One of her heroes was Einstein, who had been quoted as saying, "Logic will get you from A to B. Imagination will take you everywhere."

Now she felt at once vindicated in positing that scientists were missing the point of science; and yet, she knew she herself had been guilty of assuming what was possible and what was not.

The three Galenas smiled an identical smile. *"Indeed, Lizzie. Agents of the Alliance frequent your planet for many reasons as we prepare for the time when your dimension will qualify to become an Alliance member in full standing. This is one of the roles of agents of the Alliance, to infiltrate non-member dimensions to evaluate their potential to become members.*

"To be sure, we are careful to avoid polluting the cultures we are investigating with anything counter to their culture or level of technology, but you will have opportunities to also observe and evaluate as you go through the training that will qualify you as a full-fledged agent of the Alliance."

Once again, she faded, this time compacting the three separate forms to a humanoid shape closely resembling Minth.

"You will encounter situations and environments that are inimical to humanoid life. The Alliance does everything they can to ensure your safety, but there are many environments where the only thing standing between you and danger is your own wit, strength, and the ability to quickly evaluate your surroundings and the beings you will engage with.

"For now, I will only say that, starting in tomorrow's lesson, we will meet in the gateroom in the basement of this building. Be sure to organize the new supplies you will be adding to your MDP so you can get at them easily and

quickly at need. You have been trained in the best-use practices of your MDPs, and you will now learn that these are much more than convenient storage.

"At the end of each lesson, Professor Baird and I will be evaluating your performance and discussing our experiences. For now, we will adjourn to the outfitters and after that, you will be dismissed for the day, with the exception of your evening run with Lall."

At the outfitters, each of them was issued first aid supplies which looked a lot more like a combat medic kit, including a number of medications, both topical and internal, based on each different species' chemical makeup. Bandages were an obvious addition, but also field surgical kits, various pieces of equipment Lizzie was unfamiliar with that they were promised they would be trained to use, and body bags made each of them ponder these next steps with more than a little trepidation.

Tents and camping supplies were added, as well as rations suiting each of their nutritional needs and supplements to keep them healthy while away from "home." They were measured for clothing and several different kinds of "environmental suits" useful for various types of climate conditions, including a complete lack of oxygen.

Other equipment included binoculars like Lizzie had never seen. These could see both in complete darkness and in overwhelming light, as well as look as far away as several miles in the distance, as long as a horizon or obstacle didn't get in the way.

There were several other pieces of unexplained tech, each of which, they were assured, would be used in the course of their training. The outfitters also tested each of the emergency beacons in each MDP to be assured they not only functioned, but the readouts from them corresponded directly to the species and potential medical needs of the corresponding agent.

"These are monitored by a part of the agency responsible for tracking agent assignments. Each MDP is registered to your DNA, and none of the permissions within the MDP is available to anyone else to modify in any way.

"We would like to think that these permissions are unbreakable, but experience teaches us that no system, no matter how advanced or complex, is unbreakable. For this reason, you must practice the safety and security protocols you were taught when you were issued your MDP," the stern-faced out-fitting officer instructed them. She was a tall yellow-gold being almost as slight as a

stick figure sporting three long tripodal legs, but she had lifted large, heavy pallets of supplies as if they were feather-light.

Lizzie was more and more dazed by the variety of beings even in this small corner of the multiverse she would be traversing in her future career as an Alliance agent. She couldn't help but wonder again, if she or anyone else could hope to ever truly understand it all. However, she straightened her shoulders at this thought. She couldn't afford to let this keep her from fulfilling her commitment.

When they left the outfitters and headed back to the pod, they were quiet, and Lizzie was sure that today had been as impactful for her podmates as for herself. Even with their day-to-day exposure to beings from many dimensions, passing them in the hallways of the training building or out on the grounds or in the dining hall, today had been a turning point.

They would be going far beyond coursework and into active practice of what they were learning. For now, they were doing this as a group, but they all knew that the following term they would be paired with individual guides and sent to different parts of the dimensions without the security of their pod.

After that, who could know how often they might even ever see each other again? Lizzie realized with a jolt that this actually disturbed her. She had walked away from her college experience and the students she had spent two years with, without a backward glance or a single thought about ever staying in contact with any of them.

Now here she was, barely a few months into the training with these ten disparate, alien beings, and she was feeling concern at the idea of not continuing these relationships. In fact, she felt very similar about those in Sanglarka and Switzerland who had launched her into this course of action.

There was time before supper, and Lizzie realized she just needed to be alone for a bit to focus her thoughts. She stopped in the tree-shaded space between the pods and sat on the springy, naturally yellow grass. The others had filed into the pod before her, not noticing she hadn't followed them in.

Ynni had been very quiet through this day's experience. Lizzie reached up onto her shoulder and patted one of Ynni's soft legs that hung down onto her chest. There was almost no weight to the linkling, but she had proven herself strong and sturdy. Ynni was one more of the many marvels overwhelming her life right now.

"How are you?" she asked, as Ynni patted her hand.

"Ynni is well, Lizzie. We learned much today, did we not?"

This statement stirred something in Lizzie's mind. Of course, Ynni was participating in these classes right along with her. Obviously much of the information they were being taught would be as new to Ynni as it was to Lizzie. How had she not considered that before?

"What did you learn today, Ynni?"

"Goodness comes in many shapes, Lizzie. Also, there may be a very rocky road ahead of us. Ynni is glad we are being prepared for this. Sometimes Ynni misses her linkling family. Sometimes Ynni wonders what the multiverse has in store for two of us, linked as we are."

"I think you are right, Ynni. I am beginning to realize that I am more connected than I ever thought I could be to other beings. I had not considered that possible before. I think, when you linked to me, you changed me somehow. I am not the same person. This is probably a good thing."

"Ah, Lizzie. You are the same being as you have been since before your first consciousness in this plane of existence. You have always been and always will be. You are merely discovering your true self. Sometimes the only way that happens is when you go outside yourself. When we linked, you began to reach beyond where you were to where you are going. We will both be better now."

Lizzie nodded, considering the depths of her little companion and how seriously she may have underestimated her. Without thinking, she pulled the mbira out of her MDP and began to randomly strum and pluck the little metal tabs. The sound was soothing, and she soon realized that Ynni was crooning along.

She played, her eyes focused only on the keyboard before her, not attempting to form a known melody, but simply to enjoy the harmonizing tones of the mbira and Ynni's soft croon. She was surprised, therefore, when she realized there were more notes in the melody than she or Ynni were creating.

She paused, looking up to discover that in her revery she hadn't noticed that Gi had seated herself beside them and in her hands was a small harp, not much larger than the mbira. Gi had also paused her improvisation, looking at

Lizzie with those huge amber eyes that contrasted so vibrantly with her dark green skin.

"I didn't mean to interrupt," she sent simply. *"Your music drew me here. May I continue to play with you? I miss the music of my home."*

Lizzie nodded. She knew very little about Gi's home world. They had been discussing various home planets, but Gi had not yet made her presentation in Fin's class.

"I don't know much about the music of your home, and I am new to this instrument. I was only 'doodling,' as my mom would have said." Lizzie sent, somewhat embarrassed.

"It was perfect. Let us doodle together. Begin and I will follow. Ynni had no trouble following you. Let us make music together."

And they did. Gi and Ynni wove a descant around Lizzie's wanderings on her mbira keyboard. Once again, Lizzie got lost in the music, and she began to realize that the music she was making became more intentional as she began to see and feel the pattern of the rhythms and order of the notes.

This wasn't anything like she would have thought about learning an instrument. This was much less about musical staffs and notation and much more about the feeling and shape of the music. Where was this coming from? To her knowledge, there was no one in her family with any real talent for doing more than carrying a tune when they sang along with popular tunes, and many of them couldn't even do that.

Lizzie herself was only marginal when it came to singing. She could usually hit the right notes, but her voice was nothing anyone would want to listen to. The only performances she had ever participated in were in the chorus her music teacher had put together in elementary school. She remembered being grateful that her voice was lost among the voices around her.

But this... *this* was phenomenal. The sweet full tones of the mbira, blending with the riffing melodies of the harp and Ynni's soft soothing voice, carried them into a place that was neither here nor there. No space, no time, nothing but the music and the vibrations they were creating like a single entity, beyond individual identity, beyond any experience or thought Lizzie had ever had.

They ended as they had begun, first Lizzie, her final long note ringing, lingering and then fading into silence, followed by Ynni and finally Gi's high, quivering glissando on the harp. As they looked up, they realized that a crowd had gathered on either end of the lane between pods.

Not only her podmates, but beings from different surrounding pods stood transfixed and evidently transported, as not a single one moved or made a sound while the final notes shimmered and died on the air between them.

Lizzie didn't know what to do. Gi, however, stood and gestured to the standing crowd. *"Thank you for your kind attention to our musical ramblings,"* she sent simply.

Slowly the crowd began to disperse, obviously taking Gi's remark as a sort of gentle dismissal. Their pod, however, continued to stand there, grouped around the three of them.

Reanni was the first to move or speak. *"That was lovely. I had no idea either of you were musically inclined. Perhaps we should share our cultural music as part of our presentations in Fin's class?"*

Geln shifted their stance from foot to foot, the first time Lizzie had noticed them show any discomfort before. *"We have no sounds like these besides those made by native birds and insects or the keening of the wind. This, 'music,' did you call it? It is foreign to our culture. I would bring it home if I could."*

Lizzie put out a hand to Geln and they reached out, pulling her to her feet. She wanted to look them in the eyes, a difficult task with three faces before her, but she looked deliberately into each face and then said. *"I can't imagine a world without music, but I too have heard the music of the wind and wave and creatures of Earth in my time."*

They nodded, seemingly satisfied with her simple statement. Now, Gi stood next to her, their shoulders nearly touching as their pod gathered close around them, and what passed between them at that point shifted something in Lizzie's heart as permanently as if there had been a solemn vow between them.

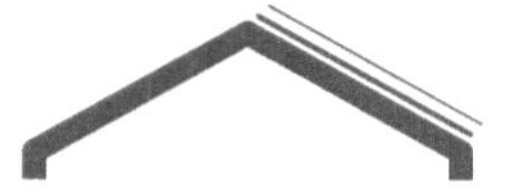

Chapter 21: Out of Nowhere

Jenny was astounded. She really didn't know anything about her aunt, especially since she had never had more than a five-minute conversation while she was alive and that only two times in her life. Reading these journal entries made her wish fervently that she had been able to get to know her better. She was so grateful that Lizzie had left these journals behind.

And now she was curious. "Lizziebot? Do we still have the mbira? Do you know where it is in the storage shed?"

"Of course, Jenny. Come, let's go find it."

They went out the French doors into the garden. Jenny fished the key out of the MDP and while opening the lock said the words that unlocked the entire contents of the shed to her personally.

Inside was the usual jumble of furniture and a collection of Lizzie's possessions, accumulated over about 60 years of adventures and exploration. All of the things in the main area of the shed were of Earthly origin. In the other locked area of the shed were things acquired from around the multiverse. Only she and Tarafau had access to that area.

However, she was pretty sure that the mbira would be in the main area. Sure enough, Lizziebot, who had been programmed with a database containing the complete inventory of the shed, went directly to a cabinet and opened a drawer. There, in a carved wooden case lined with black velvet, was the little instrument.

It was somewhat worn, polished with decades of use. Jenny lifted it out with reverent hands and tentatively plucked one of the little steel tabs. It rang with a clear and full note that hung for a moment on the air.

"Do you think she would mind if I used it?" she asked Lizziebot wistfully.

"Lizzie wanted you to have everything in this shed. It is your inheritance. I believe she would have been disappointed if you had not discovered it and learned to play it. It gave her great joy in difficult times, and its use was significant to her story."

Jenny replaced it into the case and left the storage shed with tears of joy and reverence on her face. This small instrument was a closer tie to the aunt she had begun to love and relate to after reading of her adventures thus far.

She just sat for a while in her bright living room with the mbira sitting in its case on her lap. Tidbit looked up from the window seat. "She would have been happy to see you holding it, you know. Don't be afraid to play it. It has seen many hours of use over the years. It was well made. Lizzie was always grateful to Yaw for the gift of the music she was able to create with it," *he sent.*

Jenny took it out and one by one plucked the steel tabs, enjoying the richness of each individual tone. She was able to play some scales and arpeggios easily. Unlike Lizzie, Jenny had gotten some basic piano lessons as a child. She could read music, but she could see where it wouldn't be necessary to play familiar songs on this instrument. The very action of plucking the keys and hearing the notes was very soothing.

After about an hour of "doodling," as her aunt had put it, she realized this led her to want to read more. She knew that for what was left of the time she had before she had to go back to active engagement in the Alliance, she could do nothing or think of anything until she had completed her journey with her aunt through the journals.

She was about three fourths of the way through this volume, with two more to go. It was time to read.)

The next two weeks were a whirlwind of miracles. That is what pretty much anyone would have called the jaw-dropping experiences presented to their pod. When Lizzie considered that every other being in the agent training compound was going through a similar series of instruction, she began to get the slightest inkling of the pure scope of the mission of the Alliance.

Besides traveling daily with Galena into one dimension after another, each more alien than any of them might have thought possible, they were completing their reports in Fin's class about their individual dimensions.

Lizzie had given her report without much enthusiasm. After hearing the reports her podmates had given so far, she felt Earth to be somewhat drab and uninteresting by comparison. However, to her surprise, most of her podmates had found her report as astonishing as she had thought theirs.

The details of her life experiences so far and the brief summary of Earth's history as far as she understood it herself had evidently sounded exotic and, in many cases, shocking. Most of them had been astounded by her report of two successive world wars and the devastation they had caused.

There had been definite audible sounds of shock when she described the culminating atomic attack on Japan. Lizzie realized that for a few of them, war and conflict were distant concepts. For the rest, none of them had conflicts so recent in their histories.

Fin had stood at the end of her presentation and addressed the class.

"As you may begin to appreciate, discrepancies in cultures vary so widely as to be sometimes incomprehensible. Each culture takes a different path. Often, we disagree with choices made by other cultures. However, it becomes important to realize that even cataclysm can result over time to bettering a culture through the efforts of its people.

"As you have been able to observe, Lizzie's behavior does not show a violent or contentious nature. We cannot afford, therefore, to judge an individual by the acts of a group nor a group by the acts of an outspoken minority.

"It is one of the important purposes of these courses, to make sure that every agent who represents the Alliance is clear on this point. We do not interfere, not ever, with the progress of the culture of any of the dimensions we interact with, neither those who are members of the Alliance nor those who are not.

"As you have seen in your exploration of the history of the Alliance, attempts to alter the course of other cultures have generally resulted in disaster. Thank you, Lizzie, for a succinct and effective presentation. Tomorrow, our last presentation for this section of your course will be given by Gi."

With that, he gestured a dismissal and walked from the room ahead of them, heading, Lizzie assumed, for the faculty room.

She would have liked to discuss this more with Fin, but she knew that this was his normal pattern, so she didn't feel offended by it.

"I hope I do as well as you did, Lizzie," Gi commented as they descended the stairs to the labs in the basement. *"I don't think my report will be as exciting as yours was."*

She turned to look Lizzie in the eyes. *"You have been through so much. I begin to understand some of the pain in your music."*

"Pain?"

"I won't explain right now. You'll understand better after my presentation tomorrow. I've been waiting to share with you until after that."

Lizzie didn't push her about it. She understood. Her own presentation had been a significant source of stress. She would have felt confident if the report had been on science or anything less personal. But she didn't feel she had done justice to her report on Earth. It was so intrinsically linked to so many deep feelings. And the Earth was such a big place. How could anyone give more than a cursory explanation of the diverse cultures and the sweeping history of her planet?

She also felt somewhat apologetic about the current level of technology, which would seem almost primitive to most of her podmates, or pretty much anyone in the Alliance.

Based on the questions asked after the presentation, however, she had begun to realize they were more impressed and amazed that Earth's history had been peppered with what, in hindsight and knowing what Lizzie now understood, were the multiple and constant incursions by other dimensions.

For many of them, they had only had a record of one or two visitations by dimensional beings on their planet, and more than one had discovered the dimensional portals on their own before they became gates. In these cases, they usually ran into the Dimensional Alliance instead of the other way around.

All of this went around and around in Lizzie's head as she went through her day. For the first time since she had come to agent training, she found her mind wandering in Meta's class about gate technology. She knew she really couldn't afford this, as at this point most of her classes now appended to the gates in one way or the other.

Lizzie didn't think going through the gates would ever become routine for her. The first time had been eye-opening, and her first transition with Tarafau to his home planet had opened her mind to so many possibilities.

But until she began to go through gate after gate, from one wildly differing place to another, until she had begun to meet with so many beings of different shapes and in what often seemed to Lizzie as impossible surroundings, she had not even begun to understand the task she had set herself to.

The next day, she sat in her seat in Fin's classroom with anticipation. She was not disappointed.

She knew Gi had been practicing her report in front of the mirror to mask her nervousness. She stood before them; her bright blue and yellow spiky hair deliberately arranged to become an aurora around Gi's deep green face. As usual, her erect posture and the slight tilt to her head made her seem arrogant and authoritative. Lizzie focused on her wide amber eyes as she spoke.

"My planet, Finque, in the dimension of Il, is relatively small compared to many of the planets that usually become gate planets. We have only six gates above the ground and three above the planet in space. We are a space-going people and have connections to many beings in our galaxy.

"We have yet to conquer intergalactic travel, but our scientists apply themselves to that with the view that we represent all peoples in our dimension to the Alliance.

"There are two main species on our planet, although there are multiple types of animal and plant life, and we do not know for sure that they do not possess the intelligence necessary to be involved directly in our culture.

"My species call themselves Alea. We are as you see me, with some variation in skin tone, hair and eye color, size and shape, much like Lizzie described the humans on Earth. The other main species call themselves Squeeng and populate our oceans. We are able to communicate with one another but do not generally interact unless there is a common challenge that requires us to cooperate.

"As for the Alea, we are a rustic people. We do not congregate in large cities as is common among many of your cultures. Instead, we live in concentricities, a circular formation of individual farms with a central gathering place for exchanging goods and interacting with one another.

"There are no living quarters within the center of the concentricity. Instead, when we assemble as a group for extended periods of time, we bring our tents

and encircle the gathering center as families. Within the bounds of the gathering center, temporary places are set up to share goods and services.

"We have no currency. Our trade consists of the 'sharing.' If I create something to share, I bring it to the gathering. Anyone who can use it or enjoy it is welcome to take it. Oftentimes, a well-made item passes from hand to hand, from family to family, over many years.

"If I have a service, such as repairing or labor that I can provide, agreements are made for time and materials and there is no direct trade in this matter, but the next time I need some help, someone else will likely provide it to me who has that skill or ability.

"Disagreements are handled in a council that varies from one gathering to the next. The two or several parties involved in the disagreement each choose six others to create the council, with the agreement that the decision of the council is final. Each of the contending parties is allowed a specific time to present their case, and each of the members of the sitting council are allowed to ask clarifying questions. When they are satisfied that all evidence has been presented and all questions answered, the council adjourns to a quiet place to discuss the evidence and come to a unified conclusion.

"Generally, the decision of the council is held to be final, and all parties agree to abide by their judgment. This works well for us. For those few who disagree or who continually are brought before the council, they are given a choice either to go to a retreat colony on an island in the south sea or to go to a colony on a distant planet to live among others of their disposition and preferences.

"As far as war or conflict over and above minor disagreements is concerned, we have no history of that. There was a time, as we explored space, when we felt vulnerable and put up some elaborate defenses. The organization that handles those defenses still exists, and our citizens take turns training and serving. To this point, there has been no need to employ any of it, but our space defense league remains vigilant.

"Our central government is composed of a representative from each concentricity who rotate from one year to the next. Any contributing adult may find themselves in that position, but never more than once in their life. The central council's main job is to see that roads are maintained, to organize support for communities during natural disasters, and to guide the training of our defenses.

"We have encountered many other species and cultures in our explorations of our universe, each unique and interesting in their way.

"Like the Alliance, our policy is non-interference. So far, each of the interplanetary relationships we participate in have been worthy of membership in the Alliance.

"As far as our culture is concerned, we have interests in art, craft, and music in particular. On my home planet, all of the Alea communicate via musical tones rather than anything any of you would recognize as speech. Only a small minority of us use mindspeech, more because of ability than choice. It is difficult for us to think in anything other than music.

"We had to be taught to use mindspeech in the early days of our relationship with the Alliance, long before we became members. This ability is evidently inherited from one generation to another. My father, for instance, is an agent and trained me from a young age to use mindspeech in addition to our native musical communications. I am the only one of my siblings with this ability.

"This is why I was so delighted to join Lizzie as she played her mbira. It felt so very much like home. I know we have not, up to this point, included the music of our cultures in these presentations, but to end mine, before opening up for questions, I would like to speak to you in my native language."

She removed her harp from her MDP and nodding to Professor Fin, began a slow, measured tune, allowing each set of notes to linger in the air...

... and then she began to sing. To Lizzie's shock and delight, she realized that she was singing in multiple voices at once, each harmonizing with the other precisely, conveying emotion and almost drawing pictures in the air surrounding her. Lizzie felt pathos and joy, delight and astonishment, mystery and clarity surging within her as the performance continued.

She had reluctantly taken a required quarter of music appreciation as a freshman in college and hadn't enjoyed it much. This was nothing like the classical pieces they had listened to and analyzed during that course. This was much more like the music was speaking, not to her mind, but to the very depths of her soul.

The class as a whole had been so transported that it took a while as the last note glimmered from Gi's throat and harp before they realized it had stopped. As a whole they sat there silently, stunned by what they had experienced. The music had wrapped them into it, and not just individually. Lizzie felt it had bonded them together in some way she couldn't explain.

Professor Fin rose from his chair to the side of the group and stood before them. *"That was astounding in more ways than I can say. Gi. I look forward to the time we will be allowed to visit your home. If this presentation was only a taste of your world and culture, I feel we are in for an unparalleled treat. I will postpone the questions we may have until after that time. In the meantime, for the rest of you, I recommend you reflect on this experience between now and our next session.*

"Now that we have concluded our reports by your podmates regarding their dimensions, we will be changing our class format to include visits to your podmates' origins. I know you are already being exposed to many dimensions. This exercise will allow you to realize there is a difference between simply visiting a new and unusual place and visiting a place within the context of someone you have already associated closely with. Both of these approaches have a different kind of value.

"In between visits, we will convene here to discuss our insights with a native of the dimension. At that time, each of you will have the opportunity to lead the discussion about your dimension.

"Please consult your tablets to find the scheduled day and time that corresponds to your own dimension. The various gate guardians of each of these destinations who are in charge of this type of event have already been notified and have prepared an experience at each destination unique to your particular culture.

"Go, then, to your meals, workouts, and other activities with something to contemplate between now and then."

As was his wont, he then led the way out of the classroom. Lizzie noticed her comrades were very subdued, each somewhat engaged in their own thoughts.

With this new pattern, discussion at mealtimes revolved around their experiences in various dimensions, as well as their instruction in mental training with Liliath.

"I swear, sometimes I feel like a complete idiot," Linlin confessed one day. *"It's bad enough to discover all I don't know about other dimensions and*

cultures, but to find out I don't really know much about myself is daunting, to say the least."

"I hear you," Feth chimed in with his squeaky mind voice. *"I had no idea there was so much exploration to do inside my own head. Evidently, I'm very resistant to this sort of thing."*

"We're struggling too," Geln agreed, shaking his heads in unison. *"We have three sections in our minds to deal with. We thought we think all the same things, but apparently, we do see the world slightly differently. This will be a shock to our culture, so we must thoroughly understand this before we reveal any of it to our people."*

"I'd give a lot to see the mental landscape of the dragon," added Mang, his green eyes flashing. *"Before I realized there were worlds inside my own head, I thought the concept of billions of dimensions was hard to grasp. Now I find myself wondering if there is any end to creation. I have always had trouble fixing the idea of infinity in my mind. I think we can all agree on that. And the principle that infinity stretches beyond both the smallest particle and the largest physical structure we can imagine is beyond me. I confess it makes me feel very insignificant, something I could not imagine before."*

Lizzie had to agree with all of that. Her sessions with Liliath were both instructive and intimidating. Here was something involving her brain that was more challenging than the most intensive and advanced math course in the university. The idea that her brain was capable of so much more than thought and the ordering of her body was foreign to anything humans considered as science.

The best classes at this point were the ones where they went through the gates to the various dimensions. So far, they had visited water planets, places where the intelligent life was plant-like, planets so far from the center of their solar system that light was almost a foreign concept, and even planets where Lizzie felt like she had doubled her weight in a fraction of a second as she went through the gate and before the special environmental suits kicked in with their gravitational adjustment technology.

More and more, their pod was beginning to reach out to the beings in other pods, and Lizzie was beginning to actually feel a part of something much larger than herself for perhaps the first time in her life. She recognized many of the faces, such as they were, of beings not in her classes and even knew many of their names.

However, she felt most at home with her podmates in a way she had never connected to any of her schoolmates on Earth. They laughed together, shared experiences, and now they even shared music. The one impromptu concert she, Ynni, and Gi had begun had expanded, and they were now joined by members from her pod and others.

One particular day they were playing quietly in their space under the trees between pod buildings when suddenly Ynni sat stiff upright on Lizzie's shoulder and sent a mental hiss and then a growl. This startled Lizzie so much that she stopped playing. The others hadn't noticed, as Gi was playing a particularly stirring set of arpeggios on her harp and harmonizing with her multi voice.

"What is it, Ynni?" Lizzie asked her privately. *"What's wrong?"*

"Bad one. There is a bad one amongst us. They passed by, but they are thinking bad things... most bad things. Bad things about the Alliance. Bad things about agents. So many bad things."

"Who is it?"

"I do not know. They passed by. We must tell Liliath, but not now. We must not get the attention of the bad one. Do not tell podmates. Not yet. We need Liliath's counsel."

So, Lizzie waited until the concert was over.

Chapter 22: Lizzie's Why

(Jenny looked up from the journal's yellowing pages with a start. This sounded all too familiar. She had been lulled by the seeming peace of Lizzie's experience so far. She had been excited that she would finally get the opportunity to enjoy a nearly idyllic experience of what agent training would have been like for her if she had been given that opportunity and nothing had interfered.

But she knew linklings' abilities. She knew that it was unlikely Ynni had been fooled or had imagined the threat.

She turned the page...)

Lizzie was afraid Liliath would discount Ynni's report of a "bad one." However, later when she was admitted into Liliath's office and reported the experience, Liliath questioned Ynni closely about it. It was obvious she not only believed what Ynni was saying but took it very seriously.

When Lizzie asked Liliath how such a threat was possible or even likely, Liliath replied, *"The Dimensional Alliance is not without its enemies. Most are intimidated by the combined might of the member dimensions, but now and then a group of them conspires to infiltrate or even attempt to shut down the gate system. They imagine the riches of the dimensions could be theirs if the Alliance was not there to interfere in free reign over those dimensions not prepared to defend themselves—especially those, like Earth, who are protected by the Alliance but are not official members and who do not know there is a threat.*

"In addition, not all of the beings within our membership agree on how things should be done all the time. These are generally in the minority, but their complaints are usually brought before the governing council and resolved through negotiation and reasonable concessions that may not be completely

satisfactory to both parties. In these cases, both parties agree to live by the final decision of the combined council.

"We shall put security on alert status. Ynni, if you notice this 'bad one' around again, please attempt to identify them. I know this will be difficult if you are in a gathering of any size but having a description will be paramount to catching this being or any of their potential confederates. We will be careful to notify only our security team about this, so please do not spread it. Lizzie, have you told any of your podmates about it?"

"No, we came straight here as soon as the crowd had dispersed. They know I have lessons with you, and I used that as an excuse. I wasn't sure the best way to handle it, and I was pretty sure no one else noticed anything or they would have said something. I also admit I didn't want to feel foolish if it turned out to be nothing to worry about."

"Very good. Then, for now, let's keep this between us and security. Ynni, stay on alert, please. If you need to contact me, Lizzie, simply touch the icon that will now appear in the contact list on your tablet. Don't go into detail. Simply say, 'Ynni,' and I will know. At that point I will get with you immediately. Are we clear?"

"Clear as can be, Liliath. Thank you."

"Then return to your pod, and let's hope this was just a passing thing. If it isn't, we can deal with it. Thank you for coming straight to me with this."

As she left the office, Lizzie knew that something had shifted within her. All of a sudden all of the preparations they were making, all of the self-defense and learning to control her facial expressions and the reasons for the foundation of the Dimensional Alliance became real to her in a way that none of her lessons had achieved so far.

Of course, it might be nothing. It could just be a disgruntled agent student mentally grumbling to themselves. It might never occur again. It might not be connected to any kind of a conspiracy or intent to do actual harm to the Alliance.

Nevertheless, Lizzie realized for the first time that her training as an agent was not only informational. She had thought that any threats to the Alliance were in the past, not something she might ever have to deal with herself as an agent. She knew the Alliance also had an organized army called the Troopers, but she thought this to be mainly for some vague future threat and more as a deterrent than a current necessity.

Over the next week or so, she found herself more intensely engaged in all of her lessons. Even her mental sessions with Liliath took on new meaning as she realized that protecting her mind needed to be a first priority.

Every class became more significant, more urgent. Her desire to ask questions for the pure sake of learning was transformed with intentional focus on what her instructors had to teach her. There would be plenty of time to expand her search for the answers to all of life's questions once she had mastered the skills necessary to fill her role as an agent for the Alliance.

Not only was she more intensely focused on becoming the best possible agent, but she began to understand that, regardless of the huge idea of defending the multiverse, she felt she had a specific responsibility to protect the Earth. It had not occurred to her before that some shapeless, faceless, inimical force on the edges of the multiverse might actually impact her home world.

She thought of all the Earth had been through in the past few decades and realized that those world wars and destruction were nothing compared to what a technologically superior culture could inflict on them. She pictured the entire Earth enslaved or even completely destroyed and shuddered at the thought.

While it was true that her encounter with the "bad one" might not be the runner up to anything like that, she finally thought she understood what she had signed up for and now fervently hoped that she would prove up to the task if necessary.

Therefore, it was a new Lizzie who continued her training. Mang remarked during their defense training that she had "fire" in her eyes, and all of a sudden, she found herself more engaged and attentive as Lall instructed them in new techniques.

To her distress, however, more fervor didn't necessarily translate into a higher skill level. Although she was a lot less likely to allow her thoughts to drift during the forms and sparring matches, she noted that she just didn't have the natural abilities that would make her more than an above-average fighter.

In her other classes, the kinds of questions she began to ask were changed from "why" to "how," a change that more than one of her instructors seemed to notice.

She still very much enjoyed the visits to the other podmates' dimensions and was still awed at the visits to alien dimensions led by Galena, but she also found herself paying a lot more attention to the study of what she thought of as the Dimensional Alliance constitution.

It was vital to her, as an agent, that she thoroughly understand the whys and wherefores of how the Alliance was put together.

Her pod drew closer and closer together as they visited one another's dimensions. She still had not told any of them about the "bad one," but she found herself feeling more and more protective of these beings who had become more than just teammates or friends. There was no word in her extensive vocabulary to explain this relationship, but she definitely knew that she had never felt this close even to members of her own family.

She had loved visiting Geln's dimension. It was like having triple vision to see all of the repeated faces, but each set of three, with an occasional set of four (rather like twins on Earth), were unique and had differing temperaments and abilities.

As Geln had told her, they were a very peaceful people and lovers of nature, which was not clogged by large sprawling cities. Instead, there were townships along country roads. Their visit was carefully monitored, as Geln's dimension was not a member. Therefore, they got to meet only the gate guardians and their families.

It turns out that the planet was very large and the gravity slightly stronger than most of the dimensions they had visited so far. Which explained how Geln, bulky as they were could be so light on their feet. The landmasses took up a much larger percentage of the planet's surface. When asked how the planet wasn't overwhelmed by population, the guardian in charge of the excursion simply shrugged three sets of shoulders.

"Our life spans are short compared to many in the Alliance, and most families bear only one set of children. A family, therefore, generally consists of six parents and one set of siblings. This is the natural order for us."

Geln seemed very happy to be on his planet and to introduce them to his six parents. They definitely seemed to be proud of their son(s).

Mang's dimension was so very different from anything Lizzie would have described as "elf-like." His people lived in large, extremely modern cities, similar in technology to the Dimensional Alliance headquarters city. There were farms, but the farming was done by a second race more suited to those tasks. Commerce went back and forth between the two types of beings, the rural folk exchanging for goods with what her dad would have called "city folk."

She had somehow pictured him in Tolkien-like surroundings, woodlands, playing harps and engaged in tending the land. Their guide explained it had once been that way, but that was far in their distant past. When they had established a relationship with the agrarians, it had freed them to pursue higher sciences and technology. His expression as he explained this seemed a bit haughty, as if this should have been obvious.

Minth had been sorry that he was unable to bring his podmates through his own gate. *"The environment is so highly charged that even your environmental suits would be no protection."* So, his report in Lin's class was all they had to go by.

One by one, they visited the various dimensions. Finally, there were only two left, Earth and Gi's planet, Finque.

Instead of the Switzerland gate as Lizzie had expected, they were received joyously at the Sanglarka gate by the Sanglarka team. It was definitely an impressive entrance, with the sparkling, diamond-like, snow-covered peaks surrounding the beautiful green valley with its forests and streams.

They did their workout together in the workout cycle that had become so routine for Lizzie in her pre-agent training. They ate together at a sumptuous feast with special foods that had come ahead of them. Evidently this wasn't the Sanglarka team's first time to do this for the agent training program. All of her podmates pronounced the meal well served.

They had the opportunity to watch a filmed presentation showing the many wonders of the planet, and Grenheim had answered their questions. They did their defense workout in the lodge workout room, and Oak had complimented one and all for their prowess in defensive training.

Lizzie had returned knowing that her podmates had been as impressed with her home planet and its hospitality as she had been with theirs.

The next day, before they left the pod for the journey to Gi's planet, Gi put an arm around Lizzie. Up to this time, each time they had left to visit a planet, Ynni had gone along with her reflection turned off. But Gi requested that this time, Ynni should be visible.

"My people are not shy to meet other beings, and I think most of them will be enchanted with our Ynni, especially with her beautiful singing voice. And please make sure you have your mbira. You will need it."

Lizzie did as instructed. She had anticipated this trip most of all.

They came out of the gate into what seemed like a cave, light spilling fractured into rainbows by the waterfall that shielded the gate. There was a path that took them around the veil of water into bright sunlight reflected off of a large, nearly oval pool of water surrounded by trees of a pale yellow-green.

"Welcome!" came a smooth tenor mind voice. *"I am Lolo. Please follow me and do not stray. There is no danger here, but very few of our people have mindspeech ability, and if you get lost it might be difficult for you to communicate your need to find us."*

As they spread out from the entrance, Lizzie could now see a tall green man with curly lavender hair in a distinctive blue robe that flowed to his wrists and ankles in gentle folds. It was fastened with a clasp that looked as if it was made of a blue opal in a silver setting. Lizzie guessed this ornament and the robes might be a badge of office, but she had only ever seen Gi in their standard working gear in the training compound, so she had no way of telling.

They passed through a forested area down a well-maintained path lined on either side with colorful stones. They emerged at the top of a low hill looking down onto a wide grassy plain. A stream wound through it, and from this vantage point they could also see their first glimpse of a concentricity. Radiating in a huge circle from a central cleared area surrounded by what might be fruit trees were domelike homes, each with acres of cultivated crops behind them.

Lizzie had pictured a dozen homes in a community based on Gi's report, but there were hundreds of these homes layered in a concentric circle from the central plaza-type area.

From this height, they could also hear music wafting up from below. It was like the background music for a film, never ceasing, but rising and falling in sound and intensity and tightly harmonizing like a vast choir. There had to be thousands of voices, and yet, Lizzie remembered that Gi could vocalize in multiple voices at once. Even then, the effect was mesmerizing.

After pausing to appreciate the view, they descended on a gentle path to the plain. Lizzie realized as they walked that she hadn't seen anything like a vehicle in their bird's-eye view of the concentricity.

The walk was pleasant, and their guide was silent. She assumed it was to allow them to soak in the ambient music that pleasantly surrounded them. Her companions seemed to agree, as no one seemed to be conversing in mindspeech as they walked.

Of them all, Geln seemed to be the most affected by this. His faces all reflected a combination of awe and a touch of discomfort. Lizzie remembered what he had said about the concept of music being foreign to his planet, and she could see why this must be an eye-opening experience for them. She also realized that she thought of Geln as three individuals with joined mind as opposed to one individual controlling three bodies.

She often argued with herself but wondered what an argument for Geln must be like. Their experience with Liliath made Lizzie think there was much more to Geln than met the eye.

Lolo led them to the center of the concentricity where people were beginning to gather. At the arc of the circular plaza was a raised platform. He led the group up onto the platform and gestured for them to stand and face the gathering crowd.

Still looking out towards the people assembling before them, he addressed the pod in mindspeech. *"I will be speaking to these, my people, in our language. As I address them, Gi will provide a translation for you in mindspeech. I will be assigning each of you a competent mindspeech translator so that you do not have to linger as a group but can mix individually with our people."*

Gi, who was standing next to Lizzie, nudged her and said, *"You and I will stay together. There are people to whom I would like to introduce you. The others can mix as they will."*

Lizzie nodded acceptance and Ynni added, *"Gi is a good friend and will be true. We are happy to have this link."*

The statement startled Lizzie somewhat. She hadn't thought about the fact that Ynni might decide to vet her acquaintances or that her link to Ynni might extend to people she cared about. This was somewhat disconcerting, and she wasn't quite sure how she felt about this. But Lolo was speaking...

All other voices had subsided. A bright, rich tenor voice rang out in a beautiful melody and then blended into three voices harmonizing as Gi had done.

Gi translated, *"My people, we have the honor and opportunity today to meet a small group of representatives from different dimensions than our own. Today we celebrate. Work may be laid aside. These young people are learning the necessary skills to be representatives of the Dimensional Alliance and, as such, are friends and compatriots. As they mix with you today, please show them our beating heart and give generously of your time and understanding. Do I have your agreement?"*

A great swelling chorus arose before them, melodious and grand in its enthusiasm.

"Now let's get you settled with your companions," Lolo sent, turning his back to the crowd that was once again emitting various musical tones which seemed to harmonize effortlessly with the other voices among them. *"After the mixing, we will assemble for a feast and then more entertainment."*

He introduced each of them to one of the villagers and gave Geln a choice of either one for all three or one for each of them. They chose to occupy only a single translator.

Gi tugged at Lizzie's arm. *"Come with me. I see my family, and they will want to meet you."*

She led the way down the steps of the platform to a waiting group of nearly a dozen people who were singing excitedly with one another. Lizzie noticed that Lolo was the only one in formal robes. The people around her were dressed in vibrant jewel tones, typical of country folk on her own planet on a celebration day. The women wore breeches or skirts in various styles, and the men tended more towards long tunic-like shirts and breeches.

An older version of Gi stepped forward to hug Gi, and then she turned to Lizzie, singing with a warm welcoming smile. *"Lizzie, meet my mother, Ooli."* Gi sent, at the same time singing back to her mother.

"Tell her, I am pleased to meet her," and Lizzie extended her hand. She was surprised when Ooli grasped it firmly and pulled Lizzie also into a great hug.

It turns out that members of Gi's family weren't the only huggers. Evidently there was no handshake in this culture. She noticed after receiving hug after hug from Gi's parents, siblings, and an aunt and uncle that her podmates were also on the receiving end of many hugs. This definitely tested Professor Fin's training in schooling their features, as she knew that Mang, Linlin, and Negoth only tolerated touching when it was required inself-defense classes or helping a podmate up a slope with a grasp of the hand.

Nevertheless, they accepted the offered hugs with placid expressions, although Lizzie could almost see the mental rolled eyes with every contact.

Evidently, Minth's translator had warned those he met about his particular situation of no touching, and they accepted this restriction with good grace, keeping an adequate space between him and them.

In any other crowd, the sounds emanating from such a gathering would have been tumult, but in this case, it was like being in the center of a large chorale. The music seemed to create itself from the vocal cords of hundreds of people. Lizzie could begin to see why Gi was able to harmonize with her own "doodlings" on the mbira so easily. It became obvious that these people did this instinctively and effortlessly.

Then surprisingly, a rhythmic clapping began. It was the first percussive sounds she had heard since their arrival. And further, it was coming from a circle of onlookers surrounding, of all people, Geln!

In the center of the circle were Geln, dancing gleefully and individually to the music that surrounded them. Of all the beings she associated with daily in agent training, Geln would have been the last she would have suspected of such a public display of pure joy. Their eyes were closed as they pursued their own unique choreography.

Then, to her utter astonishment, one by one, as if it had been planned, her other podmates joined Geln in the center of the circle which widened to give them space to move. Lizzie couldn't believe it as Gi tugged at her arm and Ynni sent, *"Lizzie must dance. The steps are written in your heart."*

She timidly stepped out into the circle, watching the others as she moved to the music. Each of them had a different style of movement, some fluid, some staccato, in their response to the swelling chorus.

Most striking was Reanni, her wings part of the expression of her dance. Occasionally she would leap joyously, her wings giving her the extra height other beings would lack. Her bright coloring made it even more impressive, like a Polynesian fire dancer.

She was most surprised by Mang. He was always so dignified and impersonal, but his eyes were closed, and his face was euphoric. He moved with the same grace he displayed on the practice field, but without the ferocity she was used to seeing in him.

The faces of each of her podmates expressed a joyous abandon that she had never seen in any of them before. This was more than just play or recreation. Dancing to the glorious chorus was an elevated expression of more joy than Lizzie could remember having experienced in her lifetime.

Slowly the music began to fade, and the clapping died to a single person in a slow and gentle cadence. As the dancers slowed and stopped, there was one last clap almost too quiet to hear, and all was silent.

"Come with me," Gi sent to the group. The crowd around them remained silent, and an aisle parted to allow them to follow her to an area on one side of the circle that appeared to be set up for a huge picnic. At one place in the center of it all someone had placed cushions around a low table, just barely high enough to fit their knees under. Gi gestured for them to sit.

Behind them the music of conversation began again, but it was different this time. Much like the ambient music in a restaurant or theater, it was not compelling like the music they had danced to.

As they sat, Lolo sat amongst them. *"We are so glad to have shared this with you,"* he said, looking around at each of them. *"What you have just experienced was a mass recital of the story of a time in our history when the concentricities were first constructed. This is beyond living memory, but the song tells it all. I know you could not have it translated to you. It was sung in a very condensed manner of communication among us.*

"In order to tell the story completely in mindspeech or even our normal song, it would have taken many hours.

"When you have time with Gi, perhaps she can tell you some of the stories which were included."

At this point people began bringing around large bowls of produce to place in a line down the center of the table. *"Gi assures me that the food choices we offer here are all amenable to your various constitutions. I understand that in some of your cultures, food is processed by heat and other measures. Here we do not cook our food. It is harvested in its season and served fresh from our gardens and orchards year-round."*

They waited, as they had been taught to do in their etiquette classes. This appeared to be a good choice, as suddenly a song arose again from all of the surrounding low tables which Gi translated for them.

"Creator of All Things, we thank thee. We thank thee for food and raiment and all good things which spring from the soil. We thank thee for home and community. We thank thee for all good gifts."

Then a hush fell for a moment and the ambient music rose around them, but not as intense as before. Lizzie assumed this was because, unlike mindspeech, one could not eat and swallow and continue to sing.

"When we are finished eating, you will meet with the Alliance agents who are native to our dimension, and you may ask whatever questions you wish. Afterwards, we will entertain you before we wish you farewell and good journey."

Chapter 23: Fallout

(As Jenny continued to read, enthralled by the descriptions of the many places and beings Lizzie explored, she found herself feeling a bit bereft. Her own journey had been fast and intense, and she had been given little time to explore the dimensions or to receive any detailed training. She knew there was still much ahead for her, but with the complex duties before her as the official Gatekeeper for the Dimensional Alliance, she could see no way she would ever have the opportunity to receive the detailed training Lizzie had received.

Her training would continue to be "on the job," and she also had a husband and needed at some point to deal with her dad, who was now in on her "secret identity," as he called it. They had only had a few very short telephone conversations since that day she had visited him mentally, and in her evening mental visits she had taken the time to give him a very quick rundown of what she was dealing with. He had promised not to tell another soul, but she felt like he almost wished he could also be a part of it all.

In the meantime, she had to be content with her life as it was, not as she wished it could be. Nevertheless, as Lizzie continued her account of her training, Jenny felt herself wishing she had some special ability to go back in time and experience it for herself.

As Lizzie's training continued, and as Jenny neared the last part of this journal, Jenny felt like there was something looming ahead.)

Lizzie started awake. It was still dark. The automatic lighting for wakeup time hadn't yet turned on. It was unusual for her not to sleep completely through the sleep period. By the end of each and every day, she was both physically and mentally depleted. Normally, she, like her podmates, sank onto her bed at the end of the day with a deep sigh of contentment.

What had wakened her? Ynni was still asleep on the pillow next to her. She didn't hear anything, but that wasn't surprising, with the sound barriers between the beds in the pod. She sat up, trying not to disturb Ynni, and looked around her. She could dimly discern the sleeping beings around her, lumps on each of the beds, chests rising and falling. A slight glow around Minth indicating the static field that surrounded him was the only light inside at the moment.

Then, a gentle touch on her mind. *"Lizzie, it is Liliath. I know it is very early. Please quietly wake Ynni and come. You needn't dress for the day. I will meet you in my office."*

"Ynni?" she sent softly. *"I need you to wake and come with me."*

Ynni opened huge sleepy eyes and nodded. She didn't question, and Lizzie remembered she didn't need to. The tiny linkling stretched pale green furry arms and pulled herself up onto her accustomed perch on Lizzie's shoulder.

Lizzie slipped on her socks and shoes and left the pod, closing the door quietly behind her. She shivered a bit in the cool morning air, although the dimmer of the two suns was peeking from behind the pods across the training field. The t-shirt and sweatpants she normally wore to bed were a little less covering than she would have liked, considering this was the coolest part of the day.

Nothing stirred on the grounds as she walked quickly down the path to the admin building. There was no breeze, so not even a leaf rustled around her. This made her a bit uneasy, as if she were disturbing the surface of a crystal pond of peace.

She entered the quiet building, lights turning on automatically as she passed down the long corridor to Liliath's office. She didn't knock and found Liliath waiting on her chaise.

"Thank you for your promptness. Please be seated. I am sorry to wake you, but I needed to consult with you and Ynni privately. This office is shielded to prevent potential mental eavesdropping—"

"I had no idea that was even possible!"

"Ah yes, that will be part of your next unit of training, but for now it is important that we not be overheard.

"Ynni, have you sensed the 'bad ones' lately?"

"No, Liliath, but I listen, I do. Ynni believes the bad one is not alone and means no good to the Alliance or its servants."

"Servants?"

"Those who serve the beings of the Alliance. The word is not good?"

"Excuse my prideful nature, Ynni. Of course, that does indeed describe what we do.

"I need to tell you that I have heard whispers here and there of some discord among some of the beings in some of the other pods, and some of their rancor seems to center on your pod. Lizzie, I didn't want to disturb your other podmates, but Ynni is sensitive to the thoughts of those around them. I am about to call an assembly of the trainees and their leaders, and I will be ordering the arrangement of the pods on the training ground with your pod in the center of the gathering.

"Ynni, I need you to 'listen' to the thoughts of the crowd around you. This might take a while, as there are over two hundred trainees in the training unit at any given time. Tell me how long you think you will need, and I will make sure the assembly lasts long enough to do your work."

"Ynni takes in thoughts in large groups mostly as feelings. As I feel discontent or anger, I can then focus on an individual being. But that is many, many beings. Will need at least the span of one of your hours to do this. Also, Liliath should know some beings can feel it when I probe specifically."

"I see. We must try. When we assemble, I suggest you turn your reflection off before coming out onto the training grounds. I don't wish your participation to be obvious. I don't know how many of the trainees in the camp have any idea of your abilities, and we don't want to put them on their guard if we can help it.

"Lizzie, please go back to your pod now, and try to be quiet enough not to disturb your podmates. Go back to bed until wake time."

Lizzie nodded and left. She was able to slip back into her bed without anyone noticing, but she didn't sleep a wink for what remained of the night.

The next day she tried to pretend all was normal but found herself nodding off in the middle of Professor Lulindu's lecture on the fine points of the Agent Agreement, something she would have normally paid rapt attention to, since this was the part of the interdimensional agreement that pertained most to what she could and could not do as an agent. The overall document covered many aspects, such as trade and military cooperation, how the council made its decisions, and the agreed responsibilities of Alliance members.

During their usual routine of workouts, classes and defense, she kept wondering when Liliath would call the assembly and how she might disguise the true purpose of the gathering.

When they had returned from their expedition to Negoth's dimension, which was very similar to Earth but much more advanced in technology, they were informed, as they emerged from the gate that an assembly had been called and they were to proceed to their pod, refresh themselves, and assemble at a specifically marked place in their usual pod formation.

Lizzie's belly did a flip-flop. She had been shifting from fatigue to edginess all day in anticipation of this, and now she wondered how she had managed to put herself in the middle of it. Ynni had turned her reflection off, and no one in her pod remarked on it as they left for the assembly. It wasn't unusual for Ynni to casually disappear from time to time from Lizzie's shoulder, and she didn't always accompany them to every event in training.

But Lizzie felt Ynni's tiny warm hand on her cheek as she sent to her, *"Breathe, Lizzie, and be calm. Ynni is here."*

She took a deep calming breath and did her breathing exercises as they walked to their place in the assembly. There were around two hundred trainees in their pod formations. Their stations had been marked by a small stake with a flag bearing the symbol for their pod. Lizzie's pod symbol was the silhouette of a white tree on a green background. As she glanced around, she was once again impressed by the mixture of the various sizes, shapes and colors of the beings that surrounded her pod. Their pod was roughly in the center of the gathering.

All eyes shifted upward when, out of the sky, Liliath descended to a raised podium where the professors and administrative staff were already gathered.

She was majestic. The blues started at her hind feet, which blended gently to deep greens at her head. Her eyes tended to shift in color from amber to green as her moods changed, and her extended green-veined-in-blue, nearly thirty-foot wingspan, and her tail, which could be as expressive as any cat, combined to make her more than a little formidable. If you did not know how gentle and kind she could be, anyone would have been intimidated.

She definitely knows how to make an entrance, Lizzie thought, and couldn't help but grin. No one seeing her in this way would misjudge her authority or her ability to enforce it.

"*Agent trainees,*" she began without preamble, "*I greet you from the Alliance council and wish to acknowledge those of you who are putting in such an effort as we train you to represent the Alliance. You have taken upon yourselves a significant responsibility, and we wish to honor you for it. For this reason, we wish to announce a celebration, which will be held over the next four days.*

"*This event will allow each pod to participate in various competitions and also to create a special visiting space. We will be transforming the training ground into the equivalent of a market square. Each pod will have its own booth space, which can be used for gathering, storytelling, displaying art or entertainment, and, if you wish, marketing crafts native to your dimension.*

"*All transactions will be done in Alliance credits. You will be able to draw credits from your account via your tablet. You will also get two days off of studies to plan for and prepare your booth space. Therefore, all classes for the coming two days will be postponed, including physical training.*

"*At the end of the event there will be rewards for the best booths and recognition for many of you for your diligence and hard work.*"

"*Lizzie,*" Ynni broke in, as Liliath continued to expound on the coming events, "*There are stirrings of anger and ill intent in the pod to the right and up one rank. I am sending picture thoughts to Liliath, and she has responded that you should not react in any way. She will send instructions to you via your tablet. She has identified the discontented 'bad ones,' which is the purpose of this gathering. She wishes you to pay attention carefully to your surroundings.*

"*Ynni is not to leave your side at all until this is resolved. Liliath is pleased we were able to find these but has passed no judgment until more information is gathered.*"

Lizzie was astounded that this happened so quickly. She would have never thought of discovering these people in this way. Obviously, she still had much to learn to be able to think more like an agent. She resolved to pay more attention.

When the assembly was dismissed, she walked back to her pod along with her podmates, listening only halfway to the mental chattering of the group. They seemed excited about the event and were already coming up with ideas of how to create a great booth.

Lizzie had been surprised that she had an Alliance credits account. When she asked Minth about it, he blinked in surprise. *"Oh wait, you didn't attend the first week. We were told about our Alliance credits account during the first day of orientation, and you obviously missed that part. Each of us receives a monthly stipend, which can be translated into the currency of our dimension if we wish. You probably have accumulated quite a bit, if you haven't made arrangements to transfer it to an Earth account somewhere."*

Lizzie shook her head. When she consulted her tablet and selected the icon Minth showed her, she was astounded at the quantity of credits in there. The account page showed not only credits but also the value in her native currency. Evidently, she had to go to the admin office treasurer to arrange to transfer the money to her Earth bank account. She found herself wondering how much else she might have missed in her late arrival, but she decided, that was much less important than her instructions from Liliath via Ynni.

She mostly allowed the others to enthusiastically plan the booth and activities they wanted to display. She agreed with Gi to do an impromptu concert, harp and mbira, along with Ynni and Gi's vocal accompaniment. This meant she got to practice frequently over the next two days, which was soothing.

Ynni didn't report "bad ones" at any point over the days of planning. Lizzie didn't know if this was a good thing or if it just meant that these beings were cleverer than she had hoped they would be.

It felt a little odd not to be doing their usual physical workouts, but since Mang, Linlin, and Feth had decided to do a demonstration of quarterstaff fighting, she found herself working the forms before meals every day, even though she herself would not be participating in the actual demonstration. She was actually glad for it, since she now was more motivated to get better at defense and approached it with a much more open mind.

She knew she would never be as graceful or quick as most of her podmates, but now that she was paying careful attention to the comments of the others as they diagnosed various techniques and tactics, she found it came more naturally to her. She had thought the others just had natural talent but realized that this was only one aspect. As she listened to them discussing the bouts, she realized a lot of thought and focus went into what seemed effortless to the watcher.

She and Gi took breaks to practice their music together, Ynni joining in with enthusiasm. She heard that Geln had taken a gate home to retrieve some paintings he/they had made, and Reanni was planning to present a dance native to her dimension. After having seen her in the revelry on Gi's planet, Lizzie was looking forward to it.

The spontaneous dance had surprised her so much, and she wasn't the only one. They all agreed they had been drawn into the dance by the overwhelming pull of the music and would have never done it otherwise. They had discussed the power of music more than once since then and had agreed that perhaps music of other cultures might have been good to have included in their study of dimensional cultures in Fin's class.

As they prepared, Lizzie continued feeling mild distraction and worry, constantly alert to any warnings by Ynni. She was concerned that not only had Ynni not felt any further bad feelings around them, but that Liliath had not mentioned anything to either of them about the incident at the assembly after Ynni had reported it.

She was sure that Liliath could handle anything that came up. Of course, she had a strategy in place. Of course, she was putting precautions into place, but there was no hint of any of this that Lizzie could see.

The third day after the assembly, they arose early to put together their booth presentation. Food for the next two days would be provided at various stalls throughout the square. As they worked, Lizzie was delighted with the experience, despite her worry.

Geln's artwork was mostly pastoral, beautiful scenic vistas, somewhat surprising to them all. They had not noticed this side of Geln in all the time they had spent together. It may have accounted for the fact that he had been the first to succumb to the beautiful music that day.

Negoth would be performing a series of complicated acrobatics on a balance beam that he, to their surprise, was able to pull from his MDP easily.

Minth was going to be creating a light show at the end of the day that would shine over the entire training area. He would say no more about it than that since he wanted it to be a surprise.

When they had everything in place and had uploaded the schedule of their performance events to the main computer network so it would be available to all participants, they visited some of the local food booths and sat beside their own booth, eating and waiting for the event to begin.

They had finished their booth before many of the others. They had agreed on a rotation schedule of who would attend the booth, so that each would have an opportunity to view the other displays and potentially purchase something with their well-earned credits.

Lizzie really liked the Alliance philosophy that learners should be paid for their diligence, because their training would ultimately be an advantage to the Alliance. It was a lot like soldiers being paid, if somewhat poorly, during basic training on Earth. This was much more like the university, notwithstanding the physical part of their training. Fortunately, she thought, there were no yelling drill sergeants bawling insults at them as they trained.

When a fanfare of some kind of wind instruments announced the beginning of the fair, the normally silent square burst into a quiet hubbub. Of course, mindspeech prevailed for communications, but several of the booths had displays and demonstrations that made various levels of noise, including occasional outbursts of applause or shouted encouragement during various contests.

If nothing else she had experienced so far had taught Lizzie how diverse the trainees were, this event definitely awoke a sense of awe in her, from those who reminded her of mythological creatures to forms and shapes and colors she had never imagined.

One such was a being who Minth described as a "trrfn," pronounced "terrfin." It was orblike, about six feet tall, with tentacles instead of legs which undulated along the ground to move it in one direction or another. There were no mouth or other facial features she could discern, and the deep purple iris and humongous black pupil rotated freely around the orb. Its companion was wearing an environmental suit filled with water, bubbles floating up the clear breathing tubes on either side of the helmet. This being, called a "fleon," was from a water planet and had greeted Lizzie before going to and from classes. Lizzie found herself grateful for mindspeech, as she was able to greet them warmly when they came to see Geln's painting, which seemed exotic to them, neither of their races having any reference to this kind of art.

It was about this time that Lizzie, Gi, and Ynni were scheduled to do their first music presentation. And, as it turned out, this was the reason these two had come to their booth.

Lizzie, Ynni and Gi sat on the cushions they had placed on the grass and began to play, Lizzie beginning with a few lingering individual notes on the mbira. Slowly Gi began her harp descant, mingling enticingly with the ringing notes of the mbira. Then, Ynni began to croon her own addition to the composition. When, finally, Gi added her rich multivoice harmony, they were all lifted into a blissful state.

The surrounding bustle and competing sounds seemed to fade out of their consciousness. They continued until the crescendo and then faded once again, one voice leaving at a time until Lizzie did an arpeggio followed by a glissade. The last sounds lingered for a moment on the still air.

When Lizzie looked up from this musical meditation, she saw that quite a crowd had gathered. They were each applauding in their own way, some vocally and some with staccato claps, taps, and clicks.

Lizzie, Gi, and Ynni each bowed their heads humbly in acknowledgment of the applause and set to answering questions from the group. Some few had no previous exposure to music. But many had questions about not only their instruments, but also Gi's ability to harmonize with herself.

If Lizzie had thought to bring some mbiras to sell from her booth, she would have sold several on the spot. As it was, several of the crowd singled her out later to ask if she would bring some back from her next holiday on Earth.

When Lizzie and Gi got their turn to take a stroll around the square, they were also impressed by the arts, crafts, and cultural demonstrations by their fellow agent trainees. Dancing, music, and art were common, as well as displays of different stones or plants from various dimensions.

Their booth had gone over very well, Lizzie thought. Mang, Linlin, and Feth's demonstration of defense techniques had been brilliant, each of them moving so quickly as to make it hard to follow the fight. Three on three, the three-cornered quarterstaff fight had been like a very fast-paced well-choreographed dance. After it all, Lizzie found herself feeling very inadequate in self-defense and grateful they were her podmates and she could yet learn from them.

Once again, Lizzie felt like she was not even the smallest speck on a speck in the multiverse. The incredible diversity of creation demonstrated by the fair took her breath away, and she noticed she wasn't the only one of her podmates who was silently contemplative at the end of the first day.

A few minutes before they headed to their pods to sleep, Minth ascended a ladder to the top of a small metallic tower. Banners had been strung in a circle several feet around the base of the tower to prevent anyone from coming too close.

It was twilight, and the light had faded the sky to a deep violet. He stood at the top of the tower and did something astounding. He removed his rubber boots and his gloves. He began to glow blue in the fading light, and then he started to sketch in the air above him. As he did so, patterns of light began to form, widening from the center to a circle the width of a tennis court. The patterns became more and more complex.

The entire training ground had gone completely silent. Nothing stirred. Lizzie realized that Minth was painting with light. It was like nothing she had ever seen; and, by the hushed silence around her, she was sure that she wasn't alone in this.

He sketched the skyline of a large modern city, dotting the skyline with various flying vehicles. A banner then appeared above the skyline as if held on either end by some of the flying vehicles. On it, in script none of them understood, was some kind of a motto.

The blue glowing vista lingered for a few minutes and then slowly faded away, leaving behind impressions on Lizzie's irises.

Calmly, Minth redonned his gloves and boots and climbed down the ladder. As he lit upon the ground, silence exploded into cheers of delight from all of the onlookers. Lizzie was glad he had saved the best for last. In her opinion and that of her podmates, their pod had outdone the entire assembly.

After much clamor by their fellow trainees and faculty over Minth's impressive show, they had dismantled their booth, grateful for their MDPs, which greatly reduced the work involved. Exhausted, they went to their beds in their pod, not even pausing for a quick game of cubes, which for some of them had become a nightly ritual.

The following morning, they arose, rested and ready to begin the day of competitions and the award celebration to be followed by a huge outdoor feast accompanied by music from various well-known music and dance professionals from all over the Alliance member dimensions.

One of the tournaments had been sponsored by Professor Baird. A dozen cube boards had been set up, and Minth, Reanni, Linlin, and Negoth had all signed up to participate. There were chairs set up around the perimeter of the gaming tables, and Professor Baird sat on an elevated chair so he could overlook the game play. Spectators came and went, but by the time they got to the final round, it came down to Minth and a sleekly-furred otter-like being named Belial, who had large black eyes where the irises and pupils blended together. Lizzie realized, however that he had a "tell" and hoped Minth had caught it. His long silvery whiskers twitched every time he was about to infringe on Minth's cubes, or when he spotted a clever move while Minth was deciding on his own.

Lizzie was sure her skills weren't up to the level of play in the tournament, but she had definitely learned a lot playing with her podmates outside the classroom, so she wasn't too surprised when Minth tied up Belial's tiles before the main cube was expended, stopping the game as there were no plays left to make, and Minth had scored two more matched sets than Belial.

Muttering something aloud but reaching out a furred hand to shake Minth's, Belial didn't look him in the eye as Baird announced the winner of the tournament to the excitement of Minth's podmates who had gathered in anticipation to watch the final match.

Unsurprisingly, Mang, Feth, and Linlin decided to enter the hand-to-hand self-defense competition as a team. After battling several other teams to a standstill, they lost by one point to the final team on the playing field. Nevertheless, their podmates cheered as they received second place medallions.

By the last part of the day, the pace began to slow, and they were dismissed at one point to their pods whilst the staff set up for the award ceremony and the celebratory feast. Their feelings of team spirit were at an all-time high, each of them congratulating one another on their various triumphs, large and small.

Ynni hadn't reported any "bad ones" at any point in the celebrations, even though Lizzie and Gi had traversed the training field, examining goods at the various booths and watching exotic performances by so many different types of beings that at times Lizzie's head was spinning, trying to take it all in. The more of her fellow trainees she met, the more incomprehensible it was to her that so much diversity and such vast distances could possibly be managed by any governing group, no matter how complex.

The word "science" somehow began to feel small to her and inadequate to encompass this really big concept, that creation seemed to be truly infinite and that the word "control" could no more apply to the dimensions than to, as her uncle would have said, "herding cats."

As they entered the pod and sat in the training area, with the chairs now arranged in a circle, Geln sent to the group, *"I have never had such close relationships in the past beyond my family. I hope to always remember this time together. I have reserved this painting, one for each of you, to give at this time. Please put them in your MDPs and hang them somewhere at your home base to remind you of us."* And he gestured around the circle including each of them.

He pulled a painting about the size of a piece of newsprint, neatly stretched on canvas but unframed. Lizzie was delighted to see it was like a family portrait, only instead of a formal sitting it portrayed them all sitting in the shade under the large tree between the pods, enjoying the music being played by Gi, Ynni, and Lizzie. The faces were rapt, and their pleasure and unity were as tangible as if Geln had inscribed the words at the bottom of the painting.

They were all stunned. It was evident in their faces. For a moment all three faces of Geln looked uncertain and embarrassed. Then the responses were sent all in a rush from each of them. *"Brilliant!" "Amazing!" "Beautiful!" "When did you find time to do all of that?"*

"We have been painting at home during break when you were all engaged in other activities. We even missed some of the impromptu concerts to do this. One of us watched while another of us painted." Geln replied, sighing vocally in relief that his offering wasn't being rejected. *"We have always loved painting, as there is so much beauty in the multiverse. We felt this was beauty that needed to be kept not just in memory."*

Geln handed each of them a painting, each slightly different in minor details, but all depicting the same scene. Each of them gave one of him a hug, at which Geln blushed slightly as they carefully stowed their painting in their MDPs.

It turned out that they each had actually purchased some kind of memento to give to their podmates, chosen either for a humorous shared memory or something that they felt suited their personality.

Even Ynni wasn't left out of the gifting. She crooned delightedly at each trinket. Lizzie suspected her favorite was probably the soft little blanket that was just her size that Minth had given her. At Ynni's instruction, Lizzie stowed all of her gifts into the MDP. They still had no idea where they would end up, and Lizzie had a suspicion that they wouldn't have a permanent place other than Sanglarka for a long time yet.

Sharing like this seemed to have united the pod even more than before. Lizzie would never forget all of the times they had helped, supported, and encouraged one another on this journey.

Their gifts stowed safely in their MDPs, they trooped out to the training ground where pods were beginning to assemble before the raised dais at one end of the field. Per her instructions from Liliath, once again Lizzie's pod centered themselves among the assembly, facing the dais expectantly. Lizzie had relaxed over the days of this event, but she hadn't forgotten the hidden reason for it. Ynni was alert, and that translated somehow to Lizzie's mood.

She had begun to notice that Ynni's moods often were transmitted somehow through their bond, not in words or specific thoughts, but just through feelings. For instance, she knew when Ynni was happy, excited, or focusing on something intently. At the moment, she was very focused on the minds around her. It occurred to Lizzie that large crowds like this would be somewhat stressful if Ynni wasn't able to control her ability to read thoughts. If she had no way to filter it, it would probably come across as an incoherent and overwhelming babble.

Lizzie was more and more impressed with her little companion. Just when she thought she understood the breadth and limits of Ynni's abilities, she found she had underestimated what she could do. Ynni's personality was mild and gentle; and yet, there seemed to be another side to her that Lizzie suspected would continue to amaze her the more time they spent together.

Finally, the crowd settled as Liliath made her spectacular flying entrance and alighted lightly on the podium platform. It amazed Lizzie that someone so large could be so graceful and dexterous as to not even make a sound as her huge clawed hind feet touched down.

The waiting crowd couldn't help themselves. They broke into applause and cheering. Spirits in general were high and enthusiastic. They had all benefitted from this break from their intense training schedules. And now they were less individual pods and more a congenial group of trainees, all dedicated to the same cause and with a communal experience that tied them together.

Getting the opportunity to mingle with one another on a casual basis and to learn more about each other and their associated cultures had created new friendships. Now, when they saw one another on campus or in the dining hall, they would be more likely to greet one another and begin conversations.

Regardless of Liliath's hidden intent for the event, it had definitely done much more for each of them than simply to define a potential threat to the Alliance.

"Agent Trainees of the Dimensional Alliance," Liliath began, and she immediately had their entire attention.

"It has been a delight to see you interacting with one another on so many levels. There is so much that cannot be taught in the classroom or in the field. One of those things is to recognize the beauty and potential represented in the diversity of beings and cultures in the multiverse. It is our hope that the opportunity to mingle and expose yourselves to that diversity in events such as this will prepare you for the many experiences that lay before you.

"We have seen some excellent presentations by each pod, and there is a lot to be said for how quickly you were each able to create something that allowed us a peek into your culture and the dimensions you represent.

"Now let us celebrate your excellence. Each of the instructors has decided on an award to give out, representing different aspects of the booths, presentations, and competitions during this event. I know you are all anxious to find out what they have decided. I will let them get on with it, shall I?"

With her somewhat frightening dragon smile, she moved to the side of the dais.

Each of the professors had something to say and something to give out. Best booth award went to one of the pods that had constructed a holographic museum, complete with rooms filled with artwork and sculpture. There were awards for the funniest, most informational, and best merchandise displays. Geln received an award for his artwork. All of the winners of the competitions were announced and applauded. It was good to see her podmates recognized for their talents.

Finally came awards for best presentations. Lizzie's pod received two awards. One for Minth's amazing electric art display, and the other, to Lizzie, Gi, and Ynni's surprise, for their little concert.

All during the celebrations, one part of Lizzie's mind was listening for Ynni, but no cry of "bad ones" came.

The final feast was joyful, and Lizzie began to feel that perhaps the "bad ones" incident was just an isolated event after all.

Chapter 24: Bends in the Road

(Jenny realized someone was calling her name and was startled out of her engagement in Lizzie's adventures. She knew that she was close to the end of the first journal and wanted to continue.

The voice came from the hallway, by the door to the gate office. It was Bob, Ignatius perched on his shoulder.

He was dressed in his usual uniform of jeans and a colorful t-shirt covered by a white lab coat.

"Just checking in on you, neighbor," he said with a chuckle. "Didn't mean to startle you. I'd have knocked, but that would have just been weird, coming from the gate office." His eyes were crinkled, and he chuckled, and Ignatius chuckled with him. "Just wanted to see that you are following doctor's orders."

"I was reading in Lizzie's journals. I've been taking my walks and eating well. Lizziebot has been waiting on me hand and foot, and no stress, I promise." And she put her hand up in the old girl scout gesture.

"Good enough. Where are you in Lizzie's journey? Am I in there yet?"

"Not yet. She hasn't become a guardian yet. This journal just covers her agent training. I am guessing I won't get to you until the third journal."

"Any chance I could have a gander at them at some point, after you've finished with them?"

"Sure, Bob. I think Lizzie would have liked that. When I am done with them, I am going to have Lizziebot scan them all into the database, including a version in Lizzie's handwriting. I'd be happy to send them all to you at that point."

Bob sat down on the couch across from her reading chair. "How are you doing, kiddo? You've been through a pretty rough stretch, and I know that 'shout' you did at the confrontation on the Groga planet took more out of you than we could have expected."

"Liliath warned me it might be so. Burt has been so caring and understanding, and I have a great team to back me up. I still do my nightly mental 'visits' to the various team members, and Liliath keeps me up to date. I have to say, having the journals to focus on while I wait for the go-ahead to go back to work is a real blessing. I haven't had this much time to read and enjoy a good story in over a year, and it is added spice that it's a true story about the person who set me on this journey.

"I'm beginning to realize that, as hard as it has been, no life journey is without its bumps in the road. I am learning so much that I think will make me a better gatekeeper in the long run. I only wish I had known Lizzie better before I inherited all of this."

"I think you two would have been good friends. That being said, there are definite differences between the two of you, as I am sure you are discovering," Bob said with a twitch of his moustache.

"You could say that. I don't think I have even begun to scratch the surface where Lizzie is concerned."

"Yep, she was a firecracker, that one. And such a good friend to my Cindy. Couldn't have asked for a better neighbor, even with her being gone as much as she was. At any rate, I'm off to Mervin's lab and then to conflab with Cornelium. As you know, we're working on creating a better automated monitoring system for the gates of dimensions that aren't members of the Alliance, especially gates that aren't situated to make it easy for them to have a guardian.

"We want to create new tech to locate less obvious gateways more easily, such as those underwater or buried in caves or orbiting planets. The current tech is a lot more hit-or-miss than we'd like it to be.

"Anyway, enjoy your reading. You don't have much more mandatory light duty, and then it's back into the fray."

Jenny laughed and stood to give him a parting hug. "By the way, your son dropped by the other evening to check on me as well. All he knows is that I'm recuperating from an illness, but evidently, he wants to make sure I'm okay. Is that your doing, I wonder?"

Bob chuckled again, and Ignatius's echo came right behind it. "Ask me no secrets, and I'll tell you no lies," he said with a wink. And with that, he turned and entered back through the door to the gate office.

"Now where was I?" she asked Chidwi, who was napping happily next to Tidbit on the window seat. With a sigh, Jenny sat back into her chair, found her place saved by the bookmark, and began to read.)

It was good to get back to regular workouts and classes again. The constant traveling via gates never became ordinary or mundane. Each day represented new adventures.

By this time, they had visited all of the dimensions represented by her podmates, and now they were discussing cultural differences and their observations of how their relationships continued to change, the more they knew about one another. Lizzie had the feeling that this was the true point of the exercise.

She began to realize that it was hard to actively dislike someone, the more you knew about them. You might not always agree with everything they said or did, but understanding brought a certain amount of tolerance. And it was easier to understand motivations and intent when you understood their background and cultural norms.

The week following the event was quiet, every pod going about their usual training, but she noticed there was also a lot more interaction as they passed one another in the hallways and the paths surrounding the training compound.

Some beings from the other pods started gathering at their regular music breaks in the space under the trees between the pod buildings. Lizzie and Gi had developed a musical rapport that seemed to extend beyond their own personal musical skills or inclinations. Lizzie suspected that perhaps Ynni played a part in that. Regardless, every time they played, Lizzie was transported to a place of calm and meditation.

This was reflected in Lizzie's sessions with Liliath. She hadn't asked what had happened to the group Ynni had singled out from the crowd at the assembly, assuming that if it was any of her business Liliath would tell her. Regardless, it was all she could do to keep up with her coursework and stay on top of those mental workouts.

Liliath had begun to teach Lizzie how to "armor her mind," as she put it. This involved Lizzie's learning to guard herself against various attacks, much like her physical defense practice, but in this case a mental attack might affect her either mentally or physically or both. Lizzie lamented that, either way, every day she had new bruises to show; but slowly she found she could endure both mental and physical pain as she learned to discipline her mind.

Her life in the pod would never become routine, but it was definitely more comfortable as she drew closer and closer to her podmates. For the first time in her life, she really felt a part of something she could commit to, not just out of duty. She was beginning to understand why what she was doing was important.

They were nearly to the end of this term, at which point they would all be assigned Guides and would begin to go on simple assignments in a type of internship. This would mean they wouldn't see each other as often as they would like, but the training compound and their pod building would still be their base of operations. They would see each other between assignments, but probably wouldn't have much of a chance to all gather at once.

After a particularly hard work out with Lall one day, they cleaned up and went to the dining hall. It was nice to be able to greet some of the beings they saw along the way by name. Geln seemed to be coming out of his/their shell. He would wave and smile. He had gotten a great deal of recognition due to his art and had made quite a few friends outside the pod as a result.

As they sat at their meal, the talk was all about the coming holiday when they would go home to put things in order before moving on to their agent internship.

It seemed to Lizzie, and many of her podmates agreed, that this had been a really short time to advance to the point when they would be actively going out on assignments. They all were glad it would be in the company of a Guide and speculated about what that might be like.

They agreed that after their meal they would meet under the tree, which Geln now called "our tree," to take a music break. The day was melting into evening, with one sun already disappearing beyond the horizon in a splash of golds and reds.

This time of day, most of the pods retreated to their various pod buildings to organize themselves for the coming day, to study and, for many of them, to just relax before bedtime.

Lizzie was glad, however, to just enjoy the music and the fellowship of her comrades. Lizzie's mind drifted on the music into the fading light of evening, and her eyes closed as she felt it all so deeply. The voices of Gi and Ynni, the mystical mixing of the mbira and harp and the silent but somehow noticeable energy of her podmates gathered there in the peaceful conclusion to a busy day, were all part of the melody.

However, Ynni had stopped singing and Lizzie opened her eyes. She didn't need the urgent message from Ynni about "bad ones." Surrounding them and blocking the exit from the space between the pods were several beings of various types, and their stance and posture radiated anger and danger.

The one who appeared to be the leader was as beautiful as how Lizzie might have described an elven princess. Tall and slender, with shimmering silver hair, pointed ears, and a long, tasseled tail twitching behind her, her face was a picture of rage.

"Here we have them, the little Earthling and her podmates. They're so sure of themselves. Earth isn't even an Alliance member. How they let such trash into the agent program, I have no idea, but there are plans for you and all of those like you. I am Hadron of Gingil, and you are less than the meanest slave in my kingdom.

"The dragon may think you are something, but we *know you are an infestation. Besides, even the Alliance doesn't realize the value of what they hold in their hands.*

"This stops here. When we are finished, the multiverse will have order. The multiverse will find its true destiny. Your puny little planet and those like you will find that things are about to change."

As she sent this, the entire pod were on their feet, back to back, facing the encircling, menacing trainees.

"Ynni, can you send to Liliath? Can you reach that far?" Lizzie sent to Ynni.

"Ynni does not know. I will try. I will jump down behind you and turn my reflection off. If I cannot contact her from here, I will find her and tell her what is happening."

To the group surrounding them Lizzie sent, *"What is your intent? We have done you no harm. What do you want of us?"*

"Want? Want? We want you to be gone from here. We will remove you if need be."

At a signal from Mang, suddenly every pod member held a quarterstaff in their hands in defense position. They had rehearsed this move many times, each time Lall urging them to more and more speed so that now, the staves seemed to simply appear in their hands. Many of them had complained about the repetitive exercise, but now Lizzie was grateful for his insistence.

The crowd surrounding them stepped back a pace.

"We would rather not fight you, but we will not be bullied, nor will we change our allegiance. We will be agents, and neither you nor anyone else will stop us," sent Mang calmly. *"I suggest you take your complaints to Liliath or the council. If they are just, you will get satisfaction. But I have the feeling you really don't understand the purpose of the Alliance."*

The leader of the group snorted derisively, shaking her head, her silvery hair shimmering as she did so. Lizzie wondered how such a beautiful being could be so bigoted and aggressive.

"Will you not leave then? You get this one chance to leave in peace. We do not fear your puny sticks." Hadron invoked a sword, of all things, from her MDP.

Lizzie hoped Ynni had indeed managed to make her way unnoticed from the group to run to the admin office and that she could find Liliath quickly. She knew that Ynni could outrun her, as small as she was. How long could they stall until help arrived? They were definitely outnumbered, and some of Hadron's companions were much larger than any of them.

For a moment no one spoke or moved, each party sizing up the other. Lizzie was sure that tactics were passing from one of Hadron's companions to another via mindspeech.

Mang's mind voice broke into the silence, and she knew he was only speaking to them, that the bullies surrounding them could not hear him.

"Remember our two-on-two drills. Geln, you work as a trio. The rest of us will pair up with our usual defense practice partners. Tactic three on my mark."

Lizzie and the others kept their faces placid as they received their orders, grateful now for all of Baird's constant correction.

Hadron's companions had all armed themselves, some with staves, but some with knives and clubs. Lall had drilled them over and over with their staves, fighting against various types of weapons, but this was a test Lizzie had never wanted to have. The group they faced wasn't drilling. Every face was set in anger and aggression.

Hadron's sword hands twitched a fraction of an inch toward a battle stance. Mang didn't hesitate. *"Mark!"*

At once they paired up and instigated disarming attacks and were, to a certain extent, successful. Lizzie lunged at Hadron from one side, while Gi came down with her staff from the other side with a loud crack on Hadron's sword arm, which was wide open as she tried to defend from Lizzie's thrust.

The sword only nicked Lizzie's staff, but Hadron dropped her sword and grabbed her wrist, which appeared to be broken. She couldn't reach down for the sword without leaving herself wide open, and before she could extract a new weapon from her MDP, Lizzie thrust forward into her gut. She doubled over, and Gi followed up with a hard thwack on Hadron's neck. She went down and lay still.

Lizzie felt, more than saw, the combat going on around her, as a huge troll-like creature stepped over Hadron's body as if it was so much trash on the ground. This being had a rough pebbly face with three eyes and a mouth that stretched from one ear to the other. He opened his mouth full of pointed teeth and roared, his club raised high. Lizzie ran under his arm, pivoted, and whacked him from behind, hoping to get him to turn and get some space between them and to give Gi an opportunity to charge him from behind.

From her new vantage point, facing the battle instead of having it to her back, she saw the others, and the fleeting thought that Lall would have been proud of the fight they were putting up ran through her mind; but her attention was immediately on the troll who had whipped around. She had his full attention. She had noticed in that brief moment of observing the battle that many of Hadron's group were already down, but that there were more of the enemy than her pod.

She knew she couldn't expect to hold out long against a troll carrying a club when she only had a "puny stick," but she also knew that she and Gi were quicker than he was. As if Gi had read her mind, she heard a loud crack. Gi had stationed herself behind him and had dealt him a solid blow to the back of his calves.

As he whirled to face Gi, she ducked under his club, and Lizzie followed up with a whack on his shins from behind. Now the beleaguered troll roared his displeasure and began to randomly flail his club around, hitting nothing at first, but it meant that Lizzie and Gi had to back out of the reach of the pounding weapon.

Geln had just downed their opponent, Mang had disarmed his, and it appeared the odds were shifting to the favor of the pod. Lizzie and Gi continued to circle just out of the troll's reach. Suddenly, behind Geln, a charging being who appeared to be about the same size as the individual Geln bodies, began to swell. It had no weapon, but its fists were the size of large watermelons. As it charged, it struck one of the Geln, and he went down.

Minth, who had removed his gloves and boots for the fight, reached out to the giant creature from behind and placed both hands on him. The effect was immediate and spectacular: the creature seemed to glow for a moment, his spiky hair sparkling and crackling. Its eyes went wide, and it shrank to the size of one of the Geln and then sighed and went still.

All of this happened in what appeared at once to be an age and an instant. The fight went on, and she still had a troll to deal with.

Every person in her pod was still besieged with enemies. Although somewhere in her mind Lizzie knew only a short time had passed, it felt like the battle had been going on forever.

The troll was becoming more and more of a hazard, as it was no longer concentrating on Gi and Lizzie. He laid about himself with that huge club without caring who he hit. One of his own comrades had been struck so hard that her skull was cracked, and blood streamed down her face as she collapsed.

A high-pitched wail suddenly filled the air, along with the mental cry, *"Brother, wake! You can't be dead! We need you!"* It was Geln, one of them stooping over the brother who had not roused while the other defended him stoutly and more fiercely than Lizzie would have imagined possible.

At that moment, several things happened at once. The fight became even more frenzied as her pod rallied at that pitiful cry. Lizzie, who had been temporarily stunned at the thought of one of her podmates dead, especially any of the gentle Geln, now found herself up against another club-wielding being, not as big as the troll. He leered at her, his yellow face and huge black eyes slits, and lunged at her with the club.

"Crack!" the club met her parry, once, twice, three times. At the third stroke, her staff splintered, now half its length ending at a point.

"I kill you like your friend!" her opponent sent, club raised and gloating.

"I don't think so!" she returned and in the same instant thrust her quarterstaff that had become a lance deep into the midriff of the triumphant yellow alien. The angle of her thrust was up and in, as he was taller than she. His eyes widened, went blank, and the club dropped from his hand.

From behind her came the alarm cry of an enraged Linkling. *"Ynni comes! Alert! Alert!"*

Lizzie turned to see Ynni streaking across the training ground, an angry dragon flying behind her. As relief flooded her, she felt a blow to the back of her head, and all went black.

Chapter 25: Bumps and Bruises

(Jenny gasped and put down the journal. It was late in the evening, and Chidwi was suddenly behind her on the back of the chair, patting Jenny's cheek in empathy for her shock.

Jenny remembered Tarafau had once commented that Lizzie had brought down a troll in combat, but never that she had killed. It was comforting to know that Lizzie survived to become not only an agent but a gate guardian, but she had no idea that Lizzie's agent training had turned out to be as challenging as her own journey as a fledgling gate guardian in such a different way.

She found herself remembering waking up that night when Sam had abducted her and tortured her, only to have Bob and Burt come to her rescue.

Now she related to her aunt's journey even more. It was very late; and, more than likely, if Burt had been there, she would have been told to put the journal down and go to sleep.

However, she needed to know. She could always sleep in...)

Lizzie awoke in a white room, not in her bed, and for a moment she wondered where she was. *"Lizzie is awake!"* came a celebratory exclamation from Ynni. Lizzie tried to turn her head to see her but couldn't. Her neck was in some kind of brace. Ynni's face soon appeared however, as she perched on Lizzie's chest.

"Lizzie is going to be better. Lizzie will be fine, healers say so. Lizzie must be calm, and Ynni is here to help with calm."

"Geln... is he..." Lizzie couldn't finish the sentence.

"It is sad. The one Geln has passed the veil to the next dimension, Lizzie. Brother Gelns were also injured but are healing at their home for now. The Geln body is preserved and has been taken to Geln's home. When the living Gelns have healed and are ready, they will return to mourn with their pod family."

"What happen after I was hit? I remember seeing you and Liliath coming across the training ground, and then nothing."

"We surrounded the 'bad ones,' the professors and troopers on one side and me and Liliath on the other. They stopped fighting at once when they saw Liliath. They have been taken and are being questioned by trained agents. The council is bringing representatives from their dimensions in to see if this goes farther than some dissatisfied trainees.

"Liliath has been in to see you, but you were sleeping. She will return when she knows you are awake."

"What about the rest of my podmates?"

"Gi is in the next bed, sleeping. She has a number of cuts and bruises and some internal injuries, as she was dealt more blows than you. When the troll went down, she was struck by his club. Feth has a broken arm but is healing.

"Other than some bruises, you seem to have only one injury, to the back of the head. Your podmates will be in to see you when the healer clears you for visitors."

Lizzie thought about what she could remember of the fight. It all had happened so fast, and she had only seen and heard things around the peripheral, outside of the focus Lall had trained them to achieve. She and Gi had fought as they had been taught, as a team, nearly vanquishing all of those sent against them.

She still didn't understand why it had happened and wondered what would happen next. After all, they had a dead companion to mourn, injuries that needed healing, and their training to complete. They had been scheduled for another holiday, but Lizzie doubted she would want to head home yet.

She fumed at her current helpless state, immobilized and unable to do anything but just lie there. Ynni seemed to sense this and began to croon softly. Surprisingly, Lizzie did feel her muscles begin to relax, responding not only to the soft buoyant melody, but to the waves of mental comfort Ynni was emanating.

As she lay there, a tall slender being, nearly hairless with no apparent ears or nose, came into her view. Her oval face had a bluish cast, and her eyes were large. *"I am Xia, a Drimm healer. I must examine you. It is good to see you conscious. All were concerned that the blow to your neck did too much damage. Please lie still as I check to see how you are progressing."*

Xia held up a device like a small tablet. The screen had indecipherable characters on it. She panned around Lizzie's head several times and up and down her throat, across her shoulders, and then down her torso. She then examined the results on the screen.

"You are progressing faster and beyond our original hopes for you. According to these results, the healing we have done so far has had a good effect. According to our understanding of Earth physiology, you will need to stay in the brace in bed for a few more days; then you will need to wear a support collar and shoulder brace with very light duty for at least a couple of weeks.

"You will be allowed guests, starting today, with the caution that they not over-excite you. I understand you lost a member of your pod and that they are in mourning. I also know they may have a lot to tell you about the battle you were engaged in and the parts you missed. If at any time it becomes too stressful for you, your linkling companion will notify us. Understood?"

Lizzie started to nod and then remembered she couldn't. *"Yes, Xia, I understand. Do you think there will be permanent damage? Something that would prevent me from completing my training?"*

"We do not think so, Lizzie Japhet, but it will be some time before you are healed sufficiently to engage in strenuous physical activity. You can do all other things related to your training, and appropriate assignments will be made during that healing process. At some point, you will need some physical retraining to rebuild the muscles and strengthen your neck and shoulders.

"There is a slight concussion as well that may mean you will have headaches and occasional dizziness until you are fully healed. It is encouraging that you are not only awake but alert enough to be able to ask such questions.

"If you have no more questions, I must report to the chief healer and get a message to Liliath. She is very concerned."

"Actually, what about Gi? Is she just sleeping or...?"

"Your friend Gi is sleeping after surgery and has been given a calming tea to relax her. She will recover, probably quicker than you, but she will be in our care for a few days yet. I expect she will awake soon."

Lizzie breathed a deep sigh of relief. It was bad enough they had lost a third of Geln, but to have lost Gi as well... she did not think she could have handled that.

"An apprentice healer will come in a few moments with a healing soup that you can take through a straw. I suggest you take in as much as your body will allow. The nutrients in it will speed healing. If you need us, tell your linkling. She knows how to get our attention."

And with that, Xia turned and left.

Before Lizzie could take in all that had passed between her and Xia, a woman with dark eyes and a long black braid hanging over one shoulder of her bright blue uniform came to her side with a container, out of which extended a long flexible tube.

"Your soup, Lizzie Japhet," she announced cheerfully. *"I am Cassidy. I will help you for the rest of your stay with us. I understand you are from California. I am also from Earth. My father is Shepherd, guardian of the Canada gate. I believe you have met. Because I grew up knowing what he did and having an interest in healing as well as dimensional travel, with the recommendation of my dad and the other Earth gate guardians, I came here for my medical training."*

She squeezed a bulb at the end of the tube closest to the container a few times which pumped some amber liquid within a few inches of the end of the tube which she placed in Lizzie's mouth.

"Just suck as you need to. The container is in a holder next to the bed. I've been instructed that your linkling, Ynni is it? Your linkling will be here to aid you and take away the tube when you are satisfied. I will be checking on you regularly, along with your friend, Gi. You can call out my name vocally if you need me as well. I am within hearing distance."

"Thank you, Cassidy. This is delicious, and I appreciate your help. I'll try not to be a patient who tries your patience," Lizzie sent with a smile, grateful that the tube in her mouth didn't prevent her from communicating via mindspeech.

She found that her throat was a bit sore and swallowing and using the muscles necessary to suck on the tube was a lot like any muscles would be after a long break between workouts. Nevertheless, taking breaks between swallows made it bearable.

From the bed she could not see at her left, she heard a yawn and rustling as Gi woke. *"Lizzie! You're awake! I'm so glad you made it. I was really worried when they carried you in on a stretcher soon after they put me in this bed. I didn't get a chance to see what they did to you, as they whisked me away to surgery right after. I've been awake a couple times since. Xia said they'd done their best for you and that they would have to wait to see whether it was enough. I know you can't turn your head to see me, and they won't let me out of the bed just yet, but if you could see me, you would see I am grinning like Geln on the dance floor. So sorry a third of him didn't make it."*

All of this had been said in a rush, as if she had been waiting anxiously to say it. She trilled a delighted arpeggio of sound as she spoke, ending in a more somber sustained chord. Since their visit to Gi's home world, Lizzie had asked her to sing her words as well as mindspeech, because she had found herself wishing she had the time and space someday to learn the musical language of the Finquian people. She imagined it would be very different from anything she had ever tried.

"I think I will be okay, but not up to any workouts soon," she sent back with a soft rueful laugh. It hurt to laugh, but she couldn't help herself.

"Nor me. I think they put me back together pretty well, and they said none of the injuries would cause any permanent disabilities. But it sure hurts like crazy. When you got smashed in the back of the neck by that brute, I lost focus and got slugged in the gut. Lucky for all of us Liliath came when she did. We fought a good fight, but we couldn't have held out much longer without more of us being seriously injured... or worse.

"I'm really worried about Geln. The two who are left are seriously disoriented without their brother. Of all of us, I am concerned that the wounds to their hearts might never fully heal."

Lizzie finally admitted she couldn't suck any more out of the cup and told Ynni so. Ynni gently removed the tube from her mouth and laid it next to the cup by her bed. Obviously, if she couldn't even make it through a cup of soup in one go, she had a bit more healing to do than she had hoped she would.

She wanted so badly to go to her pod to mourn with them. She was grateful that Gi, at least, was here. She hoped it wouldn't be long before her podmates would be allowed to come in for a visit. She also wanted a long talk with Liliath. She wanted to know what was happening and silently fumed that she was stuck, unable to move and do for herself.

"I'm not very good at waiting, Gi. I wish I knew what was happening out there. And I hate that we are now in a holding pattern about our training. I hope this isn't holding the others back as well."

"I don't think it will. They are giving them a break and allowing them to go home for a short holiday when they are ready. The doctors seem to think that Liliath wants the pod to continue to move forward together."

Lizzie wanted to reply that this would be good, but that she didn't want to hold the others back. However, there must have been some more of those calming herbs in the soup. She felt herself drifting off to sleep before she could finish the thought.

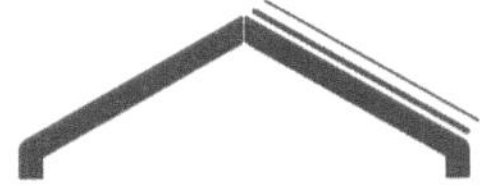

Chapter 26: The Enemy Within

(Jenny felt more connected to her aunt than she ever had. She wished she had been able to find time to read these journals earlier in her training, as short as it had been.

It was past midnight, but she was almost done with this first journal. She knew if she went to bed now, even late as it was, that she wouldn't sleep. She had been completely drawn in. She was surprised to notice that Lizziebot had let Tidbit out, and Chidwi was sound asleep on a little pillow and covered with a blanket, also Lizziebot's doing, she suspected.

Also, on the table next to her chair was a mug of hot cocoa with a peppermint stirring stick. Jenny continued to be surprised at how much attention to detail had been programmed into the little bot. There was no doubt Bob was a genius, but he paid attention to more than just the tech. He had created little bots that seemed close enough to human to make Jenny wonder just how "artificial" their intelligence actually was. A thought to pursue at another time.)

Lizzie's recuperation seemed irritatingly slow, but she tried to be tolerant of the process. Her pod had come to visit before they left for their various homes, except for Geln.

They had each told about the battle from their own perspective. Lall had come with them and had expressed pride at their performance under stressful conditions. Gi was mostly healed at this point and had also gone home.

Lizzie's healer, Xia, had told her that she would soon be able to remove the brace and they would begin gentle physical therapy to strengthen the neck muscles. The damage had not been permanent, but Lizzie was warned that during the next few months she would be excused from training workouts.

Cassidy came in a few times a day and had taken to reading *A Connecticut Yankee in King Arthur's Court* aloud to Lizzie during her breaks to entertain her. Her bright cheerful smile and the times they spent together enjoying Mark Twain's evocative descriptions of life in medieval times made the waiting much more endurable.

Then, a few days after Gi had left for home, Liliath came into the infirmary ward. Gi's bed had been moved out of the way to give room for the dragon. Liliath arched her neck to bring her head to a place where Lizzie could see her.

"Xia tells me you will get the brace off soon and that it would be okay for me to fill you in on all of the details of your recent adventure. Do you think you are up to it?"

"Yes, please! My podmates told me about how the battle ended with you, the other instructors, and Ynni charging up. That you rounded up our attackers, but nothing more. I'm just about dying for the lack of news."

Liliath chuckled, a deep rumble. *"I can imagine, knowing you as I do, that this waiting and wondering has been almost as much pain as your injuries. You really do hate not knowing pretty much anything if you can help it. So, I will tell you.*

"Ynni came charging into my office keening her alarm wail. She instantly told me what was happening. I had to alert the staff, who dismissed all of their classes to support me. They went down the path behind the pod buildings on your side of the training ground, and Ynni and I came in on the front path.

"We got there when you were all seriously engaged with your attackers. You turned to see us and were hit on the back of the head by the falling club of the person you and Gi were battling. I was too late to prevent the stroke; and Gi, who was focused on trying to help you, was slugged by a flailing club. I bellowed for them all to stop and they did, realizing that they were surrounded.

"At that point your attackers surrendered and were taken into custody. Evidently their leader, Hadron, was killed in the conflict, as were two more. Several others had to be hospitalized for various broken bones and internal injuries. Your podmates gave out many more injuries than they sustained.

"Of course, we lost a third of Geln. There will be a memorial service for the trainees in the compound as soon as you are well enough to attend and your

podmates return from their leave. So far, most of this isn't news to you, but it gets you caught up to where we are now.

"After some strenuous interrogation, we determined that this group of rebels had been building in numbers for quite a while. Your pod wasn't the only one attacked. In every case, the pods attacked had non-Alliance members.

"These rebels had formed this group for the purpose of protesting the admittance of non-Alliance members as agent trainees. They are of the opinion that this is a serious breach of security for the member dimensions, and they meant to do this to get our attention, as their representatives had complained in the past without getting the results they wished. These rebels are in the minority, and not all of them are even in agreement about this issue on their home planets.

"Of course, the stance of the Alliance in general is that having agents from non-member dimensions actually enhances security in many ways. And it is apparent that just because a dimension has achieved member status, this doesn't guarantee there won't be security breaches via any of the citizens of a member dimension.

"Regardless, their behavior, this supposed 'protest,' was not excusable by any measure. Peaceful protest is always allowed and is within the rights of any member of the Alliance, but violent actions or demonstrations are not. It is sad to think we may have enemies within our ranks, but it is not the nature of beings from different cultures to agree in all things.

"These agent trainees will be removed from the agent program and banned from any gate travel in the future unless their Alliance representative produces strong evidence as to why that ruling should be revoked. As for any punishment, this will depend on the laws of their own planet or dimension.

"And now, let's talk about you."

"About me?"

"Yes. Disregarding your physical state, Lizzie, how are you?"

"I'm not sure I understand."

"In defending yourself and your podmates, you killed other beings. The thing about killing is that there are always two wounds involved. The killing stroke always has two ends. When you kill, you are also wounded in a way that no medicine or surgery can heal.

"Even if a being's death was not your fault, even though you were only defending your life and those of your friends, you dealt a blow to yourself. The healers cannot see this kind of wound.

"So, I ask you, how are you feeling?"

"Oh, um, well... I really don't know how to feel about it. I'm not sorry for defending myself, but I never intended to kill anyone. It all happened so fast, and yet, at the time, everything seemed to slow down, like every moment was multiplied. I remember the look of shock on their face and then the eyes kind of went blank and they went down. I try not to think about it, but I do sometimes see those scenes replayed in my dreams. And lying here with nothing else to do makes it hard to not think about it, if you know what I mean."

"Indeed, Lizzie. It would be surprising if you did not relive that moment. Our mind has a way of processing the things we do not wish to think about, regardless of our wishes. It is much like the grieving process. Acknowledging that it happened, realizing you cannot change it, recognizing your role as an unwilling participant, remembering that you would have never instigated the conflict, and then believing it fully, will have to happen before you move completely beyond it.

"It may help for you to know that you are in no way at fault here. In fact, your actions probably saved more than one of your companions from injury or even death. The beings you killed wouldn't have grieved if they had killed you, and they would have continued to fight your friends after vanquishing you.

"You have done credit to your instructor, Lall. He knew that the self-defense part of your training was definitely not your favorite, but he had noticed you had been putting in much more effort in the past few weeks. Your podmates also made a valiant fight, and it was surprising that more of you were not significantly injured, as you were outnumbered two to one by much more experienced fighters, who had prepared for several weeks for this encounter.

"This being said, it appears you may be released from the infirmary in the next few days. You will be wearing a neck brace for a while afterwards but should be able to do your personal maintenance and general activities. We will be issuing you a powered hoverchair so you can get around without jarring your neck unnecessarily.

"Once you are cleared and no longer need the brace, I am recommending a few days of respite on Earth. Gaston has been informed of your situation. You

may stay in Sanglarka or in Los Angeles or visit both places if you wish. I know Miriha will be visiting you later this week, and some of your professors would like to stop in, if you would like."

"That would be wonderful, Liliath. Probably the worst pain in all of this is boredom."

"Ah, of course. We have a nice selection of science and technology training that may be absorbing for you." Liliath showed teeth in what Lizzie knew or at least hoped was a smile. *"Just mentally say, 'screen on,' and a screen will hover above you with selections of various lectures and presentations on any of thousands of topics. If you wish a specific topic, such as, say, physics or chemistry, simply think the category you desire, and selections will be automatically filtered to that category. Try it now."*

Lizzie sent, *"Screen on,"* and straight in front of her face about three feet above the bed was a screen roughly three feet wide and two feet tall. On the screen in English were a huge number of choices. She thought, *"Physics,"* and the choices, enough to take up several paginated screens, appeared before her.

She was sure the delight was probably evident on her face, because Liliath sent, *"Better?"*

"Yes, thank you! This will definitely fill in the gaps when Cassidy doesn't have time to read to me. I was going mad with boredom."

"I will leave you to it, then. I have things to do. The events of the past several days have caused great distress amongst all of the trainees, as well as the staff. I expect to see you make a full recovery. We need agents like you."

Lizzie hardly noticed her take her leave. Over the coming week, when she wasn't being treated by Xia, read to by Cassidy, or visited by various instructors, Lizzie got what could well have been several college credit hours in various scientific disciplines. She was so absorbed that she was surprised when Xia finally announced that she would not have to be in the full shoulder, neck, and head brace anymore but instead wear just a neck brace.

She would require a certain amount of physical therapy in the hospital while she adjusted to the neck brace, including getting in and out of bed, seating herself in the hoverchair, and learning to use the controls to steer the chair accurately.

It all seemed too slow to Lizzie, but she gritted her teeth and put in the effort needed to speed the process. She was learning that things didn't always happen on her timetable.

On the day she was to be released, her entire pod, including the dual Geln, showed up to escort her out of the infirmary across campus to their pod. They teased her about her cool new vehicle and her fashionable neckwear.

When they got to the pod, they all sat down in the training area, chairs in a circle. Mang began, *"We have missed you, Lizzie. We all felt it was important for us to take a moment to share our feelings about what happened and what we need to do, moving forward. There will be a memorial for Geln, later today, but this is personal, just for us. We will each take a turn, ending with Geln.*

"For me, this is concerning and instructional. I knew there was a good reason we were put through all of that physical conditioning and self-defense, but it had seemed to me to be more for testing than for any practical application. Obviously, I enjoyed it, so I didn't complain; but I had assumed, as I think many of you have, that the Alliance was this peaceful, united family of a sort.

"It had never occurred to me that there would be conflict, especially physical conflict among the members of the Alliance. But since the incident where we were all so severely tested, I am beginning to understand that the role of agent is more than ceremonial or even just for vetting non-member dimensions. It becomes clear to me that all of the etiquette and diplomacy and history and legality we have been studying are more vital than I had assumed.

"As far as I know, my dimension has no disagreements about Alliance policy, but I confess my naïveté where other dimensions are concerned.

"Probably the one thing that brought all of this into clarity is the loss of one of the trio of Geln. I confess myself still in shock, and I will have a hard time putting my grief aside to continue our training."

He reached out a hand to touch the Geln closest to him on the shoulder and bowed his head.

Each of them followed in turn. Reanni broke down in tears before she could finish. Minth actually had tiny sparks at the ends of his upstanding, nearly transparent hair as he spoke, anger evident in his every gesture. Gi sang a somber dirge aloud as she spoke solemnly about her grief for the loss of Geln. Feth, Negoth, and Linlin were brief but sincere in their agreement with Mang about their new understanding of what it might mean to be an agent and their deep sorrow regarding the death of Geln.

When it was Lizzie's turn, she had a hard time even speaking in mindspeech. Her mind was roiling. She had agreed to come into the Alliance with the sole purpose of satisfying her hunger to get her endless questions answered. She remembered her desire to want it to be more than that and Ynni's assurance that this would come, that she had it in herself to genuinely care about the commitment she had made.

"I didn't come into the training program with any zeal for their cause. I wasn't what my grandmother would have called 'a true believer.' I was emotionally stunted. I realize that now. One of the things I learned from each of you was how to actually care. If I could speak to the Geln we lost right now, it would be to thank him and all of you for teaching me the most important thing I have learned during this training.

"I do care. I can honestly say that I feel more for you than I ever felt for my own family. When I do go back home, I intend to change that. I know they care for me much more than I ever cared for them.

"My entire future is transformed from this point on. I still have a thirst for knowledge and understanding, but now my reason to know has changed. I will continue to learn all I can, but from now on it will be to make a difference for others. It is a big multiverse, so there will always be something new to learn. But more important than that, there will always be new relationships to nurture and grow. Thank you, each of you. For me, whenever I think of Geln, I will remember first and foremost that he was a friend."

Every eye was moist; and for some, like Lizzie, tears were streaming down their cheeks. Ynni was crooning softly, stroking Lizzie's short auburn hair.

Lizzie knew now that this wouldn't be the carefree adventure she had somehow envisioned. She had been naïve to think so. She would complete her training. She would be an agent with a mission.

As they all turned to Geln, Lizzie noticed to her shock that they were smiling. *"We miss our brother. It is true. We have discovered that he truly was a being in his own right and had enriched our consciousness in ways that will change how we feel and act. This is something we did not suppose.*

"However, we know he is not beyond our reach. We have clear memories of him, but it is as if he went through a gate without us, to continue his adventures.

We grieve for ourselves, but not for him. We know how he cared for each of you, and in the end, he was happy and so are we."

Chapter 27: And So Much More

(Jenny realized she was crying, tears streaming down her face and Chidwi crooning soothingly.

She skimmed through the next few weeks of training, the brief visit to home where Lizzie began the task of being more engaged with her family. She hadn't been following up with the technology she had been given to stay in touch with her parents or anyone else on Earth besides maybe Gaston, so she had much to do.

Over time, Lizzie's neck and shoulders normalized, but she couldn't do the heavily physical training. Instead, she spent that time with Liliath and Ynni, strengthening her mind and learning how to do a certain amount of physical healing using mental relaxation and other techniques previously unknown to Jenny.

Once again, Jenny realized how unique her own journey had been compared to that of other agents and guardians of the Alliance. She knew that she would have to buckle down after her brief recovery time.

She also knew she would be scolded by Burt and the others for missing so much sleep, but she would sleep a good part of the day tomorrow before starting on the next journal. For now, she read on.)

It felt so good to get that collar off. They were nearly at the end of the final term. All of them were feeling much more confident as they prepared for their internships. Curiosity was high. Where would they go? What would their assignments be? When would they be introduced to their guides?

The memorial service had been both soothing and uniting. More than ever, the members of this pod had become closer to one another than any other relationship in their lives so far.

Gi and Lizzie and Ynni, at Geln's request, had performed one of their concerts. They had considered something somber, befitting the mourning of their friend, but had finally decided on a lively, joyful outpouring such as they had experienced on Gi's planet that day Geln had been the first to succumb to the urge to dance.

Every day since then, they had fallen back into the routine of studying, working out, and the daily concerts under the tree between pods. More and more agent trainees attended, as much to show support for their valor that fateful day as to enjoy the music. Of the several attacks that had occurred, theirs had been the only one with fatalities.

At one point, Liliath had assembled all of the trainees together again, after the memorial, to be sure each of them understood what had happened, the consequences for the rebels, and how any future disagreements with Alliance policy should be handled. She praised those who had resisted valiantly and reminded them that their training would continue and to always remember the reason the Alliance had been founded in the first place.

They received a notification in Fin's class that their next study period would be in Liliath's office. Fin had nearly sparkled in his excitement.

As they trooped into the huge office, it suddenly looked a lot smaller. In addition to their entire pod, the faculty, staff, and a group of nine beings stood before them next to Liliath.

"Today you will take a big step forward in your training. Theory is important, but, as you have recently learned, there comes a time when theory must be put into practical application. Each of you have shown determination and focus in your studies. Each of you have displayed the attributes we most prize in our agents: determination, attention to detail, stamina of heart and mind, and a willingness to serve.

"Now I will introduce each of you to your guide. Your first assignment with them will be to visit their home dimension, to be introduced to their culture and meet their Dimensional Alliance representatives. You will serve for a period of time as an intern for those representatives. This will teach you more about the Alliance than anything you have yet learned in your classes.

"You will return here from time to time to check in with your faculty advisors. Your current pod building will be reserved for those times you are here,

and most of the time your visits here will coincide with one another, to allow you to stay in contact and exchange experiences.

"Each of you will be leaving today, but before you do, there will be a celebration in the dining hall for all of us to wish you well in your future endeavors."

Lizzie was sure she wasn't the only one of her podmates to be surprised by this statement. Today? Even though they all knew this was coming, they had probably thought, like her, that they would be given some time to prepare. As she considered this, she could only conclude that this was part of her training. In the future, many of her assignments might be as abruptly given as this.

The guides stepped forward, one at a time, and were introduced to their charges. Geln was assigned a single guide, and Minth's guide was actually from his own dimension, not all that surprising, under the circumstances. Lizzie had been focusing on her podmates, so that when her turn came at the very last, she was surprised to notice that the only guide left was someone she knew!

Tarafau stepped forward from behind Liliath's shoulder.

"Lizzie Japhet, you are assigned to Tarafau Bane. He has in the past been the guide to Gaston, as you know, but Gaston's level of guardianship is beyond the need for a guide. He now has an Alliance companion who will aid him in his duties. Tarafau is among one of our best agents and has been a guide for multiple Earth guardians over the years."

Multiple guardians... over the years? How old was this being with his natural shape-changing abilities?

Lizzie stepped forward and shook his hand. He was more than a little formidable, with his catlike grin exposing fangs and those pointed ears, pointed on the wrong end if he had been an elf. How had she ended up assigned to him? Her gut knotted a bit. Not at all what she had expected or imagined.

She remembered her first abrupt meeting with him, changing before her from cat to man and then whisking her off to his dimension without even the convenience of a gate and barely prevented a visible shiver. She found herself glad once again for all of the time she had spent practicing smoothing her features and not showing her initial reaction.

"I look forward to introducing you to my family, Lizzie Japhet. We hear good reports about you. Gaston is very proud to see your progress. We will visit him first and then Miriha before we go to my home. I know we will learn to work well together."

"Thank you, Tarafau. I look forward to it." Lizzie knew that wasn't entirely true, but she might as well begin practicing diplomacy now.

At that point, each of the instructors went down the line of guides and trainees who had now become their interns, shaking hands and congratulating them on making it to this stage of their training. They were quick to point out that this was just another beginning and that they would yet find themselves in their classrooms at some point at a completely new level.

They then adjourned to the dining hall, where a feast had been laid out with them each now seated next to their guides. The Geln duo sat on either side of theirs; and although Lizzie could still detect a certain sadness in their faces, they were congenial enough, and she could tell they were in a lively conversation with their guide, in addition to joining in with the pod with teasing and congratulations.

Gi and her female guide sat next to Lizzie. She seemed content with the choice and chatted amiably with Tarafau also, apparently unconcerned with Tarafau's somewhat daunting appearance.

After a fine feast, the guides insisted that Lizzie, Gi, and Ynni put on one of their concerts. They had heard about this from the other instructors, who had been attending regularly since Lizzie had gotten out of the hospital. Lizzie had wondered if this was mostly a security precaution, but evidently, they had genuinely enjoyed these musical interludes.

Lizzie thought it a fitting farewell. The music ranged in tone from wistfulness to ascending joy as the three of them expressed their feelings through their spontaneous composition. The final chord lingered shimmering on the air, and all in attendance applauded, each in their own way.

As each of them filed out with their guides, last-minute mindspeech farewells were broadcast from one and all.

"Now what?" Lizzie sent to Tarafau, wishing her mind voice didn't sound quite so plaintive.

"We head to the gate and to Miriha and Gaston to get some final counsel. We are first in the queue. After that, the three of us will head to Sanglarka, where they are waiting to congratulate you. From there we will depart to my home, where we will settle you in for your internship. I know you will miss your podmates. You have been through much more together than any of us would have expected. This makes for long-lasting bonds. Do not fear. You will see them again, sooner than you expect."

"So why are we going through the gate if you can transport to any place you wish without one?"

"Because, for one thing, it wouldn't be courteous; and secondly, not everyone knows I can do this, so we must not rely on it. You must get used to gate-use protocols, because once you are on your own, my way will not be available to you."

Lizzie had to admit this made sense. They went through the gate to Miriha's planet and were met by the gem eyes, which did their job quickly. Under the shelter of the trees, which were rustling with crooning linklings, Lizzie paused.

"Would you like to visit with your family, Ynni? We can come back for you before we go through the gate. I will only be a short walk away."

"Ynni would like that, Lizzie. Thank you."

She hopped off of Lizzie's shoulder and scrambled up a nearby tree trunk and disappeared into the leaves. *"Thank you, Lizzie,"* came a chorus of linkling mind voices, and the crooning changed to a joyous song of welcome to their returning friend.

The walk was pleasant. Various villagers nodded to them in greeting as they passed them on the street. The market square was full of people perusing goods and engaged in private mindspeech conversations, evident by body language, facial expressions and occasional gestures. They arrived at the entrance quickly enough and, when they had removed their shoes, headed up the curving staircase to Miriha's office.

As Tarafau had said, Gaston was there to greet them as the door opened automatically at their approach. He greeted Lizzie with a huge grin and a hug.

"Wow! It's so good to see you whole and healed, at least on the outside. How are you doing otherwise?"

"I am doing better than I expected to be. My podmates and all of the staff of the training center and infirmary have been amazing. It's a lot to take in, honestly, but I feel like I will be better over time. It's so good to see you, Gaston. How do you feel about me stealing your cat?"

Gaston grinned again. *"I'll be fine. They sent me a 'gardener,' a young man, or apparently young man, who is an experienced agent. He will tend my garden and keep the property in good shape. He'll be staying in the guest room and also helping Nita out as necessary. It's almost like a vacation for him, and I'm glad you got such an experienced and competent guide. Be sure to listen to him and take advantage of that experience."*

Lizzie managed not to roll her eyes at this. She had a feeling she would be hearing that a lot, and it wasn't her nature to simply bow to authority for authority's sake. But she simply nodded.

Miriha came to her then, both hands outstretched. *"I too am grateful for your safe return to us. You and Tarafau will be reporting directly to me during your internship. The fact that you have impressed a linkling puts you into a special category, as agents go. It is vital that you and she continue to train together and, since I have more experience with linklings than anyone in the Alliance, it will be up to me to help mold the two of you into an effective partnership. Does that work for you?"*

"Indeed! I'm not sure what to think about the extra attention. I'm guessing this isn't going to be anything like actual agent training "

"Not really. Based on the different professors' analysis of each of your podmates, they have been given internships most suited to their particular strengths. For you, we have some specific things in mind well suited to your temperament and interests. But for now, your internship is different than for all of your peers. You will be interacting with the five communicative species on Tarafau's planet, as well as bonding more effectively with your linkling.

"This is enough to be going on with, don't you think?"

She sent this with a wry twist to her mouth and one raised eyebrow, her eyes twinkling with mischief.

Lizzie couldn't help but laugh, and they all joined in. Tarafau's laugh was deep and rich next to Gaston's tenor.

"We will all go through the gate to Sanglarka after you go and retrieve Ynni from her friends. But first, I thought it would be a nice break for you to see the

marketplace and try some of our delicacies. There is a fruit tart that is especially nice, and we will purchase some to share with our friends in Sanglarka as well, shall we?"

They spent a pleasant afternoon admiring the many goods displayed on carts and in booths. Miriha exchanged some of Lizzie's Alliance credits for local money so Lizzie could purchase a few things. Lizzie was especially attracted to some scarves in muted colors she thought would come in handy in various ways.

In her Girl Scout days, she had been taught that a scarf, in addition to being a useful fashion accessory, could be used as an adaptable survival tool. She purchased three of them and promptly tied one around her neck, to the delight of the woman who was selling them.

After making their purchases, including a box full of the delicious tarts, and after they each tried one, they headed for the grove.

"Ynni! I'm sorry you have to leave your friends and family. Can you come with me now?"

From the canopy above her came a chittering that interrupted the ongoing crooning, and then Ynni, along with several other linklings, came scampering down the trees on either side of them.

"I would introduce my Lizzie to my family and friends," she sent. *"My mother, father, sisters, and my friends are happy Ynni and Lizzie have one another. They know we will see one another again from time to time."*

One by one, the little linklings came to Lizzie and gently touched the hand she had extended. Their tiny hands were warm and soft. With each touch came a soft mind touch as well, seemingly a greeting beyond mindspeech. The touch said many things all at once, which amounted to an acceptance into their tribe and family.

Lizzie didn't know how to respond. *"Thank you, each of you. I am honored by your acceptance and your kindness. I promise I will take good care of Ynni and will return her to you as often as I can."*

A mind chorus of agreement and joy was sent her way, and Ynni lightly leapt up to her shoulder. *"Ynni is ready. Let us go with joy."*

They walked back to the gate office, and Miriha escorted them through the gate that led to Sanglarka.

At the gate they were met by the entire Sanglarka team and all of the gate guardians as well. It appeared that this was going to be a bit more of a kerfuffle than Lizzie had expected. Each of them wore expressions of delight and welcome and joyfully escorted them down the path to the lodge.

Once inside, they were greeted by the aromas of a home-cooked feast. The outside air had been crisp and the light failing, but inside the lodge it was warm, and the rooms were ablaze with light from the lamps and fireplace.

Miriha handed her box of tarts to Livia, who exclaimed in delight. They trooped into the dining room where the long table, which usually sat a dozen people at once, had been extended to seat them all. A long runner down the center of the table contained various condiments, including Livia's amazing lingonberry jam. Two carts with various food choices, including fresh-baked fluffy rolls, sat at either end of the table, and a buffet with every salad fixing you could ask for ran along one wall. After everyone had made their dinner salads, Livia and Randall pushed the carts from one place to another, adding generous portions of each of their choices onto large plates.

Lizzie had never felt underfed at the training center dining hall, but this was glorious. All of this amazing food, the good company, and the celebratory atmosphere warmed Lizzie; heart, body, and soul. They had each, after all, had a part in giving her this opportunity in the first place.

Ynni happily nibbled on part of Lizzie's salad and a fruit tart as the rest of them included her in the general mindspeech conversations that went happily around the table. Lizzie shared some of her experiences, preferring to dwell on the funny and happy ones. Her favorite story would always be the encounter on Gi's home world, where even the most unlikely of her podmates ended up gleefully dancing to the joyful music produced by her people.

After the meal, they gathered once again in the lodge lobby chairs arranged in a large circle with the fireplace at the top of the circle and Lizzie's chair in the place of honor next to it. Yaw got out his mbira.

"I understand you have become somewhat proficient at spontaneous and instinctual composition on yours. May I have the honor of playing with you?"

She smiled at him. *"I still don't read music, but I have had some practice in impromptu music. I would love to try."*

She brought her mbira out and plucked a single key and allowed the sound to linger briefly on the air; and then, as if Gi were here in the room with her harmonizing with her multivoice, she began to express the joy and warmth of her evening with these wonderful people in the music that flowed from her heart through her fingers and into the mbira, and Ynni crooned in harmony.

Yaw joined in tentatively at first and then, as he caught the theme of the music, began to interweave his melody with hers and Ynni's.

Finally, Lizzie slowed the tempo and the music drifted to a natural conclusion, her final note blending with Yaw's and Ynni's.

She looked up with tears in her eyes to see the joy in the faces of her Earthling friends as they applauded with enthusiasm, Oak adding a high-pitched whistle. She turned to Yaw.

"Thank you for this amazing gift, Yaw. You can have no idea how much comfort I got connecting through music with my podmates and my linkling friend."

"It was well bestowed, Lizzie. My primate friends would have loved to dance to this. Fortunately, I took the initiative to record it for their enjoyment and yours in the future. I will send the file to your tablet."

Lizzie was constantly in awe of the technology that allowed this kind of thing. She looked forward to a time when things of this sort would become commonplace on her home planet. She knew the time would never come when she would take it for granted. It wasn't that long ago when she thought a record player and music from a radio were considered the height of modern luxury.

She shook her head, also remembering that not all that long ago she had been skimming around the training grounds on a hoverchair whose motor made almost no sound at all. She found herself wondering what type of technology she would encounter on Tarafau's planet. This thought made her realize they would be leaving soon.

"I want you all to know that I will do my best to be a good representative of the best part of Earth. You have all done so much for me, and I don't take it lightly," she sent to the group who were all looking intently into her face.

"I began this journey because I wanted to learn science and get the answers to my questions. I continue it because now I realize this isn't all just about me.

For the first time in my life, I see the point of being involved in something that is bigger than I am. Thank you for that."

Tarafau stood. *"I can tell Lizzie understands we must go now, and she is right. There is much to do, and it has already been a very long day for her."*

They all stood and one by one gave her a hug and a wish for success. Miriha was last. *"Lizzie, we will be speaking again soon. For now, remember that you are not alone in this. I have great expectations for you, beyond your role as an exemplary agent of the Alliance."* She hugged Lizzie, and Tarafau laid his hand on her shoulder.

Once again, they stood in the meadow surrounded by large, weaponed vehicles with a large statue of a woman, her hand held out as if beckoning. The transition was different from gate travel. They had just kind of faded from one place to the other with almost no time in between.

"Come with me," he sent, and led her out from between two of the vehicles onto a paved road that headed down a gentle slope. As they walked, she saw what she assumed were homes, only, unlike many of the places she had visited, there was no resemblance between them. For some of them, about the only thing that hinted they might be dwelling places were doors and windows. Other than that, they came in many shapes and sizes. Cylindrical, square, domelike, and even some that wouldn't have been out of place in an Earth neighborhood.

As they walked along, from time to time they encountered beings similar to Tarafau, but varying as Earthlings do in coloring, size, and apparent age. They all walked along the road, not as if it were traffic, all going in one direction on one side of the road, but some in the middle of the road, some on the sides, and in whatever direction they were heading. She saw nothing that looked like a vehicle as they strode along.

They finally came to what appeared to be a small, pale-yellow domed cottage. Tarafau led the way up a walkway lined with flowers. The edges of the property were lined with shade trees, and from this vantage point she could see a grove of tall trees beyond what might have been a large field. The lawn was closer to blue than green and looked like it might be nice to walk on, soft and springy. Round windows looked out on either side of an orange door.

Lizzie was reminded of a hobbit hole and wondered what she would find inside.

The door opened into a tiled entry hall. To the right of the hall was a round sitting room surrounded with prismed glass windows that cast dazzling rainbows over the chairs and divans of masterfully carved wood, upholstered with soft-looking fabric in muted jewel tones. Straight ahead of the entryway was a stairway that curved downward, following the curve of the room to a floor below.

Tarafau gestured for Lizzie to follow him down the stairs. This led to a much larger room that appeared to be much more casual. On one of the curved walls was a kitchen, clean and brightly lit with sunlight streaming in through a large picture window over a sink. Dividing the kitchen from the main room was what appeared to be an indoor herb garden surrounded by a counter and tall stools.

The other side of the large open room was what could only be considered a family room, but instead of couches or chairs there were huge pillow-like cushions stacked in various places around the wall. A beautiful woman who had green eyes and long wavy brown hair with gold highlights and was dressed in a flowing deep green kaftan, gracefully arose from one of the cushions and held out both hands in greeting, similar to Miriha.

"Welcome, Lizzie Japhet. I am Amenia, wife of Tarafau Bane." Her mind voice was a mellow alto. *"We are glad to have you as a guest in our home. Our children are away on holiday with their grandparents at the moment, but you will meet them in a few days. We have prepared a room for you during your stay here. I would have prepared a meal, but I understand the two of you have had plenty to eat at Sanglarka."*

"Yes, Amenia. They fed us well there. Thank you for your hospitality. This is all very new to me. Please excuse me in advance if I don't catch onto your customs right away. I am here to learn, after all."

Amenia smiled warmly, her eyes crinkling. *"Come with me, and we will get you settled in. We will be working you pretty hard, but we want you to be comfortable while you stay with us."*

She led Lizzie down a long hallway with doors on either side. Like a hobbit hole, this home was much bigger than it appeared from the street. She could see through open doorways that many of the rooms were bedrooms, but there were also a couple of rooms that looked like a study or library.

Amenia stopped at nearly the end of the hallway. She led the way through an open door into an ample bedroom with a large, curtained alcove, a desk and chair, a closet, and cabinets that Lizzie assumed functioned much like a dresser in her bedroom at home. The floor was covered with a deep forest green rug, much the same color as Amenia's kaftan. The blankets on the bed and the curtains were also in muted forest colors.

"This is lovely, Amenia, thank you. A lot more personal space than I have been accustomed to. For the last several months I've been living out of my MDP. Did Tarafau tell you how long I might be here?"

"He wasn't clear on that, Lizzie. He only said you would be with us for at least a few months and that this room would be reserved for you, since you will be coming back from time to time on various assignments. While you are here, we want you to be comfortable and feel welcomed. The bathing and hygiene room is right next to your room on the right. Does your linkling need any special accommodations?"

"She usually spends most of her time with me, but I'm sure she would love to explore some of those amazing trees behind your home. She uses the same hygiene areas as I do."

"Ynni would like to see the trees," Ynni sent to them delightedly, and Lizzie felt a little abashed that they were talking about her as if she wasn't there.

"Then let's go introduce her. Now that you know where your room is, you can settle yourself in as you go. Today will be a day of rest and getting acclimatized. Once again, your inner clock must be adjusted to a new day and night, as our days and nights differ from yours and from Alliance headquarters. Tarafau often complains that his body clock will never function normally again."

"I can relate. I understand that over time agents become more and more dependent on setting alarms unless they are in a particular assignment for an extended period of time."

As they emerged between the end of the hallway and the kitchen from a door to the outside, Lizzie took a deep breath. The air was clean, lacking any of the smells she associated with a city such as Los Angeles. It was a lot more like the air in the forests that abounded throughout the less populated areas of California, Oregon, and Washington State.

To her astonishment, the yard was about half the size of a football field. The backyard in her childhood home had been smaller than half a basketball court. The trees that encircled the grounds were a mixture of many types. Some of the smaller trees were in bloom, scenting the air delightfully. Behind them towered trees as tall as any of the sequoias native to her state.

In the center of the grounds was a firepit surrounded by low benches, and beyond them were a number of chaises just under the shade of the first layer of trees.

Amenia escorted Lizzie and Ynni to the chaises. *"Feel free, in your occasional free moments, to rest here. It is peaceful, and the air below the trees is especially invigorating."*

Ynni hopped down from Lizzie's shoulder with a croon of joy.

"Ynni must greet the treebrothers. This is okay? Lizzie is happy and safe?"

"I am safe and content, Ynni. Please take some time for yourself. I know you have missed trees. Amenia and Tarafau will take good care of me, I promise."

Without a backward glance, Ynni scampered lightly up the nearest tall tree and disappeared among its branches, finally peeking out and waving to them from high above their heads and disappearing again.

"Do you wish to stay here for a bit yourself? Or are you anxious to settle in and meet with Tarafau? He has a schedule worked out for your physical and mental training and is ready to begin whenever you are," Amenia sent as they turned away from the grove.

"I am ready to begin," Lizzie said, realizing that she really was ready and even anxious to start this new venture into the internship.

Tarafau was waiting in the family room, comfortably ensconced on one of the huge cushions. He had pulled two more from the stack and had placed them on either side of his own, facing toward a center point like a small triangle. He motioned for Lizzie and Amenia to sit; and as they did so, he turned his catlike smile on Lizzie. Those amber eyes looking out of his dark blue-black face were intense.

"Now we begin," he said, looking at each of them. *"Amenia will be helping in your advanced mental training, and at some point, she will be working with both you and Ynni to strengthen your bond. She is a counselor and advisor among our people and has other clients she sees on a regular basis.*

"You will be doing a mental and physical workout every morning and in the evening before bedtime. This will consist of the mental training first with Amenia and then workout with staves, doing the forms and eventually graduating back to sparring. I was advised by your doctors that we should postpone sparring for at least another few weeks.

"Before we begin sparring, we will return briefly to Alliance headquarters for a physical checkup. On approval from the doctor, you will have the opportunity to spar with both me and Amenia and, from time to time, others will be included.

"During the day, we will be traveling to various areas of our planet, starting with the high council. You will be attending meetings with various beings of different species. There are five species of beings able to communicate with one another on my world. You will learn of each of them, their customs and ideologies. You will learn about how our affairs are ordered and how our system of government works.

"This is the first stage of your internship. I will not go into further detail at this time, but do you have any questions?"

"Will I get to learn about your science and technology?"

Tarafau chuckled. *"Meta told me that would be your first question but definitely not your last. Indeed, you will be studying with one of my sons, as a matter of fact. Melek is a professor at our advanced science institute and will be delighted to answer your questions, as he can. I understand you always have another one to ask and another."*

Lizzie blushed and was abashed she was unguarded enough to do that. She thought that particular reaction had been trained out of her. *"I am probably more curious than is good for me, or those around me,"* she admitted. *"I am trying to learn some restraint, but it is hard."*

Amenia laughed and gently put her hand on Tarafau's shoulder. *"Curiosity is not necessarily a bad thing, but it can get you into trouble. Our Melek nearly drove us to distraction with impossible questions, and nothing was ever safe from being dissected, analyzed, and reassembled, most of the time, correctly, but there were times...,"* she trailed off with a significant look at Tarafau, who chuckled softly and shook his head, remembering.

"In any case, you will get your fair share of questions answered and even a few you hadn't thought to ask before."

For the next few weeks, they fell into a pattern of ongoing training, Tarafau escorting her to the main city that was a bit of a walk over a hill. In the distance as they rounded the top of the hill was the vast pyramidal building that housed everything from a vast marketplace to entertainment, offices, crafting shops, and the assembly hall where their council met. On the floor above the council hall were the various governmental offices and smaller meeting rooms where myriad governmental functions were managed by those elected to do so.

Lizzie was fascinated to discover that there were no elected officials in their government. Eligible candidates were selected by lottery, and each served a two-year term representing their precinct while taking a sabbatical from their usual occupations. Those terms rotated through, so that there were always experienced officers to orient and train new officers coming into the system.

Evidently, part of their schooling courses included training that would qualify them to function as representatives for their area.

Sometimes Ynni would accompany Lizzie. She was encouraged to recognize that Ynni was not only accepted but respected as a unique intelligent being. As often as the officers and other beings they met with asked Lizzie her opinion, they would ask Ynni as well.

Her daily workouts were challenging. Amenia was skilled at guiding others to learn to explore their mental gifts and expand them. Lizzie knew she would probably never be as skilled as Liliath or Amenia, but more and more she found herself able to defend her mind against mental attacks and to block physical pain, the two things they emphasized most in agent training.

The physical workouts were mostly to maintain her strength, so they did the forms with the quarterstaffs and every day ran between the monument park and the house up and down hills along the paved road. It wasn't quite as challenging as Lall's obstacle courses, but it kept her fit, and it was a good time to contemplate what she was learning.

When she and Tarafau butted heads, as they often did, Amenia could be depended on to smooth things out. Lizzie felt that Tarafau would have preferred to stay with Gaston, and they often disagreed vehemently on various political and philosophical questions. One particular day their conversation had become very heated, and Lizzie found herself wishing that they had assigned her to someone else.

Amenia had stepped in when Lizzie had banged her fist down on the kitchen table where they had been having a quick lunch before going on to their appointment with one of the council members.

"What's this? Both of you need to stop and breathe for a moment and consider whether your inflamed feelings are worthy of the topic at hand. We don't all think alike, and we don't all always agree, but no disagreement is ever resolved by angry thoughts or actions. How important is it, and what will it change if one of you is able to persuade the other to their point of view? Think! And breathe!"

After both sat and considered, they had to admit that although they didn't agree, Amenia was right. They had to work with one another, and they couldn't afford arguments about things neither of them could change or control to get in the way of their ongoing relationship.

Finally, they visited the Alliance for Lizzie's checkup. Xia gave her a clean bill of health, cautioning her and Tarafau to build back up to regular physical activity gradually. They both agreed and visited Liliath briefly before heading back to his home in a flash.

They had barely walked into the house when Amenia called them down into the family room. Ynni was sitting on the kitchen table crooning softly. *"Is something wrong?"* Lizzie sent when she saw the look on Amenia's face.

"Not exactly, but Ynni has some news. You haven't noticed she has been putting on some weight lately?"

"Actually, now that I look closely, I see it, but she hasn't been eating more than usual and she's getting plenty of exercise. Does she need to go on a diet?"

"No, I don't think so. We generally don't recommend it for pregnant mothers "

"What?"

"Ynni is expecting. Evidently she had a very warm reunion on Miriha's planet that day." Amenia sent with a wry smile.

Ynni nodded happily, patting her rounded tummy. *"We have small tribe here soon,"* she sent.

"Tribe? As in more than one?"

"Ynni thinks there are two, Lizzie."

"Soon? How soon? Do you need to go home?" Lizzie was saddened at the thought but couldn't imagine how Ynni would manage without other linklings, especially the daddy linkling.

"Not go home, but you could bring some linkling friends here to help? I know my sister and the sireling would come. Sireling would want to be with our babies."

"Of course. Tarafau, can we go now? Ynni, who should I ask for? What names?"

"Sympha is sister, and Rinn is sireling. They will hear your mind call and come. Tell them I have built a nest. They will know what that means, and they will come."

Indeed, when she and Tarafau entered the grove, the linklings responded quickly, each of the two immediately perching on Lizzie's shoulder as requested as Tarafau transported them to the grove behind his house.

Ynni was there to greet them, and they hopped down and scurried to greet her. As Lizzie watched their joyful reunion, she turned to Tarafau. Tears streamed from his amber eyes.

"Gaston always told me there was something special and unique about you, Lizzie Japhet. I admit I was hesitant to become your guide, but I recant that original impression. Interesting things happen around you. I have a feeling you have begun something much bigger than becoming an agent of the Alliance."

And as Lizzie watched the gamboling linklings run to scamper up a blooming fruit tree to where Ynni had begun her nest, like ripples in the vast pond of the multiverse, she could feel each choice she had made moving her forward.

She would always have more and more questions. She knew this was really only the beginning. The task she had set herself to learn it all was seemingly as infinite as the multiverse in all its diversity and wonders. So little time.... She had better get to work....

(When Burt returned home, he found Jenny sound asleep in her chair, the journal opened to the final page.

He shook his head, the grin effusing his face as it always did when he saw her or even when he thought of her. You're more like your aunt than you realize, my sweet, *he thought.* She could never let a question lay unanswered either.

Chidwi sat on the back of the chair looking sleepily up at him. "I hate to wake her, Chidwi, but we'd better get her to bed. She has two more journals to go, and I'm guessing she'll need her rest.")

The conclusion of the fourth book of The Dimensional Alliance series

Watch for the fifth book, "Links to Infinity" in 2022

Sign up for The Dimensional Alliance newsletter here:
DimensionalAllianceHeadquarters.com/Contact

About The Author:

Reading has always been my passion. Starting in libraries at the age of four, I have travelled near and far via the printed page, from places of ancient history to the stars and beyond. It seemed a natural thing for me to want to write as well.

Being able to go from simple day-dreaming and pretending to creating worlds of my own invention has been an ongoing passion and from my teen years I had thought that "someday" I would write books myself.

What happened to that dream? Honestly? Life happened. Out of high school I went into the military. I met my future husband, got married, had children, moved all over the place, including three years in Frankfurt, Germany, had many adventures including clowning professionally, 15 years of broadcast television as a producer/director/show-host, owned more than one business and then went through several major health challenges including breast cancer.

So, what changed? What made me decide to pursue the dream of my teen years? Let's go back a bit...
At about the age of 16 I had started having a recurring dream that pestered me most of my life. Time and time again I would discuss the dream with people I thought were wiser than me and time and time again the repeated answer came, "No idea. I've never heard of such a thing."

At age 63 after having the dream once again I decided that maybe if I wrote it down it might leave me alone. I did so and filed it on my desktop, but didn't think of it again until I started hanging out with published authors.

At the end of a recorded interview I did with Mercedes S. Lackey, after I had turned off the recording, I timidly confessed I had often considered writing a book. Mercedes leaned forward in her chair, looked me in the eye and said, "Put your butt in the chair and write!" It was some of the best advice I had ever gotten.

In search of material to write about I stumbled upon that dusty text file about my dream and the rest is history. From it came the science fiction - fantasy series "The Dimensional Alliance" beginning with "The House on Infinity Loop". I am grateful for the events leading up to setting myself upon this path. The series has the word "Infinity" in all of the titles since there seem to be an infinite number of stories I have to tell and I will continue writing them until I transition to the next dimension in some distant date.

To my readers: Never give up on your dream. The first book in this series was published two weeks before my 64th birthday. It is never too late. There are many more to come.